JOE HALDEMAN

"Haldeman writes with wit, grace, and ease.
If there was a Fort Knox
for the science fiction writers who really matter,
we'd have to lock Haldeman up there."
Stephen King

"Along with readability,
artistic integrity has been a Haldeman trademark."
Los Angeles Times Book Review

"His prose is as clear and engaging
as his ideas."
The New York Times Book Review

"Compulsively readable . . .
Haldeman does his usual expert job."
Washington Post Book World

"A mystery/SF hybrid
that exhibits the author at his most inventive . . .
Haldeman keeps the technological wonders coming,
and the action is fast and furious."
Publishers Weekly

Other Avon Books by
Joe Haldeman

ALL MY SINS REMEMBERED
MINDBRIDGE
TOOL OF THE TRADE
WAR YEAR

BUYING TIME

JOE HALDEMAN

AVON BOOKS  NEW YORK

AVON BOOKS
A division of
The Hearst Corporation
105 Madison Avenue
New York, New York 10016

Published in hardcover by William Morrow and Company, Inc.; for
information address Permissions Department, William Morrow and Company, Inc., 105 Madison Avenue, New York, New York 10016.

First Avon Books Printing: June 1990

AVON TRADEMARK REG. U.S. PAT. OFF. AND IN OTHER COUNTRIES, MARCA REGISTRADA,
HECHO EN U.S.A.

Printed in the U.S.A.

RA   10   9   8   7   6   5   4   3   2   1

*This book is dedicated to the
interesting people doing research in life
extension, cryonics, and other such
intimations of immortality.
May you outlive your critics.*

AFTER the first hundred years, some people stop taking chances. With a new young body—or at least a healthy one—every ten or twelve years, there's a strong temptation to go out and use it. But if you did try to occupy centuries climbing mountains, skin diving, abseiling, and so forth, sooner or later the force of statistics would catch up with you. The Stileman Clinics will cleanse you of cancer and sclerosis and make your vital organs and muscle and bone think they're brand-new again—but lose a wing in a sudden storm and you're as dead as any mortal. Any "ephemeral."

Dallas Barr had ignored this reality for almost a century. He had sailed around the world in a forty-foot sloop, had braved vicious currents to swim the lonely corridors of the *Titanic*, had come to terms with himself in a winterlong Antarctic vigil. On the Moon he had climbed the Straight Wall and tramped the Plato desert in search of fairy lights. He'd bought his way onto the first team to climb Olympus Mons, on Mars. Then just before his ninth rejuvenation he had been rappeling down an easy cliff in Australia's Blue Mountains when a foolproof rope snapped to give him three seconds of weightlessness and then a broken back.

That almost killed him, twice. It's hard to amass a fortune immobilized inside a body cast and either distracted by constant pain or dulled by analgesia. The ninth fortune is easier than the first, though, and a person without a knack for making money has to get used to the idea of growing old.

(Lord Stileman himself had lived only to a hundred and five, dying in the fiery wreckage of an antique racing car.

By then his clinics already were the second-wealthiest foundation in the world and only a few years away from first place.)

The only people who got immortality for free were King Richard, a few politicians and administrators, and about a hundred medical people, each of whom guarded one part of the complicated secret that was the Stileman Process. Everyone else bought the next dozen years on the same terms: all your worldly goods signed over to the foundation. And don't even reach for your checkbook if you have less than a million pounds.

Your perennial million pounds didn't buy true immortality, not in the absolute sense. The Stileman Regeneration Clinics could slow down the decay of brain tissue, but couldn't stop it altogether. Nobody had lived long enough to put it to the test, but from the clinics' extrapolations, it looked as if the upper limit would be less than a thousand years. Sooner or later your brain would fog up, and when your time came around, you wouldn't be able to find a million pounds. You would grow old and die.

Dallas Barr didn't spend much time mulling over that, even though he'd been in the first Stileman group and was therefore one of the oldest people in the world. Tightrope walkers don't worry about distance records.

When he'd hurtled down the side of that cliff, Dallas had been in the ninth year of his current rejuvenation. A disastrous poker game in Adelaide, which he'd hoped would put him over the million-pound mark, had left him with less than fifty thousand Australian dollars. He had about two years to multiply that by sixty.

Most of the people he dealt with over the next eighteen months did not know him as Dallas Barr, the rather conspicuous American playboy. Many of them did not know he was an immortal. He had a number of personas scattered around the world, most with impeccable credit references, even if they were currently short of liquid assets. He vouched for himself and then at usurious rates lent himself borrowed money, some of which was invested quietly, some conspicuously, weaving a complex skein of notes and handshakes and whispered confidences that eventually, inevitably, began to generate real money. He made his million and put it in a safe place and then spent a couple of months ensuring discreetly that when Dallas Barr walked out of that clinic young again and nearly flat broke, he wouldn't stay broke for long.

He did decide to be Dallas Barr a third time, though it meant public immortality. (He had been public once before, as Georges Andric, who ''died'' attempting to scale Everest alone.) The notoriety was sometimes pleasant and always profitable, though it involved some risk. Despite all the evidence to the contrary, there were people who thought the Stileman immortals made up an underground cabal that ruled the world. There were no statistics—if the clinics kept records, they didn't release them—but it seemed likely that the second most frequent cause of death among immortals was assassination, usually spectacular, by some crazy who thought he was saving the world from a conspiracy.

No immortal ever remembered exactly what happened during the month of rejuvenation therapy. This was for sanity more than security. The first three weeks were sustained agony, beyond imagination, being pulled apart and put back together; the last week was sleep and forgetting. When he left the Sydney clinic this ninth time Dallas Barr felt, as always, renewed but deeply rattled: a strong man of a hundred and thirty who couldn't remember the nine times he had begged for the release of death.

Stileman, Geoffrey Parke, MP, 1950–2055

Lord Stileman is, of course, best remembered as having founded the immortality clinics that still bear his name, but even before that accomplishment he was a prominent (perhaps notorious) public figure.

Born into considerable wealth, Stileman was nevertheless, from his earliest years, an outspoken enemy of privilege. As a New Labour MP, though, he turned out to be anything but doctrinaire, apparently following the dictates of his conscience even when that led him into the Tory camp. So he was never a great success as a practical politician, not being willing to compromise, but his rhetorical ability and striking camera presence made him a valuable asset to a variety of liberal and libertarian causes.

In 1991 a group of medical researchers approached him with the outline of what the Stileman Process (q.v.) would be. It was one of them, not Lord Stileman himself, who had come up with the idea of using the process as a way to delimit the accumulation of private wealth: past a certain age, in order to stay alive, a wealthy person must become a relative pauper every ten years.

Once the process had been demonstrated, Lord Stileman was in a position to effectively blackmail any person who preferred life over wealth. (Not all did at first; many fortunes were carried to the grave.) He didn't use this power to greatly increase his own wealth, but rather encouraged donations and investments in areas he was passionately involved with—the encouragement being the complex legal instrument one must sign for the second and subsequent treatments. This not only requires a large payment to the clinic, for services rendered, but disallows "certain modes of divestiture"—in plain language, you can't lend anybody, or any corporation, a significant amount of money that would be paid back after your treatment. You can't even give it away, except to approved charities and industries.

It's no exaggeration to say that, through this selective encouragement, Lord Stileman financed the British and American presence in space in the twenty-first century. Neither the Britannia satellite complex nor the ill-fated lunar colony Downside—not to mention the immortals' own quixotic enterprise *adastra*—would have been possible without the billions transferred from the estates of millionaires unwilling to give everything to the Stileman Clinics. . . .

—*American Encyclopedia*, 2068 edition

The clinic gave him a cheap bag with a change of clothes and two thousand dollars in small bills. He had a pub lunch (using the pub phone to make arrangements with a local bodyguard agency) and checked into a fleabag hotel. He sat in his room for an hour of concentrated thought, then punched up a long number from memory and had a brief conversation in Japanese. A few minutes later the phone rang, and he talked for a while in French. Then he checked his watch and went out for a paper and a pint.

Though Dallas was a fairly well-known personality in America and Britain, he felt comfortably anonymous here. The Aussies were not as easily impressed by playboy money, and at any rate the stay in the clinic had disguised him with a generally haggard look and a month of beard. He looked forward to drinking some real beer and catching up on the news unmolested. He bought a sleazy London paper and looked for an appropriate bar.

There were several places within a couple of blocks of the hotel, but none of them looked particularly safe. His love of adventure didn't extend to making himself a target for griefballs and dizneys, so he headed crosstown toward the Rocks area. The beer was more expensive there, but you wouldn't have to sit with your back to a wall.

It was broad daylight, and Dallas looked stronger than he felt, so no one gave him any trouble beyond the occasional shouted offer or challenge. He found an upper-middle-class bar with an interesting format—1930's Art Deco American—and the bouncer let him in for a mere ten dollars.

He threaded his way through the chrome and glass clutter of mostly unoccupied tables to the bar, placed his order, and unfolded the newspaper.

He didn't even get to read the headlines. While the barmaid was drawing his brew, a fat man squeezed onto the stool next to him. "Mr. Barr," he said, not a question.

Dallas sighed and looked at the man. The bodyguard wasn't due until afternoon, and probably wouldn't be fat. "I don't know you," he said, noting that the man's sloppy business suit could conceal a large weapon or two, measuring the distance to his trachea, right hand automatically tensing into a stiff blade. He had been kidnapped before.

"I don't expect you would remember. We met in Chicago." His voice dropped. "Seventy years ago."

Dallas gave the barmaid a five and told her to keep the change. He sipped the strong dark brew and studied the immortal's face. "The conference?"

"That's right. You were Andric then." The Chicago conference had been one of the last annual get-togethers before the Singapore Bombing ended the custom. Several thousand immortals in one place were too tempting a target.

"If this is a touch, you're a little premature." Immortals did borrow from one another, though it was done carefully; that had been the purpose of Dallas's call to Japan. "You must know I just got out of the clinic."

He nodded. "I've only been out a year myself." He saw Barr's look and pinched a huge wad of fat. "It's not real. Foam implant, protective coloration."

"Glad to hear it."

"There's going to be a meeting."

"I don't go to meetings anymore."

"We know. This time you must."

The barmaid came by to draw another beer. Dallas waited until she was out of earshot. "Who are 'we'? You and your implant?"

"We don't have a name. Just a group that meets here and there. Every three months or so."

"Not interested." He opened the paper and gazed at the pinup on page three.

"Maria Marconi," he said. "She'll be there."

Dallas stared at the picture. The girl was not slim or dark-haired and was probably a good deal less than a century old. "Marconi," he said. "She's still alive."

"She would like to see you."

"And I her." He turned the page noisily. "Be a good chap and tell her where I am."

"Our group has been meeting almost since Singapore."

"Do tell. How can you have gotten along all this time without me?" He started to turn the page again and the man put his hand on it. He looked up. "I'm tiring of your company."

"You can afford to be patient. Most of us would have contacted you long ago. But the group is conservative that way; if one member objects to a new person, that's enough."

"The person who was blackballing me died?"

"Yes."

For the first time Dallas showed some interest. "Was it Lobos? Sandra Bell?" The man shook his head. "Not Jim-bo Peterson?"

"No. I don't think you knew the man personally. A Russian, Dmitri Popov."

"A Soviet? Stileman must be turning in his grave."

The man smiled. "We didn't know he was a Soviet when he was asked to join. In fact, he was a deputy administrator of the American CIA."

"Ah." Dallas returned his attention to the paper. "This group of yours. I suppose you don't sit around and eat little sandwiches. Discuss poetry or footie scores."

"Nothing so wholesome."

Dallas nodded soberly. "You know what I like about this newspaper? The people who put it out know what's really important in the real world. Gossip. Sex. Small human dramas like 'I Killed My Baby and Ate It.' Like them, I don't have much stomach for politics." He shook his head. "If you people are an underground organization running the world, I wish you'd get into another line of work. You're doing a really bad job."

"If we were running the world, it would be a much safer place."

"I've probably been hearing that since before you were born. It's not true. Stileman immortality doesn't confer wisdom. We have more than our share of rich sociopaths." Dallas looked at his watch and took a deep breath. "In five minutes I'm going next door for a shave and a haircut. I'm going alone. Until then, I'll listen."

"Fair enough." The barmaid drifted by and he ordered a glass of Bundaberg. He stared at Dallas for a moment, thoughtful. "Do you worry about getting old? The brain death?"

"Not much. They say I've got another seven or eight hundred years, at least. By then they'll probably come up with something—hell, I gave a half million to that fund." The Nervous Tissue Preservation Prize was the result of a rare instance of solidarity among the maverick immortals. Each one had given 10 percent of his assets to it; the research team that could come up with a cure for entropic brain dysfunction would split a billion pounds. Immortality for a thousand people. Real immortality, barring accidents or violence.

"Yes, that's what they used to say, ten centuries, more or less." He paused, staring at Dallas. "They're wrong."

"What?"

"You don't have six or seven—" He stopped talking while the woman served him his rum. He left it untouched and continued. "You may not have even a hundred years left. Maybe not fifty."

Dallas studied his newly young hands. "Okay. You've got my attention."

LB: We should have some fireworks tonight, gentle viewers. To my right we have Dallas Barr, who is—well—Dallas *Barr*. To my left . . . [we follow LB's gaze to empty chair with grey box on seat] . . . is a thing, or man, or program that claims to be all that remains of Professor Woodward Harrison.

Box: I *am* Woodward Harrison.

Barr: Not himself nowadays.

Box: Look me up in a couple of thousand years.

LB: Professor Harrison spent most of his life perfecting a process that he called Turing Imaging. What's in that box is the Turing Image of Harrison, who died of pneumonia—old age—last month.

Box: I wore out my body, as we all do. The rest of me is still alive.

LB: Care to explain?

Box: Certainly. The Turing Image is named after Alan Turing, a mathematician who lived in the last century, one of the people who helped develop the first computers. He devised the first meaningful test for artificial intelligence: suppose you had a human being in one room and a computer in another. You can talk to either one only through a computer keyboard. The computer is programmed to act like a human, even to the extent of being able to lie and make mistakes, seeming to be slow in computations, and so forth. If, by the answers they give to any question you can come up with, you aren't able to tell which room has the human in it, then the machine has demonstrated actual artificial intelligence.

Of course, nowadays you wouldn't need a keyboard; just talk the way we're doing.

LB: That's all you actually are, then? A computer program?

Box: Well . . . what are you? Sixty liters of water and a few bucks' worth of chemicals?

Barr: That's great. A grey box programmed to do Philosophy 101.

Box: No, Mr. Barr. What I am is an actual immortal human being. You're just a man, one with enough money to get his body overhauled every ten years.

Barr: Depends on your point of view. I guess you will outlast me—as long as nobody gets mad at you and pulls the plug—but hell, so will the statue of Robert E. Lee out in front of this building. What good is hanging around forever if all you ever see is the south end of a pigeon?

Box: Ha-ha. You're right, though; no one would want to be an inanimate object. I am alive. In some ways, I am more alive than you are.

Barr: Sure.

LB: How could that be?

Box: All right. Tiptoe with me through the semantic, semiotic minefield of Philosophy 101. How many ways are there to define life?

Barr: Seven billion.

Box: True in a sense, but not relevant. Of formal definitions—in cosmology and various biological disciplines, as well as philosophy—I have access to 149, some of which overlap. [Reaction shot of Barr, eyes rolling.] I will spare you 148 of them.

The way in which I am demonstrably more alive than you is thermodynamical—

Barr: Knew you were gonna say that.

Box: Indeed.

Barr: Yeah. [Close on Barr.] You can say that if a thing is alive, then in the process of existing, it moves constantly to states with a higher degree of order. That, of course, is against the law, the Second Law of Thermodynamics. You're gonna say that since *you* go on processing information indefinitely, and since my brain isn't going to last forever, you are more alive than I am. Quod erat in your demonstratum.

Box: You have a hidden dimension, Mr. Barr. Well hidden.

Barr: Yeah. I'm fifty years older than you are, chum. I'll always be fifty years older than you.

Box: Until the day you die . . .

Dallas

THE cabby apologized to us for the noise. Before the rotor got up to speed, it made a deafening clatter. Once we were over the water it wasn't too bad.

He read back the address that he'd punched into the dash. "On the water, eh, mates?"

"I don't know. We've never been there." I'd picked up my night shift bodyguard, Merle Browning, an hour early, rather than have him find his own way to the party.

"Yeah," Merle said. "Gotta be on the water." He was an American but knew Sydney like a native. "She's got some money, livin' there."

"She a Stileman?"

"Don't know," I said quickly. Merle shot me a sleepy look.

"You guys?" asked the cabby.

"Sure," Merle said. "Couldn't find the keys to the Mercedes."

"Right," he said broadly, and shifted into overdrive. We tilted forward slightly and lifted another half meter off the water, slowly weaving around sailboats. The Opera House and skyline receded.

It was going to be interesting, though probably not as life-and-death as Lamont Randolph had made it sound initially. When I pressed him for details about the brain death emergency, he had to admit that he didn't have any; it was essentially a rumor he thought he could use to "get me interested." Not necessary, really. I would go anywhere in the world, three worlds and fifty rocks, to see Maria again.

"I got naught against 'em," the driver said. "I mean, you or me'd do the same, we had the money. No?"

"Can't take it with you," I said.

"Pre-zackly." He frowned, tapped the dash compass, steered a little to the right. "I wouldn't be so bloody stuck up about it, though. You know, most of 'em? God's gift."

"You got that right," Merle said, with a little too much sincerity.

The cabby tapped the compass again. "Goddamn computer." He reached under the dash and flicked a switch. "This is fixed fare anyhow. Swing by the free beach?"

"Anytime," Merle said. That was the nude beach on the southwest side of the Harbour. Somewhat out of the way. But of course I didn't know that.

I watched the water while the driver and Merle exchanged obvious comments. Immortality did complicate your sex life. Merle could joke about "losing track." After a hundred or so years, though, it was no joke. You meet a woman socially and, more often than not, the first moment is a mutual hear-the-wheels-turning, did-we-or-didn't-we exercise in sorting memories. Then perhaps a conspiratorial wink or squeeze—"Majorca, back in '23, wasn't it?"—or a carefully neutral friendliness while the wheels keep turning.

I was mentally reviewing the list of women I'd be likely to meet at Claudia's party—I do try to keep the past fifteen or twenty years' worth straight, anyhow—when I realized Merle had said something. "Sorry?"

"Ever come down to the beach here?"

"No . . . always mean to. Happy hunting ground."

Cabby shook his head. "Ah. All look an' no touch. Every slit brings 'er own cob, she does."

"Cob" was an oddly direct word in that context, but I knew what he meant. We were getting close enough to see a few pink dots on the rocks. Sunbathing in shadow, this late in the afternoon. The cabby said the female population, though he didn't use that term exactly, doubled when the beach was in shade. Made sense to me.

"You Yanks don't have anything like this, eh?"

"Not so public," I said, "except in California." He angled into the southernmost part of the beach, and dropped speed to where we were just barely off the water; then cruised slowly up. He and Merle waved and the shade-bathers waved back. The polite gentlemen waved their hands.

Claudia's place was about two kilometers north of the beach. It was conspicuous even from that distance. Cantilevered out over the water with no supports below, an extravagant display of space stuff. No earthly material could take the strain; it must have been those carbon filaments or something. I don't keep up on it.

A bright red warning strobed on the windshield: APPROACH LANDSIDE. With a noisy surge the cabby banked to the left and climbed, missing the roofs of cliffside dwellings by a few meters. People who had moved out here for peace and quiet.

Another red strobe: HOVER UNTIL GREEN. "God damn," he said. "Wonder what they'd do if I tried to come in?"

Merle was fascinated. "Wanna try?"

"Let's not," I said.

The cabby laughed. The vehicle bobbed in a good imitation of a small boat in a heavy sea, the rotor building up to a banshee scream. An impressive entry. APPROACH NOW, the green strobe said.

He set it down pretty smoothly on the redwood deck; blessed silence when the rotor disengaged. The tab was fifty dollars; I punched sixty, and the driver nodded vacantly, staring at our welcoming party. There was an exceedingly pretty woman, wearing about five square centimeters' more clothing than the shade-bathers, and a nice smile—and two frowning gorillas cradling H & R assault lasers. It wasn't legal for private citizens to own them in Australia.

"Mr. Barr," the young lady said, "come with me. Everyone is having drinks by the pool." She looked at Merle. "Mr. . . . ?"

"Browning. I'm Mr. Barr's bodyguard." The cabby raised a couple of eyebrows at this, and noisily engaged the rotor.

"Go with these gentlemen, please."

"Uh, I don't think—"

"It's okay, Browning," one of the gorillas said. "Body-guards got their own party." I nodded, and Merle went off, looking doubtful.

The pretty one introduced herself as Cynthia—"Call me Sin," all right—Claudia Fine's mate. Unless my instinct was off, she wasn't immortal, not yet. All original equipment. Low mileage, one owner. Oiled regularly.

The pool was spectacular, a crystal bowl a couple of meters deep by twenty in diameter, floating suspended at eye level in an elaborate sprawling rock garden. Pretty things of both genders swam naked in the clear water; whenever someone dived from the edge, the pool bobbed slightly. So it was held in place by a tractor/pressor field. Expensive.

"Dallas. It's been for*ever*!" Claudia was dressed in her usual restrained style, or undressed: nothing from the breasts up, and only a silver sheen of body metal from the bottom of her breasts down. Head shaved up to a medusa ruff crown (some electrostatic thing kept it writhing slowly).

Her kiss was strawberry. She turned around and stood gracefully on one toe, displaying. "How do you like it?"

"The face? It's . . . different." The back of her head was shaved as well, and decorated with a holo tattoo, gargoyle face with pearl teeth and shining ruby eyes. "That's the style now?"

"Not yet, dove."

Exactly one buttock was bare, healthy pink over hard muscle, but with dozens of puncture marks on the side. "What're you poking?"

"Mostly grief; a little cream tonight. Want some?"

"You know I'm not . . ." I shrugged.

"People change." She took my arm and steered me toward the bar. A nipple brushed my bare bicep and immediately sprang up hard. She giggled. "That's the cream. You should try a little. What it does to men . . ."

"I've seen what it does. No thanks."

"Regular men. Not the bangoff creeps." Terminal cream

addiction leads to pretty bizarre behavior. "Now you're gonna tell me not to poke."

"Your business. I never did understand poking, though, not when you can afford to pop or punch."

"Yeah, well. You don't understand pain."

"Tell me about it." We came up to the bar and I pointed at a small box of Foster's. "Spent nine months last year in a body cast, broken back and neck, crushed rib cage. Liver, spleen, and heart transplants. I do know pain, Claudia."

"Not the same. Not like wanting it."

"Guess not." The lager was so cold it hurt my teeth. "How much grief?"

"Forty if I cocktail it. Fifty straight."

"Good God, Claudia." Fifty-grief would be lethal to a nonaddict.

She laughed. "You're such a plank, Dal." She stirred through a silver bowl of poppers, stamps, and needles and pulled out a ten-cream. "Cream's hard to find once the party gets going. Be a gent here." She unripped my breast pocket and slipped an ampule in. "I'll come get it later." She gave my crotch a friendly squeeze and glided off. The bartender took a sudden interest in rearranging his bottles.

She stopped abruptly and walked back, standing at an awkward distance. "Uh, you just got out?"

"Tuesday."

"Need some?"

"Don't think so. Thanks for asking." Delicate business. I was almost broke, but you had to be careful about the markers you put out. Claudia wouldn't have let herself get addicted unless she was going in pretty soon. So if I took her money now, I'd be giving it back in a few months, technically in defiance of the Stileman contract. That would unnecessarily complicate things, so early in my own tenth career.

Claudia and I had lived together in New Orleans about forty years ago. She used to share my caution toward drugs. They didn't have cream back then, though, and grief was a sure killer.

Nowadays, a lot of people let themselves become addicts

before they check in for rejuvenation. The Stileman Process does cure you of physical addiction, but if it's a manifestation of some deep psychological problem, you'll of course still have the problem when you get out.

There can't be many immortals who are "natural" drug addicts, their chromosomes lined up so as to make them need it no matter what. People with that affliction don't put together their first million. People like Claudia just get physically bored, I guess. Grief turns you inside out, but nobody was ever bored by it. Cream just makes you into a sex machine, as far as I can tell: very intense orgasms refreshed at will. After a few years you're impotent without it, though; not a great selling point.

I would have thought Claudia would go for dizney, if any drug. She always liked exotic places. With dizney you can visit a dozen solar systems without leaving your chair, always different ones. Some people never quite get back, of course.

Dizney and grief are more potent to immortals than 'phems, they say; a lot of drugs affect us differently. And it varies from individual to individual; aspirin deadens my sense of smell, but I've never heard of that happening to anybody else. Eric Lundley, an Australian immortal who once was my business partner, got auditory hallucinations from antihistamines.

I wondered how many of the forty or so people here were immortals. A few I recognized; a few more were obvious from physical modifications, hardheads and strongarms. My own skull was a Kevlar replacement, but with bone and skin culture grafted over it. Real hair. If I wanted to look like someone other than Dallas Barr, it was relatively easy. Wouldn't be if the top third of my head was a shiny silver dome.

I realized that the man I was staring at, a hardhead, had detached himself from a conversation and was walking toward me. Just in time, I recognized him, and bowed ten and a half degrees.

"Sun of friendship breaking through mist," I said in pretty bad Japanese.

He answered my bow and greeting and we shook hands. Atsuji Kamachi, the first person I'd called after I got out of the clinic.

"Hardly recognized you with the silver skulkcap."

"Platinum. You should have one."

"Maybe someday." I kept the Kevlar secret. "Feel different?"

"It is colder to the touch, of course, and a bit heavier. When I hit my head on something, the sound is like a temple gong." He tapped his head twice but it just sounded like knuckles. "Inside, of course."

He looked around and lowered his voice. "I did complete the transaction that you requested." Inscrutable half-smile.

"A hundred thousand pounds?"

He shook his head. "More than ninety, less than ninety-five. As I told you, steel is soft this quarter, not only in the East."

"Which made people eager to do business, eh? Some people?"

"Some." He stroked a wisp of white beard. American and Australian immortals tended to look like tennis players and models; Oriental ones, like sages and empresses. "This Frenchman I dealt with, M. Neuville. He does not really exist, true?"

"Well . . ."

"I know the law firm is real." He spoke in an amused, conspiratorial whisper. "But that supposed fortune is so much gossamer. More margin than substance."

"Kamachi," I said with real pain in my voice.

"Ah." He held up one finger. "I ask you no questions, you tell me no lies. Is that how the saying goes?"

"Exactly."

"Know this, then." He looked to the left and right, elaborately. "A lot of steel will be sold for gossamer this week, perhaps next week. Singapore."

"Thank you."

"I am not being totally unselfish. If it were necessary for your M. Neuville to appear—in the flesh—in Singapore or Hong Kong this week, would that be possible?"

I thought fast. "What would he have to know?"

"Something about the marketing of steel—"

"Military?"

"No. General construction . . . plus the details of your late transaction."

"This Paris-Bonn-Tokyo-Singapore one?" He nodded. "By when?"

He pushed a button on his watch. "The twenty-fourth, Greenwich date. Evening in Singapore."

That was more than two days. "No problem. I may have to go to Paris tomorrow. You're still with Demarche there?"

"Immortals stay together."

"Yeah, sometimes. She can be trusted?"

"With everything, yes."

I wasn't so sure, but then I didn't have to tell her everything. "One detail. I can't fly for free—"

"Verify," he said, making a tent with his fingers, or a cage. "The transaction should have been completed by now."

I thumbed my credit card, and it flashed almost a quarter-million Australian dollars. "Okay. I'll get right on it."

Kamachi bowed and left. There was a phone by the pool, but that might be too distracting. I asked the bartender, and he directed me to a private phone in a small grotto uphill.

It was a voice-only, sitting on a concrete mushroom, too cute. I decided that in terms of security it was about as private as shouting from the rooftops, but I could make my secure call later. All I did was punch the bank and have it transfer most of the money to Switzerland, and then call a travel agent to unravel a visa for me by tomorrow. France was difficult. I had him book both the 1:00 and 6:00 P.M. suborbitals from Woomera.

When I set the receiver down, I noticed a slight tremor in the left hand. My heart was beating fast. A little adrenaline song. It felt good to be back in the saddle. Wheeling, dealing. Have to call Gabrielle LeCompe and see about hiring an actor. It wasn't quite 9:00 A.M. in France. I could call after the meeting. An actor who could learn fast and forget faster.

The beer was still cold. Almost a tenth of my fortune nailed down, and the beer was still cold. Start money rolling, and it picks up money. I probably owed Kamachi about a third of it—he wouldn't be so crude as to mention that now—but he might forgive it if this "Neuville" ruse made him enough. A good man to work with. His only principle was honor among thieves.

I sat in the grotto, finishing the beer, figuring out various angles . . . How could I use the Singapore information without jeopardizing Kamachi's margin juggling? Of course if I were a crook, and stupid, I could undercut Kamachi. Make my million, possibly, and go hide. And be found.

I had no ambition to be sushi.

The party had about doubled in size while I was gone. A little annoying; this semisecret meeting wouldn't happen until all the 'phems got liquored up and left.

Maybe not. Claudia was not known for her subtlety. Maybe at eight o'clock she'd ring a bell and chase out everyone less than a hundred years old.

I picked my way down the hill toward Lamont Randolph, the American who'd invited me here. In the bar, wearing a business suit, that artificial paunch had given him a sort of gravity. Here, wearing fluorescent shorts and huge Hawaiian shirt, he just looked outrageous. And harmless, which he'd claimed was the point.

He was talking to a beautiful woman, a head taller than he, who looked amused. I had to cough to get his attention.

"Ah, Dallas—Dallas Barr, this is Alenka Zor. She's Yugoslavian."

She touched my hand. "Slovenian, actually. We're a separate country now."

"Or again," I said. She smiled; two points.

"I've heard of you," she said. "You do all that mountain climbing and so forth."

"That's right." She was wearing an odd scent, like cumin.

"I've never understood that. An ephemeral, yes, I could

see him doing that, because he's not risking so much; decades.'' She took a sip of fruit juice, staring at me over the glass. ''You risk centuries. A millennium. Why?'

''If I could answer that, maybe I could stop doing it.'' Too glib.

''I'm sorry. An obvious question deserves an obvious answer.''

''Maybe it's because you're a Texan,'' Randolph said.

''But I'm not. I was born in New Jersey. My mother never would tell me why she named me Dallas.''

''More interesting than 'Hoboken,' '' Alenka said. ''Maybe it was the TV show.''

''No, I was over thirty when that came on.'' She nodded and lapsed into that familiar counting-back-and-subtracting look. ''A hundred and thirty-some?''

''One of the oldest,'' Randolph said.

''As far as I know, there're only four older. Not counting clinic doctors, of course.'' Most of the hundred-odd doctors had to be among the oldest, but they all were supposed to be anonymous. I'd met several through the years, who ostensibly came to me for confidential advice. Actually, I think they just had to tell someone that they were immortal.

(I used to wonder about these doctors. They have to stay near the clinics in Sydney or London, but they must have to move every ten years or so, or their neighbors would notice they weren't getting older. Surely they must sometimes run into an old chum who recognizes them from fifty years before.)

''So this meeting,'' I said to Randolph. ''We're going to—''

He held a finger to his lips. ''Not everyone here knows.'' Alenka nodded slightly. ''Not even all the immortals.''

''Do we have a secret handshake?''

''We just . . . know each other,'' Alenka said with an ambiguous smile. While I was absorbing that, wondering to what extent it was an invitation (and an invitation to what?), she hurriedly excused herself, looking off to the right.

A tall man approached from that direction, watching her go. He looked vaguely familiar.

Randolph greeted him. "Briskin."

The name clicked as I shook his hand. "Sir Charles. You were, uh, secretary of the exchequer."

"More than forty years ago. One does drag one's past around." He looked in Alenka Zor's direction and shook his head slightly. "A pity we can't truly start over each time."

There was an awkward silence. "You would be Dallas Barr." I nodded. "And Lamont Randolph." To me: "We talked for a while, where was it? . . . Grenoble."

"You have a good memory."

"Oh yes. Quite." He looked around, a little nervous, and lowered his voice. "Forgive me for being mysterious. I have to talk to both of you. But not at the same time."

Randolph nodded, perhaps knowingly, and walked off. We headed in the opposite direction, away from the crowd. "This is your first meeting," Briskin said.

"Yes."

"What do you think?"

"Reminds me of the old annual get-togethers, before Singapore. Some of them were no larger than this. Before your time."

"Yes. Same sorts of things went on?"

"Wheeling and dealing. Old friends. Maybe a little more. I take it there's some of that here, too."

He smiled. "Now you're the one who's being mysterious. Some of what?"

"You know. Political stuff, power stuff. I think Randolph believes we should be running the world. It's a shared delusion, I'm sure."

"They talk a lot about politics." He was staring at me in an odd way. "But it's all *kaffeeklatsch* noise. They're mainly concerned with making their million and keeping it safe until it's needed."

"Can't criticize anyone for that."

"But you don't do it."

"Yes, I do. In a way."

"What you don't do is make your million the same way each time. Almost everyone else does—contacts, special knowledge, and so forth. It makes sense." I shrugged. I'd heard this before. "You've made nine fortunes nine different ways."

It was more than nine fortunes, and only seven actually different ways, but I didn't correct him. "A lot of people have died of overspecialization. All the oil fortunes back in the twenties. People who bankroll fashion and entertainment enterprises. So I diversify."

"What you do is gamble. Every time you leave the clinic, you go off in a new direction." I just smiled at that. Actually, I'll often have spent several years setting up the next decade's fortune, using various identities. Learning things and making contacts. Sometimes it's just like setting up dominoes to fall. Other times . . . there can be accidents.

He was right, though, in that most people continually repeat the same basic patterns. They turn over all their assets to Stileman and then, when they walk out of the clinic, just return to the board positions or vice-chairmanships they'd vacated four weeks before. The boards would always be tickled pink to have them back—since the alternative would be their defecting to a competitor, with all those decades of inside knowledge and expertise.

I had done variations of that safe process a few times, to speed the transition from poverty to a reasonable state of wealth. But I didn't want to become an actual millionaire the same way over and over. There's real power in knowing different ways to go about it, and besides, it's diverting. I've met a number of immortals who were worse drudges than any 'phem punching a time clock, endlessly repeating the same ten-year cycle—until something goes wrong. Several hundred immortals died in the decade after cheap inertial confinement fusion was demonstrated. The world didn't immediately shut down all the fossil fuel and fission power plants, but there was rapid "negative growth." You can't make a million pounds without something to sell.

So I knew about twenty ways to climb up the ladder, and had actually made the million in seven of them. As it turned out, though, that wasn't the only reason Briskin had sought me out. He was a "power" bedbug, too, even worse than Lamont Randolph. But he had a more solid base for his delusions: an underground within this underground.

"I know some people who admire your spirit very much. They would like you to join them."

"No, thanks. This bunch uses up my 'joining' quota for the decade."

"This," he said with a gesture of dismissal, "is just a way to get together with other people who aren't going to die tomorrow. It also serves as a sort of examination area. That's why we set it up originally."

"This gets confusing. Randolph used that mysterious 'we,' too. Your 'we' is a subset of his?"

"No. Many of us are not known to other immortals." Quietly: "Some of us work for Stileman."

"Interesting." Stileman employees are given immortality on a different basis from ours. They don't have to make a million, but their rules include a prohibition against knowingly making contact with any of us clients. That's supposed to minimize corruption.

"How would you like to be independent of the necessity to make a million pounds every decade? Receive the Stileman Treatment free and clear?"

"And legally, of course," I said. He shrugged. "I don't know. I enjoy the challenge. What would I do with my time if I wasn't busy making a million pounds? More to the point, what would I have to do for your nameless bunch?"

"We have a name, the Steering Committee. It's hard to say exactly what you'd be asked—"

"What do they make you do? Steer?"

"Recruit, primarily. English-speaking people."

"And I would recruit Americans."

He didn't get the joke. "I don't think so. Perhaps financial policy. All they told me was that they thought the time had come to approach you."

We had walked off the lawn, onto the rocks that tumbled down to the water's edge. I dusted off a boulder and sat down. Briskin stood over me.

"They thought my time had come?" The water lapping

on the rocks was a soothing sound, just louder than the party murmur.

"That's right."

"So where does Fatso fit into the equation? Lamont Randolph? He seems to think my being here was all his doing."

"He agreed to be our agent, our 'blind,' if you will. He's telling anyone who will listen how clever he was."

"He's one of your Steering Committee, too?"

"Under consideration. He knows about as much as you do."

"Getting me here was a test for him?"

"In a way. We could have acted directly."

"Sure. Just give me a call."

"You told one of our members about Marconi some years ago. We found her through some . . . Italian, shall we say, connection. Lamont Randolph had done business with her last year, without actually knowing her identity, and he was on our 'possibles' list. So we used him to approach her, knowing that you'd be going into the clinic soon." He put his hands in his pockets and looked up.

"And frankly, we'd hoped you would need a little help with your million, because of the accident."

People who say "frankly" make me glow with trust. I skimmed a stone out over the water. "I don't understand why you went to all this trouble."

"If we'd simply asked, you would have refused. As you say, you're not a joiner."

"Yeah, maybe. Nothing you've said makes me real hot to make an exception."

"Well, I haven't explained—"

"Let *me* explain something," I said, standing up. "My life is already at the mercy of one secret outfit, the Stileman Foundation. So Fatso grabs me as soon as I get out of the clinic, and shoves me into the middle of another secret organization . . . the one that's out there drinking Claudia's booze.

"Now you tell me that they are just a front for the real secret organization, your Steering Committee. So now you're going to tell me there's a secret cabal in the middle of the Steering Committee?''

"No. The committee is the last of the Chinese boxes."

"How can you be sure? Anyhow, there's this Russian guy who's been blackballing me—''

"Who told you that?"

"Randolph." He nodded slowly. "So this Russian had to change his mind or die, and once he did one or the other, you were able to give Fatso the word and have him dangle Maria Marconi in front of me. And have it all timed so that I'm just out of the clinic and theoretically vulnerable to wealth.''

"No one thinks you can be bought."

"I see. You did all this to get my attention. So you can present a carefully reasoned argument that I will find irresistible.''

He looked uncomfortable. "Not just to get your attention, no . . . but I suppose we did want to demonstrate to you that we were more than an elitist debating society. That we could make things happen in the real world—like finding the woman you had lost for more than half a century.''

"Okay. Let's assume Maria does show up and, therefore, you have impressed me and earned my undying gratitude. Then what? You tell me the secret password?''

"You're not making this easy, Mr. Barr."

"Sorry. I don't have much practice at it."

He took out a cigarette and blew on its end. It sparkled into life, but he just looked at it for a moment, not smoking.

"All I can really say is that we are profoundly dissatisfied with the state of the world, we feel we have the capacity to change it, and we are currently engaged in carefully developing a consensus as to what must be done and how we should go about it. We'll work covertly within governments and transnational corporations to precipitate slowly—I emphasize, slowly—the changes we feel are necessary." He flipped the cigarette down toward the water, unsmoked. "We will do it with you or without you.''

"When do you start?"

"We've begun. Asking you and a few others is part of this stage of the plan."

"How many are you?"

"I'm not sure. Perhaps a hundred actual members, and half that number under consideration for membership."

"Doesn't sound like very many people, to rule the world."

"We only want to guide it. Forget the Star Chamber power fantasy the ephemeral papers are always dragging out. We don't have to do anything sinister. Just work collectively with our wealth and knowledge of the world."

"The knowledge better be worth a lot," I said, doing some mental arithmetic. "Because you're not talking about a great deal of wealth. Less than half a billion pounds, even if all hundred-fifty are unusually well off. You couldn't buy off the legislature of Rhode Island with that."

"You're right and wrong. We couldn't buy much with five hundred million, and we have a great deal more." He stared at me, letting that sink in. An annoying mannerism. "Do you understand? We aren't accountable to the Stileman Foundation. I'm far from being the wealthiest among us, but I personally control nearly fifty million pounds."

"Congratulations." I kicked at a rock and failed to dislodge it. "I don't know. Your outfit offers wealth, immortality, and a chance to save the world. But I already have wealth and immortality, and I never agreed with anyone's agenda for saving the world.

"You're right, though, that I had a close one last time. Being independent of the foundation's rules would be worth a lot. Maybe worth helping out with this scheme, if it's not too outrageous."

"There are other things I could tell you that would make you more enthusiastic. But the committee was quite specific as to what I was not to tell you. Until we know that you're committed."

"Fair enough. What's the next step?"

"Someone will contact you. Meanwhile, of course, you will keep this to yourself." He started back up the path.

"Oh, one thing. There will be some disturbing news tonight. If you join us, it need not affect you."

I followed him. "The business about premature brain death?"

He looked startled. "Randolph told you that?"

"He said something. Then backed off on it."

"I'll speak to him." We attempted small talk on the way back to the party without too much success. Nice weather we're having. Want to live forever?

From the edge of the lawn I scanned the crowd. There, over by the pool: a shyly raised hand, a smile breaking into a grin. "Excuse me." Maria.

I remembered holding her seventy years before, a lifetime before. Delicate, almost awkward, like a large soft bird. She was the same. I tasted salt on her cheek.

"I thought you were dead." She nodded wordlessly, her face buried in my shirt. "What happened?"

She wiped her eyes and looked up, face glowing. "This and that. What happened when?"

"You could start with after Singapore."

"Tell me what you think happened."

I took her hand and walked her over to a stone bench. I wasn't going to let go. "All I knew . . . well, I knew you had either gone underground or been . . . blown to smithereens. I looked at all the bodies and parts of bodies they found."

She grimaced. "Parts."

"Yes. There were nearly four hundred people unaccounted for. Most of them had probably been so near the blast they were simply vaporized. Some undoubtedly used the confusion as an opportunity to fade into the woodwork. I hoped that's what you had done."

"As you did, of course. 'Harlan Fitzgerald' was listed among the dead."

"Of course." She didn't continue. "You mean . . . you thought . . ."

"How could I think otherwise? The police said you were dead. They showed me—"

"The body. I'm sorry." It had been some hotel employee

about my size, decapitated and burned beyond recognition. "I left you messages. I tried to get in touch with you everywhere."

"Two days after the explosion I was in a convent outside Rome. They're the ones who took me in after my father died, when I was eleven. For ten years I counted beads and made investments for the order."

"I'm sorry."

"Don't be. It was not a bad time; I needed the quiet." She picked up a twig off the bench and broke it in two, then four. "I didn't want to recycle. I just played with the money because it absorbed me, and it was a way I could do good for the order." She arranged the four sticks in a cross, or an *X*, on her bare knee. "I expected to grow old and die there."

"But you made a million and recycled."

She laughed. "The sisters gave it to me. They said they appreciated all I'd done for them and so forth—but what it finally came down to was that I was too 'worldly.' "

"Contaminating all the virgins."

"Oh, I could tell you about virgins. Anyhow, I cared for my mother the next twenty years. She wouldn't take the Stileman Treatment. Finally she gave in, at eighty, and it killed her."

I nodded. "I've heard that story before."

"The forties were difficult in Italy. A bad time for an old person, bedridden, to be on public assistance . . . if I were to die." The Stileman contract was ruthless when it came to leaving money to relatives and friends. The foundation got it all, or you got to die wealthy. But until about thirty years ago, if you had two million and wanted to buy two treatments, that was okay. Just so long as they got it all. Now you can't even do that. It's all your money for one treatment, period.

"I've done business in Italy a hundred times since Singapore," I said. "Citrus, mercury, textiles, It's surprising we never crossed each other's paths."

"Not surprising. I've always worked through agents, and always behind a man's name. Italy is Italy."

"No worse than here."

"Better than here." She stood up and pulled on my hand, surprisingly strong. "I'm thirsty." We walked toward the bar. "I remember you talking about 'high profile' and 'low profile.' "

"Old Americanism."

"Yes. Well, for sixty-five years I had the profile of a mouse. An ant." We each picked up glasses of white wine and watched the swimmers. "I also had some Family protection at first."

I could hear the capital *F*. "Mafia."

She shrugged. "It's more complicated than that, in Italy. My uncle had connections, and of course I had money and some friends. They helped me disappear. A couple of times."

"You were afraid of the 'phems? Terrorists?"

"That was part of it. Afraid of immortals, too. And my own shadow, sometimes.

"When I came out of the clinic in '50 and found out my Mama hadn't survived the treatment—"

"That you had forced on her."

"Yes. I went into a 'descending spiral of depression.' That's what a therapist called it. Lived on favors. Went from drug therapy to commercial drugs, and wound up addicted to grief."

She had reached over the bowl of drugs to get the wine. "You shook it."

"I don't take it anymore. You're never truly cured until you die of something else. No matter what they say." Her lips touched the wine, and she put it down.

"I made my million as part of therapy. Acting normal. That was '62. Then another Stileman in '75. But that's the last one. Two or three more years and that's it."

I didn't know what to say. I spilled some wine instead.

"I'm over a hundred. I've always said that would be it."

"Nothing left you want to do?"

"Tie up loose ends." She stroked my arm. "Like you."

"I don't know about being tied up. Guess I'll try anything once."

"Silly. I've thought about getting in touch with you hundreds of times, since you came back as Dallas. I remembered that was your real name. And you don't really look that much different from Fitzgerald."

"Twenty-two years I've been Dallas. You don't make hasty decisions, do you?"

"Rarely." She kissed my cheek. "Maybe I was a little afraid it wouldn't work. You wouldn't remember, or you'd be mad. Then whom would I fantasize about?"

"Ah, the lovebirds." An acre of Hawaiian shirt appeared. "Glad you found each other."

"Lamont told me you'd be here, when we met last month in Stockholm."

I tapped a crimson butterfly somewhere over his heart. Play it dumb. "You told her I'd be here and then told me she'd be here?"

He grinned. "Matchmaking on the margin."

"But that means you knew I was in the clinic. How the hell could you find that out?"

"Well . . . we have sources." He patted me on the shoulder. "I don't mean to be mysterious. In fact, I'm not sure exactly where the information does come from."

"That's reassuring." Maybe I should ask Sir Charles. "When are we going to get down to business?"

He checked his watch. "Food in ten minutes, Claudia said. Then all the 'phems go into town; they have tickets to the Bolshoi opening."

"Could we do that instead of the meeting?"

"It'll be fun." Pat, pat again. "I have to go help." His walk looked strange, too sprightly for a plump man. The implant probably weighed only a few ounces. Maybe I should get one the next time I go private.

"He is a funny little man," Maria said.

"You met him at a party like this?"

"No, Stockholm was much more serious. He had sent me a letter . . . let me see. He said there was an 'informal discussion group' of immortals that had decided to include me. I went because I'd never been to Stockholm except to change planes."

"But what they talked about was interesting enough for you to return for more."

"Not actually. I suppose that what they discussed could be of great interest to an immortal. I'm just a well-preserved lady of a hundred and ten. Not much longer to go."

Again, an ice water splash inside me. She touched the corners of my mouth. "Smile. I told Lamont I didn't think I'd make the next one, and he asked whether he could bribe me with you being there. Funny that he should know."

"A lot of funny stuff going on. He told me I'd been blackballed for years."

She smiled quizzically. "Black balls?"

"One person had objected to my joining the group. But he died."

"I heard, yes. That Russian." Lips pursed. "That was sad, or grotesque."

"The way that he died?"

"Well . . . that he should die there, in Stockholm. It's ironic, isn't it. Just because he went to a meeting of immortals, he—"

"Wait. He died at the meeting?"

"Just after. Some kind of car accident. I read about it the next day. He was still in the Stockholm traffic net; but his car's brain went out, and I guess all the failsafes did, too.

"There was a big smell, a big stink, I mean, because he had been some kind of important government man in America. Then he defected to Russia. You must have read about it."

"No, I was in the tank."

"Oh! Of course. There were a lot of accusations. The Russians claimed the CIA had done it."

"Let me guess. The CIA said the Russians did it to make them look bad."

"Maybe. All I recall was that everybody was investigating it, but there was no conclusion. He'd gone almost straight up and fallen several kilometers into the sea, that one by Stockholm—"

"The Baltic."

"I suppose. The car seems to have exploded on the way

down, and most of the pieces sank. So you had the Americans and the Russians and the UN and the Swedish traffic people, all making wild guesses and accusations. *Dio boia!* I didn't like him very much, but that's still an awful way to die.''

I had the sudden paranoid certainty that he had been disposed of because he stood in the way of my joining the group. That was ridiculous, of course. ''He was an unpleasant guy?''

''Too pleasant. He was all over me, trying to be nice in this . . . oily Russian way. An Italian man would simply ask.''

''And keep asking,'' I said.

She smiled, teasing. ''Only to be gallant. You're too American to understand that.''

''Gallant and optimistic.''

Claudia was standing by the pool, ringing a silver bell. A procession of white-suited men and women carried steaming trays.

''You still eat like a bird?''

''Yes.'' She laughed brightly, also remembering a seventy-year-old joke. ''Half my weight in bugs every day.''

We lined up and filled plates, then tried to find places to sit. It probably amused Claudia to see a hundred expensively dressed people standing with a drink in one hand and a plate in the other, looking for a somewhat clean patch of ground to light on. I led Maria up to the telephone grotto.

The food was elegantly prepared and reasonably exotic, to non-Australians. ''You got your bugs, bird,'' I said, holding up something that looked like a cross between a crawdad and a household pest. Moreton Bay bugs, a delicacy.

''I know.'' She pried one open and speared the morsel of flesh inside. ''Chirp, chirp. You can't disgust me with that. I'll hold you down and feed you witchety grubs.''

''You've been here before.''

''I've been everywhere before.'' On that cheerful note I went down to replenish our wine.

The small chore gave me time to think some difficult thoughts. So when I returned, I wasn't completely surprised when she said, "You think I'm pretty ghastly, don't you?"

"How so?" I said, not too honestly.

"To be so matter-of-fact about dying."

"I wouldn't say matter-of-fact. I'd say positively cheerful."

"Well, yes." She intently opened her last bug, popped it into her mouth, and set down the plate. "No reason not to be cheerful. Instead of scraping together a fortune and hoarding it until it's time to go to the hospital again, all I have to do with my money is spend it. There's enough for me to live out the decade as a millionaire should."

"And then?"

"And then I die, like everybody. But not like an ephemeral . . . instead of year after year of declining powers and growing discomfort, it's over in a few days."

"Terrible days. I've seen—"

"So have I. There are drugs."

There was no real answer to that. I took a sip of the cold wine and looked at her unchanged beauty, and saw dust.

"Why don't you try to change my mind?" she said. "We were going to spend a couple of weeks together after Singapore. Let's do it now."

"Where would you like to go?"

"I don't know. You have a special place?"

"Any place would be."

"Be serious, Casanova. Perhaps somewhere you've never gone?"

I looked up into the darkening sky. "Well, *adastra* would be different. Feel like throwing money away?"

"That would be fun. You make the arrangements; I'll fly us up."

"Good. Early next week." *Adastra* was the ongoing starship project. Like most immortals, I'd invested some money in it, one incarnation or another, but I'd never been up to walk around in it, or float around. They'd only had life support inside for a year or so, and didn't encourage casual visitors. It probably was the one place Maria hadn't been.

"You have your own ship, or rent?" I asked.

"A nice Bugatti that I more or less own. Stileman got it nine years ago; I bought it back last year." That was a familiar pattern.

"White Sands?"

She shook her head emphatically. "Too crowded. Maui."

"Money to burn?"

"Be nice to me and I'll leave you some." A creepy thought. She would be allowed to.

She had to raise her voice to be heard over the clatter of a couple of dozen cabs approaching the front of the house. "That would be Claudia getting rid of the 'phems. Shall we move on down to the meeting?"

"Sure." She took my arm and squeezed softly against it. "Sorry that I seem morbid. I'll try not to bring it up."

As it turned out, she wouldn't have to.

Geoffrey Lorne-Smythe, London Physician, Dead at 136

(Reuters, 19 Sept.) Geoffrey Lorne-Smythe, one of the founding members of the Stileman Foundation, died last night, apparently the victim of a cerebral hemorrhage. A housekeeper discovered the body early this morning, and, as stipulated in Dr. Lorne-Smythe's will, he remanded the body to the custody of the London Stileman Clinic for analysis. (The Metropolitan Police Authority were invited to witness the autopsy, and confirmed that there was no evidence of foul play.)

A clinic spokesman, warning that test results are as yet inconclusive, said that Dr. Lorne-Smythe evidently perished as a delayed result of a head injury suffered last year while playing polo. . . .

Dallas and Maria stood at the entrance to the mansion's great room and, along with everyone else, silently read the obituary that glowed down from the wall screen. Most of the furniture was occupied; they sat together on the floor by the glass wall that overlooked the harbor. The slight buzz of conversation stopped when Lamont Randolph stood up and escorted a frail-looking gentleman dressed in evening clothes to the front of the room.

"My friends," Randolph said, "allow me to introduce Mr. Ian Montville, who was the head of Dr. Lorne-Smythe's household at the time of his death. Mr. Montville was in Australia representing the estate's interests here, and kindly consented to speak to us confidentially."

"Yes." The old man cleared his throat and continued in a clear voice evidently accustomed to giving orders. "Dr. Lorne-Smythe did request that I contact you in the event of his death. I believe that there are only two other foundation members among your . . . anonymous group. The Doctor was not sure that the foundation would be frank with you. He wanted to be assured that all of you were aware of the details of his . . . decline. As unpleasant as it may be to communicate them.

"About four months ago, the Doctor told me he was forced to admit a sudden and apparently continuing advent of mental confusion. I had noticed, of course, having been in the family's service for nearly fifty years. The Doctor had been forgetful and physically rather clumsy. I had put it off to the absence of his wife, though, who had been vacationing on the Moon for some weeks.

"He confided, however, that the mental decline was far more profound than simple absentmindedness. He was unable to read either Japanese or Chinese, in both of which he had been fluent, and could speak only a few phrases. He still had French, which he had learned as a child, and German, from his university studies.

"More seriously, he found it increasingly difficult to understand his own investment patterns. He had kept notes in a kind of shorthand that was rapidly becoming opaque. I sat with him for several days, attempting to decode his records page by page. A great deal was lost. If any of you know of direct dealings with the Doctor which have not yet been regularized by the estate, please be in touch with me."

Montville poured a glass of ice water from a tinkling pitcher and drank half of it.

"He assumed it was brain death, entropic brain dysfunction, or so he said. If I may be permitted a personal observation . . . I could never have imagined Dr. Lorne-Smythe giving in, not even to this certainty of death. But he did become quite meek in his last days, withdrawn and uncommunicative even with Mrs. Lorne-Smythe. To all appearances he did give up, though of course he wasn't really the Doctor anymore.

"From the time he first noticed symptoms of decline—which was eight days before he confided in me—until the morning of his death, was only a fortnight. It was not a terrible way to die, but of course was centuries premature. I never conceived of outliving him."

He picked up the glass and stared at the ice, swirling it. "Poor man. I honestly do wish it had been me instead."

Maria

DALLAS was of course upset by the news—or by the evidence, I should say, since Mr. Randolph had hinted to him the day before that there was bad news waiting at Claudia's.

He was older than the doctor.

I held his hand while the aged servant was talking. Although his expression didn't change one iota during the speech, his skin grew cold and damp. He is probably a formidable man to face over a card table, or a conference table. I suppose most of us have some talent in that direction.

Mr. Randolph led a short discussion afterward, the essence of which was that we should all find out what we could and then meet again later. The Slovenian woman Alenka Zor offered the use of her Dubrovnik villa in two weeks. She is very beautiful, and I did not care for the looks she exchanged with Dallas. Is there something between them? It can wait, woman. Be patient. Less than a year and he's all yours.

Maybe I shouldn't have lied to Dallas about the time. It just came out that way. I guess I said "two or three years" to give him some hope.

The doctor last week said six months, maybe eight. It makes me feel free.

People who lived near Sydney and London were going to push as hard as they could for inside information. The two surviving foundation members—one of whom was a doctor—who had come to other meetings of this group were this evening conspicuously absent. People grumbled about that; one woman used the lovely archaic term "stonewall-ing," which Dallas had to explain to me. Nobody men-tioned the possibility that one or both of the foundation members might be too ill to come, dying of advanced age. I didn't bring it up.

Dallas volunteered to pass the word to the immortals working in *adastra* and see whether any of them had news or ideas. That had the immediate result of getting us visas (the rest of the world may call it a half-built spaceship, but the people aboard call it a country), since the chairman of their Earthbound board was in the room. That probably saved us a day of red tape before our trip.

The prospect of going aboard *adastra* gave me an unaccustomed feeling of anticipation. Space travel is no novelty to me—I've taken the Bugatti as far as Ganymede Station—but I've never seen *adastra*. On reflection, it did annoy me a little to realize that Dallas had chosen the starship as a sort of tacit argument that there might be things for which it could be worthwhile to greatly, abnormally, prolong life. But I had already covered that in my mind.

I think Dallas may make the same mistake other immor-tals have made, thinking that I'm existentially (as well as experientially) naive because of having spent a large part of my life sequestered in some convent—either a solid one of stone and tradition or the no less real fence of secrecy, *omertà*, that has characterized my business dealings and social life, or nonexistence, since I left behind the skirts of the Church. It is a mistake I capitalize on. I know the world well, and, from decades of isolated contemplation, I know the map of my own mind as well, far better than most people know theirs. And I don't fear death, God's last gift, which gives me a kind of freedom that people like Dallas can never have. I feel sorry for him as much as he feels sorry for me.

The Stileman Process makes life sweeter, but it isn't immortality, and I think the Church was justified when it declared that using the term in that context was a venial sin. To find actual immortality, you have to die. If that's false, and if everyone since Peter has been lying or fantasizing, when you die it's just like turning off a switch—then when I die I will be losing nothing of value.

At the end of the evening, Claudia brought out an "entertainment" that was designed to shock us, and succeeded. The sport of boxing is still legal up in Queensland, a state to the north; she imported a pair of athletes who proceeded to beat each other senseless, for our edification. They were not, as I remembered from childhood (and Dallas confirmed), protected by gloves and helmets. Claudia cheerfully pointed out that most of them suffer irreversible brain damage before they retire.

Dallas and I collected our bodyguards and shared a cab back to the city. He was staying at the old Regent and, of course, made it clear that I was welcome to move in with him; plenty of room in the suite and so forth. I pleaded too many loose ends to be tied up before we left, though actually, as he must have known, most of it was electronic business that could be done from any safe phone. I suppose he thought I was being coy, and that must be partly true, though the image of a century-old coquette is ghastly. It's mostly to indulge a lifelong habit of meditation before change. This would be a large change.

Besides, our first time should be in zero gravity. They say it's amusing. I have never even "done it" in the water.

A QUIET DECLARATION OF TASTE.

The Bugatti Galileo is not the marque for everyone. Yachts costing considerably less may draw the eye with modish styling: may impress the simply impressionable with exaggerated claims of sustained high acceleration and extended range. (The discerning customer, however, will of course ignore the claims of advertising and ask to see the ship's individual bonded certification.*)

You will find that no yacht, of whatever price, exceeds the Bugatti Galileo in actual maximum range and sustained acceleration. No yacht can outperform the Galileo.

Only Bugatti provides twin inertial confinement fusion engines, for both sustained power and insurance against engine failure. (Yachts with less range may not need the insurance, but with Galileo the adventurous may explore the far reaches of the asteroid belt, and even beyond—well outside the range of any service and emergency vehicles.)

The Bugatti is for those who agree that space travel should be more than an orbital shortcut over the oceans or the occasional weekend on the Moon.

Bugatti—for those who know that life is always new when there are new worlds to conquer.

---

* Required in Common Europe and North and South America. Dealers in other locations may not be required to carry certification, though all Bugatti dealers do so as a matter of policy.

Dallas arrived in Hawaii two days early, the Singapore business having been less complicated than Kamachi had predicted. Already worth a quarter million pounds, less than a week out of the clinic, Dallas let himself relax. One day for beaches and bars, the next for morning skin diving, alone, and an aimless dawdle through the forest preserve on Kauai.

As arranged, he met Maria outside Spaceport Maui at noon the next day. After a quick bad lunch at the cafeteria, she led him to the runway, where the Bugatti sat like a shiny black panther poised to leap. Dallas was impressed.

"I've never owned one quite this elegant," he said, running his hand along the sweep of the carbon filament wing, careful not to cut himself on the edge. "You actually took it all the way to Jupiter?"

"I did," she said, looking pleased. "The company said that's the farthest anyone has gone in one of theirs."

"I can imagine. It's so small." The entire ship was less than twenty meters long, half of that engine and fuel tanks. "Where'd you carry the extra fuel?"

She opened the sliding air lock door; the inner door irised automatically, a luxury Dallas thought he would rather do without. "Right along here," she said, gesturing. "I had them take out the passenger seat, shower, and galley, and put in a ten-thousand-liter auxiliary tank."

"That's about double?"

"Almost. Anyhow, I filled it up at the Exxon dump in high orbit, then did a long burn to Ceres; topped off the tanks there, then burned and deburned to Ganymede Station, where I refueled again."

"Enjoy Novysibirsk?"

"I enjoyed bathing, after three weeks. Showering in one-twentieth gee is a strange experience. Novysibirsk is strange, too, especially Ceres. Sort of a male world. Like the old cowboy movies, but with modern conveniences. And vices."

"Never been there. Sounds dangerous."

"Not at all, really. If you're not a cowboy yourself."

"Yeah, I imagine." The mounting ladder was automatic, too. They climbed inside.

It was small but opulent. The acceleration couches in front were upholstered in milk-white leather. The floor, which of course would see little use, was covered with a custom-designed Oriental carpet. The galley had an Italian coffee machine and a large wine rack that rotated slowly, to keep the corks from drying out in zerogee. An ebony-and-bone screen gave privacy to the head and shower. The walls, panelled in warm grey silk, were graced by antique Japanese watercolors.

"You stripped all this down for the Jupiter flight?"

"All except the paintings. If I were to do it again, I would leave in the coffee machine, I think; the instant was so bad I stopped drinking it. Long solo flights are easier with coffee."

"With wine, too, I should think."

She laughed. "Grappa. Less redundant water mass." Maria could stand up straight, walking to the couches; Dallas had to stoop slightly. "Use the head if you want."

"I'll wait for zerogee. More of a challenge." (That was another refinement. Most spaceship heads were fan-operated; worthless in gravity.) They started strapping in. "Better tell me where the barf bags are, though."

"Under the left armrest. You get space-sick, *pobrecito*?"

"No, the shots work for me, for the balance problem. It's just Maui."

"We're safer than White Sands." She saw he was strapped in and fed the engines a few drops of fuel. There was a high-pitched hiss and they rolled forward. "Four times safer, launch by launch."

"Statistics," Dallas said, staring out the cockpit as the hangar door rolled open for them. "If I die in a launch, I want it to be my own fault. Not some damned sea gull."

She smiled over at him. "They fixed that. There hasn't been a bird on the track in years."

"Yeah, right." Dallas took out a barf bag and tucked it under a shoulder strap. "Years."

Dallas

It wasn't very rational of me to feel more nervous at Maui. You aren't really in control during boost phase from Sands either; anything serious that goes wrong will be over in a microsecond.

But rolling down that track pinned down by five gees of electromagnetic acceleration—and then being suddenly flung free—well, it may save fuel, but if you can buy a spaceship you can afford a little extra gas.

There were three others in the queue ahead of us—a Mercedes and two dumbos, a shiny NASA one and a beat-up rocknik one. A nice long wait for Maria to get weighed and do redundant system checks, and for me to sit and try to think about something else.

It takes about three minutes at this end, mostly to evacuate the big air lock chamber. Then a short countdown and you spend more than a minute mashed under five gees, total silence and darkness (except for the entertaining spurious colors your crushed eyeballs generate), and then— save for a few milliseconds as you flash through the automated air locks at the exit—you're suddenly screaming through thin air at about ten times the speed of sound.

"You going to kick in while you're still in the tube?" You're allowed to if your exhaust volume is small enough.

"The last few seconds, yes. It's more comfortable that way, don't you think?"

"Yeah." Otherwise you have a second or so to free fall, and then the jets kick in. Feels something like falling off the high board and hitting the water in a belly flop.

Finally a light blinked green, and we rolled into the black

mouth of the air lock. It closed behind us and the only light was the cluster of instruments in front of Maria, a collection of dim green and orange blobs. There was a loud clunk and then the hammering of a pump that got quieter as it sucked the air out.

"Ready?" Maria said.

"Oh yeah. Looking forward to it." I did literally look forward, to keep from spraining my neck, and reached back to smooth down any wrinkles in the cloth of my shirt. Maria did the same: it can be like a dull knife blade pressed down on your kidney.

Then a faint metallic voice counted down from ten. I took a deep breath and belatedly remembered I should have hyperventilated. Then we started rolling.

They'd improved the start a little since the last time I'd been talked into leaving from Maui. It wasn't a sudden five-gee slap but, rather, a slow buildup over several seconds. The giant eased himself onto your chest, stomach, and abdomen in almost total silence. People amused by knuckle-poppings and eructations must find the onset of acceleration hilarious.

It felt as if I could breathe only a fraction of a cupful of air at a time, and only take it halfway down my throat at that. I knew that the panic screaming in my brain was just a result of too much carbon dioxide in the blood—the skin diver's first response (diving without a breather), which he learns to ignore. It's easier to ignore in the water. I wished I could see the clock that Maria was probably staring at. I wished I could see Maria. Not enough to risk a broken neck, though.

I felt a welcome increase of crush—Maria's engines adding their bit—and we were suddenly dazzled by noontime sun in a cloudless sky of deepest ultramarine. Straps cut into shoulders and waist with the sudden braking, hitting air; then the comparatively soft weight of about three gees, headed up.

Maria flipped a few switches, the snaps loud in the thin cockpit air. "You okay?"

"Fine." I lifted a heavy arm and laboriously returned the

barf bag to its home. I couldn't tell whether she had seen the gesture.

The sky got steadily darker as we blasted up and to the east; the ocean horizon's curvature became more pronounced. Then we were finally weightless. My stomach did a reflex "uh-oh" but decided to relax.

Maria unbuckled fast, saying something in Italian, and smoothly kicked off back to the head. A lot of women have that problem with sustained high acceleration. I couldn't feel too superior, lying there dopey with a kicked-in-the-balls malaise. I should get one of those fancy hydraulic suits.

Some more Italian from the head, and a girlish laugh. Then the toilet cycled, and the screen clicked open and shut, and she swam back to the cockpit.

"What's so funny?"

She stopped her forward progress with a light palm touch to the control board and hovered next to me. "I'm tattooed . . . look at this." She slipped open the throat of her blouse and lifted the bra to show how its lace edge had imprinted a pattern on the top of her breast. "It's down below, too. Never wear frilly underwear in five gees."

"I'll keep that in mind." I made a grab for her, more than half in earnest.

"No time." She gave me a peck on the forehead and pushed off, back to her place. "Should be coming in pretty soon."

You could see *adastra*'s support structures for several minutes before the ship itself was visible: shiny, perfectly round bubbles of hydrogen and oxygen, gleaming metal stock, girders, floating in clustered jumbles like huge jackstraws.

The ship would eventually be a streamlined wedge, streamlining being necessary even in "empty" space, if you go fast enough. They were planning to top out at about three one-hundredths of the speed of light. Most of the wedge right now was a gossamer skeleton, just becoming visible when Maria touched the yaw jets and the sight slid away to port.

She stared at the stern monitor and tapped the yaw jets again at just the right moment; no wasting fuel by nudging back and forth. The blinking red light of *adastra*'s dock drifted to the center of the screen and stopped directly on the vernier line. "Very nice," I said.

She smiled and nodded. "Let's see how close they let me get before they—"

The radio came on, suddenly loud. "Bugatti one-six-four-nine-I-T, slow down! You're closing at over eighty."

"Seventy-eight," she said sotto voce. "Will comply." She gave the main jet a long and a short. "How's that?" she asked the radio. "I can't go any slower. We're not *that* immortal."

"Well done. Prepare to surrender control in approximately ninety seconds."

Docking in low orbit is fairly complicated, since any appreciable change in velocity results in a new orbit. (That's true farther out, of course, but it's less pronounced.) You can't just aim for the dock; you'll miss entirely or even crash.

Eyeballing it, you want to fiddle pitch and yaw so that the "horizontal" vernier of your stern monitor lines up with the plane of your orbit, with the dock an appropriate distance above or below. If the dock's dead on the "vertical" line, you should be able to come in with just the main jet. In practice, you have to be damned good to do it. It looked as if Maria could have, if *adastra* had let her. Like most large structures, though, it controlled final approach.

I cinched my straps tight and so did Maria. The radar-feedback computers that take care of the last couple of hundred meters aren't subtle or gentle. They don't want to have to turn you around, so they tend to give you one big blast and then a series of short ones.

This time it was only two. The first one rattled my teeth, and the second was hardly noticeable. Then we tapped the dock and padded clamps closed on us with a creaking sound.

Maria closed down the board and unstrapped in a hurry, kicked off, and drifted sternward. "We may have to move pretty fast. Some docks don't seal too well against a hull curvature this extreme." She came back shepherding both our bags.

"Okay. I'll be ready to jump."

"One way or the other." She took my hand and we kicked over to the door. "Follow what I do, though. If the leak's too bad I'll zip up and go back inside—it's a fast door; you wouldn't want to be caught on the wrong side of it."

There was a scrape and a rattle from outside, and then a "bing-bong" that signaled mating was complete. We squeezed into the broom-closet air lock space and sealed the door behind us. Her left hand over the red emergency slap plate, she thumbed the OPEN button.

My ears popped. There was a loud hiss of escaping air, and a red light was blinking stroboscopically. Maria kicked off in a slow graceful roll, suitcase held to her chest, and I followed with a headfirst uphill dive. It was cold, maybe ten below, but the accordion dock was only about five meters long. The opposite air lock opened as we approached, closed behind us, and cycled quickly.

A smiling, handsome man was waiting for us. I wondered whether it would have been a woman for a male pilot.

"I hope the holding slips are heated," Maria said to him. "If my ship gets that cold, you're going to owe me for several million lire worth of leather upholstery and vintage wine."

The man nodded without changing expression. "It will be no problem," he said with a surprising Russian—rocknik?—accent. "Your visas, please?" We handed them over, along with passports. He kept nodding as he inspected them, initialed a couple of places, and handed them back.

"You have no objection to sharing living quarters?" We didn't. "Good. Follow me, please. Leave your baggage."

Moving with exaggerated slowness for the benefit of those of us who had not brachiated for several million years, he glided from handhold to handhold, following a line of blue tape labeled "TO HUB."

This part of *adastra* was presumably unfinished, just a gloomy volume of indeterminate hugeness. It appeared to be the space between the inner and outer hulls of the ship, curved metal surfaces separated by about ten meters. Occasional light showed a sparse forest of spidery girders stretching off in every direction.

"This whole volume can't be pressurized," Maria said. "Not all around the ship."

"No. One sector at a time, as it is being worked upon. Follow me."

This was fairly daunting. A tunnel barely wider than my shoulders, totally dark. Claustrophobes need not apply to *adastra*. He clipped a flashlight to his belt so that Maria could gauge her distance as we glided up or down. I maintained my distance from Maria by the simple expedient of colliding with her periodically.

"We are approaching a membrane," he said, and disappeared with a fluttering sound. Then Maria and I went through, into light and sudden pain. Inner ear. I pinched my nostrils shut and blew slightly, gestured; she did the same and thanked me.

This tube was not quite so narrow, and was translucent and glowing deep red. Previously the air had had the thin sharp smell of low-pressure oxygen, seasoned with grease and welding flux. Now the air was thicker, more humid, as if people might live here. I looked toward my feet as we moved away from the "membrane." It was just a series of flexible baffles slit along most of two diameters. I'd read about them somewhere, a kind of air lock between areas of high and low pressure. A little leaky but simple and fast. If one side had a sudden drop in pressure, the whole thing would collapse into an impermeable seal.

I wondered why the red light. Maybe to trigger some pre-infantile birth canal memory. The side of the tube was wet, with condensation, and warm. You couldn't have seen in there, could you? I don't remember that far back.

I looked up at Maria and forgave myself a temporary obsession with female parts. What sort of attraction was this, born of four days together, that lasted and grew for seventy years? We had joked about it, and said some obvious things, and never seriously used the word "love." How could I love someone knowing I would lose her in a year or two; how could she love someone and still want to die? But if it wasn't love, we were both in serious trouble. Glandular regression to puberty. I couldn't wait to get my hands on her.

Watson Hygiene Account

Tentative script for Dallas Barr 40-second endorsement

HIGH SCALE—

A marina, night, full moon. Good-looking man and woman, clothing informal but expensive and sexy, walking along the dock hand in hand. They're talking in whispers. They approach his yacht, which has one dim interior light, and stop. She hesitates, nods.

He helps her down into the yacht. Backlit, we see her begin to undress. The light goes out.

Dallas Barr walks along the dock, following their path. As he approaches the yacht, we hear a glissando of silvery laughter.

Barr turns. MEDIUM CLOSE-UP as he speaks.

     Barr
Lucky man, eh?
   (*The laugh again*)
Not so lucky.

ANOTHER ANGLE: BOAT STARTS TO ROCK SLIGHTLY

     Barr, cont.
She has AIDS X. In two
months he'll be dead.

(*Beat*)
She's not out to get him.
She doesn't know she
has it. She won't have
any symptoms until a
month after he's dead.
Then she'll die, too . . .
along with everyone else
she's been
intimate with since June.

ANOTHER ANGLE: SOUNDS OF LOVEMAKING

Barr, cont.
Everyone who didn't use
Airskins.

He holds an Airskin up, draped over his palm; a pencil spot (polarized to give rainbow reflection) picks it up.

BCU AIRSKIN

Barr (V.O.), cont.
Not just a condom—it
had better *not* be, since
it costs ten times as
much—the Airskin is
only a few molecules
thick, invisible except for
the blue ring around the
end. It protects you
absolutely, by
electrostatic repulsion.

Airskin . . .

(*He drops it; camera*
FOLLOWS *as it drifts down.*)

all you feel is safe.

LOW SCALE to follow

Maria was looking forward to getting her hands on Dallas, too, but first they had to survive an "orientation discussion." Nobody was allowed to visit *adastra* simply in exchange for paying the most expensive hotel bills in the history of the universe. You had to let yourself be educated, and you had to "become part of" the project, by donating a few symbolic hours of volunteer labor.

The corridor abruptly widened into a large cylindrical room, which the leader identified as Hub One. There were six doors leading down, or up, to the various levels. One door was an empty yawning elevator shaft; the others had ladders. He pointed at one labeled "Spoke Five."

"They're waiting for you at Level Four," he said. "I'll go transfer your luggage to your room. Leave your shoes here." He floated between Dallas and Maria, grabbed a handhold, and flew back the way they had come.

"Level Four, Spoke Five, Hub One," Dallas said. "I think I prefer 248 Main Street."

"Don't be silly. When people live here, they'll just say four-five-one or something. Nobody could ever get lost." She opened the door and started up the ladder.

Dallas followed carefully. "Sometimes it's fun to be lost."

It was about a hundred meters to Level Four, an effortless glide. It would be a good bit of exercise for fitness extremists, and people afraid of elevators, once the ship had gravity.

The reception room at Level Four was designed to impress millionaires, the only people who would ever see it. The walls were a continuous abstract pattern of inlaid wood, from all the forests of Earth; the floor a tiled mosaic from

Pompeii; the ceiling a Michelangelo fresco. The centerpiece was Rodin's sculpture "Eternal Spring," a young man and woman passionately entangled, pulling their humanity from a base of cold rock.

There were three people in the room, a woman with a name tag and two other customers. Ignoring the museum-quality furniture all around the room, they were standing in the half-crouch posture that's natural for zerogee.

About a third of the floor, where they were standing, was covered with a Stiktite mat. The woman looked their way and held up two pairs of slippers. "Marconi and Barr?"

"No," Dallas said. "This plane is going to Cuba."

"Pardon me?"

"Old joke." As he floated by the Rodin, he brushed the marble with his fingers. "I remember when you bought this. There was hell to pay."

She shrugged. "It's the most appropriate piece of art in the world, for us to take. And they needed hard currency."

Maria and Dallas rotated slowly in the air, putting on the slippers, and then the three helped them down to the mat.

The woman with the name tag was Melissa Abraham. The other two were Bill and Doris Baron.

"Brother and sister, or married?" Maria asked.

"Married." Dallas and Maria nodded politely. There were lots of sibling immortals, since it was about the best way to spend a large inheritance, but married ones were rare. (Besides the obvious problems, there was the practical one that each person had to maintain a separate fortune; neither one could bail the other out if he or she didn't make a million.) "Seventy-one years," Doris said. "Two Stilemans apiece."

"The Barons arrived this morning," Abraham said. "We asked that they wait a few hours so as to join you for this introduction." The two exchanged a look that left no doubt as to what they had done during those hours.

"So this is the sales pitch?" Dallas said.

"Well . . . not really. The four of you have already contributed more than ten million dollars to the project. We assume you have some faith in it."

"Or at least money to throw away," Dallas said. "Better you guys than the foundation."

"You've never thought of coming along?" she asked.

Dallas looked around. "To tell the truth, I never took it that seriously before. It wasn't this real."

"We're going," Doris said. Bill nodded.

"I don't know. Giving up a lot, everything for a blind gamble. Nobody can say whether it will even get you out of the solar system, let alone eighteen light-years."

"There's no really new technology involved," Abraham said. "It's just bigger than existing structures and vehicles."

"A thousand times bigger," Maria said.

"That's true. I know it's like saying that because we can build a tree house, give us the money and we can build a skyscraper. We get that line from 'phems pretty often. I don't think the project would ever have started, if we'd had to rely on 'phem money."

"Immortals are more optimistic," Maria said.

"We have time to be." She obviously hadn't heard the news. "Let me make us some coffee."

She walked over to the nearest wall, the rest of them following in a chorus of Stiktite rips.

The coffee machine was a larger version of the one that graced Maria's Bugatti, an eight-armed centrifuge of teak and gleaming brass. Abraham asked about cream and sugar and punched a sequence of buttons. The machine counted out the right number of beans and ground them with a startling shriek. Boiling water hissed and the aroma of coffee permeated the room, sudden and strong because of the low air pressure.

The machine spun a few times and filled five bulbs of Waterford crystal. Dallas had to laugh when she handed one to him.

"You folks sure know how to economize."

"It's not just to impress people. We're not coming back, after all. The things we take along should remind us of the best our past could offer."

The rest of the hour was not too excruciating—though,

contrary to Abraham's protestation, it was indeed a sales job. They especially wanted to get Dallas on their list, since he was one of the most public immortals.

He was interested in an abstract way, but said it would be another few hundred years before he ran out of things to do in this solar system. Maybe he'd come join them later.

Abraham showed them around the parts of the living area that were pressurized, as yet less than one percent of the total. Then they crowded into a repair tug and circumnavigated the skeleton of the ship.

Most of the outside work was being done by robots, and Abraham seemed to think that that gave the project a high degree of predictability. She said *adastra* would be ready to go in fourteen years and three months. Dallas offered to bet her a million dollars on the spot that it would be late.

Finally, they were released. Abraham called someone and found out their room was Suite B, Hub One, Spoke Four, Level Four. They may have set a speed record for nonresidents.

Maria

I'VE only had a few lovers, usually not immortals, and my memories of the last time with Dallas couldn't be trusted. That was a long time ago and I was star-struck.

He first made love 112 years ago. By now that woman's grandchildren could be dead of old age.

There's not much he doesn't know. His sophistication with my body might have been disconcerting if it hadn't been offset by his own evident impatience. The Stileman Treatment does wonders for a man's plumbing; it sets his clock back to about age twenty. Which might have been embarrassing if it hadn't also been funny, in a grotesque way.

It's hard for a couple to "stay together" in zero gravity; the first minute or so requires certain adjustments, finding a proper rhythm. But we didn't have a minute. I was obviously Dallas's first woman since he'd left the clinic, and he had all the staying power of an excited rabbit. While we were still in the you-hold-still-while-I-move-a-little-this-way stage, his time was up. So instead of relaxing in a warm postcoital glow, we had to swim around the suite with tissues, chasing down threads of ejaculate, which quickly spun out to gossamer fineness. I got some in my hair.

The shower was just big enough for two friendly people who like steam baths with a draft. It was a coffin-for-two cylinder with an air vent at the bottom, to substitute for gravity. (Of course it would be a regular drain once the ship was spinning. I wondered how much of our hundred thousand dollars per night paid for temporary amenities like that.) The shampoo was not remarkably effective, I suppose because the water had to be quickly recycled, but it did the minimum necessary.

Of course, after the shower Dallas was up and ready again. He promised to be careful, and he was, and the only problem with the whole thing was trying to stay reasonably dignified during dinner afterward. Not running off before dessert.

The food was unremarkable, but the company of Bill and Doris was interesting. Bill had made his first million in asteroid mining, during the confusing free-for-all period between the invention of the fusion drive and the rockniks' November Revolution. He had the luck to stumble onto a silver variegate, an asteroid with a vein of pure silver.

So they both were able to stay immortal without too much effort, so long as no one else found their asteroid. Once each decade, as soon as they get out of the clinic, they go to Novysibirsk, find their private asteroid, and carve out a couple of million pounds' worth of silver. Their craft is completely stealthed; no one can track them to the rock by radar.

It's a clever way around the Stileman rules. It's not like saving assets illegally, because they don't own the asteroid. All they own is the knowledge of its orbital elements. They were on their way out there now.

After dinner we went back to our suite, to play with a bottle of wine and each other. You shake globs of wine out of the bottle and chase them around with straws. You don't do it with clothes on.

Oral sex can be exotic in zerogee, floating in the middle of the room with the lights off, your lover a disembodied presence who contacts you only with his kiss. Ghost lover, succubus.

We also had time to talk, actually the first time since Claudia's party that we've been together and not busy getting this or that done. I asked him why he seemed so unconcerned about the new brain death revelation, and after a long pause, he told me about the Steering Committee and the "inside" information he had from Charles Briskin.

I almost wished he hadn't told me. I'm one-fourth

Sicilian, and I take the business of secrets very seriously. True, Briskin hadn't said, "Keep this to yourself, or else"—but he probably hadn't thought he had to say it.

Dallas laughed at himself for having felt a twinge of paranoia over the Russian's death. I didn't think it was paranoiac at all, or funny.

"The timing is too neat," I said. "The way of dying is too suspicious. Don't you think they're capable of getting rid of someone who is retarding their progress?"

"Come on, Maria. It's just an old-boy network." He explained that Americanism to me. "They don't have to kill a member to get rid of him."

"It's the only sure way to keep the secret safe."

"You're making too much of it."

"If I am, then you're brewing a paradox. They're not powerful enough to engineer a murder, but they are powerful enough to know the real story behind Lorne-Smythe's death."

"They could be powerful in knowledge, in connections, without being desperadoes."

"*Ostia!* Which one of us comes from a convent?"

"Mafia maid." I let the matter drop. Perhaps I should have been more insistent.

The next day we did our symbolic token of labor aboard *adastra*. They assumed we didn't have any useful construction skills (which was more or less true in my case, but Dallas had built two houses himself), so they put us where we couldn't do much damage, painting a bulkhead and each other.

There was no excuse for not doing a perfect job, except that it was zero gravity and neither of us had ever seen a pressure-roller before. If you set the pressure too low, or roll too fast, you get a streaky mess that has to be gone over again. But if you set the pressure too high, you make little solar systems of paint planets that go spinning away. That's why one person rolls while the other stands by with two sponges.

(Dallas thought a vacuum cleaner arrangement would work better. Vacuum is one thing they have in abundance.)

When we weren't taking advantage of weightlessness and privacy, we spent a lot of time talking, usually in the observation room at the end of the axial corridor, half the time watching Earth race by a couple of hundred kilometers below us, half the time staring into the depths of the sky. The ship was pointed at Cassiopeia, and there was a little telescope you could use to look at Eta Cass, the star they were going to. It was a double star, very pretty; purple and gold. (Dallas said there are no purple stars, but I know purple when I see it.) The sky was beautiful in that direction, the Milky Way billowing as you can never see it on Earth. There was a lovely twin star cluster near Eta Cass.

By now Dallas knew me well enough not to try to argue me into going back to the clinic, but he wasn't above trying to ply me with numinism. Dying meant leaving all this beauty behind; it could be mine for another thousand years or more.

Of course no one knows what beauty might be on the other side, but I knew *him* well enough not to pursue that. He was surprised when I quoted the King James Bible at him: "The heavens declare the glory of God; and the firmament showeth his handiwork." That's how I learned English, reading that old translation of the Bible: my father had learned that way, and he wanted to share it with me. When he died, I continued.

(A psychiatrist once theorized at me that this was the root of my religious feeling; that it was a way of coping with my father's dying and deserting me. It doesn't seem likely, but even if it were true, you could argue right back that my father was taken from me under such circumstances in order to crystallize my nascent faith.)

Sleeping is wonderful in zero gravity. In a ship you have to slip into constraints, since you don't want to drift into any buttons or switches, but aboard *adastra* we could just float there. Dallas is a heavier sleeper than I am, and he sleeps longer, so I was able to watch him for hours. I would have guessed that people would contract toward a fetal position, but they don't, or at least Dallas doesn't. He floats with arms flung out, as if in supplication, his legs bowed like a jockey's. Once he appeared to be having an interesting dream; I quietly joined it as incubus.

I find myself being the devil's advocate in this enterprise, defending *adastra* against Dallas's cynicism and rationalism. Ignore the hardware; ignore the species-imperialism and dominance aspects. *Adastra* is a testament to faith, which Dallas mistrusts, his own more than anyone else's.

The central personnel problem, for instance, in keeping everyone alive for a few centuries: the Stileman Foundation has to agree to train a hundred or so doctors to send along to administer the treatment. So far it hasn't agreed to supply the people, and Dallas says it never will: it has nothing to gain and a thousand customers to lose.

I think they just haven't come up with the right price yet. It won't be money.

(The woman Abraham thinks that these artificial-intelligence TI, touring image or whatever, computer things, might be the answer to that. They could make carbon copies of all hundred doctors and take them along as cybernetic consultants.)

It seems to me that a more daunting problem would be what in the world those thousand or so people are going to do when they get to Eta Cass. They all will have plenty of talent in making fortunes, but what else? The supposition is that they'll have centuries to study farming, construction engineering, and so forth. But I don't know. There's a lot more to growing things, for instance, than just knowing what to do—the fruit trees I was in charge of at the convent nearly perished before Sister Petra took over. Petra was mentally retarded but things grew for her.

I'm told that engineering is the same, in that you must have a "feel" for it. Out of a thousand financiers and children of rich people, how many do you suppose will be able to make a machine behave? Enough to build a world from scratch?

I suppose they could go at it gradually, living in orbit for generations, tended by the machines that took care of them en route, while chosen pioneers down below learned how to cope with the planet. When I was a little girl, people talked about doing that here—building permanent cities in orbit, a hundred times the size of *adastra*. The rockniks might have that many people now, nearly a hundred thousand, living permanently in space—but it's a sprawling slum, nothing like the gorgeous postmodernist architectural fantasies I studied for that school report when I was ten. Maybe they would have been built if America hadn't had all that trouble in the nineties. Dallas said it wasn't likely, since the cities were supposed to have paid for themselves by selling solar energy, which couldn't compete with cheap fusion. I don't know. Money makes money.

Even if it would work here, though, it would still be a chancy way to live eighteen light-years away. A long wait for spare parts, if something breaks down.

Still, I wouldn't be surprised if Dallas were to go in spite of his protestations. I would almost go too if I were still here. New worlds to conquer, as they say.

We had to leave a day earlier than planned; the committee wanted Dallas (and everyone in their group who'd had more than seven Stileman treatments) to undergo a battery of tests before the Dubrovnik meeting.

He's been thinking about it, and is more worried than he wants me to know. It shows on his face when he doesn't know I'm looking.

I pray for him not to die before he's ready. Prayer is not one of his own tools, I suspect. We haven't talked much about religion, beyond his curiosity about my years in the convent, and perhaps that's best. It's not as if we were going to marry and raise a family.

The London hospital visit took less than an hour, just a few measurements and samples. Some of the samples, though, were no fun for him to give—kidney and liver cells and a little scrape from the prostate—so Dallas stayed in London for a day or so of bed rest, while Maria went to Italy for two board meetings, and up to Switzerland to talk to the people who were turning her real estate into cash.

Dallas's day of bed rest was also active. From his secured suite in the Savoy he worked on the consequences of the

Singapore steel scam, calling in and debriefing the French actor whom Mme. Demarche had hired to impersonate Neuville. He paid off the actor and Demarche, and then tracked down Kamachi, whose tip had started the whole thing, in Rangoon. In return for a half dozen names and prices, Kamachi transferred £200,000 to Dallas's Zurich account.

So the lovers were apart, but their fortunes cuddled together in Switzerland.

Dallas

I was looking forward to Dubrovnik, not having been there this century. The weather was good all over southern Europe, so instead of flying, I rented a high-speed floater and put it on automatic pilot. Spent the morning skimming just under the speed of sound, from Dover, around Gibraltar, through the Mediterranean, up the Adriatic. Enjoying being alone. I listened to most of Mozart's piano concertos and thought a lot about Maria, coming to no conclusion.

Her agent had booked us into a faded-modern extravaganza of wood and glass that clung to the side of a cliff just south of the old walled city. I admired the view from the balcony for a few minutes, then changed some money at the desk and took a water taxi into Old Town.

Nothing had changed much in the sixty years I'd been away, which was not surprising. They had a lot invested in staying picturesque.

With two hours to kill before the meeting, I took a slow stroll along the top of the medieval fortification that encloses the city. Not ancient by the standards of nearby Rome and Greece, it did seem old to me—older than it had last time.

That had been five years after Singapore, five years after I'd lost Maria. I had almost stopped thinking about her by then. What I do remember thinking, a child of seventy, was that in another thousand years I would be half as old as these walls, with some prospect of outlasting them. Stone will crumble.

So now what? Tonight would tell, probably. Assuming I know whom to believe.

I went down to the Placa, the main thoroughfare, and looked for a trinket to give Maria. She'd insisted on paying all of the *adastra* hotel bill, $400,000 American. (It would have taken half my money at the time, but she didn't even ask.) I found a small cross carved out of Martian lapis lazuli, which would go well with her eyes, and had it mounted as a necklace.

The only Slavic language I speak is Russian, and I'd been warned not to use it in Dalmatia. So with English and German and a lot of arm-waving and pointing, I found my way to Alenka Zor's "villa" at the end of Kneza Damjana Jude—actually an apartment carved out of the limestone supporting the city's walls, a dozen large rooms arranged in an eccentric L. It appeared to have views of both the city and the ocean, though I thought one of them had to be a holo; maybe both. (This "illusion of an illusion" was one reason Zor had bought the place. She amused herself later on by opening both windows; the views were real. The asymmetry and false feeling of being underground confused your orientation.) The view from the ocean side was so conventionally charming that Alenka facetiously apologized for subjecting us to the picture postcard cliché: a magnificent old castle perched on an island of black rock, glowing in the light of the setting sun.

Nearly all of the thirty or so people there at this hour were American, British, or Australian, being true to our cultures by showing up more or less on time. Maria might be another forty-five minutes even if she'd just had to cross the street. Having to cross the sea could make it an hour.

I was surprised and pleased to see Eric Lundley there. Surprised because he hadn't been at Claudia's party, though he lives just outside of Sydney, in the Blue Mountains.

Eric and I had been business partners in real estate and currency manipulation about forty years ago, before I became Dallas Barr again. We kept in touch sporadically; he was the guy I could always call if I needed a gloss on molecular biology or the sex lives of the Jacobean dramatists.

Eric had found an interesting way around one of the

Stileman rules. He was queer for books, the actual physical things of paper and leather and so forth. About the time we were together he was building an extra fortune, several million Australian dollars, with the express purpose of pulling together the largest private book collection in the hemisphere. He put it in a comfortable building up in the Blue Mountains, in the middle of nowhere—and then donated it to the Stileman Foundation. Since it was an outright gift, he was able to put various strictures on its use. Any immortal can study there, even live there. But it can't be approached by floater; you have to walk two uphill miles through heavy forest. When you get there, you have a few hundred thousand books, but not much else: no phone, and no food other than what you packed in. It's never very crowded.

So when Eric gets out of the clinic, he makes his million as quickly as possible, puts it in the bank, and lives off the interest, renting a small place near the library to serve as a mail drop. Then he lives with his books for a decade or so. About a year before he goes into the clinic, he plugs himself into that weird outfit in Vegas and has his Turing Image updated. (He might be the only Stileman immortal who also has a TI, since it takes fifteen or more years to complete the initial programming. I've always assumed he did it so that if he forgets something, he can consult himself. . . .)

It's a strange sort of passion, but more constructive than most. And it certainly makes him a handy person to know.

He hadn't seen me come in. I circled the room and sneaked up behind him. "Eric," I said quickly, "which American President invested in dirigibles for interstate transport?"

"Roosevelt. The second," he said without turning around. "Must be you, Andric—I mean Dallas."

We shook hands. "This is where we're supposed to say, 'You haven't changed a bit,' " he said.

"Never seen your chin before." He used to have a full red beard; now it was freckles. "How come you didn't make the meeting last week? It was right next door."

"Can't stand Claudia. No offense; I know you used to—"

"Long time ago. Little too strange for me now."

He nodded, looking around. "Been coming to these things long?"

"No. Claudia's was my first."

"Would've been mine, too." He pointed his glass at Briskin. "Sir Charles wrote last month, explaining about the mob and inviting me. Now I wish I'd been there. Quite a bombshell they dropped."

"Know more tonight." I wondered whether Briskin had planned to invite Eric into the Steering Committee. Probably.

"Interesting that we were both asked at the same time," Eric said.

"I was told that the guy who was blackballing me died. Dmitri Popov."

"Really. Now that's interesting. Didn't know he was immortal."

"You knew him?"

"Not personally . . . but we had some indirect dealings. That was before anyone knew he was Russian."

"When he was with the CIA."

Eric shrugged. "He was in the information business; I'm in the information business. We traded."

"You have hidden depths, Eric."

"Virtual abysses. That's probably it, though. We didn't part on friendly terms." He looked around the room, thoughtful. "I wonder how many people were invited to this little tea party when he died."

"And whether it was an accident?"

"Oh, it was no accident. But I just assumed it was the intelligence community, one side or the other, or maybe both, who did the deed."

"You know that for sure, or is it an opinion?"

"Anyone who knows Volvo floaters knows they can't do that on their own. It was a real clumsy cover-up. I guess you were still in the tank?"

"Until last month, yeah."

"You ought to go back and read about it. I know you

don't follow news, but this item was pretty interesting.''

"I don't know, Eric. If this outfit gets rid of members who have inconvenient opinions, maybe it's time for us to tiptoe out the back way.''

"No, we ought to study it and see if there's any link.'' His eyes brightened with the prospect of research. "It's like your president, Kennedy, when he was assassinated. Was that before your time?''

"I was thirteen or fourteen.''

"Same kind of thing, on a bigger scale. Anyone who knew military weapons knew that the assassin couldn't have done what he did with the weapon he was supposed to have used—an Olympic-class marksman with sniper experience couldn't have done it. But it was seventy years before the whole truth finally came out.''

"When there was nobody left in power who could be affected by it.''

"Exactly. Likewise, the investigation of this one seems to have trailed off into nothing. No doubt impeded by misinformation and bribes.''

"No doubt.''

"I do have a lot of stuff on it here and there in the library. Maybe we ought to get together on it and do some headscratching. For insurance.''

"Yeah, let's.'' I saw Maria and waved. "You know Maria Marconi?''

"Nope.''

"She was the bait they used to lure me in.'' She came over and I made introductions.

She handed me an envelope. "You were in and out too fast, Dallas. The bellman had a message for you.''

Cream-colored expensive stock, the envelope sealed with wax and marked by a signet ring. I opened it:

Dear Dallas,
I feel foolish resorting to this but have never completely trusted electronic security.

There is something about this business that I don't like. Various things that may or may not have to do with one another. Taken separately, they are innocent enough, but considered together they begin to stink.

Anyhow, I would like the benefit of your experience. Please contact me here as soon as you come back to Earth.

With an access of paranoia, I remain

Your friend,
Lamont Randolph

I showed the note to Eric and Maria. "Looks like there's a lot of this going around."

Eric read it carefully. "This guy here tonight?"

"I haven't seen him."

"From the tone of the message," Maria said, "you might expect him not to come. He struck me as a man who wouldn't take chances." To Eric: "He's the one who supposedly lured me into this organization for the purpose of luring Dallas. Though it turns out he was just following orders."

"Too much intrigue in this mob," Eric said. "Maybe you're right, Dallas. Let's quit and start our own secret organization."

"Think I'll give him a call."

Alenka directed us to a phone she said was secure (though she said it with a shrug), and I punched up the number on the hotel stationery.

A tired-looking stranger's face appeared on the screen. "Lieutenant Cook, Homicide."

"Sorry. I was calling 5283-7752x205."

"That's right," he said, brightening. "The penthouse at the Royal Sydney Hotel. Show yourself, please."

I clicked it off. "Could they trace it here?" Maria asked.

"In the States they could."

"Not in Australia," Eric said, "not legally. So this Lamont Randolph either was killed or he killed somebody else."

"Was there anything in the Sydney papers?"

"I don't read the Sydney papers. We could punch them up here, though."

It took a few minutes to get the phone's data acquisition talents to agree to speak English—it wanted to speak Slovenian, Alenka's language, rather than Serbo-Croatian. We finally got it to deliver the front page of the Sydney *Herald* for the last few days. On the day of the note:

IMMORTAL DIES IN PLUNGE
FROM BALCONY WINDOW

POLICE: NOT MURDER?

28 NOV (ANZP) At 6:13 this morning Lamont Randolph, 89, "jumped-fell-or-was-pushed" from the balcony of his luxurious apartment in the Rocks. He fell into a stream of light traffic and was immediately struck by a tank truck. His body was dragged more than 50 meters before the driver could bring the vehicle under control. He was pronounced dead on the scene by traffic paramedics from the downtown barracks.

POLICE CHIEF: "SUICIDE UNLIKELY"

Police declined to speculate about the nature of the incident beyond a few simple observations. Lieutenant Harley Cook, the 12th Precinct's chief of homicide, admitted: "It seems unlikely that the man would have jumped. A wealthy person has access to many less harrowing ways to end it all, and besides, there was no note and, as far as we can tell from a few interviews, none of the psychological precursors to suicide."

Lieutenant Cook refused to call it homicide, though. "The hotel's security is impressive; you can't just take an elevator up to the penthouse. At the time of Randolph's death there was a bodyguard on duty in the foyer that provides the only entrance to the living quarters.

"The balcony has a low railing; one could conceivably be pacing and absentmindedly stumble over it. Or he could have been sleepwalking." With the press of further questioning from reporters, Lieutenant Cook ended the interview.

JUST HAD THIRD STILEMAN

Lamont Randolph had received the Stileman Treatment three times, most recently last November. For more than

thirty years he has been on the board of directors of
General Nutrition, an American firm whose Pacific base
of operations is in Syndey. . . .

My first instinct was to tiptoe out the door and disappear,
but we agreed that that would be too conspicuous. Besides,
it might be handy to know what we were supposed to
believe about Lorne-Smythe's death.

So we circulated separately for an hour, each of us paying
special attention to what sort of chat was going on around
Sir Charles Briskin. With Maria he was neutrally friendly;
with Eric he was somewhat formal; with me he communi-
cated a conspiratorial "watch what happens next" attitude.

The news of Lamont Randolph's death percolated through
the rooms. It was especially jarring since to some extent he
must have been on everyone's minds, having led last week's
discussion and, with Alenka Zor, invited them here.

At nine Alenka asked everyone into the dining room,
where the heavy elegant furniture had been moved aside and
dozens of folding chairs set up.

Sir Charles unnecessarily introduced himself and said a
few words about poor Lamont Randolph. "As to the
unlikelihood of suicide," he said, "we, of course, know a
few things that the authorities do not. And perhaps Randolph, in the course of his investigation . . . perhaps he
learned something that we do not know."

He paused to let that settle in. "Randolph was coordi-
nating data and opinions gathered in his region, which, of
course, includes the Sydney clinic. He had contacts within
the clinic, legal and otherwise."

"Just one minute," said a man with a clotted German
accent. "You're trying to say that . . . this thing that
Randolph learned was so depressing that it drove him to
take his own life?"

"Only recognizing the possibility," Briskin said.

"That's fantastic," Alenka Zor said. "He was no hypersensitive child."

Briskin looked uncomfortable. "As may be. It's only
peripherally relevant—"

"The hell you say," said a woman with a Texas accent. "What if he learned too much and the foundation had him killed? That's pretty damn relevant."

"It doesn't seem plausible—"

"The hell it don't! If I needed somebody put away like that, not sayin' I ever did, that bodyguard in another room wouldn't cut no ice. Just land a good man on the roof, have him climb down to the penthouse balcony, do the dirty deed, run back up to the roof, walk down a couple flights, then take the elevator down and walk out. Nobody in the lobby; they're all outside on the sidewalk, busy gawkin'." She paused in the speculating silence. "Go ahead and tell me the foundation couldn't do that."

"Of course it could," Briskin said. "If it wanted to, it could have everyone in this room killed. But that's not the way it does business."

"Perhaps its business has changed," Alenka said. "If he could prove it is offering only a hundred years, not a thousand—"

"All right. It's possible. Anything is possible. Let's concentrate on what is known." He glared around the room for a moment. "Let me introduce Dr. Joseph Reingold. Head neurologist for the London clinic. I don't have to tell you what he is risking by being here." Reingold was a short, pudgy, balding man. Like many secret immortals, he had chosen an apparent age and physiognomy that would draw no special attention.

"It would have been a terrible risk," Reingold said, "a month ago, three weeks ago. But now everything is changing; everything has to be reconsidered. Including foundation policy separating us from our clients. Because we all have to work very fast."

"It's true then?" Alenka said.

Reingold nodded. The room was still as a held breath. "Apparently Dr. Lorne-Smythe did die of entropic brain dysfunction. It is possible," he said over the sudden murmur, "*is possible* that his death was an anomaly. That something unique to his medical history accelerated the aging process."

"The polo accident," Briskin said.

"Possibly. Not likely. Hundreds of immortals have had mild concussions." He pointed at me. "You're Dallas Barr. How many concussions have you . . . brought upon yourself?"

"Maybe half a dozen," I said. "Seven, eight." Across the room Kamachi smiled and touched his silver dome.

"And you're one of the oldest. You're more than fifty years older than I am."

"Two years younger than Lorne-Smythe." I said quietly.

The doctor nodded. "You and about twenty of the oldest immortals visited the London clinic over the past week, cooperating in a series of tests. We have no early conclusions, I'm afraid—in fact, no clear indication as to in which direction we ought to proceed. Other than obvious concern over the physiology of the brain."

"So we're no different from . . ." I gestured toward the company assembled; some of them flinched.

"Not much different from our controls, who are people with one Stileman. Slightly less brain mass than you used to have; more convolutions. We can't tell too much without dissection, though." He inadequately concealed his enthusiasm over the prospect.

"Until Lorne-Smythe died, entropic brain dysfunction was just a name for something we knew would happen eventually. A disease with no examples. The thousand-year prognosis was an educated guess; no one would have been too surprised if the true figure were five hundred years—or two thousand, for that matter. If Lorne-Smythe is typical, though, our model of the aging brain is drastically wrong."

He went on to repeat the same things over a couple of times, reinforced by impressive charts and graphs and some grisly holos of autopsies. There were differences between Lorne-Smythe and me that I'd call important. We were close to the same calendar age, but he'd had only seven Stilemans to my nine. He'd had his first one in his seventies; I was only forty-seven for mine.

And I had the protection of the Steering Committee. Maybe.

The meeting was understandably subdued after Reingold finished. Maria took my hand and murmured something; Eric patted me on the shoulder. Otherwise, people avoided me, since I had been singled out as the oldest there. As if they could catch the brain death if I sneezed.

Briskin made a discreet signal and walked toward the balcony. I followed him a minute later, trying to look reasonably nonchalant. What'll it be, Charlie? Months, or centuries?

There was a light rain falling, but it wasn't cold enough to be uncomfortable. There was no one else outside.

"Frightening business," Briskin said. I didn't say anything. "Though perhaps it . . . need not affect you."

"What, it was faked?"

"Not really. Lorne-Smythe did die of entropic brain dysfunction. But not because he was old. Not because of a polo accident."

"You mean, your people—"

"Allow me not to say just now. I don't know everything about it, and I'm not authorized to tell you all of what I do know."

The castle view that had been so tritely pretty in the setting sun was equally trite now in its gothic menace: sickly bluish light from the obscured full moon showing angry breakers awash over the jagged black cliff base, the castle visible only in vague outline, save for one pale glowing window.

Briskin waved a cigarette alight and cupped it against the mist. A trick of the breeze enveloped me in smoke, and I coughed reflexively. He apologized.

I should have been more careful, more circumspect. But there was an overwhelming feeling of unreality about it, an actual physical feeling, as if my feet weren't quite touching the ground, as if my head were impossibly light and large. Maybe the wine and slivovitz had something to do with it; maybe the nicotine and whatever else was in Briskin's smoke. But instead of nodding sagely and letting Briskin finish his speech, this is what I said:

"Look. In words of one syllable, answer me this: Did

your Steering Committee kill Geoffrey Lorne-Smythe?''

He took a long drag on the cigarette, and the red glow reflected from his cupped palm showed most of his face, but his expression revealed nothing.

"Surely you can answer yes or no."

"No," he said. "I can't answer."

He wanted me to be afraid then, and I should have been. Instead, I was annoyed. "What about the Russian, then? Popov. Everybody knows it was no accident. Did you—"

"Who have you been talking to?" His voice was suddenly harsh, commanding.

"Lamont Randolph, for one." I laughed recklessly. "Getting so that immortals have a shorter life expectancy than 'phems.''

"You think we did that, too."

"I don't know what the hell to think. You've never told me anything specific, just vague innuendos of vast power and wealth."

"I tell you exactly what—"

"And what that Texan lady said about the Stileman Foundation applies even more to your secret outfit. It wouldn't be hard to kill Randolph if you thought he was dangerous. To have him killed by some third party."

Briskin nodded slowly, started to say something, then turned and walked back inside.

The feeling of unreality persisted. Real life isn't like this. Secret organizations don't arrange assassinations and make them look like accidents and suicides.

I leaned back against the cold metal railing, looking into the brightly lit room. The Texan lady was deep in grim discussion with Kamachi. A trickle of cold water ran down my back.

Who was I kidding? I knew Kamachi had killed, for extreme business reasons. Maybe the Texan had, too; she implied it. Even if this Steering Committee was nothing more than a bunch of fantasizing power brokers with delusions of world conquest, they could certainly take care of me, permanently.

Too comfortable for too long. Not creature comforts, but complacency in my view of the universe, where I fitted into it, how things worked and my measure of control over them.

And a short memory. My first million had been in marijuana, illegal at the time, running it by boat or plane from the Caribbean islands into the southern states of America. A criminal then, I knew of people who would murder anyone for a fee. Satisfaction and confidentiality guaranteed. Sliding scale, depending on the customer's assets and the victim's accessibility.

Jim Nicholson, a guy we called Smiley, claimed to do that for a living. One drunk night he told us how much he'd charge to "mortalize" each of us. I was the cheapest victim, twenty-five hundred dollars. Easy to set up. My carrying a gun didn't count. I was too trusting, he said.

And maybe a little stupid, too.

Maria stepped out on the balcony and slid the door shut behind her. She shivered, and I slipped my jacket over her bare shoulders. The lacy black Italian dress flattered her delicate figure but couldn't have helped much against the weather.

"Find out anything useful from Sir Charles?"

"Yeah. I owe you an apology."

"How so?"

"Sir Charles's bunch, the Steering Committee. They're about as bad as you were afraid they would be."

She turned and looked back into the room. "Wonder where he went?"

"Just stepped out to round up a death squad."

She looked at me curiously. "I wouldn't joke about it. What did he say?"

"He was careful not to say anything specific. Just scare the hell out of me with pregnant silences."

"What did you ask him?"

"Well . . . whether his committee had killed Lorne-Smythe—"

"Dallas!"

"—and Lamont Randolph, and Popov."

She turned to look into the room again. "How could a person make millions of pounds without knowing when to keep his mouth shut?"

"I guess he got to me. Or the whole situation got to me. I had to know."

"He'll *get* to you, all right." She reached into her purse and pulled out a small black caller. "Where's your bodyguard?"

"Back in London." They're not legal in Yugoslavia.

"Mine's offshore. Is there anything back at the hotel that you can't live without?"

"No, but . . ." She pushed the call button. "You actually think they—"

"I came prepared for the worst, Dallas. Maybe Sir Charles did, too."

"In case I didn't pass muster. Held my mouth wrong."

"You can't afford to be sarcastic." The caller whispered, and she spoke some rapid Italian into it, a dialect I couldn't follow. "Eric's probably in danger, too, by association. The three of us are going to casually wander out, go down to the quay, and hire a random water taxi. My bodyguard's waiting for us off Lopud Island, about a kilometer north of it."

"And from there?"

"We'll discuss that later." She opened the door and pushed me through.

Sir Charles was still missing. We separated Eric from a conversation and steered him toward his coat as I whispered, "Maria thinks the shit has hit the fan." He didn't need any details.

It took us less than ten minutes to walk from Zor's place to the public quay. We got in the first taxi on line and asked the driver to take us to the Lafodia Hotel on Lopud. The idea was to let him call in that destination and then, before we arrived, to pay a good-size bribe to have him swing around to the other side of the island.

We made stilted small talk for a few minutes, and then Maria reached by me to tap on the plastic partition behind the driver's head. We were a minute or so away from the island. The driver dropped the taxi down to a hovering idle, turned on the inside light, slid the partition open, and turned to face us.

Without changing expression, he brought out a large-bore pistol and shot Eric point-blank in the face.

I'm no fighter but I've been an athlete for a century and, so soon after rejuvenation, have the reflexes of a nervous rattlesnake. Without thinking, I'd grabbed the pistol barrel instantly, felt the shock as he fired, yanked it from his grasp, reversed it, and fired back. His chest and throat exploded in a bloom of blood and shredded flesh. The taxi stalled and fell to the water.

Eric was just gone. The blast had disintegrated him from the neck up. I'd seen death before, even violent death, but nothing like this. His hands were twitching open and closed. Blood jetted from a neck artery, splashing against the roof and rear window of the cab. His shoulders worked as if he were trying to express something.

Then the blood stopped spurting, and the body relaxed into death. I turned to Maria.

She seemed paralyzed, eyes wide in a glazed stare, not looking at either of the dead men. Her skin was so pale as to be almost blue. The front of her elegant dress was spattered with dots and streaks of crimson, and so was her hair.

She unsnapped her purse and slowly brought the caller to her lips. "There has been an accident," she said in slow Italian, in a monotone. "We're on the water, on the other side of the island."

I looked at the weapon in my hand. It was what American police call a crowdpleaser, a sort of hand-size sawed-off shotgun. Past three or four feet, the pellets evaporate harmlessly. At close range it has the force of a hand grenade.

From the elbow down, my arm was dripping blood.

"Is it still loaded?" Maria asked in a weirdly calm voice. "I mean, how many shots does it have left?" With some difficulty I found an ejecting lever and chipped a thumbnail pushing it in the wrong direction. Then the cassette slid out and I held it up to the light. Three shells. I slid it back in and stuck the weapon in my waistband. Wiped my hand on the upholstery.

The taxi rocked in the gentle waves. The only sound was blood dripping. "Poor Eric," I said, to say something.

"It's over for him," she said, and looked out the window.

I had the odd sensation of knowing that I should feel sick, but feeling almost okay, in spite of everything. Even somewhat elated, light-headed. Maybe some soldiers feel this way once they give up all hope of survival. I didn't know whether I had hours left, or minutes, or days. But I had no doubt they were going to get me. And Maria. Maybe we would make it a harder job than they expected.

A light approached from the other side of the island and became two headlights as it drew closer. I put my hand on the pistol butt. "Is that your guy?"

She nodded and carefully opened the door on her side. An emergency air bag was keeping us well out of the water. She waved into the headlights, and the other vehicle, a Mercedes limo, pulled up alongside.

Her bodyguard wasn't a "guy." She was a big woman, blond and deep-voiced. She croaked *"Dio Cristo!"* when she saw the carnage, then helped both of us transfer from one bobbing vehicle to the other. After a whispered conference with Maria, she produced a handgun and fired at the air bag. It deflated with a loud sigh. The taxi tipped up and slid into the dark water, its headlights visible for a few seconds.

"—To your home, my lady?" the bodyguard asked.

"—No. Head for Rome—no . . . Palermo. I have to think." The limo surged forward, and we both sank back into the overstuffed cushions. "—Turn off the lights, if it's not too unsafe." In the last of the light I saw tears starting.

They agreed that it would be ridiculous to make long-range plans. The first order of business was to sink out of sight. Sicily seemed marginally safer than Rome, as a jumping-off place to get to the States. (The United States would be their best bet since Dallas's Americanness was too conspicuous; they could disguise his famous face, but he'd still stand out too much in the European underworld.)

The bodyguard, Cleta, left them in a run-down seaside motel a couple of dozen kilometers outside Palermo. Before dawn she returned with changes of clothing for both of them, suitcases, American passports, rather roundabout tickets to the Conch Republic, and US$47,000. She'd had to sell the Mercedes for less than half what it would have been worth in a legal transaction. Maria thanked her and gave her ten grand severance pay and hush money, and promised to rehire her when this all blew over.

It was never going to blow over, of course. That's a problem when your enemies are immortal. There was no place on Earth where they could be safe.

Area and Population of the Worlds

CONTINENT	Area (1,000 sq. mi.)	% of Earth	POPULATION [est., millions]				
			1900	1950	2000	2050	2075
North America	9,400	16.2	106	219	380	410	420
South America	6,900	11.9	38	111	258	600	880
Europe	3,800	6.6	400	530	720	750	790
Asia	17,250	29.8	932	1,418	2,433	3,015	3,224
Africa	11,700	20.2	118	199	390	570	630
Oceana	3,300	5.7	6	13	30	50	73
Antarctica	4,400	9.3	—	—	>0.1	0.1	0.2
Earth	57,850	—	1,600	2,490	4,211	5,395	6,017

Off Earth:	area	(2075.0, actual numbers)
Cislunar space	—	1,390
Moon	4,890	436
Mars	18,700	129
Novysibirsk	*	110,000†

* Ceres has a diameter of 640 miles; the other asteroids are 360 miles or less in diameter.
† Estimates range from 85,000 to 150,000.
Source: Rand McNally & Co.

Maria

I think Dallas wanted to go to the Conch Republic because that was the last place he had worked as an actual criminal. Supposedly he would know how to act and so forth . . . though the fact that a hundred years had passed since his experience might dilute its value—like Jesse Jim time-traveling to join the Al Capone gang, or something.

We both were still numb with the shock of Eric's sudden death; the sudden transformation of this thing from hypothetical fancy to brutal fact, when we boarded the economy flight out of Palermo. It was a weekender "gasbag," Dallas's choice as the least likely mode of transport for a couple of rich people running for their lives. Also grotesquely inappropriate for a somber or a careful mood.

A chatty hostess on the floater bus that carried us up to the tethered gasbag described the thousand-and-one delights that awaited us there: four "gourmet" restaurants; live entertainment; all kinds of gambling, perfectly legal. She didn't have to mention the drugs and prostitution, also legal. Or at least not *il*legal, in the airspace no-man's-land between countries.

Our room was a tiny cubicle, mostly bed and mirrors, expensive. The real economy passengers didn't invest in them, figuring to stay up the full twenty-four hours, taking advantage of the ship's diversions (of course, they would make enough by sensible gambling to pay for everything).

We sat on the bed for a few minutes and watched Palermo recede. "Shall we go try our luck?" I said. "The tables will open once we're seven miles out."

"You go without me, hon. I want to rest awhile." Short,

prearranged conversation, working on the assumption that the rooms were bugged. The fine old Family that obviously ran the ship wouldn't be above filing people's pillow talk for future reference.

Dallas would have to spend the whole trip in the tiny room and other safe places, if I could find some. The woman sitting next to us on the bus had gushed about how much he look like Dallas Barr. A little of that could go a long way toward guaranteeing us a welcoming committee at the other end.

My job on this first expedition was to scout out places where we might safely talk, or where Dallas could at least stretch his legs unobserved. And bring back something to eat.

It was hard to concentrate even on the simple task of walking from place to place, asking myself, "Would he be seen here?/could we talk here?," because my mind kept reeling back to that moment of terrible violence. So abrupt, so senseless, so evil. And now Dallas and I will end that way, too. Yea though I walk through the valley of the shadow of death. I will fear no evil. For Thou art with me. Thou art with me.

The casinos would not do, and although two of the restaurants offered "private" booths, they would surely be no more private than the sleeping cubicles. The observation deck was too open, and of course we couldn't go to a show and talk.

I finally came upon a nearly ideal place, the swimming pool. It was satisfyingly loud, with background noise from the engines and air conditioning, as well as the water sloshing around and people splashing and shouting. The echoing din would normally have driven me away, but now it was perfect. And I had never before, as an adult, been undressed in front of strangers, but I realized that nakedness was a rather good disguise for Dallas; we don't visualize famous people without their clothes on, at least not with any accuracy.

At a buffet line I assembled us each a plate of salad, bread, meats, and cheese. Famished, I wolfed down a piece of ham while waiting behind a dawdling woman—and then the image of Eric blowing apart, meat, came back suddenly, and I almost vomited. I swallowed hard a few times, and it finally stayed put; but my appetite was gone.

A waiter stopped me at the door and said he would be glad to carry the plates to my "suite." I said he needn't bother, and he insisted, still politely but with enough of an edge that I finally understood. He didn't want us to walk off the ship with their valuable pseudoceram plates and stainless flatware. Walking back to the cubicle behind him, I was first amused, then angry in a petty way, and then provisionally sympathetic. Possibly he didn't enjoy this part of the job. If he did, I should find room in my heart to pity him.

The emotional distraction took away the nausea, anyhow, and I was able to nibble a little food with Dallas. We made small talk and watched the ocean roll by a kilometer below, while he polished off his plate and then half of mine.

"Didn't feel like eating?" he said, hand poised over the last chicken piece.

"Not really." He swooped and snatched it. "Actually . . . I feel like swimming."

He gave me a significant look. "Long dive."

"No, silly, they have a pool. Australian style; you'll like it."

"Pretty raucous?" I nodded. "Let's go get wet."

There were forty or fifty people in the pool area, many of whom would have benefited from a few acres of clothing. They added little to the scenery but did help the noise level. Dallas and I put our clothes in a locker and slipped into the deep end. We held on to the pool's edge and inched into a corner. Nothing suspicious about a "young" couple huddling there and whispering.

"So this island we're going to," I said, "it's not really part of the United States?"

"Depends on who you ask. About fifty years ago the Conchs formally seceded from the country and changed the name to the Conch Republic. Neither the U.S. government nor the state of Florida admitted the validity of the act.

Florida cut off their freshwater pipeline; the Conchs retaliated by kicking out all the tourists and blowing up the bridge that connected them to the mainland.''

"Sounds American," I said. "I do remember something about it."

"It wasn't all that impulsive, either. A lot of people in the power structure were happy to have an officially outlaw state nearby. For hiding ill-gotten gains, currency manipulation, and so forth. So the federal government keeps protesting, dunning the Conchs for unpaid taxes and demanding extradition this and reciprocity that. But it never does anything that might actually change the status quo.''

We both winced as a huge man dove over our heads. When the tidal wave subsided, Dallas continued.

"It's a good situation for us because we can do everything by cash and not raise any eyebrows. Sooner or later we can be smuggled into the States, with new identities already in place.''

"All right . . . and then what?" I shouldn't have said it.

He stared out over the pool's deck, looking at nothing. "Yeah. Then what.''

"You have ten or twelve years before your next Stileman. You show up at the clinic for the treatment—assuming you can put together a million pounds without being Dallas Barr—and they'll immediately identify you. No disguise is going to hide your chromosome pattern."

"So I have ten or twelve years to beat them," he said quietly. "Or to wait for them to beat themselves, more likely—but I'm thinking more in terms of two or three years. Your time, not mine."

He waited for me to say something. I just looked at him. A part of me wanted to be honest, end the charade right here. Tell him one year would be too long. But I just looked at him.

"We have two basic courses of action," he said. "One of action, really; one of inaction."

"Hide or attack," I said.

"That's right. Though we can ambush them from hiding without too much risk. Send messages to as many Stileman officials as we can locate, describing what happened. Telling everything I learned or could infer from Briskin. Or I could try to go public, use my famous mug—''

"No. Even if it worked, they'd get to you."

"Maybe not, if I set it up right."

"No! You can't act as if they used any common sense, any caution. The way Sir Charles set up our assassination, he obviously didn't waste any time weighing the possible consequences."

"Went ahead and did it." Dallas looked thoughtful. "Yeah. For safety's sake, we have to assume they'll do anything to get us. Even though Briskin may be the only really crazy one."

A giggling couple rushed by over us, bound for an obvious destination. I watched the man's erect penis bouncing and felt a sudden internal squeeze. Dry mouth.

Dallas followed my stare and laughed. "They don't have things like that in the convent?"

I tried to think of a funny reply, but nothing came. I rubbed his smooth bicep. "Let's go back."

Watson Hygiene Account

Tentative script for Dallas Barr 40-second endorsement

LOW SCALE—

A man and a woman, both a little overweight but still attractive, sit on a couch watching the cube. Clothes, furniture, surroundings all low-middle.

We see that they're watching a sex show (maybe a *Holes 'n' Poles* excerpt if we can work up account reciprocity). He slides his hand into her blouse

     Man
  Come on, Margie . . .

>   Woman
> I dunno . . . maybe I
> shouldn't. . . .

>   Man
> Come on . . . I'm dyin'—

>   Woman
> If you think it'd be all
> right . . .

A flurry of activity as they undress each other in haste.

Dallas Barr's speech starts as a VOICE-OVER; after a second, the POV drops to the cube and shows his face.

>   Barr
> Lucky cob, eh? Talked
> the slit into it.

REVERSE ANGLE; she's wriggling out of underclothes.

>   Barr, cont.
> Said he was dyin' for it . . .

CLOSE shot of penetration

>   Barr, cont.
> He will, all right. Die for it.
> Her ass has the X; Brand X.

BIG CLOSE-UP from the side, plunging penis

>   Barr, cont.
> He's not wearing anything.
> Two months, his blade'll
> rot and fall off. Another
> month and he's dead.

POV back to Barr. He holds up a three-pack of
Airskins in one hand and a single one in the other,
draped over his palm. A pencil spot (polarized to give
rainbow reflection) picks it up in front of the dark b.g.

> Barr, cont.
> Airskins. Twenty bucks a pop.
> Can't feel 'em; can't see 'em except
> for the blue ring.
>
> Guaranteed to save your life . . .
>
> unless her husband shows up.
> Then you're on your own.

They tethered the gasbag hovering over a marina, and a
floater took people down in groups of thirty to Mallory
Square, on the west end of the island. In the customs shed
there, those who were headed on to the United States got
into a TRANSIT PASSENGER line, for the usual red tape and
waiting. There was no line for CONCH REPUBLIC, just an exit
door and a table with a rubber stamp, in case you wanted to
decorate your own passport.

Although the island was a congenial place for criminals—
affluent ones, at any rate—it was not at all lawless. It had
police and courts and its own truncated version of Florida
law. For six weeks following Secession, a local bar named
Sloppy Joe's had used as its sole source of entertainment a
group of lawyers giving a marathon reading of the Florida
statutes. They would read a law and call for a voice vote
from the patrons of the bar. If the people in their wisdom
rejected the law, it was torn out of the book. Of course,
you also lost whatever was on the other side of the last
page.

The result was a strange hybrid of Novysibirsk-style
anarchy and conventional American law. You could walk
naked down the street carrying a gun, but you couldn't spit
on the sidewalk. You could be a fugitive from justice in
sixteen countries and go anywhere on the island

unmolested—but so could all the bounty hunters and undercover cops who followed you.

For the average tourist it was no more dangerous than New Orleans or Alaska; it was as pretty as the former and as loose as the latter. Reconstructed or scrupulously preserved nineteenth- and early-twentieth-century buildings sat well back from wide streets lined with tropical flowering trees and palms. Silvery awnings shading the streets from the tropical sun seemed to be a modern concession to comfort, but they were actually there for security, so people could come and go without being monitored from orbit. The government of the United States was not the only party interested in those comings and goings; the Mafia had a satellite, and so did several conglomerates.

But the salt air was like spice and the light was liquid gold. The food and drink were Caribbean, and so was the pace of life. *Mañana,* if we get around to it. Sometimes there were gunfights, true; but they were usually professionals, and hitting bystanders was a serious misdemeanor.

Dallas

As soon as we checked into the hotel, I took the crowd-pleaser down to a gun shop and found a holster to fit the awkward thing. I also bought a three-shot "homer" hidden inside a pen barrel. That's a small heatseeker that's good out to about a hundred meters if your target's unambiguous. Maria didn't want any weapons, but I forced a nonlethal stinger on her, a pocket model that she could put in her purse and forget about.

Maria went down to the library to get the Stileman committee addresses we needed (the Conch phone system is deliberately primitive, not hooked up to any datanets) while I went off to find some money and a good laundry.

Getting the money was straightforward. There's a store-front message service on Duval Street where I traded my thumbprint for a fifty-year-old key. The key fit a deposit box in a bank on the other side of town. The box was halfway through its ninety-nine-year lease; I'd filled it up the year after Secession. It held six kilogram ingots of gold, a ten-carat diamond of the first water, and three packages of one hundred uncirculated thousand-dollar bills. I took the bills, the diamond, and two ingots.

The gun felt awkward. Too big; too conspicuous. I bought an oversized Hawaiian shirt to wear over it but that made it even worse, like a growth on my hip I was trying to conceal. I went into Friendly Mike's Death Shoppe to make a trade.

In the other gun shop the salespeople had been heavily armed; Friendly Mike didn't have any obvious weapon. He didn't need one. Only three people were allowed in the shop at a time, and each of us was tracked by one of three automated lasers, their mountings making ominous greased-metal whirrings as we moved.

He was a huge, rounded cone of fat, like a slightly mobile Buddha, perched heavily on a four-wheeled stool between the register and a glass counter full of small weapons. Small black eyes sunk deep in fat, missing nothing.

"Dallas Barr," he said in a stagy deep voice.

"Nice to be recognized."

"Maybe sometimes."

I stopped a safe distance away. If he fell on you, that would be the end. "I want to trade in a gun. Do I just pull it out, or will that get me fried?"

"Go ahead. I'm in control."

I handed him the crowdpleaser, butt first. His pudgy hands were surprisingly agile, spinning it around, inspecting it from every angle. He opened the receiver a centimeter. "Shouldn't carry a round in the chamber. Blow your leg off." He sniffed the muzzle delicately.

"Hm." He set it down on the glass and stared at it. "Normally, I could give you five or six hundred, trade-in."

"Normally?"

"Yeah. Don't like to carry stuff I know was used in a crime. Cops come by, I sort of have to give it to them."

"Crime?" I could feel my knees turning to water.

"Double murder in Yugoslavia. You forget already?" I shook my head. "We hear as fast as anybody. Interpol, in your case."

"I killed one man in self-defense."

"Hey. I'm not here to judge. Just explaining store policy." He handed it back. "You want some advice?"

"Sure."

"I'll sell you anything you want. But the first thing you want is to go to a laundry. Get rid of that face." He extracted a card from his vest. "Betsy Wolf. She's real good and I get a ten percent kickback."

The address seemed to float shimmering over the card, an expensive refinement. A warning to prospective customers, not to expect bargains. "Thanks. I'll check her out."

"There's no reward on you, yet. Interpol doesn't always carry that, though."

"That was crossing my mind, yeah. Thanks." The Conch Republic had rather more bounty hunters than preachers. I walked fast through the chalky heat to the address, an oceanfront highrise. "Elizabeth Wolf, Beauty Consultants" took up the whole top floor.

The elevator told me how many weapons I was carrying and opened a box in its wall for me to deposit them. It locked the box and coded it to my thumbprint, supposedly. There were nine boxes. "What if more than nine armed people come through here at the same time?"

"I do not know how to answer that question," it said. I was obscurely glad. The door opened into an elegant reception area, glass walls on the right overlooking the ocean, and on the left, a holo reproduction of nineteenth-century Key West. An aerial view from before the time of airplanes.

The receptionist looked up, and for a fraction of an instant there was the familiar I-know-you-You-must-be-someone-famous expression, which faded immediately and was replaced by something professional. "May I help you?"

We established that my name was Morris Niemand and that I wanted to see Dr. Wolf and I didn't have an appointment. While we were discussing the impossibility of my seeing her right away, Dr. Wolf buzzed the desk and said send him in.

The inner office, actually several rooms, was all white and chrome and smelled faintly of isopropyl alcohol and old-fashioned starched sheets. Uniform white light radiated from the ceiling and the upper half of the walls.

Dr. Wolf came in, and it was my turn to be surprised. I recognized her from the Sydney party. I felt very unarmed.

She tried to suppress a smile and failed. "Small world, isn't it? Mr. Niemand."

"I guess I'd better go somewhere else."

"You could. But anybody you find on the island who's any good is going to be immortal. It's a profitable enterprise.'' She took me by the elbow and walked me across the room. ''Any good or not, they're going to recognize you.''

She sat me down on a stool and put a finger under my chin. ''Look straight ahead. Chin up.''

''Wait. I'm not sure—''

''I keep no records, cash on the barrelhead, very bad long-term memory. I'm already forgetting what you used to look like. Smile—no, naturally.''

''What kind of cash?'' I said, smiling. A holo camera came down from the ceiling and circled me silently.

''Permanent change?''

''No.''

''How much cash you have? Now don't smile.''

''Forty or fifty thousand.'' The camera went around again.

''Last of the big-time spenders, eh? Follow me.'' We went into a low room that had a row of chairs facing a large holo cube. She took the first chair and unfolded a keyboard on her lap. An image of my head appeared from floor to ceiling.

''Where'll you be going?''

''Uh . . . I don't know.''

''Don't be coy. For fifty thousand I can make you black or oriental. That's the easiest kind of misdirection. But there are places where either might be a disadvantage.'' She herself was black. ''I assume you've learned to handle places where being *white* is a disadvantage.''

''I'm not being coy. I haven't had time to plan.'' I could afford to tell her something. ''There are people after me with guns. They don't want to talk about it. Rightly or wrongly, they're not afraid of the law.''

''Stilemans?''

''At least one of them.''

''And you can't go to the law yourself.'' She was staring thoughtfully at the image.

''No. Not just like that. Eventually.''

She nodded and tapped a few keys on the console. ''Here.'' My face rippled hugely around chin, cheeks, brow. Then it was somebody else's face.

"That would do fine."

"Four nonmetallic pressor and tractor inserts. Good for about two years; then your face starts to sag back to normal. I can take them out or recharge them, no fee. Course, when you go into rejuvenation, they'll be found. Likewise any kind of facial surgery."

"That's it for fifty grand?"

"No. I'll throw in new identity papers, change your skin color and hair. Height and posture. You want a new dick?"

"What?"

"Blade, dork, penis. One-eyed trouser mouse. It's as individual as the face. You can imagine circumstances where a man might want it disguised." Deadpan. "Give me a first. Say you want it shortened."

"Yeah, well . . . not this time. What about the voice?"

"I wouldn't advise it, unless the ones after you have known you a long time. Most people, it really wears you down, trying to keep a new voice in mind twenty-four hours a day. It's conspicuous when you slip."

"But I've been on the cube a lot."

"Without the face, people won't recognize the voice. It's real white bread, you don't mind me saying. Might be different if you had a funny way of speaking or a strong regional accent."

"Okay. How long does it take?"

"Hour. Then another hour for the local anesthetic to wear off."

"Eighty grand for two?"

She cocked her head at me. "You want it done twice?"

"I mean a package deal. I have a woman with me; they're after her, too."

"Anything special about her?"

I smiled. "Oh yes."

"That's not what I mean. If she's seven feet tall or weighs three hundred pounds, we're in a whole different category."

"No. She *is* beautiful, in a classic Mediterranean way. Like Enrica del Vecchio."

"Beauty's easy to fix." That gave me a little chill. "Is she also a public figure, at all?"

"No; in fact, she's been a recluse for . . . many years. But we have to assume the people who're after me will recognize her."

"Okay. Eighty thousand?" She thought for a moment. "Slow day. I guess so."

I took one of the packages of bills out of the bag I was carrying, broke the plastic, counted out twenty, and gave her the remainder. "Must not take you long to make your million."

"Almost a year, actually." She quickly counted them out in piles of ten. "Lots of overhead. Protection and all."

Satisfied, she stacked the bills together and rolled them into a thick wad, with which she pointed to a door. "You go in there and shower, put all your stuff in the safe. The guns you were carrying ought to be in there by now. Ever kill anybody?"

"Day before yesterday."

"Jesus. Well, I won't tell you your business."

"It's not my regular business. Any advice is welcome."

"Get rid of that hog-leg. The crowdpleaser. I don't know any more about guns than the next cosmetic surgeon, but I know that that one's a death warrant. It's good out to four or five feet, then nothing, right?"

"Guess so. I've only used it once."

"This town's full of people who'll stand six feet away and shoot you between the eyes, just to be cute. I mean it."

"Point well taken. I'll hide the thing."

"Good." She patted me on the shoulder. "I need repeat customers. You go get cleaned up and we'll freeze your face."

The only person who knew me in both incarnations was Dr. Wolf herself. I never passed the receptionist again and the pair who dressed and coached me, Jules and Julie, only saw me after the implants and skin dye.

From Anglo-Saxon to Mediterranean in two hours. I had

olive skin and a force-grown moustache, generous but neatly trimmed, meeting salt-and-pepper sideburns that ran all the way down the line of my jaw. Long dark hair parted on the side, which felt odd but was obviously right. Lifts in my shoes made me walk rather forward, on the balls of my feet, and added an inch to my height. White raw silk business suit, more obviously expensive than I would choose to wear, also right. They tried to get me to smoke a long, slender cigar, but it made me sneeze. Lost the habit a century ago; the craving, maybe thirty years later.

Julie spent half an hour coaching me with makeup. For at least a week, I'd have to cover up bruises on cheekbones and chin, where the tractors and pressors were inserted. After that I would use less, but to stay in character I should always have a little bit of powder. Cassius "Cash" Donato, my papers said I was. American, fortunately. I felt about as Italian as a hamburger pizza.

Looking in the mirror was disturbing. The reflection really was a total stranger; she'd even changed the color of my irises, to black. The small tractors that drew up the skin of my cheeks were resting on my cheekbones, their bulk giving my face a triangular aspect that didn't look too handsome. The two chin pressors created a dimple line and forced both sides of my chin out a centimeter or so.

As the anesthetic wore off, it felt as if someone with an impossibly light touch had a hand on each cheek, pushing slightly in and up. Jules said I wouldn't notice it after a couple of days. It also felt as if I had been punched in the face three times, but they gave me a pill for that.

I went back to Friendly Mike's and the fat man didn't recognize me, or he concealed it well, while I bought a stinger with an ankle holster and a six-pack of shatterguns, one-shot. When I bought six shells for the crowdpleaser, he gave me a curious look and said, "Two in one day."

I went back to the motel and took the steps two at a time. Put the card in the door and slammed into a wall of pain.

Having been hit by a stinger twice before, I knew what was happening and what to do. Don't move a muscle. Be over in ten minutes or so. Don't panic. People panic and die of shock, in agony.

Stinger's a neurological weapon that has something to do with the skeleton. Anything you do that changes the angle between two bones makes the joint between them fire up. The greater the change in angle, the more pain.

Shallow breathing a constant ache. The small adjustments necessary to stay upright made a sparkle of twinges in knees, pelvis, shoulders, back, neck.

Last time it happened, I let myself fall over, thinking it would be easier to not move if I were lying down. The pain of falling wasn't worth it. My attackers were also unnecessarily rough, emptying my pockets.

(They had shoved me around and laughed at my trying not to cry out, which cost them. They didn't know who they were robbing. I tracked them down through some lowlife friends and had their hands and knees broken, shattered with a steel pipe.)

Of course I knew it wasn't hitters this time. My own stupidity. There was Maria, half hidden behind the easy chair, stinger raised to fire again. No. It's me.

"No," I said, keeping my jaw clenched. "Don't! It's me, Dallas."

She threw down the stinger. "Of course it is!" She ran toward me.

"Don't touch." She stopped; I'd told her about the weapon's effects. "Okay. Take out the needle. Help me lie down." The short needle that contained the stinger juice was marked with a length of fluorescent orange thread.

She thought I meant lie down on the bed, and that was painful. Strong woman, though, to carry a rigid man my size ten, ouch, twelve steps. She spent a few minutes at first repeating how sorry she was and how effective the disguise was, and then just waited with her hand resting lightly on my shoulder.

It wears off all at once, like a wave of sparks unrolling from the scalp and toes to the chest and radiating out. I sat up slowly and rubbed at the stiffness. "You did right. I should've called."

"I saw you running up and thought . . . I didn't know *what* to think. Just remembered that . . . man in the taxi."

She looked like she was getting ready to cry. I pulled her over to me. "Yeah. You did right."

She extricated herself, not crying, and helped me off with my jacket. "Lie down, I'll rub your back." I did, gratefully. "You know, I've always hired people to do that sort of thing, *protettori*. If you want me to go armed, you'll have to be more careful about surprising me."

"Right. Won't give you any hand grenades."

"I'm serious." Her fingers dug in hard. "You can't know how I'm going to act because *I* don't know how I'm going to act."

"That's why the stinger's good. You can shoot first and explain yourself later. Or be in the next county by the time it wears off and they call the police."

I told her a little about Dr. Wolf; her appointment was in forty-five minutes. We would meet back here and go out for dinner. I would not shoot her as she came in the door. She told me to get some sleep and left. I had to call her back; she'd forgotten the stinger.

I really felt like relaxing in a hot tub, but didn't want to go through the trouble of reapplying the makeup. Then realized I could use the practice, while it was still fresh in my memory.

Told the tub medium-hot with bubbles and got a beer out of the refrigerator, nine dollars American. I laid out all the armament on the vanity and undressed the strange dark body. Set a shattergun on the edge of the tub. If anyone came through the door I would take out him *and* the door, and part of the wall, and whoever was behind him. You can't reload a shattergun, but neither can you miss.

Slid into the soapy water and asked for classical music. Predictably familiar Brahms. The bubbles were odd, not like soap at all, but a kind of long-lasting slippery foam. I remembered an ad for the stuff, sexy to some people. It would wash off in the shower.

Leafed through *What's On?*, a promotional magazine describing the island's various attractions. A casino where you have to be in costume or naked. An underwater brothel. A raw-meat restaurant, guaranteed fresh and free of parasites, Try Our Caveman Special. Maybe not.

I was dozing, magazine drowned under the weirdly permanent layer of bubbles, when Maria came back. I heard the door squeak and shouted that I was in the tub. She didn't answer; feeling foolish, I picked up the shattergun, getting suds all over it. Hiding it. She opened the bathroom door.

"Nice." Good disguise; she was still beautiful, but black. Helmet of short frizzy hair. She smiled, and I noticed three things simultaneously:

Her teeth were different. Why?

She was shorter. How?

Her right hand was hidden by the doorjamb. It appeared with a pistol. My thumb twitched.

There was a deafening explosion and she disappeared in a cloud of smoke and debris. I scrambled to get out of the tub, slipped and cracked my forehead on the faucet, managed to stay conscious. Groped through the dust and smoke for the crowdpleaser and another shattergun.

I stood there in the ringing silence for long seconds, dripping, expecting to die. But there was nobody else. All over the living room, blood sucked up plaster dust, turning into brown clay. On the floor, intestines and liver and one whole lung rendered starkly diagrammatic by the dust, like a brutal sculpture. Feet still in shoes, jagged shinbones sticking out. Behind the couch I found the biggest piece: head, shoulders, and one intact arm, still holding the pistol. Her eyes had exploded and an impossible length of tongue lolled in the dust. I staggered back almost to the toilet and vomited.

The shattergun doesn't have a projectile as such. Shaped like a saucer with a handle, you aim it in the unfriendly direction and press the button, and it launches a pattern of ten or a dozen little bombs, shaped charges. They go about a foot and explode, making an expanding hemispherical shell of hypersonic turbulence that's devastating indoors. Mine had little stickers on them warning the stupid-but-rich NOT FOR USE IN VACUUM.

Most places, if you blew someone into dirty shreds with the sound of a spaceship exploding, you might draw some attention. In the Conch Republic people had more interesting things to do.

The police eventually showed up, moving with understandable caution. By then I was dressed, glad we'd left the suitcases closed. They used a shouter and requested that I come through the door with my hands on my head. I did. The door itself was down on the other side of the parking lot, splintered and bowed slightly with the pressure of the shock wave, blood slick on one side.

"Anybody else in there?"

I couldn't see who was talking or where he might be hidden. "No. Not alive."

"How many dead?"

"Just one. Woman tried to kill me."

"Yeah, pal. That's what they all say." Two men and a woman, in heavy armor, appeared from behind parked floaters. They advanced on me with heavyweight lasers. Aiming lights danced on my chest.

One had lieutenant's bars. "Self-defense, eh? You know her?"

"Huh-uh."

He climbed up the steps while the other two stayed below. Gestured me back into the shambles.

"This is what's left of her." I showed him the thing behind the couch.

"Oh yeah, Jesus. Sally Murchison." He looked at me sideways. "You Mafia?"

"What?"

"No offense, just that Sally comes pretty high. Came. She had a sort of bug up her butt about the Mafia, though." He spoke into his ring. "This is Freeman on that seven-twelve. Let's get a meat wagon with a Delta Echo team. And a shovel." His face went blank, listening. "No judge, no. Self-defense. Check for a bond under Murchison.

"No prob about Sally," he said to me. "Business is business. But somebody's got to pay for the room." He looked around critically. "You couldn'ta used a pistol."

"Bad shot." That wasn't true.

"Yeah." He took out a pad of forms. "Name."

"I don't have to tell you, do I?"

"Huh-uh. You can get shot resisting arrest, too."

I tried to remember my new name and drew a total blank. I handed him my passport.

"Cassius, eh? Lean and hungry look?"

I nodded. "People call me Cash."

"Yeah? Gonna call you Broke after this." He copied the name and passport number onto the pad. "Got a damage evaluation team comin' out with the hearse. Might be smart if you settle with the innkeeper soon as you get a number. Then fade real fast. Whoever's after you can afford the best. Price of Sally, they could have fifty meatbrains walkin' around with your picture in their pocket. Maybe they do."

He looked down at the gruesome mess and smiled. "Sally, she was one hell of a party girl. Off duty, y'know. She liked cops." There was a tiny chime sound. He put a finger to his ear and nodded. "You're in luck. Whoever hired Sally posted a damage bond. Plenty to cover this."

He handed back my passport. "Maybe you want a souvenir?" He held up the pad.

"How much?"

"Five grand and I tear it up. Ten, and the record shows we carried you out with Sally."

"This is an expensive town."

He shrugged. "Make it eight. Eight, and you're covered all the way to the incinerator."

"As Cash Donato?"

"Whatever name you registered under. Gotta keep the computer happy."

"Harry Morris Williams." That was the name on the passport Cleta had conjured for me.

I took out my fat wallet and counted eight from the thick stack of K's.

He watched with interest and accepted the money thoughtfully, then gave me the two pages off the top of the pad. "Maybe for another ten I could find out who hired her."

"Thanks anyhow. I've got a pretty good idea."

"Guess you would." He turned his back. "Better fade."

I strapped on the ankle holster and shoveled the rest of the artillery into my suitcase. Lugged both bags down to the sidewalk and called Dr. Wolf's office from a public phone. Left a message for the "current female client" to wait outside for Cash to pick her up, Waved at cabs for a couple of minutes. The hearse, a black unmarked van, floated up and parked under the blown-out room. Two men came out, one carrying a shovel and a long-handled scoop. I started walking, and of course, a cab pulled up of its own accord. The driver wanted to know what all the excitement was; I told him I was just passing through.

Left our suitcases at a bed-and-breakfast a few blocks from the doctor's office, loaded up a shopping bag, and walked over. I might not have recognized her, blond and blue-eyed and angular, if I hadn't gone through a similar transformation myself.

She didn't recognize me at first either.

"Maria?"

"Dallas! You took long enough. Men keep propositioning me."

"Understandable." They had put her in a teasing translucent white shift cut loosely in the bodice and slit up the side. It did look like a working girl's uniform.

We started walking. "Why didn't you wait at the motel?"

"We don't have a room there anymore." She listened in silence while I explained.

She looked pale. "This has not been one of your best ideas, Dallas. You said we'd be safe for weeks, months."

"We might be, now. If they do think she got me."

"Sure. Let's take all of your weapons down to the pawnshop."

"Not yet." I stopped in my tracks. "Damn. This means we can't send the letters. Some of them are sure to go to people who are on the Steering Committee, people who think I'm dead."

She nodded but then said, "No . . . you can write 'These

letters are to be sent in the event of my death.' Then have them remailed the way you said, from Arizona or someplace.''

''That's good. Shouldn't even have to remail them, since this is the place where I died.'' We came up to a bench, COURTESY OF EDY'S GARDEN OF EATIN', and I sat down. ''I should have thought of that. Damn.''

''You're still upset. It's understandable.''

''Before, too. I'm not thinking fast enough or well enough. We don't get too many mistakes.''

''Me, too. The terrible pictures in my head, I can't seem to concentrate on anything.''

''Yeah, Eric. What we *need* is Eric. He could always—''

We looked at each other simultaneously. The Turing Image. ''We can have his mind,'' she said. ''We should call anyhow and tell him, tell it, what happened.''

''I wonder. Guess we should.''

''Would it be safe? I mean, could they trace it?''

More thinking. ''About as safe as any kind of telecommunication. We used to use it as a kind of message center so as not to disturb each other with calls. We assumed it was completely safe.''

''Scrambled circuit?''

''Yeah, but the main thing was that it knew me as well as Eric did, in terms of recall. If somebody claimed to be me, it could ask the name of my nephew's wife's dog, or whatever.''

''Let's do it.''

''Now?''

''We have to do *some*thing! Not just wait around for them to find us again.''

I had a strong temptation to point out that a couple of days ago, all she wanted to do was hang around waiting to die. ''Used to be a scramble station down on Caroline Street. Check it out.''

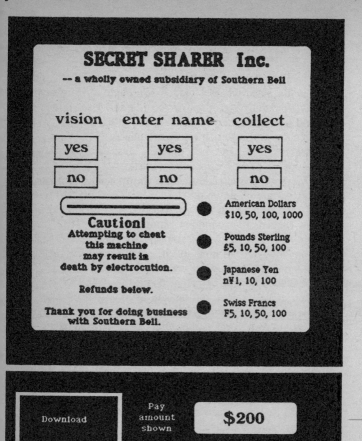

Operator: The two hundred dollars gives you credit for twenty minutes. Please be prompt in inserting additional money should you exceed this time.

Dallas: 5213-555-0936XLUNDLEY.

Eric: Who are you and why won't you show yourself?

Dallas: It's Dallas. But I don't look like him.

Eric: Okay. Who was your girlfriend in 1974, when you were arrested?

Dallas: Mavis Bertram.

Eric: Is it true that women whose names begin with MA always have large breasts?

Dallas: You couldn't tell by Mavis.

Eric: Long time no see. Still no see. You calling to tell me I'm dead?

Dallas: Among other things, yes. I didn't know it was public knowledge.

Eric: It isn't, yet. I have access to some resources that are generally closed.

Dallas: Police files?

Eric: Yes.

Dallas: So you know I supposedly killed you.

Eric: Damned unfriendly, if you ask me.

Dallas: Any clue to who actually did it? Who was behind it?

Eric: No, all I have is the announcement, like a wanted poster. Were you there?

Dallas: It was a cabdriver, a water taxi in Dubrovnik. He killed you and then I killed him.

Eric: Always the man of action.

Dallas: You don't have any emotional reaction at all?

Eric: Oh, I do. "Feel" rather than "think." Without any accompanying somatic sensation, of course; hard to explain. And it's over in microseconds. But that's a long time for me.

Eric was my only relative. Maybe what I feel is like what Eric would have felt if he'd had a twin brother who was murdered. Grief and a desire for revenge. Perhaps you would help?

Dallas: As much as I can. Right now we're just trying to stay alive; we were trailed here by another assassin. The

	people involved are powerful, maybe more powerful even than the Stileman Foundation. Which they have infiltrated.
Eric:	Questions: Who are "we"? Where is "here"? Conch Republic, I assume.
Dallas:	Yeah, it's the Conch Republic; Maria Marconi is the woman with me. You don't know her; Eric met her just before he died.
Eric:	Maria Marconi, born 1970, Rome. Father and siblings perished in 1980 earthquake. First Stileman 2015 in conjunction with treatment for uterine cancer. Four subsequent treatments, as of 2063. Dress size 10, and so forth.

In this way I do know her. Eric managed to hardwire me into the Stileman archives for a tenth of a second twenty years ago. So I have a lot of biographical data about people who were immortals then.

Like Charles Briskin.

Dallas:	You seem to be a jump ahead of me.
Eric:	I could even stay ahead of Eric sometimes. Inferring Briskin because Eric asked about him before he left for Dubrovnik. He was concerned about an "inner circle" Briskin had invited him to join.
Dallas:	It's called the Steering Committee. Do you have anything on it?
Eric:	No.
Dallas:	He claims to have about a hundred immortals who have managed to subvert the rules on accumulation of wealth. They want to change the world.
Eric:	Starting out with killing anybody who stands in the way of their agenda. Sounds vaguely familiar.

This is not safe. The scrambled link is okay, but we have to assume that they can get to me physically, get to the actual crystal, once they find out that I exist and have an interest in them.

Download me. By the time you do, I'll have built a false data structure here, one that hasn't talked to you and that was not alerted by Eric before he went to

> Dubrovnik.
>
> You have to leave the Conch Republic as soon as practical. I would have known that you'd go there because Stileman records show that's where you keep your illegal money. Briskin probably has access to the same information.

Dallas: Have to put in another grand note for the download. Ready?

Eric: A zillion nanoseconds ago.

Dallas guided the K-note through the slot, and a data crystal rattled into the download bin.

"Stileman knows about your illegal resources?" Maria said.

"I've wondered about that." He fished out the crystal, looked at it, and sealed it in a pocket. "Always seemed to me that they'd wink at a million or so. They don't want to lose customers."

He picked up the heavy shopping bag. "Besides, they claim to have the best economists in the world, or the most, keeping track of where every penny goes. If they ignored the underground economy, they could never get the books to balance."

They went down Caroline a couple of blocks to a Holo Shack and picked up a portable reader for the crystal. Then they further covered their trail by abandoning the suitcases left at the bed-and-breakfast and moving into another motel room. They had to buy new clothing anyhow, to match the more flamboyant exteriors Dr. Wolf had given them, and Dallas had taken the precaution of carrying along the crowdpleaser and shatterguns in the shopping bag. All they had to replace were some cosmetics and shaving gear.

Flamboyant clothes were easy to find in the Conch Republic. Dallas held his taste in check and let the clerks advise him. Maria just bought two duplicates of what she was wearing, available everywhere, and a conservative business suit, which took some looking for. They got back to the motel in time to sit on the balcony and watch the sun go down. Dallas brought out cold drinks and the Holo Shack reader.

"Before you conjure up Eric again," Maria said, "think about paradoxes."

"How so?"

"Suppose Briskin did get to Eric before we did. Convinced him that we, or you, actually did kill Eric, the real Eric. Then what you have in your pocket is not an ally, but a possible betrayer."

"Seems farfetched. This Eric *knows* me."

"He's not human, though. He's a logical structure; to him, you and Briskin are both inputs. Maybe the one who gets to him first determines how he'll interpret the second one."

"No, they're smarter than that. I talked to the first one made, Woodward Harrison, about twenty years ago. You remember the *Lloyd Barnes Show*?"

"Scandalmonger."

"Right. He was trying to get an argument going between me and Harrison's Turing Image. Think the TI won, made me look like a fatuous bully. Even that first one was pretty subtle."

"So you don't think Eric's could have been subverted?"

"I don't think so. I never talked to Eric about the possibility. Be willing to bet he built in safeguards, if he thought there was any danger."

"Let's be careful for a while, though."

"Sure." I put a utility crystal in the reader. "Check this thing out before we put Eric in it." It buzzed a query tone, and I said, "Local news."

The small screen flickered and filled up with a smiling computer-generated face, two dimensions. "News time! A courtesy of Bailey's Bar and Massage Parlor. Go to Bailey's if you want that . . . waterfront feel. Tourist or native?"

"Native."

"Today it was partly cloudy and hot, with occasional murders. I mean five dead in less than one hour, in three apparently unrelated incidents.

"At noon there was a prearranged duel between Jake Freeman and Hugo Moran, over some slit who don't want to be named. Hope she likes Jake, because Hugo's feedin' the fishies.

"Hugo was the challenger, and Jake's choice of weapons was knives, underwater. Hugo was a charter pilot and Jake works in underwater salvage and demolition. Fair's fair, huh Jake?

"Next, at about twelve-thirty, was a contract job that fucked up, and I mean fu-u-u-ucked up. If you were tryin' to get some sleep at the El Rancho Motel, you didn't get any. That little noise they heard all the way to Tampa was a shattergun backfire. I mean, welcome to Hamburger Island! The pieces belonged to Harry Morris Williams, a guest in our fair city, and Sally Murchison, a high-class hit slit who used to have a spotless record. Police say Mafia and the Mafia says 'Ay! No-a comment!'

"Then a fenderbender on A1A turned into a bloodbath, as differences of opinion developed concerning—" Maria leaned over and turned off the machine.

"That was you."

"Me and the cop and eight grand. Told you about the shatterguns."

She swallowed, nodded. "It actually blew her into pieces."

"Yeah. Can't say I'm getting used to the sight."

"Guess you'd better show me how they work."

Dallas had one in his jacket pocket. He showed her how to use both safeties and the trigger. "We can tape down the safeties and rig it as a booby trap. Protect us while we're sleeping."

"Disintegrate a nosy hotel maid? No thanks."

"With luck, we won't be in hotels much longer. Find someplace safe and stay there awhile."

"Someplace safe." She shook her head. "You think we'll find that in the United States?"

"I don't know. Out in the country, maybe." He studied the dark gray clouds billowing in from the northwest. "Maybe we'll get a storm tonight." Dallas had told her that their best time to be smuggled into the States would be during a heavy storm. There were a hundred eyes looking down on the Conch Republic; most of them couldn't see through clouds. He turned on the reader and said "Weather."

A different computer face appeared. "Today's weather is brought to you by God—just kidding, folks!—is brought to you by Southern Custom Transportation. We'll drop you and your cargo anywhere in the southern United States or Caribbean, rain or shine, day or night. Our Midnight Special is a fully stealthed, radarproof nuclear submarine, a reliable Russian model that survived the Khomeini Wars.

"Looks like a hundred percent chance of rain tonight, though whether it'll be heavy enough to hide behind, we won't know till later. It's a low-acid rain, pH six-point-eight, so you don't have to take in the daisies.

"Surprise, tomorrow will be sunny and hot. High tide tonight at seven forty-nine, low tide two fifty-five in the A.M. See you there!"

Dallas switched cubes and Eric's face appeared on the small screen, with a bushy red beard. "I've been thinking about your problem," he said.

"Good," Dallas said. "Come up with anything?"

"Yes, but you won't like it. Follow this train of logic. First, you have to assume, in the absence of evidence to the contrary, that Briskin's committee people have access to all of the Stileman Foundation resources."

"We had been assuming that," Dallas said.

"On top of that, though, they evidently recognize no legal constraints on their use of these resources. So we have to assume, as you said earlier, they're actually *more* powerful than the Stileman Foundation. What we must do, then, is assemble a list, a set of places where you could be certain that the Stileman Foundation couldn't get hold of you. Then discard from that list the places where the constraints on the foundation are merely legal, matters of treaty or contract."

"Such as here," Maria said.

"Conch Republic, yes, and Alaska, for the same reason. They can't legally extradite you, but neither can they be prosecuted for gunning you down, as long as they follow the local customs."

The image of Eric held up two fingers. "The two large places where you could go are, obviously, the Soviet Union and Khomeini."

"An armed camp and a radioactive desert. Wonderful."

"Khomeini's impractical because half the population would kill you out of hand for being obvious infidels. The Soviet Union would be possible, but only if you were willing to drop completely out of sight, becoming peasants. People who live comfortably are too conspicuous, and the police are easily corrupted."

"We'll keep it as a possibility," Dallas said. "We both speak some Russian."

"There are a few small places where the Stileman Foundation is forbidden. The Seychelles and Vatican City are the only ones where your lives wouldn't be in constant peril from the natives. I'd say neither of them is large enough for you to become anonymous, though with Maria's Italian and her convent background, she might be able to fade into the woodwork in Vatican City."

"It would be too open, though," Maria said. "Like trying to hide out in a museum."

"But it's mostly indoors," Dallas said. "That would protect you from satellite observation."

"Which is the reason I reluctantly disqualified the Australian outback and the American wilderness. People wandering out in the bush are routinely scanned and identified by various government agencies. It's done automatically, and their identities go into artificial intelligence routines, like yours truly, who decide whether a merely human official ought to be notified."

"That might be all right, though, with Dallas and me having new identities."

"The problem with that is the only way to test it is to go wandering out into the world and see whether anybody shows up to kill you."

"Which makes a good argument for staying here awhile," Dallas said. "If they don't come after us here, they won't do it in the States. Here, we can shoot back."

The image smiled, spookily accurate. "In most of the States you can shoot back, too. But twice they've sent single assassins after you, and twice you've killed them. I think they'll try something else next time. Floater bomb, poison gas. Maybe fry you from orbit with a laser."

"You always were a cheerful son of a bitch, Eric."

"Always. But you see what I'm building up to?"

"Space," Maria said. "No place to hide on Earth."

"Specifically, Novysibirsk. Cislunar space is just a suburb of Earth. Downside is practically a Stileman colony, and all roads on Luna lead to Downside. Mars, anyone who's not part of an expedition would have to bring his own food, water, and oxygen. The outer planets are even worse, if you could get to them. So it has to be the asteroid belt."

"Just great," Dallas said. "Outlaws and anarchists."

---

3. Ceres/Novysibirsk

Most commercial travelers to Novysibirsk limit themselves to Ceres or the gravity "worlds" Mir and Upyours. People who do a lot of business in Novy, though, learn that it can be worth the extra trouble and discomfort to seek out the primary source or end user. Ceres has a "value added tax," Mir has a "gravity charge," and Upyours a "rakeoff," all of which amount to a 10 percent across-the-board charge on all transactions, from both buyer and seller.

If you are willing to put up with microgravity and can operate without docking and load transfer facilities, then the direct route may be for you. But both buyer and seller beware! Novysibirsk *is* in a formal state of anarchy, and although most of the people you will deal with are honorable, if you feel you've been cheated, your only recourse is a jury-of-peers arbitration tradition—which will decide in favor of the rocknik almost every time. Make sure all your deals are settled and recorded with third parties on Earth and in Novy before you leave.

The possibility of violence must be mentioned, if only to counteract the widely held misapprehension that Novysibirsk has a sort of "Wild West" attitude toward crime. Occasional incidents of shoot-out duels and spacings are given disproportionate attention in the media. Most people do go armed (though normally with sublethal weapons), and arguments can escalate. There is also the possibility of immediate "justice" if a person is observed committing rape of a woman, cold-blooded murder, or holing, which is any sort of deliberate damage to a structure that results in loss of air or water. There is a positive side to this, of course. It's been twenty-five years since Novy's last rape.

   To the typical visitor, one with no criminal tendencies, Novy is a safe and civilized place.

   —*Barron's 2082 Commercial Travelers' Handbook*

Maria

"It's not such a bad place," I said. "You've never been there."

"Well . . . no . . ."

I could see he was marshaling an argument. "Excuse us, Eric. We have to talk." I reached for the reader.

"Please wait." That was strange. I'd never had a machine tell me not to turn it off before. "One more thing first. I won't go through all the logic, but there's only one safe way for you to get off the planet. Rocket jocks."

"What?" Dallas said.

Eric smiled. "See you." He turned himself off.

Dallas tapped the blank screen. "I wonder if a Turing Image can go insane. It wants us to take a homemade spaceship to a place overrun by trigger-happy ex-Communist anarchists. For our safety."

"They're not 'trigger-happy,' " I said. "That's only a cliché for the soaps, crazy anarchists. They're nice people."

"I'll concede that. But have you ever met a rocket jock? *That's* crazy. Go up in a spaceship you built yourself."

"You see what he means, though. A commercial flight would be risky, put us in the information net. And they're sure to have my Bugatti watched."

"Yeah," he admitted. "It's probably booby-trapped six ways from Sunday by now." He rattled ice cubes and peered into the empty glass. "Refill?"

I handed him mine. "Half." He took them back into the room.

I watched the storm gathering, all charcoal and alizarin in

the last rays of the sun. Dallas was jittery. Well, it had been a sufficiency of evil, these past two days. I felt more numb than scared. The rum was helping that.

Dallas handed me the cold metal glass. "You've been there, the asteroids."

"Ceres and Mir. That's like saying you've been to the United States if you've seen only New York and Chicago."

"I suppose we'd want to go to Ceres. One of the big ones."

"Perhaps not." The storm was starting, below the horizon. Dim blue flashes, whisper of thunder. "If we went to a place with only a dozen people, we'd certainly know when someone new showed up."

"Yeah. But I'd go stir-crazy."

"There is that." I didn't know the phrase, but knew what he meant. "Ceres is like this place, a little smaller."

"Less water."

"Things take a long time to drop, too. I mean it is an actual city. Even Mir is more like an outpost, a frontier town." I sipped the dark rum. Molasses perfume, lime tang. "But that's what I would like, I think. Go from little place to little place."

"That's what you'd like." He suddenly swallowed half his drink in two gulps, something I'd never seen him do before, and glared at the sunset. To keep from glaring at me.

"I know you don't like spaceflight—"

"I don't like *air* flight! These rocket jocks . . ." He shook his head, almost took another drink. "I told you about the airplane crash?"

"Not since Singapore. Seventy years ago. It was in a jungle?"

"Mangrove swamp. Only forty, fifty kilometers northeast of here, in fact. We were making a delivery, ten big bales of marijuana. There was a little uninhabited island where we had people waiting with a boat. The idea was to come in low and dead slow over the island, and just open the cargo doors, bank, and tip the stuff out."

"Bank?"

"Like yawing in a spaceship." He rotated a hand. "Tilting.

"That part of it went all right. The island was where it was supposed to be; our accomplices signaled us with a flashlight. Doors open, bales out. Treetop level, right on target.

"The plane was an old DC-3 that my partner had put together from several old wrecks. He was inordinately proud of his skill as a pilot and a mechanic. Like your rocket jocks."

"So it crashed."

"Stalled, first. We were supposed to go up, up, and away, back to Jamaica; but he gave them the gas, and both engines sputtered out.

"There was a two-lane asphalt road, A1A, not much more than a kilometer away. He thought he could make it, gliding, land there—it was three in the morning—torch the plane, and hope the guys in the boat would come get us." He took a drink, this time only a sip.

"Wrong on all counts. We lost altitude too fast and clipped a treetop with the right wing. Crashed nosefirst into the shallow water."

"The pilot?"

"He was unconscious or dead, I couldn't see. I smelled gas fumes and panicked. Good thing. I kicked the windshield out and slid down, started running, slogging. The old crate went up in a fireball."

"Did the men in the boat—"

"They took off for open water. Couldn't blame them. It didn't look like anybody could've survived. Probably too shallow to bring the boat in, anyhow. When I caught up with them in Key West they looked like they'd seen a ghost."

He looked a little like a ghost now. "Still . . . airplanes aren't spaceships. Spaceships are safer."

"Sure. Twenty-some years later. Working on my first legal million. My firm was a subcontractor to the American space agency, NASA, supplying the pulse-code modulation master unit for the space shuttle. I got a pass to the VIP stands to watch the thing take off. That was the *Challenger*. Remember?''

''The one that blew up on television. I was fifteen.''

''I could feel the shock wave on my face. One hell of a safe spaceship.''

''But again, that was chemical fuel. There is no way an inertial confinement fusion engine could explode like that.''

''You're the expert.'' He finished the drink and stood up, not too steadily. ''One more an' then a nap. Call the submarine guy. You want?''

''Another half—oh, bring the bottle out. We'll watch the storm.''

''Good idea. Maybe get struck by lightning. Save everybody a lot of trouble.'' He mumbled something about sending a kid up in a crate like that. Bubble gum and baling wire.

The rocket jocks aren't all that crude, but he was right about the overall situation. Nurse a homemade spaceship to the very edge of the human envelope. Evade a bunch of killers by going to a place where killing is a socially acceptable response to insult. Where rum is ridiculously expensive.

It would be an interesting challenge to get there. A difficult trip even for the five-billion-lire Bugatti. But if we didn't make it, well, space is not a bad place to end. The cold airless dark where God lives.

Not butchered by animals.

1 December 2080

The Hon. William Mason (Comm., MA)
House of Representatives
Washington, D.C.

Dear Dr. Mason:

If you are reading this letter I am no longer alive. It is one of forty-seven copies I have asked to be mailed in the event of my dying violently or under otherwise suspicious circumstances.

I was killed by fellow Stileman immortal Charles Briskin. My death was a minor act in a conspiracy designed to take over the Stileman Foundation, and eventually the world. (Briskin's so-called "Steering Committee" has also disposed of at least three other immortals: Eric Lundley, Lamont Randolph, and Dmitri Popov.)

This letter is going to every member of the Board of Governors of the Stileman Foundation. Some of you are no doubt allies of Briskin. Possibly all of you. If no obvious action is taken within the next month, then the person who mailed these letters will mail another batch—this time 183 of them, to every major news medium in the world.

I was invited to join the Steering Committee. When I declined, on April 14 of this year, an attempt was made on my life in Dubrovnik, Yugoslavia. The assassin was successful in killing Eric Lundley, a crime for which I was later accused. (The accusation is ridiculous; Eric and I were friends and partners through four Stileman rejuvenations.)

My agent will be watching for a public statement from the foundation about Briskin and the Steering Committee. Preferably something that clears my name of murder. Otherwise, you're going to be the center of some very unwelcome attention.

Sincerely,
Dallas Barr

They caught the stealthed submarine a little after midnight, gale-force winds surging needle blasts of heavy rain across the island, lightning crazing the blackness. The ship wallowed and bobbed dizzily through the shallows, following channels to deep water, but gave a smooth ride once it was under the surface. When they came up two hours later in a cove south of Miami, the storm had abated to a steady driving rain. Six of them went ashore in a half-swamped inflatable raft with too small a motor, homing in on a dim blinking light inside a dilapidated boathouse. They were met by a taciturn man who said he would take them into town in the morning. Meanwhile, sleep in the boathouse.

It was less than ideal for sleep, a leaky roof dripping from a dozen places, small creatures scuttling in the darkness. Possibly all six of them were fleeing for their lives. That could also encourage insomnia. Dallas and Maria found a place that was only damp and tried to get some rest, Dallas with his back against the plank wall and Maria with her head on his lap. By dawn she was snoring softly. Dallas was wide awake, having nightmares.

Dallas

OUR host was a small-scale farmer, backyard full of elephant garlic and marijuana bushes. His primary vehicle was a school bus so ancient that it had no automation other than a failsafe—and the failsafe kicked in twice, grounding us, when the "gawd damn muthuh-in' ser-kit bray-uk-uhs" acted up. I felt conspicuous in the antique, but once we had joined the stream of rush-hour traffic we didn't stand out so much. It's not a wealthy area; there were a lot of old wrecks putting along.

The other four refugees were headed for Ciudad Miami, the more prosperous Spanish-speaking quarter. Maria and I got off earlier, in the seedy University Heights area where I once lived.

There's no university there anymore, and "heights" is not a word you could accurately apply to any part of Florida. The people who live there call it Puny Uni or Burnout. Half of it was gutted by fires in the Food Riots, and nobody's rushed in to rebuild.

I had the farmer drop us at the Big Tweety Motel, which featured a neon baby bird boasting "Kleen Cheep Rooms." If anyone looked for us there, we would deserve whatever they had in mind.

It did cost less than a twentieth of what we'd paid in the Conch Republic, and indeed it was clean, ozone-smelling. Small, windowless, a hard bed with a picture of Jesus nailed over it. Combination shower stall and toilet, to save time. While Maria was using it, I checked the one drawer. Gideon Bible with the cover torn off, decorated with some obscene cartoons, pretty well done. Feeling vaguely guilty for being amused by it, I put it away before Maria came out.

I stretched out on the short bed, feet hanging over the end, and the sleepless night suddenly caught up with me. Maria eased in next to me while I was floating on the edge of sleep and kissed my cheek lightly.

It was early afternoon when I woke. Maria had gone out quietly and found bread, cheese, sausage, wine. No cups or plates; I cut things up with my clasp knife and we passed the bottle back and forth. Strong American cheddar and garlicky German sausage. It was the best meal I'd had since before Dubrovnik.

"Maybe we should rest a few days," I said. "Lay low. The police report and the letter ought to throw them off the trail. Maybe for good."

"I don't know," she said, intent on peeling the casing from a sausage. "We'll have a lot of time in space where we won't be able to do anything *but* rest. And we'll know we're safe, there. Anyplace on Earth, one of them might be waiting behind any door we open."

"It's possible," I admitted. "See what Eric says?" She nodded and I got the reader out of our suitcase.

"Hello there," the image said. "Still on the island?"

"No, we had a handy storm and slipped out."

"Good. Shall we go about getting you a spaceship?"

Maria allowed herself a small smile. "I was thinking about hiding out for a while first. Get our bearings, rest up."

"Whatever you want. But if I were you I'd get the hell out. You're probably still in Florida, right?"

"Well. . . ."

"If I can figure that out, so can Briskin. You should've gotten on the tube straight off the boat. Go to Montana or someplace."

"He thinks I'm dead. Body, police report, everything."

"If you can buy a cop, Briskin can outbid you. Besides, he's probably figured out that Maria's with you—did you supply a body for her, too?"

"No."

"She's just as dangerous to them as you are, now. The best thing you could do is leave a delayed-action time bomb, publicity, and go to high ground as soon as possible."

"We've set up the time bomb," I said, and explained about the letter. "I thought we might want to wait around and see what happens."

"I think you'd better not. If you're headed for Novysibirsk and suddenly hear that Briskin and his gang have been arrested and thrown in jail, you can always turn around and come home. What you *can't* do is get away once they've found you."

"Two against one," Maria said.

They were right, of course. "All right, damn it. How do we go about hiring this patched-up hodgepodge of a spaceship?"

"Just tell me how much you can afford and hook me up to NatNet. It has a rocket jock exchange magazine called *Crash & Burn*."

"Sense of humor, wonderful." I emptied out my purse, and so did Maria. We did a quick count. "Comes to two hundred grand and some change, and two kilos of gold. They're worth a couple of hundred grand, themselves."

"As of noon, two hundred and thirteen thousand and eight hundred dollars. You'll probably want to take that to Novysibirsk, though. Metal's more reliable than currency out there. That's enough to live well on for a couple of years—insofar as anyone lives well there."

"Best done quickly." I picked up a few small bills and Eric. It was too warm for a jacket, but I put it on for the shattergun in the pocket. "See a pay phone while you were out?"

"There's a power station on the corner, up to the right. I think there was one there."

The bright glare of the afternoon sun made my eyes water. I sneezed three times.

Smell of old smoke. It couldn't still be around, after

ninety years. Maybe they burn sections off every now and then, for old times' sake.

The power station didn't look too good. There was nobody visible, customer or proprietor, but there were two floaters being charged, one in the quick-fill bay. I wouldn't leave one alone in this neighborhood. Then the door to the toilet opened and the customer came out; at the same time I noticed the cashier, a holo simulacrum hard to see in this light. I chided myself for paranoia and went to the phone over by the slow-charge bay.

The smallest I had was a ten, and it was more than enough. I hooked Eric up and the end-of-transaction signal chimed in less than a second.

"Gots a brain in there, hmm?" I turned; it was the man I'd thought was the customer. A head taller than I was and muscular. "Fast one, too. Le's have a lookie." He had his hand out and a smile that was slightly horrible, incisors replaced with metal fangs. Both earlobes had been cropped off, and he had ritual X scars on the cheeks, one under each eye. He was also missing the last joint on each little finger. All of the mutilations were probably signs of rank.

"¿No comprende anglais?" He waggled his hand impatiently. "¡Dame el lector, cabrón!"

"I'll give you something," I said, and hauled out the shattergun.

"O-o-ooh," he crooned, mocking. "If that real, it ain't legal. You don' look like no croid, though. So mus' not be real."

He took a step toward me, and I took a step toward him, thrusting the weapon forward. "Try it, shitbrain." He leaned back, still with the lopsided carnivorous grin, and I heard or sensed something behind me, spun around, and ducked just under a swinging metal pipe. The pipe clanged against the wall, and I swung the reader up hard between the second guy's legs. He dropped the pipe and grabbed his groin, staggering. I punched him as hard as I could on the bridge of his nose with my elbow, knocking him down, and spun back around.

The ugly one was in a crouch that could have been defense or offense. My thumb was still hovering over the shattergun's button. "You've got about two seconds to be missing. Or I'm gonna do the world a favor."

"No you not," he said quietly.

"Blow you to shreds."

"No you not. You blow that thing, you got rats from six precincts on you ass before the dus' settle. 'Prendo you don' want that."

"It'd be worth it."

" 'Prendo not." He inched toward me, his hands making slow circles.

It was an impasse, all right, but only a temporary one. I had the little tangler clipped to my inside pocket. I set down the reader to free my right hand. "Here. Just don't hurt me."

He stood up and strode toward me. "That's more—" The tangler hit him as he was reaching for the reader. He twitched convulsively and fell right on top of it, screaming. Then he arched his back and tried to lie still, knowing what had happened. I had to move him to retrieve Eric, of course, which caused more screams and an outpouring of sincere invective in two languages.

I ran back toward the motel. "What the hell is going on?" Eric asked.

"You almost had a new companion. Where are we headed?"

"New Mexico, probably. We ought to talk about it."

"Better just get on the tube. Attracting too much attention." The screaming had stopped, though, and so far no floaters with sirens. Screams were probably not all that rare here.

Note from Eric: This beauty has been on the market for 19 months, price dropping from $300K. The Europas were disasters, but with the AMC plant it should be a good machine.

Maria had not used the American tube system since the year it first opened, when it was one of the great engineering marvels of the world. It gave the Americans an actual freedom to travel that many of them thought was implicit in their Constitution, since it made a trip across the country only a little more expensive than a trip across town. Unfortunately, it soon became part of the underworld, figuratively as well as literally. People could get to Denver for ten dollars apiece—but they had to hire two hundred-dollar bodyguards before daring to go downstairs.

The guards were big men, black and white, in sleek black Pinkerton bulletproofs, armed with saps and zaps, crowd-pleasers, an assault rifle, and a sawed-off shotgun.

The black man took the money and two return tickets. "We get on the other side of Security, y'all stay between us all the time. Shootin' starts, you just get down and cover your head. Carryin' a weapon?"

"Shattergun and a stinger," Dallas said. "Some other stuff in the suitcase."

He raised an eyebrow. "Don' wanna use the shattergun down there. Break somethin', they jus' put you *down*, I mean the feds. Wanna put it in your suitcase anyway, get through Security."

"Stinger, too," the white man said. "Keep it on the outside, where you can get to it, though."

"Had some trouble this station couple days ago. Buncha griefballs jumped us, plastic knives. Hurt a customer. Hadda kill two."

"You get in trouble for that?" Dallas asked.

"Unh-unh," the black man said. "Save the rats some work. They like ta give us a medal."

They went through the metal and explosive detector,

which noted the weapons in their luggage and bond-locked it until Denver. Down the escalator into a brightly lit slum. A couple of dozen idlers, dull eyes and bright, watched them descend. There were four other bodyguards; they all exchanged nods.

"This don' look too bad," the black man said. "None of our favorites." There was trash everywhere, bottles and needles.

In one corner an old man masturbated a handful of blood. The white guard kicked a bottle at him. "Give it a rest, Pops. Ya broke it again." Pops ignored the advice.

Five cars showed up right on time; the Atlanta shuttle, twenty-two minutes after the hour. The cars were fairly clean, each with eight rows of three overstuffed "seats," upended couches, half of them occupied. They waited outside the Atlanta/St. Louis car while most of the passengers filed out, and then were admitted, one at a time, as the door read their tickets, bodyguards last.

When they'd all backed into place, standing facing the direction of travel, a holo woman floated high in front. "Please do not interfere with the seat restraints." A cage of stiff belts snaked out to enclose each traveler as the car rolled into darkness. They click-whirred through an air lock. "There will be approximately one hundred seconds of acceleration now. For your comfort and safety you may wish to remain facing straight ahead." In absolute silence an invisible three-gee hand pressed down on them. "Then, after four minutes' coasting, we will reverse the seats and decelerate for another hundred seconds. This will be Atlanta. Please remain in your seats for rerouting to St. Louis. Thank you and have a *nice* day." She faded and was replaced by a holo extolling the virtues of Atlanta.

Maria

THE whole trip to Denver took less than thirty minutes, though I wouldn't have minded spending more time and traveling in less frightening surroundings. In Denver we rented a floater and skimmed down to White Sands. It was beautiful desert, but both of us napped through part of it, the floater on auto.

The owner of the used GenDyne/AMC hybrid said he would meet us at the White Sands parking area, coordinates G-35, spot so-and-so, the static test stand. We were a little early, but he was waiting for us.

Lester Jacobssen was a surprise to me. All the rocket jocks I'd met were young or immortal. Jacobssen looked about ninety and not likely to make ninety-one. He was in a motorized wheelchair, dwarfed in the shade of a huge white Stetson.

We identified ourselves as Jack and Mary Culpepper. In fact, he was ninety-two, as he pointed out in his second breath, born in 1988, "the last year America had a sane President." That meant something to Dallas; he laughed along with the old man. I was busy trying to smile and fight the coldness inside, that sometimes comes unexpectedly. I was eighteen when he was born. I could have a child this old, if I could have had a child. My knees trembled with the familiar memory of the deep cold mortal pain, the botched operation that sent me to the Stileman Clinic. The cancer in my womb that was suddenly everywhere. "Sorry?"

"I said you'd like to see it, wouldn't you? Before you pay all that money?" He had a querulous, uncertain voice. The businesswoman in me cut thirty thousand off the price, maybe forty. This was a man who needed money, I supposed for a Stileman.

"Of course. The outside first."

It was an old-fashioned dropnose design, as were all the pre-'75 GenDynes, with stubby Thermlar wing covers retrofitted. Its shortcomings in that regime were unimportant to us, since we'd be going through the atmosphere only twice.

I ran a thumbnail along the not-too-shiny skin. "The hull's pretty badly pitted." I took a small magnifying glass out of my purse—glad for the first time in ten years to have it—and peered at the skin. You couldn't see anything. "Look at this, Jack."

Dallas took the glass and stared at the featureless smooth silver. He nodded soberly. "Gonna cost a pile."

"The last time I had it plated it was only eight thousand," Jacobssen protested.

"Yeah, well, that was a long time ago. Obviously." Dallas handed back the glass and sighted down the hull. "Jesus, I don't know about these dropnose jobs."

I picked up the strategy hint from his tone of voice. "Now, Jack. We knew all the Europas were dropnose."

"Europas, yeah." He nodded absently. "We used to call 'em Fireballs."

"That's why I switched out the power train," Jacobssen said, almost whining. "You can't *git* anything more reliable than that AMC."

"Maybe not in America."

"You said you wanted to buy American this time," I said with a slightly bitchy attitude. The old man turned to me hopefully. "Could we see the inside, Mr. Jacobssen?"

"Sure, I'll—"

"Just a goddamned minute," Dallas said. "I'm not through here." He walked around the ship for precisely one God damned minute, peering into the reaction chamber, fingering the recessed landing lights. He kicked the tires on the landing gear.

Frigid air spilled out when the air lock irised open. The old man rolled onto a wheelchair lift, and up and in, and we followed him.

The inside was not as comfortable as my Bugatti. You don't expect even old spaceships to be shabby, since they aren't lived in that much and don't have to contend with the kind of entropy, dust and gravity and sunlight, that wears down an earthbound room. But this one did show its years and kilometers; it could have used a bit of paint and lacquer and reupholstery. A squirt of deodorant wouldn't have hurt. I felt a little pity for the old man. He couldn't see that a thousand dollars spent on cosmetics would have paid back twentyfold in his asking price.

I think that's characteristic of rocket jocks, though. The inside can look like a parrot's cage if the power train is a percent or two over the original specs.

The emergency equipment bay had an inspection seal on it that was nine years old. I popped it and took out the two space suits, standard Soviet one-size-fits-nobody military issue. They smelled slightly of Lysol and had permanent creases where they'd been folded. "You've never used these?"

"Nope," he said proudly. "Never had a speck of trouble."

"Good thing," Dallas said. "Suits could blow at those creases. Shoulda rolled 'em."

"They came with the ship that way." Dallas shrugged.

I rolled the suits and put them back, then shuffled sideways to get past the two men and sit down in the acceleration couch. It was slick plastic and not clean; made my skin crawl. We couldn't afford the Bugatti glove leather, but I'd have to find something.

Like most American marques, the control boards were overautomated and underinstrumented. Except in one particular: "Where's the cube interface?"

"Don't have no *cube* interface."

"But the advertisement said you had AI navigation and communication."

"Yeah," Dallas said. "What're you tryin'—"

"It does, it *does!* Sixth-generation Japanese, but it's *resident*. You don't need no cube."

"It was made before the cube standard, is what you mean."

"I like it better."

I didn't. With a cube interface, we could have had Eric as an AI backup. "Does it have a vocal I/O?"

"Sure, the red TALK button down in the corner of the right panel."

I pushed it. "Good morning," it said. "May I be of service?"

Dallas cringed. "It's afternoon. Goddamned Japanese accent."

"Maybe it's morning in Japan," Jacobssen said lamely.

"Can you talk to another computer?" I asked it.

"Of course, my lady. In eight languages."

Dallas rolled his eyes. "I'll go get Eric."

Jacobssen was visibly relieved to have Dallas gone. "You got somebody else with you?"

"In a way. He lives in the computer."

"A course. Heard a those."

I studied the controls. "Have you ever docked this thing cold? Without target feedback control?"

"Well . . . don't know where I'd do that, you know? Used to take it all the time to the Moon and went out to Deimos a couple times. That's all feedback, even the fuel dump."

"I see."

"Where you fixin' to go, you need to dock cold?"

Lying is the best policy. "We thought we might do some Earth-orbit prospecting. Check out old satellites for salvage."

"Ah. They're all picked over."

"It would just be for fun."

"Funny idea of fun," he griped, supersalesman. "The Moon, now. That's my idea of a place."

Dallas came back and gave me a little nod, signifying that Eric had been primed. I turned him on and said, "Talk to the autopilot, Eric. Try Japanese."

"Okay." What followed was one of those strange computer-to-computer things. I can follow technical Japanese pretty well, though not as well as Dallas, and for about ten seconds I could understand their exchange about the machine's experience and capabilities. But they talked faster and faster, until it was like a couple of Japanese chipmunks scolding each other, and finally just a warbling bleedle-eep-bleep that could have been any language.

Eric came back down to earth suddenly. "I don't think I would buy it, Mary."

"Why not?"

"He's too old a program, sixth-generation. I don't know about his responses to some of my queries. . . ."

"You can reprogram the autopilot," Jacobssen said. "I could cut the price enough to pay for that."

I tried not to smile. We had flushed the quarry and he was moving into range. "It's not that simple."

"No, it isn't," Eric said. "The pilot *is* the ship, to a large extent. If you switch out the pilot you have to retrain the ship. It takes time and money."

"Look." He was actually sweating in the refrigerated air. "Can we talk without the computer?"

"Sure," Dallas said, straight-faced. I turned Eric off.

"You're both immortals, aren't you?" We nodded. "So look. I want the treatment, the Stileman, and I don't have time to fuss and fiddle."

"You have an appointment?" Dallas asked.

"Tentative. I have to show financial proof by the fourth of next month." He spun the wheelchair around so he was looking away from us, out the small porthole by the galley. He was silent for a moment.

"We weren't going to do it, me and Edna. Edna was my wife, we never had enough to both do it, or even one of us. So I lost her seventeen years ago, and I figured, well, you know. Join her before too long.

"But that's a funny thing about money, isn't it? You work all your life and can't quite make it, but then you relax and don't give a shit, excuse me ma'am, and it just rolls in. Couple of years ago I was in spittin' distance of a million pounds. Started to think about the Stileman.

"Then I got this cancer of the pancreas. Sort of puts a

time limit on it.'' His voice was trembling. ''Couple of weeks I got to go to London . . . or go to bed.''

This was not an act. ''How much do you have?'' I asked.

He fumbled with his credit flash, having to punch in a correction twice, then held it up to me: £893,667.

''So you need a little over a hundred thousand pounds,'' Dallas said. ''Call it a hundred and fifty-five thousand dollars, this morning's exchange rate.''

He checked the flash and nodded cautiously.

''We could do it,'' I said to Dallas.

''I don't know. Let's check the thrust.''

''The thrust is fine,'' Jacobssen said, relief palpable in his voice, as if he hadn't just talked himself out of thirty thousand dollars. ''It's rated five gees max, fuel consumption twelve microAvs per second. Go ahead and crank her up. Guarantee she'll crack max.''

I turned the key and gave it the tiniest drip of fuel. The engine hissed outside and there was a creaking sound, the ship settling forward into the arms of the testing bed.

''Feels solid,'' Dallas said, confirming that we hadn't gone sliding across the New Mexico desert. ''Give it to her.''

''Just a second.'' I pushed the TALK button. ''Display the testing bed data, please.'' A screen lit up in front of me with the sigil of the U.S. Department of Transportation. I slammed the manual control as hard as I could, all the way forward—American control sticks have this annoying resistance built in, so you'll feel as if you're really *doing* something—and the gee number climbed up to 5.0 in about three seconds, the engine's whine going to a roar and then a scream. Then it crept up to 5.4 over the next ten seconds. That was impressive, both for the speed of onset and the fact that it exceeded its rating by eight percent. I cut it off and nodded to Dallas.

''Okay, then,'' he said. ''We won't haggle. We'll go one sixty-eight, give you plenty of walking-around money between now and your Stileman.''

''It's a deal.'' He reached under his chair seat and brought out a stiff envelope with all the paper work. Eric notarized the bill of sale and recorded it with White Sands, Washington, and Geneva.

Jacobssen's eyes bugged out when Dallas produced the money in currency. American currency, unlike Italian, has magnetic encoding you can check with your credit flash, and he apologized for checking out a few random bills—but after all, um, paper money . . . He didn't want to say that only criminals closed deals with bales of currency. Dallas told him it was "mad money" we'd won gambling up in Vegas; using it this way, we wouldn't have to pay taxes. The title transfer on a used machine can be for "one dollar and other assets, real and intangible." He seemed a little relieved at that, and at my suggesting that he go ahead and check out every bill; we weren't taking off this very minute. Besides, the transaction was contingent on a test flight, one orbit.

(It seemed odd to me that the money would change hands *first,* though of course it made perfect sense from the seller's standpoint. Otherwise, if we crashed trying it out, he would have no spaceship, no money, and a staggering lawsuit from the damage that "his" negligence caused. From our side of the transaction, well, I supposed we could still get our money back if the ship crashed.)

I had Dallas take the floater back to Hertz while I kept an eye on the ground crew, who extricated the Europa from the test bed and prepared it for takeoff. The old man evidently did check every one of the 168 bills, meanwhile.

When the machine was properly pointed down the hangar access lane, I got inside, to wait for Dallas in the air conditioning. I turned on Eric.

"Good job," I said. "We knocked him down thirty-two thousand."

"What . . . you mean you actually bought that old crate?"

Interesting feeling, a mixture of chagrin and fear. "Oh, no. I thought you were . . . I thought Dallas told you to bluff!"

"He did, but I wasn't. I suppose we should have had some signal. He turned me off before I could elaborate.

That brain is less than useful. It gives wrong answers and defends them.

"The previous owner may have been unaware of this. His flight log, ever since the AMC power source was installed, shows nothing that would challenge even a beginning pilot. He was under external control almost all of the time, so the AI unit hardly had a chance to wake up."

"Is there anything we can do about it?"

"I don't know. Dallas didn't used to be a very good pilot. You are, evidently."

"I am. But I'm accustomed to the best equipment; that makes it easy."

"This should be an interesting challenge, then. I can help you with orbital elements and such, and Old Brainless-san there might be able to do shared-control radar feedback things. That's the only way they'll let you near Ceres."

"That's what they say. Though I could probably do it without the feedback; when I got my license first they still made you dock cold."

The air lock irised, and Dallas swung in. "Let's go!"

"Bad news," I said, and told him about Eric's reservations. Eric elaborated that the AI unit was probably worse than useless, since it had plenty of speed and computational power, but its personality interfered with its professional judgment.

"If you bought a new GenDyne, anything after '72, the AI commo and guidance wouldn't have a Turing Image imposed. That was a marketing ploy for a few years; people felt more comfortable with a 'person' in charge." I'd never heard of that, but then I didn't follow American fads.

"But it's not a big danger, is it?" Dallas said. "You've driven ships without artificial intelligence. You didn't use AI docking with *adastra*, did you?"

"It's in the circuit as a failsafe. If I'd made a large error, it would've sent an overriding command." Some rocket jocks made fun of European sports ships like mine, since they gave you the feeling of seat-of-the-pants control without actually putting you at risk, if you should make a drastic error. The AI failsafe makes decisions a million times faster than you can push a button.

But I've always liked the feeling, the illusion, of being in charge. So now it might pay off. "Let's take on some fuel and get our basic stores aboard, go up and try a couple of orbits. If it doesn't work out, if I don't like the way it handles, we can cancel the deal and start over."

"Better hurry, then. Want the guy to be alive when we come back."

Nobody with any sense goes up, even just to low Earth orbit, without a week's worth of air, water, and food. It would be embarrassing to run out of air, waiting for a service vehicle to find you.

We went ahead and filled up everything, including fuel, since you get better prices with large quantities. If we decided to cancel the deal and buy another, we could transfer the stores easily enough. Most rocket jocks kept their vehicles at White Sands. Maui costs a great deal more for parking and will refuse any ship that doesn't have the Faraday cage and trolley adapter for the launch tube.

I could read Dallas's thoughts as we looked over the menus for the dehydrated meals. Space is not the place for people accustomed to dining, rather than feeding.

He was more in his element at the duty-free store. We allotted a hundred kilos for trade goods, things in demand in Novysibirsk that can't be made there. Caviar, single-malt Scotch whisky, pheromone enhancers. It was obvious from the clerk's innuendo that we could have bought narcotics. Neither Dallas nor I was interested in spreading that kind of wealth. (For the last few months I've carried a spike of fifty-grief in my purse, though, in case the final days become unbearable.)

It took several hours to get the ship loaded, and we were getting tired. But we decided to go on with the test, then park it and allow ourselves a good night's sleep at the Hilton. It would be a long time before we had starched sheets and room service again.

I asked Dallas whether he would like to stay dirtside

while I tested it out. He gave it a moment of hard thought, and looked wistfully over at the Hilton. "No. If something happens, it happens to both of us." A reassuring sentiment.

So we sealed it up and I was given clearance and rolled over to the east-west runway. There was no queue, but we had to wait for an empty window. Several police floaters crossed our path in formation, which gave me a little twinge of apprehension, and then we got the count, at twelve seconds. I keyed in Goofy, the name Dallas had given the incompetent AI interface, and indeed it was up to the job of sending us off at the right microsecond.

Five gees is uncomfortable, but it saves fuel. After about three minutes we had orbit insertion and tapered down to weightlessness. On the starboard horizon the parched desert was just giving way to the green-and-glitter oasis of Greater Dallas. Dallas looked down at his namesake and his greenish pallor turned to a healthier paleness. "Everything seems to work okay?"

The instruments didn't show anything wrong, but then a lot of them were just warning lights: if this light goes on, learn to breathe vacuum. "It held maximum acceleration well. We'll try an orbit change once we get on the other side." I slid back the plate exposing the keyboard on the right armrest and tapped out some numbers. Then I turned on Goofy.

"May I be of service?" it hissed.

"Yes. When we pass anti-Sands I want a circular orbit, our apogee raised a thousand kays. Period of acceleration timed so that half the increase is done before anti-Sands, and half after we pass it. Confirm and clear."

"Confirmed, but may I ask what our destination is?"

"No, you may not."

"Knowing our destination would allow me to refine your calculations and save fuel."

"Confirm and clear."

"I *said* confirmed." There was a slight pause. "We are cleared with White Sands. Acceleration to commence in forty-eight minutes."

I turned it off. "Cheeky bastard," Dallas said. I called a human at White Sands and verified that we'd been given clearance. It would be wonderful to have a midair collision because your ship's navigation system suffered a personality problem.

"I'm going back to check the stores," I said, unbuckling. A warning light went on, which startled me. Then I realized it was telling me that I had unbuckled. *Warning! The pilot has abandoned her post!* "Get you anything?"

"A beer, yeah." I stretched, glad to be in free fall again, and used the headrest of the couch to push off back to the pantry.

Dallas had done a good job of packing; everything was still stacked neatly. A loose piece of equipment falling a meter or two at five gees could do a lot of damage, even if nothing in your cargo was intrinsically dangerous. Ours included shatterguns and a crowdpleaser.

We'd taken on a fourth of our drinking water as beer and wine. It would all be recycled pee by the time we got to Ceres, anyhow. There were several brands, color-coded in rectangular boxes in the cooler. "Green one, or what?"

"Green's fine." I carried it up to him and almost warned him not to open it right away, but decided that would be patronizing, and braced myself for the mess. Five gees, after all. He parked it in the air in front of him, though, and let it settle.

God forgive me the sin of pride. Dallas acts like a neophyte in blast phase, but he does have thousands of hours in space. Some remarkably brave hours, like going to Mars before it was open. Chasing down the will-o'-wisps in Plato and the Alpine Valley; that must have been back when Downside was just a supply dump.

"See what's on the news?"

"Sure." I asked the cube for the news, and when it queried for a subject, Dallas said, "Stileman Foundation." We were in for a shock.

"An important news item associated with the Stileman Foundation broke little more than an hour ago. A prominent immortal, Dallas Barr, has gone on a murderous rampage, apparently because of a brain disease brought on by aging. . . .''

Dallas looked at me and nodded with a grim expression.

"Murdered by the mad immortal are fellow immortals Eric Lundley and Lamont Randolph, both of Australia; Krsto Vozac of Yugoslavia; and Sally Murchison, a private detective in the Conch Republic. Also feared dead is the Italian immortal Maria Marconi.

"In all likelihood, Barr had his physical appearance radically changed in the Conch Republic, so the accompanying picture may be of little value. Do not attempt to apprehend him. He is heavily armed and has killed friend and stranger alike.''

"Depth,'' Dallas said quietly.

"The first murder, which occurred in Sydney last Thursday, was contrived to look like an accident, or suicide. Barr had met Lamont Randolph at a party a few days before and evidently developed an intense dislike for him. Barr dropped in on him for an evening 'social call,' and while they were having drinks on the balcony of his penthouse, Barr pushed Randolph to his death on the pavement a hundred meters below.

"The next day, after a social gathering of immortals in Dubrovnik, Yugoslavia (which, ironically, had been organized partly by Randolph), Barr struck again, murdering his longtime friend and business partner Eric Lundley, as well as a water taxi driver, both with point-blank pistol fire. Then he sank the taxi and evidently swam for shore.

"According to at least one witness, there was another passenger in the taxi, the beautiful Italian immortal Maria Marconi.'' A picture of what I used to look like appeared on the screen. "Yugoslavian authorities are still searching for her body, which may have been displaced dozens of kilometers by ocean currents.''

"Tonight she sleeps with the fishes,'' Dallas said with what I think was supposed to be an Italian accent.

"Don't be ghastly.''

"They must all be in on it. More.''

The screen showed a picture of an intense-looking,

attractive black woman. "Interpol traced Barr to the anarchic Conch Republic, and contracted the services there of Sally Murchison, a private detective. She tracked Barr to a midtown motel, but he was either waiting for her or had set a trap. She entered and was immediately blown to pieces by the blast from a shattergun.

"It seems unlikely that Barr remained in the Conch Republic after this murder. He arranged to make it look as if he had himself perished in the blast, and apparently slipped off the island the night of December first. He could be anywhere in the world by now and, as noted earlier, could look like anyone. But according to the Stileman Foundation, he has at most only a few weeks to live, the victim of entropic brain dysfunction."

Dallas reached over and pushed the D-select button. "Depth on entropic brain dysfunction."

"Entropic brain dysfunction, EBD, was originally thought to be the only limit on the effectiveness of the Stileman immortality process. It is not possible for the body to produce new nervous tissue, new brain cells, after infancy, and various environmental factors cause constant destruction of these cells.

"Some of these factors have to do with individual behavior, or misbehavior—drinking alcohol and taking certain narcotics, especially grief and dizney—but other factors are inevitably a part of living, such as exposure to radiation from natural causes, industrial sources, and residue from the Khomeini Wars.

"Part of the Stileman Process works directly on EBD by somehow increasing the efficiency of the cerebral cortex. Exactly how this is done is a closely guarded secret.

"Until recently, it was believed that the process would be effective for at least a thousand years, and this may still be true in the majority of cases. But in the past month it has failed in two of the oldest Stileman immortals, and Stileman scientists are working overtime, trying to uncover some factor in the heredity or medical history of these two men that would make them anomalies. Both had been physically active, even athletic, for over a century; both had suffered several concussions. Both were Anglo-Saxon males with no previous history of mental problems.

"The first victim, Lord Geoffrey Lorne-Smythe, suffered a fate similar to normal senility, though it progressed much faster than it would in a normal person. The second, Dallas Barr, has become psychotic, accusing the Stileman Foundation of trying to kill him while he himself circles the world on a murderous rampage." The end-of-level pattern came on the screen.

"Better watch out," Dallas said. "You're circling the world with me."

"I wonder what Lorne-Smythe did to oppose them. How they induced the senility."

"God knows. What I'm afraid of is it's something they did during his last time at the clinic; maybe they did it to me, too. Briskin said I didn't have anything to worry about if I stuck with the Steering Committee. Maybe I'm harboring some sort of medical time bomb, and only they have the antidote."

"In which case, there isn't any sense in worrying about it."

He shrugged. "Yeah. I guess this means no Hilton."

"No." I bit my lip and tried to control the tremor in my voice. I had seen Earth for the last time. "We'd better compute an orbit." I turned on the machine. "Cancel the last correction. We want to go to Novysibirsk."

"Why?"

I sat there with my mouth open for a moment. "Business," Dallas said.

"It is impossible to go anywhere in Novysibirsk and return on the fuel you have. You'll have to buy DT-3 in Novysibirsk, where it is very expensive."

"We'll go anyway," I said. "Which is closer, Ceres or Mir?"

"Mir is closer. But you can get to Ceres on less fuel, by slingshotting Mars."

"Show me the plot."

A diagram appeared on the screen. "These elements are computed assuming you will first rise to HEO and refuel."

"No." Trying to pay cash for fuel at the HEO dump would be as good as announcing our identity. "Circularize this orbit and we will leave from here. Give Sands our—"

"You must not do that," the machine scolded. "DT-3 costs $1453 per liter in HEO and $2500 in Ceres."

"Execute the command," I said. "Tell Sands that our destination is Mars. Verify."

It seemed to take a long time. "Verified. Under protest. Acceleration will commence in nineteen minutes."

"What does 'under protest' mean?" Dallas said.

"Only that my flight log affirms that I gave you the proper advice, and you ignored it."

Dallas glared at it. "You could be replaced by an abacus."

"I could not." It turned itself off.

He carefully punched the beer open. "Gonna be a long one."

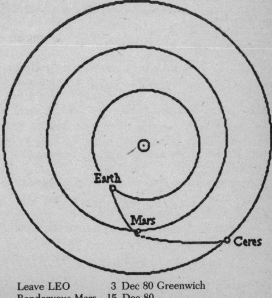

Leave LEO   3 Dec 80 Greenwich
Rendezvous Mars   15 Dec 80
Arrive Ceres   7 Jan 81 (8 yanvár Novysibirsk)

The first flight to Ceres took seven years, there and back, and lost four crew members to murder and suicide. Maria and Dallas discussed this in a lighthearted way at the beginning of their six-week trip. They were looking forward to the intimacy and isolation, and when they wanted time alone, they could draw a curtain between the two acceleration couches and meditate upon the unmoving stars. There would be no shortage of things to *do,* even though the ship was fully automated, since they could tie into public data links for millions of uncopyrighted books and movies (no credit account to pay for anything new). If either of them had any fears of not enjoying six weeks locked up in a padded mausoleum sharing another person's body odors, they didn't voice those fears.

In fact, they wouldn't have time to be bored, or annoyed, or fly off the handle. Things would all too soon become interesting.

Dallas

FIREBALL was a pretty quiet ship under half-gee acceleration, just a faint hiss and a few creaks and ticks to keep you nervous. We cranked for over five hours, most of which time I gratefully slept. Woke up fast when acceleration stopped, of course. It's exactly the sensation of falling out of bed. And off a cliff.

Maria reached over and grabbed my arm, which was probably waving around somewhat as I plummeted to my doom. "Wake up, Dallas. It's only zerogee." She unbuckled and did a stretch-and-tumble. "Race you to the head." I decided to be gallant and let her go. Five hours is a long time for a woman. But it's a long time for a beer drinker, too.

The toilet's gimballed so you can use it during acceleration, and there are handholds leading to the head, but it looked like you would have to be a gymnast to get into and out of the acceleration couch. And I supposed Maria didn't want to be away from the controls during blast. *I* didn't want her to be.

Waiting, I toggled the viewscreen to look aft and was startled at how small Earth seemed so soon, only a little bigger than the crescent Moon does dirtside. Shouldn't have been surprised, but I hadn't been out this far in twenty years. The Moon was a dull fingernail clipping almost lost in the Sun's glare.

I unbuckled and tried out my "space legs," as they say, though legs in zerogee are about as useful as your appendix. The cabin was small enough to be easy to get around in, and the Naugahyde padding on the walls was loose and tacky enough to give you a good grip for starting and stopping. Tacky in both senses of the word. I knew that we would grow to hate beige.

I took my turn at the head, forgetting the Stiktite slippers and so demonstrating one of Newton's laws in a disconcerting way. Zerogee's easier than a rotating environment, though. The head at LEO Cyanamid used to have a red *X* to the right of the urinal with a sign saying AIM HERE, STUPID.

"Why don't you bring back some wine," Maria said. "Let's celebrate." I selected a package of white Burgundy, Montagny '78. Good year but a bad container. Did they age it in the plastic, or had it been transferred from a glass bottle? I didn't want to know.

I squeezed a bubble out and we drank it with straws, the way we had in *adastra*. It wasn't bad. "So far so good," I said.

"We're still in one piece. I should check and see if the piece is where it's supposed to be." She turned on the computer.

"May I be of service?"

"I want to take two position checks, with respect to the Sun and two stars. Give me—"

"That will not be necessary. We are on course."

"I need the practice. Let me have first Aldebaran, then Spica, then the Sun." While she was getting Eric from the storage locker between us, a star field appeared on the viewscreen, dominated by a bright orange one in the center. Various numbers and acronyms glowed at the bottom of the screen. I could recognize VWRTSOL and AWRTSOL as being velocity and angle with respect to the Sun, and time and elapsed time were clear. The rest I would have to figure out.

She plugged him in, and Eric's face appeared in a small superimposed square. "Space, eh? Moving fast, that's good."

"We want to do a redundancy check on the ship's computer," she said. "Can you verify whether we're on the proper course?"

"Only to a certain extent. I don't have any independent

sensory input. So all I can do is take the same numbers it starts with and see whether I come up with the same results."

"That's enough. We're more worried about the logic than the data." She and Eric talked arcsines and such to each other for a while. I worked on the bubble of Burgundy. From each according to his abilities, to each according to his needs.

Maria looked up and there was a slight edge in her voice. "Could you do this if something happened to me?"

"Oh yeah. I'd have to punch up a handbook. It's been a long time." I brushed away some mental cobwebs. "Let me see . . . you get the angles between your direction of travel and two stars, and then a sun vector, distance and speed. Couldn't do it without a computer, though."

"Not many people could."

"Good to seven nines," Eric said. "You'll want to correct at least once before the Mars swingby, of course, but this will definitely get you there."

I punched up the news and there was no essential change. Still after me, but only on the Earth. The newsie said that I could stay in the Conch Republic indefinitely, if the identity laundering had been done well. Typical 'phem fallacy, "indefinitely." If I wanted to live more than ten years, I had to go to either Sydney or London—where they'd know who I really was ninety seconds after the first blood sample.

"I wonder," Maria said. "If they actually are still looking for a single person, then traveling together is a sort of camouflage."

"I wouldn't count on it. Since they managed to track us to the Conch Republic, they probably know I wasn't alone on the airship. They have their own reasons for keeping you a secret."

She nodded slowly. "I suppose it would be harder for them to characterize you as a homicidal maniac if you have a willing companion." She reached back and unclasped a barrette, then plumped her hair out into a golden halo, smiled. "God knows I'm willing."

*   *   *

Space travel is both the fastest and slowest form of locomotion in human history. For most of the next eleven days, the Earth was a blue star behind them and Mars was a red star in front, and the only change in the scenery was that one gradually got dimmer while the other gradually got brighter. If you measured it, you could have told that the Sun's filter-darkened disc was diminishing, too. Otherwise, everything stayed the same. The unblinking stars, more or less eternal.

Eric pointed out that his attitude toward the astronomical universe was profoundly different, now that he was no longer flesh and blood. With instruments of any subtlety, he could detect the movement of stars from month to month; he could ''watch'' the waxing and waning of variable stars. These were real in a way they could never have been when he was limited to the human perception of the rate of time's passing, and to the grossness of human senses. To him the universe was a throbbing, living thing—which he had known intellectually, before. Now he could watch it happen.

About a day before swingby, the scenery available to the merely human passengers started to change perceptibly, with Mars showing a small disc. Dallas was relieved to have a visible sign of their progress. Maria's feelings were complicated.

Maria

WITH the approach of swingby, I had a sense of foreboding, which I dismissed as reluctance to have anything alter the status quo. The eleven days had been a small miracle, time out of time for both of us. Not just respite from our troubles.

This love confuses me. Can you, should you, separate your body from your mind from your heart? Your spirit. Other times in my life I've felt there were different kinds of love working at the same time: I could love a man with my mind and loins, and separately love Christ with my spirit, and when the two loves clashed later, in the confessional and penance, there was a rightness and a comfort to that; even to the guilt. This love with Dallas is disturbing in its pervasive unity, even while it's exhilarating; almost as if he were invading the place that holds my love of God.

In a century of life I've only been swept away like this one time, and it wasn't a man. After the earthquake that killed my father and brothers, when I was sent to the convent to live, I spent nearly all my waking hours in prayer, praying for the souls of my father and my brothers, and for poor Mother—and poor me!—but mostly trying to understand through prayer how God could have let this happen. My knees swelled up and cracked and bled, and finally the sisters had to carry me to my cell, where they set up a small shrine, and I continued to pray lying down. And though I wasn't given any answers more satisfying than the ones in the catechism, what I did find was ultimately as comforting, though it can't really be put into words. A union with the mystery, an ecstatic union which, as King James has it, surpasseth all understanding.

I'm not ignorant, and I know now that some component of my rapture was slippery adolescent sexuality, redirected. A virgin's diffuse orgasms. But I also know that God gave us all this complicated plumbing and wiring for a reason, and suspect that it bloomed then in my case to help me through my grief. Dallas would say the stress triggered a body change. I think both statements are the same.

But these eleven days. We've worn clothes only while Eric was with us, which is so absurd it's given us both giggles. We could do anything in front of Eric, even the things I only have Latin words for, and it would just be data to him. Or it might be cruel, if you can be cruel to a circuit, reminding him of things he can never have again.

When Mars started to show a visible disc, I went over all the calculations once more from the beginning, independently of the ship's computer. Eric and I matched the computer's results to eight significant figures.

The swingby business would be simpler if Mars didn't have an atmosphere. In fact, it's denser than Earth's at high altitudes, since the more massive planet has a steeper density gradient. It's still just a few molecules here and there, but we'll be cutting through at nearly a hundred kilometers per second. When I made a similar maneuver in the Bugatti, on the way to Ganymede, I noticed some vibration due to turbulence. And the Bugatti isn't dropnose, which might or might not make a difference.

Two hours before swingby, I made a small course correction that would take us over the north pole; we wanted to bend our trajectory down under the plane of the ecliptic, to point toward Ceres. Mars was about the size of the full moon from Earth, and seemed to grow as we watched, though I knew that was an illusion.

"Should we have the space suits out? Even put them on?" Dallas asked. I had told him about the turbulence.

"I wouldn't bother . . . there's no real danger." Actually, the reason I wouldn't bother was because if something happened, that would be it. We'd be a loose collection of pieces spinning away from Mars at somewhere between 96 and 120 kilometers per second. Impossible to catch up with.

I would just as soon not be in a space suit, waiting to run out of air.

As it turned out, the situation was not so clear-cut.

I kept Dallas busy by making sure all the hatches were battened down, litter secured, especially. We needed a short burn, a "kick," at perimartian, and you wouldn't want a plastic straw to come hurtling toward you at five gees.

I deliberately didn't have us strap in too early, remembering my own trapped feeling, thirty years ago, as Mars loomed closer and closer. You're going about twenty times as fast as instinct, or intuition, says you should be, since we're accustomed to low Earth orbit. It feels like you're going to crash.

"Two minutes," I said. "Better strap up." When Dallas was secure, I told the ship to initiate the attitude adjustment, which was larger than I'd expected. Mars swung and Dallas flinched.

The planet was getting bigger every second, no illusion. The polar cap came rolling over the horizon toward us. I asked for a ten-second countdown before the burn.

"One month," Dallas said.

"What?"

"Today's the fifteenth; it's been exactly one month since Claudia's party." He reached over and stroked my arm. The machine started counting. I blinked back tears.

Dallas

THE swingby was pretty terrifying even before we knew about the damage. A hundred kilometers a second is a lot faster than I had ever gone before—Mars seemed to hurl itself at us; it looked as if we were going to plow into the polar cap. Goofy started counting down. At "three" we hit turbulence.

It was like a bumpy road in an old-fashioned car, not a floater. Really bad bumps, like the potholes you'd run over and wonder whether they meant a new axle. I saw the sudden fear on Maria's face, and my own heart nearly stopped. She looked at me and started to say something, and then the acceleration of the precalculated kick pressed us both deep into our couches.

For ten seconds the ship bobbed and shook while the engine screamed and the martian landscape sped by underneath us. When the engine cut out suddenly, there was one last shudder, and then the neutral silence and stillness of free fall.

Maria cleared her throat. "That wasn't supposed to happen." She squeezed her arms gently, painfully. "*Ostia!* I feel like I've fallen down a long flight of stairs."

"Yeah, two weeks lounging around in zerogee." Where it hurt me most didn't bother her at all, she lacking testicles.

She undid her straps, wincing, reading my mind, or body: "Be glad you don't have breasts." She thumbed the computer. "Give us a general systems check. Was anything damaged by the vibration?"

No answer.

She turned it off and on again. "Testing. Do you hear me?"

Nothing. "Try Eric?" I said. She nodded and I turned him on. "We just came out of swingby and looks like we lost Goofy. Would there be any danger, plugging you into him?"

"No. Just use the data channel we did before, with the navigation." I jacked him in, and his reply came before my hand had moved back six inches.

"It looks like he's there but we can't get to him. He's drawing a normal amount of power but has no data input or output."

"Fix?"

"Maybe somebody could. It might just be a loose connection or a simple component that got zapped. There's no way for me to tell from here." The bearded image shook its head back and forth once. "He's trapped in there deaf and dumb and blind. And he was crazy before. He's probably not going to be of any more use to you. Maybe you ought to just power him down."

"You make it sound like euthanasia."

"Only in a sense. Presumably he's not the only copy."

"Boys," Maria said, "I think we have a bigger problem than that." She pointed at the console, where a red light was blinking. "It says 'life support malfunction.' "

"Doesn't say what?"

"No. I imagine we're supposed to ask the computer."

"Perhaps it considers Goofy to be part of the life support system," Eric said, "even though it surely has backup computers, not burdened with personalities."

"We could look it up in the manual," I said, "but I'll bet the only way to get to the manual is through Goofy."

"Does it seem colder to you?" Maria asked, almost in a whisper.

"It isn't," Eric said. "That's psychosomatic. Your autonomic nervous system. It's been twenty-four degrees centigrade since you woke up this morning."

"I guess so." She rubbed her palms together and blew

between them. "Sweating . . . wait! There *is* a manual, a paper one." She pushed herself up so hard she hit her head and knees on the soft ceiling. "Back with the space suits."

She went aft to the emergency equipment bay—a closet barely big enough for two space suits and two people, heavily shielded against solar flares—and floated back with a slim booklet, looking disappointed as she riffled through it. "It isn't very detailed. I don't know that it will be much help." She passed it fluttering to me.

It was even shorter than it looked, since the text was repeated in five languages and a lot of the illustrations were little more than decoration. "Looks more like a sales brochure than a manual."

"You're losing air," Eric said.

"What?"

"This reader you've got me in has a weather recorder. Every three minutes it reports temperature, humidity, and barometric pressure. Your air pressure is down a measurable amount."

"How much?" Maria asked.

"One twentieth of one percent. If you were on Earth, I would say take out the umbrellas. Front coming in."

"Popped something."

"Or hit something," Eric said. "Did you hear anything that might have been a micrometeorite impact?"

"It was pretty noisy around perimartian. We could've hit a brick and not noticed."

"Turbulence," Maria said.

"Interesting. Well, if you were holed, the puncture is probably under the vinyl somewhere fore."

"Devil to find," I said.

"One of you would have to go outside." That sounded too interesting, with those old commie space suits. "But since the hull is seamless, if you did pop something under stress, it must be either around the air lock, the viewports, or possibly the shieldwall. You could find the leak with a cigarette."

"We don't smoke," Maria said.

"Pity. It could save your life."

Same old Eric. "There's probably a detector punk in the first-aid kit," Maria said, and pushed herself back toward the emergency bay.

"How long do we have?"

"I don't know. It's a differential equation, since the rate of loss is a function of the amount of loss, complicated by turbulence. If it were a linear relationship, then based on the information I have, you would lose half your air in about fifty hours."

"It shouldn't be any problem, then."

"I hope not. It would get lonely without you."

The punk gave us some problems at first. It was a long stick of what appeared to be sawdust and glue. Burnt at one end, so it had been used before. But whoever used it had thrown away the instructions.

The igniter was a battery with a resistance coil and a button. Push the button, it glows red; stick the punk into it, and you're rewarded with a sputter of jasmine smoke. Then it dampens out.

On the third try we realized that the punk puts itself out, generating a little shell of carbon dioxide around the coal, if you don't start waving it around as soon as it lights. Maria was embarrassed; she'd seen a demonstration tape of that when she was in school.

That brought me up short for a moment. How many of us are left who went to school before spaceflight was common? A few hundred? A few dozen?

After we figured it out, it only took a couple of minutes to find the leak, around the aft viewport. Long enough to tire of the cloying jasmine perfume.

The aft viewport had been installed by Mr. Jacobssen himself, so you could enjoy the view while waiting for rations to heat.

You could just feel the breeze of the air going out with the palm of your hand. It was along the top of the viewport, but I epoxied it all around just in case, and the air pressure stabilized. Then we got down to the real problem: how the hell could we get where we were aiming?

A high-energy orbit like ours requires frequent small

corrections and rather delicate timing. Ceres trundles around the Sun at a measly eighteen kilometers per second; we were playing catch-up at nearly six times that speed. The rule of thumb is to make a correction when two-thirds of the distance has been covered, then another when two-thirds of the remaining distance is covered, and so on. Sooner or later you decelerate, since the folks on Ceres have enough craters already, and the process starts over with a more modest closing velocity. The later you decelerate, the more economical.

The first problem was finding Ceres. Normally you would just call them up and get on a carrier beam; their instruments would interact with yours and bring you in with maximum safety and economy. But that took AI on both ends, so we would have to just follow the beam, Maria piloting manually. In either case, there was a charge for the service. We had a quarter million in gold and trade goods, not to mention fifty-five thousand-dollar bills, but not a dime in electronic credit.

"You call them," Maria said. "Some of them are old-fashioned about dealing with women."

Eric gave me the frequency, and I thought for a minute. "This is Fireball 2368 New Mexico calling Ceres Flight Control. Cassius Donato piloting.

"We have two little problems here. First, main computer's out; we'll have to follow your carrier in and perform the rendezvous manually. Second, we don't have any line of credit, but we have plenty of cash and trade goods. We'll pay for the carrier after we get to Ceres. Awaiting reply."

We were about twelve light-minutes away. I set up the little magnetic chessboard. We let Eric watch on the condition that he was not to say anything.

Ceres called back in a little less than half an hour, no picture. "Okay, Fireball, we dopplered you outa Mars swingby at eighty-two klicks, our vector. Whatsa hurry, goz?

"You do have two little problems. One, no way nobody does a manual rendezvous with Ceres. If you was dopplered a tenth of a klick and had a long white beard by the time you got here, we'd still shoot you outa the sky. We *live* here, goz; we just *get* one bad landing. You get within ten thousand klicks of rendezvous and we got a five-gigawatt mining laser, turn you inta plasma. Nothin' personal.

"That don't mean you can't use the carrier wave; you just gotta stop short and get towed in by somebody who can lock into our feedback loop. That's your second problem: you got to make a deal with somebody here to pay for your carrier and at least make a deposit on the tug.

"Passive carrier wave's five thousand rubles, that's with flight params ad lib. You can call around or you can make a deal with me, Big Dick Goodwin. You agree to pay me six, cash, I put down your five. You don't pay, I kill you.

"Most of that's docking fee and landing tax. You could save twelve hundred with a visual approach, generate your own params, but hey. Make a mistake and I gotta fry you.

"For the tug, you got a choice of maybe ten, twelve free-lancers, depending on how big Fireball is. I called a friend, Blinky Bukowski, and he offers his services for twenty thousand. That ain't a bad deal, goz, but call around.

"You didn't say what flavor cash you got. Today it's 1.8504 rubles to the pound, 1.0974 to the dollar, 1.5657 to the mark. If you got kopeks or Earth rubles or any kinda soft currency, bring a wheelbarrow of it an' maybe we'll talk. Otherwise I'll get a witness an' we freeze the transaction at today's rate.

"What say, goz? We in business?" The standard "awaiting reply" symbol appeared on the screen.

"That's $23,692.36," Eric said. "I'd try a counteroffer."

Maria nodded. "At least round them down. What does each number come to in dollars?" Eric displayed $5,467.47• $18,224.89.

"The carrier fee's not negotiable, but everything else is. Tug fee seems high. Any information, Eric?"

"No—it would be about a quarter that in cislunar space, but you can't make comparisons."

"I say we should be generous on the one that has his fee,

and push the other one down," Maria said. "Tell him he can have six thousand if he can get the tug down to fifteen."

It was an interesting way to bargain, twenty or thirty minutes per offer. Epistolary haggling, passing notes. We finished the chess game, me winning for a change, and eventually did get the tug fee down to sixteen thousand dollars. Eric said that we should bill Mitsubishi for it, if we get out of this alive.

MANIAC STILL AT LARGE!!

DEATH TOLL MOUNTS TO NINE!!

Dallas Barr, international playboy immortal, has been charged with four other murders in a sex-and-death trip that spans the planet and boggles the mind!

Four belated poisoning deaths bring to a total of nine the hapless victims of Barr's jealous rage. Police from four countries have pieced together this gruesome scenario:

At a party in Sydney, Australia, Dallas Barr met Maria Marconi, a mystery woman from his distant past. They had been lovers in 2010, but for seventy years he thought she was dead.

Passion rekindled, the two millionaires retired to *adastra*, the immortal elitist starship that is also the world's most exclusive and expensive hotel. Whatever they did there had to be worth $100,000 a day!

LESBIAN NYMPHO!!

Little did Dallas know that his newly rediscovered heartthrob was a pansexual nymphomaniac, willing to try anything twice!! It fell to the unfortunate Lamont Randolph to pass the news on to him.

From personal, confidential testimony of other immortals, police have figured out that Randolph (fellow immortal and veep of General Nutrition in Australia) had been one of Marconi's lovers in the past, but was jilted in favor of a woman! He had befriended Barr the previous week, and wanted to make sure he knew what was going on!

Randolph evidently gave Barr the lowdown about both of the women from firsthand experience—a three-way bedfest with French immortal Gabrielle Lecompe! He also told Barr about the other immortals she'd opened with: Texas industrialist Helga Moss, Nigerian economist Yakubu Shagari, Alaskan book-maker Sonny Gaines, and Dallas's old partner, Aus-tralian Eric Lundley. All of them were doomed.

LUNATIC RAGE!!

Far from being grateful for the information, Barr became enraged, and pushed Randolph off the pent-house balcony to his death 170 feet below! After that he returned to his London hotel room (having left no trace of his hop to Australia and back) and then proceeded to a get-together of immortals in Du-brovnik, Yugoslavia. There he cold-bloodedly mur-dered four of Marconi's lovers, by doctoring their drinks with a slow-acting nerve poison! (The poison was manufactured by Sedlidge Bionica, a firm he founded thirty years ago!)

Then Barr left the party with his old "friend" Eric Lundley, along with the luscious and lascivious Maria Marconi. They hired a water taxi back to their hotel—but they never made it! In the middle of the Adriatic Sea Barr pulled out a gun and murdered both immor-tals in cold blood, and then assassinated the taxi driver as well.

PERFECT ESCAPE!!

Barr sank the taxi in deep water and swam back to the mainland. By the time the first body floated ashore, he had fled, and was safe in the notorious Conch Republic.

Unable to extradite the murderer from the anarchic island, authorities hired a local private detective to track him down. She became Barr's ninth victim when a clever booby trap blew her to pieces!

Barr's appearance may have changed radically—rich criminals often go to the Conch Republic for total identity "laundering"—and by now he could be anywhere in the world! If you run into someone who you think is Dallas Barr, *do not attempt to apprehend him!!* Immediately contact the local police—then take cover!!

—From *Allplanet Fax & Pix,* December 4, 2080

Dallas and Maria could read day-old newspapers and week-old magazines by punching them up from a public library data base. None of the news reports they read, from sensational tabloid to stuffy current-events analysis journal, said anything about the possibility that they might have escaped Earth. Of course that didn't mean that no one suspected, or possibly even knew for sure. The Stileman Foundation appeared to have the media well under control. As the weeks went by, their story drifted from page one back toward oblivion.

Maria

OUR flight profile originally called for forty-five minutes of deceleration at three gees, uncomfortable but not dangerous, saving fuel. The tugboat captain Blinky Bukowski was waiting for us about twelve thousand klicks from Ceres. He was actually in Ceres orbit, of course, but the period of the orbit was over two hundred hours, creeping along at about a hundred meters per second.

He talked through the prerendezvous phase with me, and I was comfortable with his competence. He tilted the plane of his parking orbit to match ours, and then timed its circularization so that we both ought to arrive at about the same spot at about the same time. We didn't plan on mechanical failure, though, least of all of a dramatic kind.

Ceres had been an invisible mote through most of our journey. It was visible the last few days, finally becoming the brightest thing in the sky, and growing into a disc.

It was the size of a Klondike dollar when I flipped us around. Dallas and I strapped ourselves in and waited for the count from Blinky's computer. I would have to initiate the deceleration manually, which could introduce an error of as much as a tenth or twentieth of a second. A timer would cut it off forty-five minutes and nineteen seconds later, whether or not I was paying attention, or conscious. Then we would look around for Blinky.

The three gees wasn't too bad. I was tired, though, and closed my eyes after a few minutes, which could have been fatal. But my ears popped suddenly, and I forced my eyes open.

The "life-support malfunction" light was on.

I touched the emergency shutoff button on the armrest and we were weightless. "What's that?" Dallas said, his voice oddly distant.

"Losing air." We both looked back at the galley viewport—this time it was the bottom of the "custom-installed" window, and it had popped out so far we could see a thin black crescent of space from across the cabin. Air rushed through it in a constant low sigh.

I was out of my straps first. "Get the suits," I said unnecessarily, and kicked toward the porthole, ripping off my blouse to stuff in the gap.

There was quite a bit of wind; enough, I was afraid, to suck the blouse on through, but it did hold. It was fairly porous material, though, and I could feel that we were still losing air fast. I told Dallas, and as he brought the space suits over, he stopped at the refrigerator for a beer. That was perplexing, until he shook it up, popped it, and saturated the cloth. It frosted over into a solid mass.

But we had already lost too much air. I was gasping as if I had run several kilometers. Black dots swarmed in front of my eyes and my hands and arms felt palsied. It seemed very cold.

The Russian suits are made to go on quickly: main zipper; gloves; helmet lock. But you have to undress first. I had on dancing tights, and although I could force my thumbs under the waistband, I couldn't seem to get them down. I was both frightened and somehow giddy, almost giggling at the absurdity of not being able to perform this simple act. Dallas slipped out of his jumpsuit and swam over to help me. I had never seen a man shrink in the cold, of course, and that did make me giggle. Dallas had taken my pants off a few times before, but never with a penis only three centimeters long.

He guided my legs and arms into the suit's overlong sleeves, closed the main zipper, fitted the helmet, and locked it on. Frigid oxygen filled the suit, and a splitting earache immediately sobered me up. I swallowed hard and yawned, and it went away. Yawning filled my lungs with

Lysol vapor, though, and I started coughing, each cough an echoing explosion in the plastic globe. The smell made my gorge rise, but I choked it back in time. Bad enough to have the faceplate clouded with water vapor and saliva specks. A splash of vomit would be death for both of us, the choice between my flying blind choking or trying to survive near-vacuum long enough to clean my helmet.

The time! I gestured wildly at Dallas and kicked back to the acceleration couch as fast as I could. We had decelerated for only a couple of minutes and were hurtling toward Ceres at more than seventy-five kilometers per second. We couldn't radio them to explain, and even if we could, I doubted that Big Dick what's-his-name could be talked out of blasting us if we came too close.

At least one thing was working; a green light next to the red one meant that the lost air was being replaced.

Dallas was fast getting dressed. I wasn't even completely strapped in when he came forward; I grabbed at him and we touched helmets.

"Have to make up for lost time. Get ready for five gees. We'll do it for a few minutes and then cut back to three. We'll come up short, too far out from Ceres; but by then the ship will be repressurized, and we can start over."

"You're the boss." His voice sounded like he was in another room.

I tried to think. The timer said 42:01, so we had decelerated for a little more than three minutes before I shut it off. No way to tell exactly how long we'd been in free fall; at least another three minutes. Juggle numbers. Distance with respect to Ceres is $D = D_o - v_o t + at^2$, but it's not that simple; every time you change acceleration you're in a new regime. I was too foggy to plug the numbers in anyhow. I typed in "4:00" for the five-gee correction and when Dallas gave me his hand signal I pulled the stick back hard, all the way.

The pain was so sudden and intense it gave me a rush of adrenaline. The life-support unit on the upper back of the space suit kept me from conforming to the acceleration couch properly; it was as if a hundred-kilogram weight had suddenly dropped between the shoulder blades. I blacke out, thinking *Dallas will go under, too.*

Woke up with Dallas shaking me. "How long on three gees?" he shouted from that other room.

"Thirty-eight minutes," I dragged out from somewhere. He punched it in and I reached for the vernier stick, and stopped myself just in time before pulling it back. Wouldn't want to fling Dallas back toward the wine rack at three gees.

Wrong ship. No wine rack on this piece of junk. The black dots swimming had company now, brilliant purple flowers opening and closing. Hard white stars sparkled. I yawned every couple of seconds. Dallas gave the sign and I closed the frozen lump of my hand around the vernier, and pulled it back to the faint click-stop at 3.0 gees.

Three wasn't nearly as bad as five. But I yawned with almost every breath now. I couldn't feel my arms and legs beyond elbows and knees. My buttocks and breasts felt icy.

Ostia. The suit was leaking. But the green light was still on; pretty soon the cabin would be up to a livable pressure. If nothing else went wrong. I watched the minutes creep away. Somewhere around thirty I passed out again.

I woke up slightly in luscious free fall. Dallas was whispering from far away, but all I could see was pale white. Ice crystals, I realized, on the inside of my faceplate. The suit wasn't working well at all. Dallas said the porthole was gone.

No air outside? I could breathe, though. I went back to sleep.

Eric: Mayday, Ceres.
Ceres: You got Big Dick Goodwin at Ceres Flight Control. An' you *Fireball* 2368?
Eric: Affirmative, *Fireball.*
Ceres: So what happened to, uh, Cassius Donato? Who're you?
Eric: I'm Eric Lundley, a passenger. Donato is here but can't speak to you; the ship's lost all of its air and the emergency suits don't have working radios.

Ceres: Anyone dead?

Eric: Not yet. One passenger has a defective suit; Donato
has just wrapped her in a thermal blanket, but we
need to get her out of this bucket as soon as possible.

Ceres: I don' know. How close is the tug?

Blinky: Blinky here. Shit, I couldn' even find 'em an't the
transmission. Lemme doppler. What's yer amplitude
on the transmission, Big Dick?

Ceres: Twenty-three-point-eighty-one mikes.

Blinky: Jus' second, punch it in . . . shit. Okay, Fireball.
Eighty, ninety minutes before I can get to you. Hold
on that long?

Eric: Suppose we'll have to.

Ceres: Hey. I'm slow, but I an't that slow. How we know
this an't a mutiny situation? I mean, you can talk to
us, but the captain can't. There's no air but you look
okay, beard an' all. You even *look* like a fuckin'
pirate.

Eric: I'm not exactly human. I'm a Turing Image. I find a
lack of air invigorating. If I could communicate with
Mr. Donato, I would have him come over and wave
hello. Alas, we're not jacked up together, and otherwise, our only link is acoustic.

Ceres: If the screen's on, I could hold up a written message.

Eric: And he would eventually see it. Right now he's
absorbed in trying to glue a plate over the porthole
that blew out. It won't do much good, though. I
believe the ship's life-support system tried to com-
pensate for the drop in pressure by pushing more
and more air into the system. I don't think there's any
left.

Blinky: This is gonna cost, ya know. I gotta do a fuckin' EVA?

Eric: We'll give you two thousand extra.

Blinky: Hell, I dunno. Maybe five thousand.

Eric: Mr. Bukowski. It's either two thousand or I go on a
general frequency and offer fifteen hundred or the
lowest bid.

Ceres: I'd do it, Blinky. Two thousand, that's eighteen
hundred twenty-two rubles. An't so bad.

Blinky: Shit. Guess not. Keep the mike open; I'll come in
when we make visual.

Eric: Thank you, Mr. Bukowski. Ceres, will you write a
note explaining things, and hold it up to the lens?

Ceres: Yeah. Gotta find the pad.

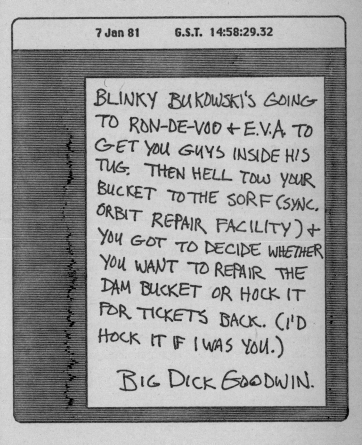

7 Jan 81   G.S.T. 14:58:29.32

BLINKY BUKOWSKI'S GOING
TO RON-DE-VOO & E.V.A. TO
GET YOU GUYS INSIDE HIS
TUG. THEN HE'LL TOW YOUR
BUCKET TO THE SORF (SYNC.
ORBIT REPAIR FACILITY) &
YOU GOT TO DECIDE WHETHER
YOU WANT TO REPAIR THE
DAM BUCKET OR HOCK IT
FOR TICKETS BACK. (I'D
HOCK IT IF I WAS YOU.)

BIG DICK GOODWIN.

Dallas

I peeked inside the blanket and Maria's body heat had thawed out her faceplate, but she looked awful. Eyes half shut, mouth open and slack, panting shallowly. She was pale and her lips were turning purple.

At least the air pressure was enough to sustain her. I saw a woman die of slow decompression on the Moon from what turned out to have been a simple maintenance oversight. We tried to carry her back but we were two hours from help. She died choking on bloody foam from her lungs.

So the problem with the suit wasn't a leak. We probably had zero pressure in the cabin ten seconds after the porthole popped. The oxygen supply in our suits is cryogenic and uses a preheater, which must have been the problem. The air was coming into her suit from the l/s unit too cold. I couldn't see any way to investigate it without disassembling the unit.

I wrapped the thermal blanket around as tight as I could with three bungees, which is what I should have done in the first place. But the frost was so frightening that all I could think of was to warm her, holding her. Which was stupid. If my suit was radiating that much heat, I'd have a frost-covered faceplate myself.

I did know enough not to rub. That was one useful thing I learned in the army. If you rub the fingers of a frostbite victim, you could wind up with a handful of loose fingers. Takes forever to grow them back, hurts like hell.

Tried to stop the porthole leak by gluing a dinner plate over the hole with epoxy. It didn't do a damned thing.

Green light merrily blazing, l/s pumping right along, not a molecule of air left in the reserves. I pulled the fuse so the damned system wouldn't burn itself out, pumping vacuum.

Spent a long time then watching Maria, holding her, trying to will her awake and warm. I almost missed the note. A few seconds after I saw it, it disappeared. Incoming message logo, then Eric's picture took up one corner of the screen, which was otherwise dominated by a close-up portrait of a bearlike individual, unshaven and wearing a cap that said COKE IZ FIZZ, who blinked both eyes simultaneously once each three seconds, staring. Our mercenary savior.

I waved at him and he waved back. What would have happened if I hadn't been prepared? If somebody suddenly started cutting through the air lock with a jigsaw laser? Five shatterguns and a crowdpleaser in the pantry.

(Ah, but the shatterguns are NOT FOR USE IN VACUUM. They would make a nice bright flash, announcing your unfriendliness and impotence simultaneously.)

As it was, I opened the inner air lock door, but the outer one was stuck closed because of some brilliant failsafe sensor, so Gospodin Blinky had to jigsaw through.

The short EVA was no problem. The vessels were about thirty meters apart, but he'd strung a cable. I put one arm around Maria, looped the other around the cable, and kicked off. Blinky brought Eric.

Worried as I was about Maria, the sudden beauty outside was still overwhelming. I haven't done enough space to become jaded. Ceres looked like a caricature of the Moon, outsized craters blistering an absolute crescent; you could only tell it was a sphere by the absence of stars behind the shadow side. In the other direction Jupiter blazed copper-gold, close enough to tell that it was round, which I'd never seen before.

And the stars were as always. Looking at them, you could almost understand religion.

The tug was just an ICF engine bolted to a steel platform with tanks of this and that, heavy-duty winches, and a cartoon of Blinky with the slogan HIRE A MUTANT. The life-support module was smaller than Fireball's cabin. But warmer.

It was not a time for modesty. As soon as the inner door closed, I stripped Maria out of the frigid suit. Blinky removed his helmet and gloves and took a soft Woolweave blanket off his restrainer bunk for her, and although he stared at her nakedness, I think he stares at everything.

She was shockingly pale, with waxy patches on her cheeks, breasts, buttocks. In semiconsciousness, she looked old and tired.

"That's frostbite, goz," he said. "We better get her some advice." He punched up a doctor and described the situation. She had us take Maria's temperature; it was high enough to rule out hypothermia, more life-threatening than frostbite. She said that if there was no obvious breathing problem and a regular pulse, then the main thing was to warm her up slowly. She suggested that I get inside the blanket with Maria, and hold her without rubbing; administer a strong pain-killer as soon as she was awake enough to complain. Blinky gave me a Morphoze popper out of his first-aid kit.

Being bundled together gave me a strangely asexual, almost maternal feeling. Front to back, I alternated warming her face and her breasts by pressing with my hands, resisting the impulse to rub. Freezing my pelvis against her icy behind.

Once he was satisfied that we were doing all that could be done, Blinky suited up again and went out to rig the tow. He couldn't just attach the cable and blast off, because the towed ship would swing into his ICF exhaust, which was a little hotter than the interior of the Sun. So he winched Fireball straight up underneath the platform, where there were padded clamps of various sizes. He clamped it in and headed toward Ceres with a tenth-gee acceleration.

It was twenty-five double-kays, he said cheerfully, 2.8 hours. Might as well relax and enjoy it.

I wasn't as good at calculations as Maria, but I could divide 25,000 by 125. At our top speed we would have covered the distance in 200 seconds. How the mighty have decelerated.

Maria woke up moaning and I put her back to sleep with the popper. Blinky spends a lot of time at 0.1 gee, so he has an actual floor with a rug and an Earth-style bunk, which he offered to us. I said I didn't think I could sleep, so he said fine: wake me up in an hour and ten minutes. He'd been up for more than a day. He let her have the bunk and curled up on the rug.

Maria had thrown off her blanket and didn't look good. All of her skin was swollen, angry red, and there were blisters on her cheeks and breasts. The doctor had said to expect blisters and leave them alone. Her skin felt hot, so I didn't replace the blanket.

With an hour to kill, I turned on the monitor and started flipping through menus. *Novysibirsk News* was refreshingly empty: notices of financial transactions; shuttle schedules; a cranky letter-to-the-editor column. Nik Morenski complained that Ceres had become unlivably crowded and we ought to start getting together about an immigration policy. Feedback was 18 percent for, 73 percent against, 9 percent who gives a shit. The editor said that Morenski was a second-generation native, so don't pay any attention to him. Cosmic rays had rotted his brain.

In the classified advertisements, under "Announcements," was a notice that the Stileman Foundation would pay a million pounds for the capture and Earthside delivery of Dallas Barr. Nice to feel wanted. At least it didn't say "dead or alive."

Which brought me back to wondering what we were going to do. If it were only me in the equation, I would say hole up and wait, at least for a few years. Briskin seemed too unstable to keep a complicated enterprise going for long; surely not everyone on the Steering Committee was a homicidal megalomaniac; once it was generally known what lengths he had gone to, he'd be out.

But I still had hopes of converting Maria back to life. That meant we only had a couple of years, tops.

Our letter accusing Briskin of murder went to all forty-seven members of the foundation's Board of Governors. None of them had done anything, except Briskin, who got his hands on a copy and presented it as evidence of my paranoia. Possibilities:

1. The governors all are members of the Steering Committee, and we're dead meat.
2. The Steering Committee got to them before we did, warning them that I'd gone berserk and so forth. Briskin is one of them, after all; he's been on the board since the thirties.

Besides, news of the Yugoslavia murders would have gotten to them before the letter, along with the supposition that I had murdered two or three people in cold blood. It could be that even without any intervention from the Steering Committee, the board members would dismiss the letter as the raving of a madman.

(Of course, there was always the possibility that not just Briskin, not just the Steering Committee, but everyone on the board as well—they were *all* crazy! Maybe there was a time bomb in the Stileman Process that unhinged you after a certain number of years. So where did that leave me?)

Maybe I did sound like a lunatic in that letter. I wanted to check it. Eric could have pulled it out of his memory instantly; but he was over next to Maria, and I didn't want to disturb her. Some news journal had printed the text of the letter, I remembered, probably *NorthAm NewsChex*. I started sorting through its last few weeks' editions, checking everything that had "Dallas Barr" in the text.

I turned up in the oddest places, including a food column. This was after they "discovered" I had poisoned all those people. A columnist with a warped sense of propriety had contacted Alenka Zor's caterer, and reproduced a last-meal menu.

A *Sports Illustrated* writer had had herself dropped at the spot where the taxi sank, along with a spotter in a boat, and had swum to shore. She reported that it would have been an easy job for a person with my athletic background. Since she had done the swim naked, she earned a picture and paragraph in *NorthAm*.

Eventually I found the letter. I had to admit its tone could be interpreted as paranoid. If you already knew I was a dangerous psychopath, it wouldn't do anything to change your mind.

"Lookin' for the million pounds?" Blinky was reading the screen over my shoulder. "He might be gettin' here anytime." He reached past me to open a cabinet door, and pulled out a glass bottle with a Wild Turkey label, but with a colorless fluid inside, not whiskey. "Couldn't sleep." He pulled the cork and tipped the bottle toward me. "Home-made vodka?"

"No thanks. Wonder why they think he'd come out here."

He shook some vodka into a jigger glass and let the glass fall while he replaced the cork. I supposed his habits were geared for this tenth-gee, or for Ceres, at a thirtieth. Things do take their time falling. "They're jus' coverin' bases. They don' know *where* the hell he is."

He had a funny way of drinking: jerk the glass away a couple of centimeters; lean forward to sip as the vodka creeps over the rim; then bring the glass back to its original position. Didn't spill a drop.

"He's probably still in the Conch Republic," I said. "Safest place for him to be. No sense in leaving."

"Novy'd be safe, too," Blinky said. "Except for that million. Lotsa guys go after that. Lotsa guys sell their mother for that."

"I guess." Including Blinky, one assumed. "You know, we've been following it all the way out. We were in cislunar when it happened, the murders."

"You're Stilemans," he said, and I nodded; most people who travel space for fun are. "Know the guy?"

"Met a few times. Didn't *seem* like a maniac." In for a penny, in for a pound. "We were drinking buddies for a week forty, fifty years ago, in Australia. Felt like I knew him pretty well, then. I just don't buy it."

"Me neither. Fuckin' foundation. They want his ass, set him up. Don't kid yourself. Between them an' the Mafia, an't a dime's diff." He took another three-step sip. "Every ten years I go down, give 'em my fuckin' money, get the treatment. Hustle back here." He made an economical gesture. "Don' own this crate. Me an' Big Dick, he's a Stileman, too, an' we're five years outa phase with each other. Papers on the crate, it belongs to a third party who don' exist. So I run it a couple years while Big Dick does the mike down at Flight Control. Then we switch. More money up here, more fun down there."

"No trouble making your million?"

"Hell, no. Couple of years, then jus' spend it. Lots to spend it on down there."

"You like it up here, though."

"Oh yeah." He sat down, an odd contortion that involved gripping the Stiktite with the sides of his slippers. He had let go of the jigger and sat with his hand out, waiting for it to fall. He spoke carefully. "I like it. You meet the most interesting people."

He looked at me, and didn't blink. He knew. "Bet you do."

He caught the glass and considered it. "While I was hookin' up the winch, I took th' liberty of checkin' out yer stores. Didn' take nothin', you don' mind."

I nodded.

"You got that crowdpleaser, buncha shatterguns. I could get you real money for them."

"Sure."

"Good weapons for Novy. Do the job but don't punch any holes in the wall. You make a hole, y'know—they push you through it."

"That's why I brought them."

"I saw the pictures in the news, that Dallas guy used a shattergun on the . . . what do they call 'em? Woman who kills for a living."

"Hit slit."

"Right. Blew the door out. Blew it right across the fuckin' parking lot. Wouldn't happen here." He blinked twice. "Every place people live here is a pressure vessel. You know engineering?"

"Some."

"Tension, compression. Everything flexes. Didn't flex, it'd leak. So shattergun's okay."

"Thanks. I'll remember that."

He finished the jigger and licked the inside in a curiously delicate way. "If I was Dallas Barr, I'd be real careful. Ten percent of the people here are Stilemans, and some of them are really sweatin' for their million. The others are *all* sweatin'."

"Yeah. If I meet him, I'll tell him not to wear a name tag."

"You do that." He flexed and stood up like a genie, floating, legs crossed, and put the jigger and the bottle back in the cabinet. "Little shuteye."

"Get you at 1400."

"Thanks." He put a toe down to the floor, pushed off with a little Stiktite rip, then rose and fell in a graceful parabola toward the rug near where Maria was sleeping. He landed horizontally with his eyes closed.

The Come & Get was the first commercial establishment that most people saw in Novysibirsk, since its only competitors on the northern end of the corridor were a mining office and a general store with no windows. The Come & Get had windows.

"My goodness," Maria said weakly. She had spent two days in the orbital aid station, and her skin was still burning from the frostbite. What she saw made it hotter, blushing. "This wasn't here last time."

"I heard they liked tattoos," Dallas said. There were three naked women in three display windows. One was doing a crossword puzzle, one was watching the cube, and one was watching Dallas, intently, with a schoolgirl's dimpled smile. Her legs were parted to expose the symmetrical tattoo of a black hairy spider, four jointed legs extending down either thigh, green jeweled eyes mounted somehow over the pink slit of the mouth.

The Come & Get

101 Tsiolkovski
Ceres
Novysibirsk

A Long Standing Sexual Establishment

*If you're sick enough to want it,
we're sick enough to sell it to you*

Basic Menu

American	R 100
French	50 (deetee 75)
Greek	125 (female 150)
British	150
Hydraulics	125
First aid*	200
Fist aid*	250
Bad boy*	150
Dress-up	add 10%
Extra partner	add 75% het, 50% home
Extra customer	add 125%
Watcher supplied	add 20% (cube R 75, quality guaranteed)
Just watch	varies
Zerogee	partner's r/t plus 10% plus R 60/hr. prorated
Gravity	add 50%

Anything else by arrangement. Anything.

No Tipping!

* Liability release required, pervert.

"Is that sexy?" Maria asked.

"It's . . . different." The woman watching the cube uncrossed her legs and faced them, drawing up her knees so they could see that she had both male and female organs. "So is that."

"I didn't know people came like that," Maria said. Dallas looked at her and decided she couldn't have meant it as a joke. He took her arm gently and steered her on down the corridor, each careful step a slow glide of six or eight meters.

They had left most of their trade goods and the gold in a bonded warehouse in Ceres-synchronous orbit, next to the aid station and the repair facility where Fireball was being patched up and overhauled. Dallas carried a bag with weapons, the diamond, all their currency, and one precious bottle of Glenmorangie Scotch whisky. At his insistence, Maria wore a stinger clipped to her belt; he wore the holstered crowdpleaser. She carried the reader with Eric under her arm.

It was 0745, and the corridors were just starting to fill up with people on their way to this and that. Traffic along Tsiolkovski, the main avenue, sorted itself out into five narrow lanes. At both edges of the corridor was a strip of Stiktite; window-shoppers and cautious people tiptoed along there, putting one foot down before lifting the other. There was a center lane marked with red and white stripes, where people moved fast and took their chances, trying not to hit the ceiling four meters up, or the people coming from the opposite direction. Dallas and Maria had crept along the Stiktite at first, but now were loping down the moderate-speed lane next to the candy-striped one, feeling clumsy but looking graceful.

The main corridor, Tsiolkovski, displayed an interesting mix of residences and shops, the high-rent district. Entrances were ornately decorated and most of them featured ostentatious displays of elements imported from Earth: a large round antique stained glass window; a massive hand-carved door from Spain; a bonsai garden; a Vegas brothel holo. Most of these belonged to Stilemans who, like the Barons they'd met in *adastra*, made their money here but spent most of their time on Earth. Some of those places were for rent, which was going to be their first stop. A public hotel didn't sound like a good idea for a person with a million-pound price on his head.

Dallas took a map card out of his breast pocket and checked it with one eye. "Second left up here." They almost went down in a heap, trying to stop and turn, but managed, laughing. They turned down a side corridor, Seventh, that opened between a French- or New Orleans-style residence and a greengrocer who was setting out a display of hydroponic fruit, too large and too perfect.

The address of the rental agent was −141 Seventh, which meant his door was 141 meters down Seventh, to the west of Tsiolkovski. The entrances became less ostentatious as you went along, and the agent's was next to last, ten meters from the grey slag wall that ended the corridor. The sign hanging over the entrance said PETER'S PIECE OF THE ROCK—0900–1700, but the door was open, so they went in. The place was completely devoid of decoration: white walls, green Stiktite floor, two hard chairs facing a desk with a keyboard. There was a vague mint smell, probably air freshener. A rear door opened: Peter Quinn.

"Goz Donato, Goza Vaughn. Come in, come in." He was a small bent bald man, evidently in his late seventies. "Thought you might be on the first shuttle, so I opened a little early. Sit, sit."

Sitting was not something you did spontaneously in a thirtieth of a gee. Rather than hover expectantly over the seat, they followed the agent's example and grabbed their chair arms with both hands and forcefully inserted themselves.

"Sunburn, gozpoda?"

"No, Mr. Quinn. Frostbite; I had a suit malfunction."

"Oh my. I suppose everybody tells you how lucky you are. To be alive. Isn't that absurd?" He unlocked the keyboard and tapped one button; the wall to his left became a two-dimensional picture of a living room. The furnishings were simple but the view was interesting, a panorama of the asteroid's surface.

"This is one thing I have; I have, oh, forty-eight properties you could rent for maybe up to a year, some of them for a few years. How long are you staying?"

"We don't really know yet," Dallas said. "We want to look around, check out some other rocks. We may be staying here; we may be using Ceres just as a home base while we explore. For how short a period of time can we rent?"

"Short is no problem. Short is *expensive*, but it's no problem. Can I be direct?"

"Sure."

"I'm in this business fifty years, here and dirtside. You learn to size people up, what they think they can afford, what they *can* afford. Let me guess."

Dallas spread his hands.

"You're both Stilemans. Believe me, you don't have to be one to spot one." He raised a finger. "But that does not mean you're going to spend a lot of money. People don't make money by spending it, not spending it on apartments. People make money by . . . well, to be polite, by driving a hard bargain."

"By screwing other people," Dallas said. "To be impolite."

"Definitely. But like that verb, it works best if the other party *also* feels he or she has gotten a good deal. *Good* business, the kind of business I like to do, is when this is actually true: you get a bargain; I make an unseemly profit."

"So what do you have in mind?" Maria said.

"Look at this place." He tapped two numbers on the keyboard. "Is this nice, or what?" Like the previous one, it had a view of the glorious sky and bleak landscape, but the furnishings were plush, greys set against vibrant colors, pleasingly coordinated.

"Is that a holo view?" Maria asked.

"No, it's a real window. Upstairs living room. No problem with solar flares; the bedroom, kitchen, and dining area are all under two meters of rock. Automatic alarm system, you got ten or fifteen minutes to walk downstairs."

"So what makes it a great deal?" Dallas said.

"The woman who owns it is gone for five years, maybe seven. I'm supposed to close it up, shut down the life support. Put everything in storage that doesn't like hard vacuum. That's a fixed expense. You rent the place for five minutes or five years, it's all profit to me."

"What you mean is, she didn't say you could rent it."

He shrugged. "She didn't say I couldn't. You sign a bond saying everything will be the way she left it, or you pay through the nose."

"I don't know," Dallas said. "Signing a bond doesn't bother me; we aren't going to damage anything. But it's her property. It can't be legal."

"This is Novysibirsk." He smiled a display of teeth much younger than he was. "What is this word 'legal'?"

"That's literally right," Maria said. "If her bond with him didn't forbid renting—"

"Even if it *did*," he said, "and I didn't get caught, there would be no problem. I wouldn't do it, ethics, but if I did—no problem! This rock is either devoid of civilization or the pinnacle of it, depending on your point of view."

"Which is your point of view?" Dallas asked, smiling.

"Devoid. But who needs civilization?"

"So you must have several properties like this," Maria said.

"Well . . . no. This is the only one I have where the client neglected to stipulate rental terms. She wanted to save money and not use a lawyer." He shrugged elaborately. "So I ask you. Whose fault is it if I make a few rubles? Who's hurt? She still doesn't have to pay the lawyer's fees."

"How much do you want?" Dallas asked.

"Big deposit, low rent. Rent gets lower, the longer you have it." He leaned back, which made his knees float up and bump the underside of the desk. "If you only have it for a short time, it's a thousand rubles a week. After four, it's two thousand a month. After two months, fifteen hundred. That's cheap for Ceres."

Dallas nodded. "And the deposit?"

"A hundred thousand."

"We're not gonna set fire to the place."

"Look at it from my perspective. It's a long way down. You know how much it would cost me to replace a simple two-ruble glass? I *would* have to replace it. She can't know the place was rented."

"I wonder," Maria said. "Suppose she found out. What would she do?"

"This is Ceres. She could go down to the landing dock and pick up some lowlife and pay him fifty rubles to give me a vacuum lesson. As in breathing vacuum? At my age, I don't think I could learn."

"She wouldn't do that," Dallas said. "She'd squeeze you for the money."

"Ceres. You get your random arbitrageurs. They decide you don't get your money. Then what do you do?"

"Not murder."

He shrugged. "She's an interesting woman. Sort of a cross between Cleopatra and Attila the Hun. I do need a deposit."

Dallas reached in the bag and brought out the diamond in its velvet box. He opened it like an egg, a hand span above the desk, giving the diamond a little spin. It glittered hypnotically as it slowly fell, spraying color.

"I don't know much about jewelry," Quinn said.

"Ten carats, standard brilliant, first water. It was appraised at eighty thousand dollars twenty years ago. Worth a lot more than a hundred thousand rubles now."

"I'd have to have somebody look at it."

"That's okay. We'd have to look at the apartment, too. Why don't we do both at the same time."

He pursed his lips and nodded. "Let me have your thumbs." He took their thumbprints on a Xerocard and phoned them to the apartment, so it would let them in. "I can have an appraiser come in at lunchtime, if not sooner. We could close the deal this afternoon, if the terms are agreeable."

"After we see the place," Dallas said. "Then we can talk about terms."

The apartment was luxurious, unusually so for being well away from Tsiolkovski. The address was 220 Thirty-fourth, and all the rest of East Thirty-fourth Corridor was taken up by hydroponics and a chicken farm. So it was as close to living "out in the country" as you could get in Ceres.

The floor upstairs was Persian-carpeted, which was ostentatious both in terms of money and as a statement that the owner was an Old Hand. It was hard for a tyro to move around a room without Stiktite on the floor. You tended to fetch up against the picture windows.

It even had an air lock, which Quinn said was "almost unique." There were only about a dozen private air locks on the whole asteroid, since they had to have elaborate failsafes. It wouldn't do for someone to go out and forget to close the door.

Downstairs was more comfortable, more utilitarian. One luxury was a water bed, which tied up a few hundred rubles' worth of water. Dallas suggested they try it out, but Maria was too tired, still feeling weak from the frostbite.

On their way back to Quinn's they stopped at a pseudo-Mexican restaurant that featured cabrito, roast goat. Dallas and Maria opted for the vegetarian plates instead, which cost two orders of magnitude less, and perused the local classified ads to get a sense of what people were paying for rent. Quinn's terms didn't seem unreasonable by comparison.

Waiting for their meal, Dallas had the reader in his lap and was scrolling, reading out the classified ads to Maria. He suddenly stopped and stared.

"I'll be damned. Look at this." He passed the reader to Maria:

To the nice couple we met on *adastra*: A little bird tells us you're in trouble and might be someplace in Novy. If you need a couple of friends, give us a buzz at (Ceres) 34-833.—Bill and Doris

"It is tempting, isn't it?" She handed the reader back. "But we don't want to drag them into this mess."

"We might have to." Dallas pushed the REMEMBER button and said "Barons" to the machine.

Their meals came, couscous with a variety of steamed vegetables. Dallas tore into his like the starving creature that he was, but Maria ate hesitantly and excused herself after a couple of minutes.

She came back from the toilet pale and trembling. "Still not completely recovered," she said. "You go ahead and finish mine."

"Should we find a doctor?"

"No. They said I'd be weak for a while."

"You might have picked something up at the aid station."

"Picked up?" She looked at him quizzically. "Oh, you mean a virus or something."

"There were lots of sick people there. Oddly enough."

"If it gets worse, all right." She picked up the wineglass and took a careful sip, but then put it down a little too fast. The wine lagged behind the container; she retrieved most of it.

"Do you get the feeling that you're stuck in a slow-motion movie?"

She gave him a weary smile. "Often."

*

Dallas

WHEN we got back to Peter Quinn's office, he was at his desk, ready and waiting. "Nice place, eh?"

"It will do. You have the diamond appraised?"

He took the velvet box out of a vest pocket and opened it, admiring the stone. "This is a remarkable piece, evidently. I mean, *beautiful*, that I can tell myself. But my friend says remarkable. If you got it for eighty thousand, you got a real bargain."

I shrugged. I'd paid almost three times that much, illegal cash. "That's what it was appraised at, 'way back when. You know Earth. Of course, I paid more, in order to hang on to it through the Stileman shakedown."

" 'Away back when,' yes; twenty years." He set the diamond exactly halfway between us. "I sent a holo to the International Diamond Registry in Antwerp. The last owner of record was a Stileman, Russell Coville. He happens to be in Novy, out at 127 Johanna. I wouldn't live there on a bet. It goes around once each forty minutes, your own shadow makes you dizzy."

"You talked to him?" Good old Russell.

"He says he sold it to Dallas Barr."

Quickly: "That's who *I* bought it from. You can understand why I don't want to sell it on Earth."

"Oh yes." He leaned back. "I took the liberty of assuming that was the case, and that's what I told Mr. Coville." I nodded, not trusting myself to say anything. "If you *were* Dallas Barr, it wouldn't do me that much good.

The million pounds, the Stileman Treatment. I've been off Earth for too long, haven't kept up with my exercise. Couldn't handle gravity. My heart would stop before the shuttle did.

"I stay here, I've got twenty years, thirty, maybe more. Maybe a lot more. You hear things; things are happening."

"That's good."

"You've got several alternatives. Antwerp says on Earth you might get $175,000 for this. That's 160,000 rubles minus some change. If you were to offer it for, say, one-forty, you'd have a dozen people lining up. You'd probably get the one-sixty if you held out."

"That's good to know."

"But you'd probably be kidnapped or dead the next day. The connection with Dallas Barr would not stay secret, and there are some desperate people here, predators."

"The other alternatives?"

"You could have the stone broken up. My friend could have it done confidentially; this is not something outside his experience. You would have four largish stones and some gravel, assuming no accidents: aggregate value perhaps 60,000 rubles."

"That might be best."

"*Or*—or you could just leave it with me. In lieu of a damage deposit. If everything blows over, you get the diamond back, you haven't lost a kopek. If someone mistakenly kills you, thinking you are Dallas Barr, or kidnaps you . . . the stone wouldn't be worth anything to you anyhow. Would it?"

"Aren't you taking an awful chance? What if I *were* Dallas Barr? Sitting across from you with a crowdpleaser on my belt. A dangerous psychotic murderer."

He didn't say anything for a moment, and when he spoke, there was a quaver of tension in his voice. "So all of life is a gamble. You would live longer if you hid under the bed and never came out. But I've never hidden . . . and I don't believe everything I read in the papers." He sat forward. "What I believe is the things I read *between* the lines. Who owns this paper? Who wants you to think what?"

Maria cleared her throat. "I think we have to trust him."

He nodded to her and looked back at me. "I told you I'm in this business fifty years, real estate. Before that, would you believe it? I was a social worker. New York, what was left of it."

"Bad times, fifty years ago."

"Good times for a boy who wants to change the world. A lot of the world needed changing."

"Still does."

"More worlds now. Ten years I beat my head against the wall. Against the system. I was an old man at thirty." He smiled. "And a young man at sixty, when I sold everything and came out here. But by then I'd learned: nobody *changes* the system. Not unless you're a Hitler or a Khomeini. And even then, the system eats you. You change it, but you don't change it into what you wanted." He looked at Maria again, intently. "I'm not old compared to you two. But it *is* trust, gospoda; that's the one thing I learned in eighty years. The system does whatever history makes it do, and the same kind of dreary criminals take charge, generation after generation. But *we* can be better than that, one at a time, two at a time; family, friends, business associates. We can beat the system bit by bit, in our own little spheres, being human with each other. And learning to know the predators when we see them, of course, the ones you can't be human with, and handling them."

Maybe he was a kindly old man and maybe he was a cynical hypocrite trying to lull us into vulnerability. In either case, we had only two reasonable courses of action: go along with him or get rid of him.

If he were going to betray us, he would have done it already. So maybe when we got back to the apartment, the "villa," there would be an assassin waiting, or some foundation goon. I did doubt it; he seemed to be a straight character.

Besides, I'd done enough killing for one lifetime. "Okay. You have a piece of paper for us to look at?"

"Here. Save paper." He turned on the holo apparatus and a standard rental agreement appeared on the wall, with the numbers he'd mentioned.

"Tell you what. Let's not haggle." I took out the bottle of Glenmorangie and set it on his desk. "Twenty percent off, all the way down the line."

He considered that. "I'm not a Scotch drinker. But let's not haggle. Ten percent."

"Fifteen," I said, and reached for the bottle.

He grabbed it. "Fifteen and the Scotch." He smiled. "Never too old to learn a new vice."

"Deal." The old bastard knew it was worth two hundred rubles. If we stayed less than a month, that would more than make up the difference. "If we're screwing each other, I guess this is the foreplay?"

Our large bags were being held at the shuttle depot; I called from Quinn's office, and they arrived only a couple of minutes after we got to the villa.

Maria wanted to lie down, but first I made her memorize the various places I stashed the shatterguns: one per room, easily accessible but out of sight. I decided not to try anything fancy in the way of booby traps. Just have a weapon fairly close to hand wherever you were. That had saved my life in the Conch Republic, where, it was becoming apparent, we had been in less danger of discovery. Old Quinn knew who I was, and so did Blinky, and the appraiser most likely had figured out we were here, even if Quinn hadn't revealed anything. Not forgetting Russell Coville, who could put two and two together and also would sell his own mother into white slavery. Bill and Doris Baron suspected we were here—was that just from the foundation ad, or did they know something a thousand other people did? Best to assume the worst.

While she slept, I turned on Eric and filled him in about what had happened since we came down from synchronous orbit. We agreed that the safest thing to do would be to move to a smaller asteroid as soon as Fireball was ready, and not tell anyone that we'd gone or where we were going.

Then I went down to the water bed, where Maria was sprawled naked, gently snoring. She was still beautiful, though the frostbite had given her skin an odd color and texture. I undressed and slipped in next to her.

When I touched her she went into convulsions; her body started bucking in and out of a crouched fetal position, floating in midair after having risen with the first twitch.

I wrapped her in a blanket and held her, and the convulsions quieted down and stopped. But she wouldn't wake up enough to respond to any questions. Her eyes wouldn't focus; her breath was sour and hot.

I pulled on my clothes and checked the map card. There was a clinic at Twentieth and Tsiolkovski. Quicker to carry her there than wait for whatever Ceres used for ambulances, so I wrapped the blanket tight and ran her outside.

A selfish thought that couldn't be avoided: this was fine timing. The last thing we needed—*I* needed—was to be tied down by a serious illness.

I should have guessed how serious it was.

Novysibirsk Medical Services
Ceres Center

DATE: 10 yanvár 81

CLIENT'S NAME: Selena Vaughn

SPONSOR (if other than self): Cassius Donato

REASON FOR ADMISSION: Frostbite complications, general debility

Disposition/Prognosis

Suit malfunction caused reversible frostbite. Patient recovering well from this. Continue pain medication as needed.

Patient is a Stileman rejuvenee whose current period of rejuvenation has almost expired. Early stages of deterioration evident in skin and muscle tone, considerably accelerated by the trauma of frostbite. In three to four weeks her condition will begin to deteriorate rapidly.

Recommendation/Rx

80 ea. 6 mg. Neophet; 30 ea. sandman gen. Euthanasia per patient's desires, no later than 10 févral.

CHARGE: R50.00 / $US 54.87 currency

PHYSICIAN/PARAMEDIC:

Sarah P. Eaton MD

Maria

THEY thought I was asleep, and whispered. I had my back to them but could see Dallas in the examining room mirror. He looked at the bill, turned pale, leaned slowly against the wall.

"This can't be right."

"Today's exchange rate." The doctor was an attractive woman with long flowing white hair, who looked under thirty, except for the eyes, penetrating and sad and old.

"I mean . . ."

"Oh, I know what you mean. My specialty is Stileman physiology. There's no mistake. She didn't tell you she was getting close to her time?"

"She said two or three years . . . I wouldn't have brought her if I . . . she can't get back to Earth."

"She knew how much time she had when she left. You start to feel it the last few months."

He shook his head. "I know. Went down to the wire last time."

"She out of money?"

"No. She just . . ." He shrugged.

I turned around, slowly. Hot skin hurt under the scratchy hospital robe. "We have to talk . . . Cash." Almost said his real name.

"Be down the hall," the doctor said, and left. Dallas was at my side in one drifting step, half the room long.

"Dallas," I whispered, "Dallas." Trying to slow down my spinning mind, focus on the speech I'd been rehearsing for weeks. "I don't know how to ask you this."

"Anything," he said gently.

"I have to get back," I said. "Somewhere between Earth and here I . . . stopped wanting to die. I want to live with you, go on living. . . ."

He was crying. He jerked his head sharply, and the tears spun away from his face, tiny crystal spheres.

I touched his face. "It's a terrible gamble. But we don't know for sure that they're after me. You could stay here; I can run the Fireball alone."

He was shaking his head, not looking at me. "I'm sorry I lied. I was just protecting you."

"You . . . you can't do it."

"Of course I can. I've done it alone before."

His teeth were clenched, voice hoarse: "Don't have *time!*"

"Yes, I do. Five to seven months. Even saving fuel, I can get there in—" He thrust the hospital printout at me.

It took a few moments to register. That was me they were talking about.

Euthanasia in four weeks.

"This is wrong. This has to be wrong." But my body told me otherwise.

Dallas and I walked back to the villa together in almost total silence. What could we say? When we got there I wanted to hold him, and talk, and cry, but that had to be later, after I had a chance to be by myself for an hour or two, and reason things out. He understood. Aloneness is one thing we all understand better than normal people. I went to the downstairs bathroom and turned out the light.

The drugs had me buzzing and glowing. They gave me a four-week supply of Neophets to keep me charged up, as well as sandman for sleep. They wouldn't do that on Earth. They should. A terminal Stileman tends to surrender psychologically, spiritually, to the diffuse malaise that grows on you as all the body's systems realize that time is running out. And then one system after another collapses. They can hook you up to an artificial heart and lung, and bypass your kidneys and liver with machines, but that's unnecessary cruelty. Eventually the catalog of maladies includes cancer, and within a day, within hours, it's corroding you everywhere. Or your brain blows a fuse, if you're lucky. They don't yet know how to do a brain bypass, unless you count things like Eric.

There was a hospice associated with the convent where I was hiding, back in the twenties. We had a succession of terminal Stilemans because of the Italian national lottery. You win a thousand million lire and the most valuable thing you can buy with it is life . . . but you can't buy the financial acumen necessary to finance a second treatment, or the luck to win the lottery again.

So we'd get these suddenly old men and women. I treated a number of them with "accidental" overdoses of painkiller, when it came to the last week. That's no more murder than my spike of fifty-grief is suicide. It's pain management. Not all of the sisters would have agreed.

On the way to Mars, Dallas had argued about suicide with me. If suicide were a mortal sin, how could I justify refusing my sixth or nth Stileman, knowing that the refusal would result in sure death? The Church took care of that in the twentieth century, though, allowing people to refuse dramatic treatment if its purpose was merely to postpone natural death. The Stileman Treatment is a hundred separate "heroic measures," against a condition that otherwise has a recovery rate of exactly zero. Not counting Lazarus.

If on the other side I come to judgment and it turns out that I was wrong, and have committed a mortal sin, then I've been wrong about more important things in this life, and it won't make any difference.

Trying to subtract the drug, to find out how I really feel. I have thought about this time, and even looked forward to it. I'm surprised and chagrined at the spectrum of fears, petty and huge. Fear of incontinence, the embarrassment. On the way here I sneezed and wet myself a little. Sickness; specific anxiety about vomiting—which resonates both with that gagging at the smell of Lysol when I put the suit's helmet on and with the way so many of those old people died, choking, "inspiration of vomitus." Fear of all the pain, and breaking down under it, shaming Dallas.

Fear of death. The darkness, not being.

Which means, I must say it to myself, fear of loss of faith. At this threshold. My hundred-year-old brain has heard all the arguments about the existence of God, and my hundred-year-old heart has survived them. Until now, when I need the faith the most. All that magnificent edifice, all the strength and span of it, how could I lose its sustenance now?

Maybe my brain's been affected by the debilitation process. But it doesn't feel like the brain.

The darkness in the bathroom was not soothing anymore. I turned on the light and took a moment to despise the animated corpse in the mirror, and then went upstairs to Dallas.

The Stileman Foundation
1000 King Street
Sydney, Australia

The long habit of living indisposeth us for dying.
—SIR THOMAS BROWNE

PRESS RELEASE

9 January 2081

1158 GST

HEAD: STILEMAN HEAD VARGAS DIES AFTER MADRID ATTACK
   STRINKS: STILEMAN/VARGAS/MADRID/VIOLENCE (SPAIN)/
       NOBEL PRIZE/GUNS

Raphael Vargas, chairman of the Stileman Foundation for the past seven years, was gravely injured by gunfire last night when he resisted a purse snatcher in downtown Madrid, and he died this morning at 0943 Greenwich time. A bystander, who is being sought by Madrid police, shot and killed the purse snatcher in a brief exchange of gunfire that resulted in no other injuries on the nearly deserted side street.

Vargas will be remembered as a humane and energetic leader who sought to promote understanding between Stileman "immortals" and the main stream of humanity. It was he who instituted the Stileman Achievement Award, which offers free life extension to Nobel Prizewinners in all categories.

(Vargas's death will cause an ironic exchange of a type that's not uncommon when Stileman rejuvenees die of accidents or violence. His closest living relative is a son who, aged 101, is a senile old man living in a rest home in his native Barcelona. The son will inherit Vargas's fortune, estimated at more than ten million pesetas, and so will himself be eligible for the Stileman Treatment.) GOTO BRANCH HEAD **1.1?**

Branch head 1.2: Sir Charles Briskin Named Successor

STRINKS: STILEMAN/BRISKIN/U.K. GOVT./VARGAS

Sir Charles Briskin, who was secretary of the exchequer for the United Kingdom from the reestablishment of that office in 2030 until 2038, has agreed to take up the position of chairman of the board of this foundation, following the sudden untimely death of Raphael Vargas. Besides his obvious professional qualifications, Sir Charles brings to the office a unique academic orientation, having earned both a doctorate in economics from Cambridge and a doctorate in history from Harvard University, in the United States. His undergraduate preparation, at Trinity College, Dublin, was in political science and economics.

Born in 1960 in Belfast, Sir Charles was knighted in 2035 after his bold wage and price control scheme helped Britain avert the runaway inflation that destroyed the economies, and brought down the governments, of most EEC member nations that year.

Sir Charles has had seven Stileman Treatments, beginning in 2004. He has been a member of the foundation's Board of Governors for nearly fifty years and was the natural choice when the board assembled this morning to name a successor to Raphael Vargas.

subbranch head 1.21: The Dallas Barr Situation

Of the current Stileman crisis, new Stileman Foundation Chairman Sir Charles Briskin says: "This teaches us that we must never become complacent about our understanding of the medical processes involved in the Stileman Treatment. Both the premature death of Geoffrey Lorne-Smythe and the outrageous homicidal behavior of Dallas Barr apparently have been the result of repeated head injuries, which in each rejuvenation session seemed to have healed enough not to require attention. How wrong we were.

"The oldest Stileman veterans should be closely monitored as they go through their thirteenth decade. Also, it should go without saying that all of us must opt for surgical replacement of the skull, the so-called hardhead prosthesis, the next time we go in for rejuvenation—not only for our own safety but also for the general welfare, ephemeral as well as immortal. We can't afford any more Dallas Barrs.

"The reward of £1,000,000 for Mr. Barr's apprehension remains in effect. We don't wish to harm him, of course, but hope that the study of his condition may prevent its recurrence.

"Fortunately, the enlightened state of Yugoslavia, within whose borders Barr committed two cold-blooded murders, has long outlawed capital punishment. Authorities there have agreed to allow Stileman scientists to study Barr during his incarceration there. . . ."

The other seven board members finished reading the press release and so signified by nodding, sipping water, scribbling.

"It's good, Charles," said a tall black man, "but do you think the statement about Dallas Barr is really necessary?"

"Perhaps not," Briskin said. "It's a matter of personal concern to me, since we were acquaintances. I would hate to see him hurt someone else."

"I believe it is a good idea," said a French woman, "in the sense of public service. While we have the people's general attention, to remind them of the danger."

Atsuji Kamachi nodded, his silver dome glittering from unseen lights. "So unexpected, so sad. Have you any idea where he could be?"

"I don't have any special relationship with Interpol," Briskin said. "I think they traced him to the Conch Republic and then lost him. I would suspect he's in America someplace."

"I would be inclined to think otherwise," Kamachi said, "from more than forty years of dealings with him. He is comfortable in many places; speaks many languages well. In America his face is too well known.''

"They say he probably changed his face in the Conch Republic. He could look like anyone.''

"Of course.'' Kamachi stifled a yawn. "I am not thinking too well. It is four in the morning here.''

"I suppose that's all of the business,'' Briskin said. "Let's adjourn until next week. Meet, say, at midnight Greenwich, between the twelfth and thirteenth.'' The seven consulted calendars, nodded assent, and one by one their holograms faded.

Briskin sat alone at the end of the long mahogany desk. He looked around the large dimly lit room: an ancient tapestry; oversized oil portraits in ornate gilded frames; large crystal chandelier flickering with archaic gaslight, a stupefyingly expensive affectation. He nodded at no one and spoke into the air. "Cease recording. I'll have supper here at eight-thirty. Alone.''

"May I decant a '63 Ausone at eight-fifteen?'' the air asked.

"Do.'' Briskin stood up. "I'll be in the library with two gentlemen. We are not to be disturbed or recorded.''

"Very well, sir.'' As he walked down the corridor to the library, Briskin allowed himself a broad smile. It vanished when he opened the door.

One of the men, handsome and muscular, with an insolent air, was sprawled on the couch reading a magazine that was inappropriate for the Victorian room. Queen Victoria would have fainted at the cover illustration, which depicted oral sex. The other man, small and strikingly ugly, was reading the spines of the rows of leather-bound books. Both of them had glasses of brandy. Briskin nodded at them, went to the sideboard, and poured himself a measure from the crystal decanter.

"Didn't think you'd mind if we had a drink,'' the ugly one said.

"No, of course not. You're sure you weren't followed?''

"No way,'' the other said. He had a southern American accent, soft and sweet. "We did like you said. Took the floater down the game trail far as we could, parked, then watched for an hour from cover, then walked the three miles here. That first mile was a bitch."

"The blizzard is over, is it not?"

"Still blowin' snow around. Somethin' new to me. Can't say as I like it."

"It's even colder where you're going. Do you both have experience with spaceflight?"

"Yeah," they said in unison.

"There is a commercial flight to Novysibirsk, to Ceres, leaving HEO on the twelfth. You're to be on it, with the identities I established for you."

"That's where Barr and the woman went?" the ugly man asked. His accent was harsher, New England winters.

"It's likely but not certain. Barr owned a diamond that wound up there, in the possession of a real estate agent. At least an agent called Antwerp about it. It's possible he could have sold it in the States right after the murders, and the person he sold it to might have gone straight to Novysibirsk and bought property. Possible. Not very likely, though."

"If he's there, we'll find him," the handsome man drawled. "Guess we check out this real estate agent."

"That would be sensible. His name is Peter Quinn."

"Is he important?" the ugly one asked. "I mean, suppose we have to . . . hurt him."

"Do what you will." Briskin took a huge sniff of the brandy, then a sip. "This brandy's a hundred and five years old. Is that older than you?"

"Barely. I'm a hundred and three." He looked at Briskin sardonically. "I'll answer the other question. 'Why do you look like that when you could look like anybody?' The personal answer is that I like to look like myself. The professional answer is that nobody expects an immortal to look like a toad."

"I can tell you're immortal."

"Any immortal can, after a few years." He pointed at the other. "And you can tell Golden Boy is a 'phem."

"For a while yet," he said. "That's what the million's for."

"Murray amuses me," the ugly one said. "I want him to stay around, stay pretty. Is that shocking?"

"I am mortified," Briskin said, rolling his eyes. "I've never met an actual homosexual before."

"But he ain't," Murray said. "It'd be okay with me, but he ain't." The ugly one shrugged.

"Try to bring them both back alive. If you have to kill the woman, well, you have to, but Barr is of no value to me dead." He pointed at Murray. "Bring me Barr and you're immortal. Otherwise you'll grow old and die. You might not even get that old."

The man made no effort to conceal his hostility. "I'll bring him."

Dallas and Maria missed the news of Briskin's suspicious takeover, understandably, since it happened the day they found out she was going to die.

The scene is a cliché of modern tragedy (fear of science having superseded our fear of the gods): young lovers facing a terminal prognosis. In this case the young lovers were also ancient, which tempered and complicated their reactions. Four and five billion people had died in their lifetimes: thousands of them with names, hundreds of them friends, some of them lovers. They beat death, every ten or twelve years, but they also had to live side by side with it.

Conventionally Anglo-Saxon, Dallas stopped crying after less than a minute. Sufficiently Italian, Maria did not, and perhaps she wasn't crying for her own impending death so much as for the abrupt and tragic death of this new love. Old and new. She had calmed to an occasional dab and sniffle by the time they returned to the villa and she excused herself downstairs.

When she came back up from the cellar darkness, floating over the ramp, she found darkness upstairs as well. Dallas was vaguely silhouetted at the window, staring out over the dim blasted landscape of Ceres, a ghostly jumble of rocks and crater walls glowing pale gold in the light of Jupiter.

"Night comes fast," she said. Dallas nodded in the

darkness. "I'm sorry. This is the worst thing I've ever done in my life."

"Dying is the worst thing that most people do."

"Lying to you." She put a hand on each shoulder, from behind, and leaned her forehead against the back of his neck. "I was afraid . . . afraid you could talk me out of it. If you'd known how little time was left."

"So the time scale has changed," he said quietly. "All of a sudden I'm faced with losing you. I suspected that you would . . . go your way, and I *would* lose you. But I expected to have years to get used to it. This is too quick, too much."

"I'm sorry." She was trembling. *"Mea culpa.* I was going to . . . once we were settled here, I was going to talk to you about it, figure out a way to get back and take the chance."

He turned around and squeezed her, hard enough to make her gasp. "Maybe there is some way."

"No. Not to get to Earth from here in three weeks. I've gone over the numbers . . . over and over in my head. Can't be done."

"Here. Sit on the couch?" They did a clumsy pas de deux and collapsed in slow motion toward the cushions. Dallas touched a lamp on the way down. In the warm pink glow they both looked healthier than they felt.

The reader was on the coffee table. "Let's see what Eric says."

"No harm in it."

He turned it on. "Eric—we have a real problem."

Eric

Location 220 44th Corridor,
Ceres • temperature 21° • pressure
0.6 atm. • p O$_2$ 120 mm Hg • input
state *on* • both Dallas & Maria
appear to have been crying remarkable for Dallas of course Maria
even cries alone *Eric* which is   Eric—

appropriate both in terms of her
personality & her culture • wish we
had met when *we* I was solid I   **we**
would have a more comprehensive
picture of what she was like & so
be more of *have* a help in this cur-   **have**
rent pancake • did not mention to
Dallas the fact that her frostbite
trauma might accel *a* erate the   **a**
aging process but he didn't ask & I
think he has enough trouble • that's
probably what this *real* is   **real**
about • he's going to say
"problem" now as in
Eric-we-have-a-reeeal-problem • &
the probability is *problem* large   **problem.**
that the problem he perceives is
only the visible part of the
iceberg • output state *on:*

Okay. I'm all ears.

input state *on:* • so to speak although I don't speak any more or
less than *Maria's* I hear   **Maria's**
actually • from the sad expressions
I assume that Maria's been given a
negative prognosis *frostbite* proba-   **frostbite**
bly when she went in for a follow-
up at the hospital here • no it was
more likely an emergency since
has Dallas didn't mention any   **has**
follow-up when he updated me
three hours ago • if that's the case
I wonder *triggered* what they think   **triggered**
I can do for them • maybe they just
have to talk to someone • I know
the feeling • *the* wish they'd plug   **the**
me into a datanet for a few
seconds every now & then • on the
ship I *degenerative* could stay   **degenerative**
plugged in to the public-access nets

all the time • phase—early frostbite has triggered the *phase* degenerative phase early • it was like walking around a party full of eclectic interesting people • maybe *early.* they'll find a place here where I can sit & listen • output state *on:*

phase

early.

I'm sorry. How long do you have?

input state *on:* • if she has *four* time to get back to Earth, she can be extremely public about it & say she escaped from the foul clutches of *weeks* Dallas Barr, man about town & part-time murdering maniac • might just be able to get back to Earth *only* in 28 days in Fireball, but it's close • even with the boost from Mars it took us 35 days • call it forty days *three* without • fuel mass required goes roughly by the square so need 2.04 times the fuel with maximum *until* acceleration • doubt that there's room for the extra tankage • wait, he's going to say only three weeks really *it's* so that's 3.63 times the fuel • absolutely no way even if she had her Bugatti • only-three-until-it's-too-late *irreversible* sometimes your word choice surprises me, Dallas • that probably means you actually have to trim a few more days off to give her time for the song and dance • output state *on:*

Four

weeks;

only

three

until

it's

irreversible.

I'm afraid you can't make Fireball get to Earth in that short a time. You'd need to increase the

**fuel at least fourfold, & you
would have to maintain five gees
for two long periods.**

input state *on:* now Maria speaks *I*
leaning forward • look at her new
face, but I always bitmap it and
reprocess so she looks like she
really looks like • I don't really
blame him for getting all human
over her though I was always par-
tial *know* to blondes, none of
whom was to my knowledge much
of a spaceship pilot • wish they
wouldn't turn me *is* off when they
got down to biology but I suppose
civilization must be served • well
in some supposedly *there* civilized
places supposedly civilized people
pay to be watched • is there any
historical precedent *any* for that,
rather than the other way around?
SEARCH nothing in *my* memory wish
they would *other* hook me up to a
generalized relational database • I
feel deaf dumb & blind • way is-
there-any-other *way* way • does she
mean alternative transportation or
another way out of her predica-
ment? SEARCH output mode *on:*

I

know.

Is

there

any

other

way?

**Drones used for document ex-
change have done Earth/Ceres in
as little as seven days. But their
rates of acceleration would be
intolerable to you, and the fuel/
payload ratio would be unrealis-
tic considering the necessity of
life support.**

But that's not what you mean.

input mode *on:* is there any other *no* way • some way the degeneration process could be slowed here on Ceres • good excuse to be *some* plugged into a database, but first a quick tree off my own memory:

No;

some

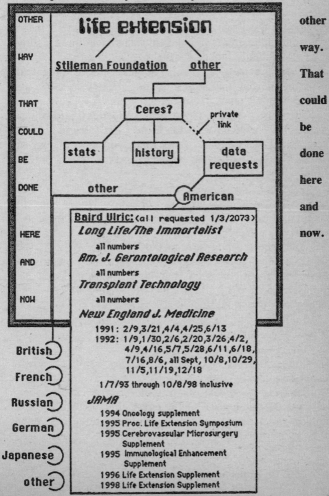

other

way.

That

could

be

done

here

and

now.

Dallas

SOMETIMES the lifelike way that Eric's image acted made you admire the programming genius that went into creating a TI. He actually looked startled.

"There's something here," he said. "Something that could be of great importance to you."

Maria didn't react. "What is it?"

"Eric, the flesh-and-blood Eric, had extensive dealings with a Novy scientist or doctor, Baird Ulric, back in '73. He shipped him more than twenty thousand pages of journal articles, in twelve languages—actual paper copies from his library."

"Why in heaven's name would he do that?" Maria said.

"So there would be no record of the exchange. They all seem to be about life extension and gerontological research."

"Then there *would* be a record," I said. "Whether he owned a paper copy or an electronic one. The foundation's draconian about controlling that kind of information."

"But it's all old stuff. Nothing after late 1998."

"What good would that do?"

"I don't know. Maybe it's just of historical interest. But it was important enough for him not to tell me about it."

"Or trivial enough."

"It doesn't work that way. Most of my memory space is taken up with trivialities.

"He spent two weeks on this project but never mentioned it, so I reconstructed it by interrogating his library and copier, which have a rudimentary kind of intelligence, or at least memory."

200

"Why would he keep it secret from you?"

"We discussed the possibility of the foundation, or some other authority, taking physical possession of me, of the crystal, and analyzing it to see what Eric was up to. I thought I had convinced Eric that I had adequate safeguards, but every now and then something like this came up. I could usually figure it out."

You don't think of TIs as being capable of, "programmed for," initiative, but of course they are. Eric's TI had been on its own since November. "You're sure the foundation couldn't get it out of you?"

"What could they do? Force bamboo splinters under my fingernails? Actually, the copy that's sitting down in New York has all of the forbidden links erased. I could do it to this copy in a millisecond, too, and in the process also destroy the logical structures that allow me to take the action. Leaving no trace."

"You're as devious as the real Eric."

"Ah, but I *am* the real Eric, now." He raised both eyebrows in a characteristic bug-eyed expression. "Shall we see if we can find Gospodin Ulric?"

I took the reader into the kitchen and plugged it into the data jack. The directory listed Baird Ulric at the address of the clinic we'd just left.

It rang for almost a minute before a harried and shaggy man appeared on the screen. "Ulric." He leaned forward. *"Lundley?* Eric Lundley? But you're supposed to be . . ."

"Eric is dead. I'm his Turing Image."

"Oh." He pointed. "You're the Stileman with frostbite who Liz treated this afternoon."

"Small world," Maria said.

"Biggest one we have." He looked up, toward the corner where Eric's image would be superimposed. "I think I know what you want to talk about," he said slowly. "But let's not talk about it over the phone. You have dinner plans?"

"No," we said in a three-voice chorus, though Eric probably did have plans: electrons du jour.

He looked at his watch. "Meet me at the entrance to the

clinic at nineteen-thirty. We'll figure out a place to go." He rang off.

"The plot thickens," Eric said. "He thinks the foundation has his phone tapped?"

"I suppose it's a reasonable assumption," I said, "if they have any idea of"—I suddenly had a being-listened-to feeling in the middle of my back—"the hilarious way he does crossword puzzles."

"His fiduciary penchant for rudimentary needlepoint," Eric said.

Maria nodded. "The random way he parts his beard." But it was too late for that, actually. If they had been listening earlier, whoever "they" were, they were probably on their way.

It was more than an hour until 1930, and the clinic was only ten minutes away; but we all had the sudden urge to take a stroll.

Ulric stepped through the door at exactly 1930, saw us, and motioned to his left. We walked part of a block and turned into a place called Sadie's Grill ("Ridiculously Expensive Food Prepared the Way We Feel Like Doing It").

Very loud classical music; about twenty booths in a late-twentieth chrome/glass/fake plant decor. "This is as safe as any place," Ulric said. We slid into the first unoccupied booth. My skin rippled and the music dwindled to an almost inaudible whisper. The restaurant outside the booth became a flowing blur.

"Pressor field," Maria said. "Are all the booths like this?"

"All the ones on this side. You pay a security surcharge. Paranoia tax."

A waiter was right behind us. He had to lean over the table, and push his head inside the pressor field, to be heard. Ulric ordered for us, a pitcher of wine and four house specials; Liz Eastwood, the doctor who'd examined Maria, would be joining us.

"First let me tell you what I infer. Then you tell me what you infer."

"Okay."

"Since you're carrying Eric Lundley's TI around with you, one can assume that (A) you're Dallas Barr, and (B) you didn't kill Eric." He looked at me expectantly.

"That is an inference. A couple of them."

He bowed toward Maria. "And *you* are the infamous lesbian nymphomaniac Maria Marconi, somehow returned from the dead. Possibly neither lesbian nor nymphomaniac."

Maria looked at me. "If I were Dallas Barr," I said to Ulric, "I'd be a fool to admit it. There's a million-pound price on his head."

"I don't need a million pounds. I'll prove it by paying for dinner. So what have *you* inferred?"

Eric cut in. "Less, and nothing particularly dramatic. Peculiar, rather than dramatic. What I have are citations for twenty thousand eight hundred seventy-four journals, none of them less than eighty-two years old. Eric Lundley acquired paper copies of them and shipped them to you, probably at considerable expense."

"Actually, he could only locate three fourths of them. But yes, it cost a couple of million rubles, dollars."

"That was nine years ago. For you to have read them all, you would have to go through more than fifteen a day. The ones in Chinese and Arabic probably take longer than the ones in English, too."

"I did read eight or ten a day, for several years, but only the ones in my specialty, immune system disorders."

"But they're all so old," I said. "What good is antique medical knowledge?"

He looked thoughtful and his brow furrowed. "You must have it half figured out already. But this is something we never talk to . . . outsiders about. You confirm that you *are* Dallas Barr. Then I'll take a chance."

I considered it. "Okay. I'm Dallas Barr. But you'll never get a million pounds for the knowledge. I have a crowd-pleaser under the table, aimed at your abdomen."

"You'd fit in real well here," he said without changing expression. "There's no formal record anywhere in the solar system of my interest in immunology. I'm supposedly a general practitioner.''

"Okay."

"Liz Eastwood, similarly, has spent a quarter of a century immersed in gerontological oncology. There's no record of her ever even having requested a journal article on the subject.''

"Clever," Eric said.

"What?" I said.

"There are more than a hundred doctors and medical technicians on this asteroid," Ulric said. "We essentially give health care in our spare time; some of us make a living in something other than medicine. Every one of us has a ghost specialty." He leaned forward. "What we are doing is rediscovering the Stileman Process. Secretly."

I could feel the sudden electricity from Maria. Neither of us dared ask.

"The foundation owns every particle of research on anything related to life extension that's been done over the past ninety years. It's all proprietary. You want to work in one of those fields, you have to work for them. You work for them and they have your ass in a vise. If you make anything public, they can deny you life extension. They can murder you, plain and simple. And legally."

"But they haven't bothered to nail down the old work," Eric said. "The work that actually led up to the original Stileman Process."

"We don't know. That's why we had, um, *you* try to find paper copies of everything." He turned to me. "Eric Lundley had the largest private collection of bound journals—actual physical books of magazines—in the world. He was always extending his collection. So he could search out volumes of things like the *Journal of the American Medical Association* without arousing suspicion."

"So what you did was go back in time," I said. "Put yourself in the shoes of the original researchers, and reconstruct what they did."

"It was easier than that," he said. "No false modesty;

medicine hasn't stood still in the past hundred years. There are a lot of ancillary things we all learned in medical school, that evolved from the original Stileman research. But that is essentially what we've done. Are doing.''

"Does it work?" Maria said, in a voice more calm than mine would have been. The waiter came with the wine and we both jumped as he leaned into the field.

"It's startling the first time," he said. "Thank you for not knocking anything over." He poured three glasses, expertly shaking globs of wine out of the carafe (cutting off the right amount with a knife blade), and disappeared back into the blur.

"Not yet." Maria had been holding my hand; I felt the pressure slacken. The aroma of the wine was strong inside the enclosure. We all reached for our glasses. "But." He sipped. "But maybe." He glanced outside, moved over, and Liz Eastwood slipped into the shell.

She looked at us intently. "You've told them?"

"Some. Maria, we have two chimpanzees we're watching very closely. The plan was that if they were still okay three years after going through the process, two years from now, then we would try a human volunteer. Probably a Stileman who wasn't able to raise his million—partly for clinical reasons and partly because, well, he wouldn't be risking that much."

"I'll do it."

"It's not that simple," Eastwood said. "Did you talk about her chances?"

"No," Ulric said.

Eastwood carefully poured herself some wine. "Fifty-fifty would be optimistic. Especially since you're already dying."

"So I have nothing to lose."

"Only your mind." She took a sip and continued in a quiet voice. "You are fed and emptied by tubes. You're on constant dialysis. You have a major operation every few days for at least eight weeks. Your bones are cracked and the marrow replaced. We pull out your intestines and check every inch. Remove and replace your breasts. Open your skull and fool with the brain. We do awful things to your throat and sinuses while you stay alive on oxygen piped into your lungs through tubes. Every organ gets looked at, fixed up, and put back. Then we skin you alive, one area at a time, and grow new skin. We have to do everything slowly and carefully. It's probably as bad as any torture ever devised by man.''

"They do all that in the Stileman Clinics," I said.

"But they know how to make you forget," Ulric said. "We don't. It's as simple as that."

"We'll use palliatives, anesthetics, tranquilizers. Up to a point, chemistry can help you deal with the pain and the unrelenting awfulness of it. But only up to a point."

"Even if we could guarantee your life," Ulric said, "we can't guarantee your sanity."

"All right," Maria said in a small voice. "You've done your job. I'm terrified. But I still want to go ahead with it."

"We could start tomorrow morning," Eastwood said. "As long as the cancer hasn't set in. I didn't find gross abnormalities today; inspection palpation, samples. Have you ever had cancer?"

"In 2015. Ovarian."

Eastwood had started to take a drink. She set it down. "Did it metastasize?"

"Yes. That's why I got the Stileman Treatment in the first place."

"When was the last time you ate?"

"I . . . tried to eat lunch but nothing would stay down."

"Okay." Eastwood wiped her hands on her napkin. "I think we'd just as well get started. You don't have much of an appetite anyhow, do you?" Maria shook her head silently. "Tell Henry to hang on to my dinner. I'll be back around midnight."

I got out to let Maria out of the booth. She hugged and kissed me, trembling, then put a finger on my lips. "Don't say anything. I'll see you."

I watched the doctor lead her out and slid back into the silence. "That's wise," Ulric said. "If she's started to metastasize, it wouldn't be worth putting her through the trouble. We'd chase cancers for a couple of weeks and lose her anyhow.''

I looked out through the window but couldn't see her for the blur.

Selena Vaughn Shift Schedule
(problems, call Baird now)

Schedule will be updated after each major op.
Try to keep your own schedule loose.

This is the big test.

11 yanvár	General oncology inspection, cleanup	Eastwood Belyayev Lewis Swim
13 yanvár	(Predicated on above) blood switchout, dialysis	Zholobov Shower Hurd

—Beregovoy and McAtee on call for mesenteries until fevrál—

14 yanvár	Liver 1	Perkins Titov Taral
15 yanvár	Immune system 1	Ulric Morvich
16 yanvár	Immune system 2	Ulric Booker
18 yanvár	Liver 2	Perkins Taral
21 yanvár	Colon, large intestine	Arcaro Prior Shatalov Winkfield
{21–22 yanvár Liver 3 if necessary		Perkins etc.}
22 yanvár	Gallbladder	Bierman Gorbatko Stout
23 yanvár	Pancreas	Artyukhin Borel Knapp

24 {yanvár	Is. Lang. if indicated	Borel etc.}
25 yanvár	Small intestine	Prior
		D. Wright
27 yanvár	Kidneys 1	Goodale
		Koonze
28 yanvár	Kidneys 2	Goodale
		McCreary
30 yanvár	Bladder	Hartack
		Volkov
1 fevrál	Other urinary	Rukavnikov
		York
2 fevrál	Adrenals	Kurtsinger
		P. Ivanov
4 fevrál	Marrow team	Bierman
	(adjust as needed)	Sande
		Feoktistov
		Volynov
		Kiley
		Ben Ali
		Hanford
8 fevrál	Lower circulatory	Lang
		V. Wright
10 fevrál	Parathyroids	Cordeo
		Titov
12 fevrál	Thyroid	Titov
		Garner
13 fevrál	Corp. luteum (ovaries n/a)	Minder
14 fevrál	Duodenum	Sarafanov
		Kurtsinger
		Velasquez
15 fevrál	Other stomach	Velasquez
		Klimuk
		Legarova
17 fevrál	Pituitary body ant.	Alan
		Dale
		Dzhanibekov
	Pituitary body post.	James
		Z. Ivanov
20 fevrál	Esophagus	Yegorov
		Rolfe
21 fevrál	Pharynx	Ussery
		Adams

22 fevrál	Sinuses	Turcotte
		Ryumin
23 fevrál	Cardiopulmonary team	Lazarev
		Romanenko
		Dodson
		Franklin
		Shoemaker
		Rider
26 fevrál	Ears	Lyakhov
		Boland
27 fevrál	Eyes	Dobrovolska
		Notler
		Booker
		Rot2
28 fevrál	Mouth (teeth all implants)	McHargue
29 fevrál	Salivary glands	Barton

Schedule for mart (and apryél if necessary) will be posted mid-fevrál.

Dallas

I wasn't able to see her for ten days. Then they'd call me every few days, whenever she had lucid periods relatively free from pain.

They gave her back her real appearance, removing the flesh tractors that had changed the shape of her face and body, which was comforting to both of us at first. Later it became disturbing, much more so for her than for me, the again familiar face daily becoming more haggard and old, not only from the constant pain and anxiety but also as a natural effect of the Stileman Treatment's wearing off. Baird juggled the order of therapies so she could have facial plastic surgery as soon as it was practical.

The visits were more for my benefit than hers. Sometimes we could talk, but she had difficulty concentrating and often would lapse into confusion or fall asleep. She did a good job of being brave, though she seemed always on the verge of collapse. Once she did crack and began crying hysterically; a doctor gave her a shot and she relaxed into sleep. I wondered whether it would have been better to let her cry.

After a while I was on the verge of cracking myself, under the unrelenting pressure of helplessness. Baird offered me mood drugs, which I refused on principle for too long. Finally he said he wouldn't let me see her if I didn't take something; my gloominess was going to retard her progress.

By the end of February I had to stop seeing her anyhow; they had to put her into total biotic isolation for a couple of weeks, trying to control a runaway combination of infections that cropped up after the heart/lung team had finished with her. Baird said it was not any more dangerous than most of the planned therapies, but it did slow them down.

Other than taking those occasional trips to the hospital, I stayed locked up in the villa. I had spent one day, right after they started on Maria, in frantic commerce: I sold most of our trade goods, paid off two months' rent, and filled the pantry with food and drink.

I bought more weapons and spent a lot of time sitting in the darkness watching the street. Too many people knew who I was. Sooner or later someone would come to collect me. I had to have an off-duty doctor or nurse drop in every night to stand guard while I slept, or tried to sleep.

Sometimes people would come by during the day: Baird or Liz or, oddly, Big Dick Goodman, who was one of Baird's fellow conspirators against the Stileman Foundation.

Goodman was over seven feet tall, slender as a blade of grass but with an oversized head. He had more motivation than most Stilemans to help Baird. The last time he'd gone to the clinic he'd almost died because of the stress of spending six weeks in Earth gravity. There wouldn't be a next time. He gobbled calcium and protein and exercised daily, but he couldn't seem to build up bone and muscle mass. Born on Ceres, it was as if his body had decided he was going to be an actual extraterrestrial. They had called him Lysenko in school.

I liked him. He was coarse and played dumb but was well read and had a gruesome sense of humor.

On the tenth of March Dick showed up with Baird. I liked Baird, too, but never liked to see him during the day. I was always afraid he'd be bringing news.

It was good news this time. "It looks as if we have the infections beaten. They're working on the inner and middle ears this afternoon. Maybe you could see her tonight, before we go on to the next phase."

"Fine. Just going to pick up where the schedule left off, eyes next?"

"Yeah, that's Winnie Dobrovolska's team; pretty easy stuff, but she won't be seeing much until next week." We floated in toward the kitchen, Dick homing in on the refrigerator.

"You guys wanna beer?" I took one but Baird said coffee; he'd been up for twenty hours and still had to do ward rounds.

I squeezed out a cup of coffee and zapped it. "Good time for her not to be able to see," Baird said, "and for you not to see her. Finish up all the facial surgery."

"I always feel like it's bad luck to ask how she's doing."

"So don't ask, I'll tell you." He took a sip of coffee and let go of the cup while he concentrated on sitting down. "That's why I came. It looks like coasting downhill from here. There's some painful stuff left, but nothing particularly life-threatening." He caught the cup and looked at his watch. "In eleven days, if there aren't any complications, we should be able to remove the zipper and glue her up." She had a plastic zipper from the base of her chin to her pubic bone. "After that we do the skin replacement, which has to hurt, but she'll know then that she's made it."

"And then . . ."

"That's why we're here," Dick said. "We gotta talk about 'and then.' "

"How we'll go about dropping our bombshell. How we're going to use you and Maria."

"My notoriety, okay; we talked about that. I'm willing to do anything so long as it doesn't expose her to physical danger."

They looked at each other and Baird let out a tired sigh. "There will be danger for all of us. There's something we haven't told you; something that not even all of the medical people know."

"Foundation's been fuckin' with us," Dick said. "They been murderin' us."

"The ten- to twelve-year cycle is artificially induced. There's no reason the rejuvenation can't last seventy, eighty years or more."

That was more than interesting. "What do they do to us?"

"Something to do with the spleen; we're not sure exactly

what. It's always atrophied when you do an autopsy of an ex-Stileman who's died because of running out of money, but it seems normal for a Stileman who dies accidentally. Before the terminal degeneration has started."

"You'd think that would be common knowledge," I said.

"Would if you could get it published," Dick said.

"What actually kills you is not the spleen specifically, but a generalized breakdown of the immune system. That's my bailiwick; that's how I got started on this project."

"It's pretty neat," Dick said, "pretty cute. They go to old Stileman 'way back then and make the spleen booby trap part of the package. He's this wet-handkerchief liberal who an't ever recovered from bein' born rich. They give him the magic wand: wave this an' nobody's ever gonna be super-rich again. Except they're willin' to die for it. More than *die*. Give up immortality."

"You can see why the limitation was necessary for the economic scheme to work at all," Baird said. "If the first millionaire clients had traded their fortunes for seventy or eighty years instead of ten, the Stileman Foundation could never have grown so powerful so fast. They'd all be millionaires again in a few years, and then have most of a century to extend and consolidate their fortunes. They could in actual truth rule all of the world—including, eventually, the Stileman Foundation itself."

That was a lot to sort out. "So the foundation will be out to get you, not just because you can underbid them."

"We can expose them. The basis of their financial power is murder and deceit. Even if they owned every legislature and judiciary in the world, and they don't—that wouldn't protect them from the wrath of their own clients. The ten thousand wealthiest people in the solar system."

"Slow down now," I said. "We don't know that all of the foundation is in on it. You say some of your own doctors don't know. What would be the minimum number who are in the know on Earth—just the spleen doctors and the immunologists?"

"And the overall coordinator, whoever my counterpart is

there. Of course, like me, he could be one of the immunologists.''

"But nobody on the board is necessarily part of it. They go in the clinic every ten years like everybody else.''

"Go in an' play *cards* for six weeks,'' Dick said.

"Presumably everyone who was in on the original proposal knew about the artificial limitation. Most of them must still be alive, some of them either on the board or serving as silent partners. I would be very surprised if everybody on the board did not know all about it. Probably everyone high up in Briskin's Steering Committee, too.''

"I wonder. He never dangled that in front of me, the possibility of a longer time between rejuvenations. But he did say there were things he wasn't allowed to tell me.''

"So who knows?'' Baird said. "Literally, who? We ought to play it safe and assume *everybody* knows.''

Dick shook his head. "Careful. We could maybe pick up some allies, you know? Half the board might be holdin' out on the other half.''

"Good point. We'll keep that in mind.'' He sipped the coffee and blew on it. "So we've got four things: The truth about the murders you're accused of. Existence of the Steering Committee. The foundation's cynical manipulation of the Stileman Process. Our duplication of it. They're all strongly or weakly linked. But it seems to me we ought to feed them to the media one piece at a time. We don't want to drop all the information at once.''

"People's lips only move so fast,'' Dick said. "Average person's attention span couldn't handle it all.''

We thought together for a minute. Dick belched by way of preamble. "You got the order right. We show 'em Dal an' Maria to get their attention. And Eric's TI. Maria's old bodyguard, if they haven't got to her.''

"This gets the 'phems interested. Here's two of Dal's victims, one alive and one not, sayin' he's innocent and not crazy. They point the collective finger at Briskin and also accuse him of murderin' the Russian and the Strine.

"How come he murdered 'em? Hold on to your hats.

Conspiracy time, Steering Committee. That gets the Stilemans interested.''

"Hold it," I said. "Do we have anything on the Steering Committee other than my word against theirs? Against Briskin's?"

"Corroborative testimony," Baird said. "You can't be the only one they approached who had second thoughts."

"Yeah," Dick said, "and even if nobody comes for'd right away, they will after we drop our little bomb. Foundation got you by the *spleen!* Here's chapter an' verse."

"I don't know about that one," I said, devil's advocate as usual in these discussions. "That's going to be pretty technical stuff. They'll have scientists lined up twice around the block to prove you're lying."

"That's when we produce Maria's records and show that we can duplicate the process, without the ten- to twelve-year limitation."

"Which won't be proven for thirteen years. By which time I will have died in jail."

"You an't gonna chicken out."

"Who said anything about that? I just don't want you guys to think that Maria and I are only going to walk out on a stage, take a bow, and then go on with our business. Just going back to Earth, even if we didn't announce who we were, will be like playing catch with hand grenades."

"The public announcement should make you safe, at least from assassination."

"If the camera's plugged in."

We had discussed this part of it before. Maria and I did have to go back to Earth. The foundation had an octopus grip on the news media. If Baird were to broadcast from here, his story would be released as NUTSO ROCKNIK CLAIMS STILEMAN HOAX, appearing in all the finest tabloids, and nowhere else. And not even the tabloids would report the subsequent bloodbath on Ceres.

The plan was for Fireball to return to Earth with somebody else piloting. Maria and I would go back as unregistered hitchhikers a couple of days before, on a stealthed vessel that might be able to slip into White Sands as if it were returning from the Moon.

If we were caught, the pilot could claim he was returning me for the reward, and we might get uncensored air time anyhow. If things went as planned, though, we'd set up a controlled press release situation, with enough money spread around to guarantee us at least a few minutes of uninterrupted multichannel broadcasting. The foundation couldn't edit us out of existence after we'd gone out live on a dozen local stations all over the country.

"So what's our timetable look like now?"

Baird shrugged. "Depends on how long it takes until Maria's surgically clean enough for a few gees' acceleration. Maybe four weeks after she's released, maybe three, depends. Mental recuperation might take longer than physical; nobody's ever gone through this before. It's still up in the air."

Dick cleared his throat. "Doc, you said we was gonna—"

"That's right. Look, Dallas. Suppose, uh, in the eventuality that . . ."

"We an't talked about what would happen if she dies. Would you still be with us?"

I had thought about it. "Yes. I wouldn't have so much news value, assuming you'd have to wait until you had a successful patient. The patient wouldn't have as much news value as Maria, either. But we'd have plenty of time to work out—"

Baird's caller beeped. He twisted his ring. "Ulric."

"Code two in the OR," a squeaky voice said. "Your patient Vaughn."

"Who's on it?"

"Dr. Franklin's team."

"If there's any problem, patch him through. Otherwise I won't bother him."

"Very well, Doctor." It beeped off. He looked up at me, brow furrowed. "That's remarkable timing."

Then I recalled that Maria was there as Selena Vaughn. "It's serious?"

"Yes and no. It's sort of expected, and it's happened to her once before. Heart stopped. Good thing the zipper's still—"

"*Heart* stopped? She died?"

"No, not at all. Well, only technically. She didn't feel anything, under anesthetic for the ears. They just pull down the zipper and stimulate the heart into beating again."

"It's not a big deal, then?"

"Well . . . best if it doesn't happen again."

Maria

I'D read that some people who died on the operating table and were brought back claimed to have had out-of-body experiences while they were dead. I wouldn't have minded that. My body would have been a good place to be out of, then.

I died four times. It was not a big deal clinically, Dr. Ulric said. I suppose it's philosophically trivial, too, since they just start you up again. Not like being thrown into a hole in the ground to rot. And not like resurrection.

But it had religious meaning to me, finally; a negative kind of religious meaning. I can't believe anymore. I can't believe in God. Something broke in me; something became clear.

It was the last time I died, and the only time it happened while I was conscious. I was supposed to be out of danger, no matter how much it hurt.

They were replacing my skin, and had completed the first part successfully, from the soles of the feet on up past the knees. For the second part they stripped all the skin and scars, stitches and scabs from thighs, buttocks, abdomen. The only part of me that didn't hurt down there was the soft tissue of the womb entrance, which had already been scourged. Where this all had started, sixty-some years ago.

I think someone made a mistake with the anesthetic, and someone who was supposed to be monitoring me wasn't there. Maybe the same person.

I was lying suspended in the pressor field, surrounded by panels of instruments, invaded by tubes, feeling a familiar constant throbbing pain like a bad burn, which I had more

218

or less become used to in the first phase, when it suddenly began to get worse. Each minute the pain doubled and doubled again. I prayed and cried and prayed and screamed—and then there was a new pain, like a thick spike driven down hard into my chest, and then an electric jolt spasming along my left arm, and I knew I was having a heart attack, a bad one, and no zipper this time.

I tried to get my breath, but my lungs wouldn't do anything. Red lights flashing and a very quiet bell. The room around me started to go black, and I knew with sudden horrifying finality that all the weeks of prayer here had been nothing but habit, while my mind was asking *Eli, Eli, lama sabachthani?*, a million times, why hast thou forsaken me?, and quietly coming to the reasonable conclusion that there was no one, nothing, up there to answer. All the sophistries reconciling a loving, compassionate God with a world full of injustice and pain became just that: sophistries—and I was alone in the last instant of my life, trying to scream with no air, and from the next instant would be nonexistent for the rest of eternity.

Some time later I woke up to normal pain and a fresh scar on my chest, a big ugly one taped shut, and Drs. Lazarev and Ulric communicating the remarkable news that I'd just survived yet another heart attack.

Well, some of me had survived. God used to be part of me.

The rest of the time was just pain, and disorientation. I lost track of the days, but monitored my progress by how far up the pain had crawled, the skin replacement. I think Dallas came in often. Finally the pain got to the top of my neck and held still, fading upwards away from breasts, shoulders; finally just a tired, sunburned feeling. They unwrapped the mummy windings to reveal a body that glowed pink and tight, not a wrinkle nor a hair, like a large and sexually precocious infant's.

I think they overestimated the psychological trauma of being able to remember the pain, the helplessness, the anxiety. Perhaps we may remember it from regular Stilemans, at some level. The reptilian or the limbic brain, do they have memories? Maybe all of the nervous system remembers things in some primitive way.

Worse things happen, anyhow.

I did have a recurrent nightmare where the surgical zipper was back in place and I managed to free my hands and unzip myself and scoop out my insides and throw them all around that awful room, dying but feeling wonderful. The organs looked like the holos in a life sciences textbook that used to give me nightmares when I was a young girl in *ginnasio*. Real ones look worse.

The dream stopped once I was well enough to make love with Dallas, so I suppose it's pretty obvious what that zipper really was, and it was infinitely better to have him opening it.

I hope he's still alive.

I wish it were him with me in this tiny space instead of this awful filthy little man.

I wish the nightmare hadn't come true that way. I can't make myself stop seeing it. I'm afraid I may lose my mind before we get to Earth. "Lose one's mind" is an odd idiom. There are parts of this mind I would love to misplace. The colors were so bright with my new eyes, bright blood and strings and globs of yellow fat the blue and grey guts and brains sparkling splinters of bone

---

CRIMEWATCH CERES

25 apryél

RESIDENCE BURGLARY

0944 Somebody broke into Hod Abramson's place and stole two signed & numbered Picasso lithographs, each worth about forty thousand rubles. If somebody's dumb enough to try to sell them to you, you might give Hod a call at 37/995. Ask him what a good price would be.

DUEL (MURDER?)

1334 This one depends on who you ask. Just outside the Loony Toonz Café, right after having lunch together, Robert Hughes killed Vladimir Repka with a knife. Robert says it was a duel and Vladimir an't talking. Two of the wounds were in the back, which Robert says was just good technique, a clinch. No eyewitnesses. Vladimir's wife says Robert owed them money. Check your mail for jury call.

SPACESHIP THEFT

1449 Routine position check of parked properties at the Synchronous Orbit Repair Facility revealed that a small craft belonging to Baird Ulric was missing. Maintenance had been completed on it but Ulric was leaving it at SORF until next week. The craft is a stealthed four-passenger Rocketdyne. Being stealthed, it could be anywhere. Let's everybody send a sympathy card to Baird, who shouldn't of left it unlocked.

STOP THE GODDAMN PRESSES
DOUBLE MURDER

2319 People investigating one hell of a noise at 220 34th found that the people renting the place had redecorated it with blood and guts. At least one person, apparently impossible to identify, was blown to bits by some sort of concussion weapon. Another was lying dead in the hallway without a mark on him, possibly killed by the same blast. Quick check with our mayhem editor says could happen, maybe. Stay tuned on this one, boys and girls.

There was enough blood and gore around for several corpses, but they only found two hands and two feet. And Dallas, who was unmarked but obviously dead. They scraped most of the remains up into a bag for the recycler and were going to do a double garbage run, John Doe and Cassius Donato, when one of the volunteers noticed that Dallas's eyes were open and wet. People who've been dead for a while may have open eyes, but they have a peculiar dull, sunken aspect, like fish eyes in a market, and Dallas remained unrecycled because this woman had seen that and remembered it.

They left the rest of the garbage and carried his apparently lifeless form down to the clinic, unaware that his heart was beating slightly six times a minute. A nurse took a sample of cool blood and ran it through the machine. He couldn't interpret the results, so he called the hematologist Tolliver Bierman, who was startled to see that the patient, or corpse, was Dallas, with whom he had spent a few pleasant evenings. Then he puzzled through the large molecules the machine had flagged, and was relieved. It was just a zombi analog.

Zombi, officially called Vitaslow, was a fantastically expensive drug with one clinical application and a certain usefulness to the criminal world. It would put a person into suspended animation for five or six days, slowing down everything while you waited for a transplant to become available, for instance. It was also handy if you wanted to stuff somebody into the trunk of a floater for a few days or mail him bulk rate to the Moon. Or have him enjoy being buried while wide-awake, or cremated.

Dallas

THIS zombi shit gave me some idea of what Eric must feel like, locked up in that box thinking. I never wanted to make a TI before, and I doubly don't want to now. Don't want to put my ghost through that after I'm dead.

Your brain just races out of control. You can see and hear, after a fashion (sounds are lowered in pitch and stre-e-etched out), but you don't feel anything, or taste or smell. And all you can see is what you're pointed at; you can't move your eyes.

I was pointed at the door when the guy went after Maria. He took about a day to step over me and get into position. Hiding in the hallway, he fired one slow dart, which must have missed. He stepped inside the bedroom, gliding for about five minutes, took aim while he was in the air, and disintegrated in slow motion. The explosion from the shattergun sounded to me like tons of gravel rolling down a metal chute.

It must have hit him off center, because most of his right side stayed intact. It was sort of fascinating to watch. The shock wave ripped his clothes off and an instant later he popped open like a soft vegetable stomped. The skin pulled away in large sheets twined with shredded clothing, and his body spun, spraying blood and pulverized organs, and the reflected shock wave picked me up and thumped me against the ceiling somehow. It didn't hurt, but I saw a bright blue flash and passed out. I woke up on the floor again, facedown, so I never saw what happened to Maria.

I slept and woke and slept and woke, always waking to the monotonous sight of out-of-focus Stiktite. Ages later somebody slowly turned me over, looked at me, and left. I couldn't see anything but the ceiling for about a year. People were talking, but I couldn't make out any words in the low growl.

I studied the streaks of blood on the ceiling. You don't normally think about how blurry things are outside of the very center of your field of vision. I was allowed to think about that for a few weeks. I blinked once, which took about a minute. That gave me a rough measure of how much time was slowed down. If it takes you a tenth of a second to blink, then I was cranking along at about one five- or six-hundredth of the normal rate.

I didn't think about zombi at the time. I thought this was what you got when you died.

A woman I vaguely remembered from the hospital crawled into view and stared at me for a long time. I tried to make myself blink, but no go. With infinite slowness she reached down to touch my face, my chin; I think she wiggled my head. The part of the ceiling I was looking at rocked back and forth gracefully. She growled something and picked me up, all six pounds of me. Two and a half kilograms.

We proceeded to the clinic. I am the universe's authority on East Thirty-fourth Corridor, having studied it for a month or so as this woman ran, towing me toward Tsiolkovski. I know a lot about those two blocks of the main drag, too.

It dawned on me that this was something other than death, or she wouldn't be in such a languid hurry. Zombi slows down your reasoning somewhat, and blocks out big chunks of memory—I should have remembered about zombi from magazine articles, and I even had a German business partner who'd been kidnapped with its aid a couple of dozen years before; but those were blanked-out areas.

Weeks of running down hospital corridors. A blood test that I unfortunately could watch, longer than a Wagnerian opera and even more tiring. They leaned me up in a corner and finally a guy I recognized as a blood doctor crept into the room. Seasons changed while he surveyed a wall

monitor. Then he studied a trayful of poppers, looked at one
for a long, long time, then ambled over and gave me a pop.

The world came back in a blast of smell and pain: the
antiseptic/cotton/alcohol/blood/cold metal hospital smell;
tiny pain from the popper and big ache on the top of my
head. I reached back and felt an egg-sized bump; no blood
on my fingers.

"Somebody popped you with zombi," the doctor said.
"The effect is like—"

"Yeah, I know. Where's Maria?"

He shrugged and looked at the other people. "You were
the only one there," said the woman who had brought me
to the clinic. "You and that corpse you spread all over two
rooms. What did you use, concussion grenade?"

"Shattergun, Maria used it."

"There were footprints in the blood," a man said.
"Somebody was walking around right afterwards."

"It sure as hell wasn't me."

We hurried back to the villa and did find a few footprints,
easy to differentiate from the investigators', since the blood
was partly dry by the time they showed up. There were
three small footprints going toward the bed, then several
overlapping while he stood at the bed and did something,
two footprints leaving; three in the hall. The woman who'd
noticed I was still alive pointed out that these footprints
were slightly more distinct; he was probably carrying
Maria.

We followed the footprints up the ramp and into the
living room, where six of them besmirched the Persian rug.
They led to the air lock and stopped.

"He couldn't have been wearing a space suit downstairs," I said. "They don't make boots that small."

"Maybe he had one stashed inside the air lock," the
woman said. "Maybe one for her, too."

"I don't see how. You can't open it from the outside."

"Maybe he had an outside accomplice."

"But where could they *take* her?"

"Maybe they just wanted to dispose of the body." I
looked at her. "Oh. Sorry."

Report of Outside Investigation
ad hoc Vigilante Committee
Big Dick Goodman, head
21 apryél

This is a sketch of what we saw outside of the air lock on top
of 220 34th, being rented by Cassius Donato and Selena
Vaughn, who have one big housecleaning bill ahead of them.

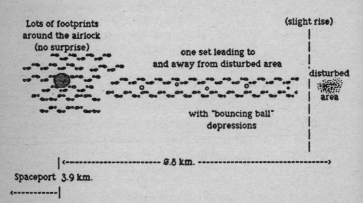

The disturbed area on the other side of the rise could of been
caused by a small spacecraft landing and taking off. We got a
call in to the Akademia Nauk sizemologiests, however the hell
you spell it, and they're gonna find out whether there was a
pair of taps there between 2200 and midnight last night.

I wouldn't of been able to see a ship sitting there from the
ground control station 4.7 klicks away, on account of the rise,
and a pretty good pilot could probably bring it in and take off
again without anybody noticing except they were out walking
around outside.

The footprints going to and from the disturbed area are
different sizes, with the ones going to it on top. So it's gotta at
least be a floater or something. What must've happened was
that someone landed it and came over to wait by the air lock.
Then this guy comes up with Vaughn, dead or unconscious,

probably with the zomby stuff. He lets the other guy in and probably gets a space suit from him. Plus one of those plastic EVA rescue balls. He stuffs Vaughn in there, which makes the circular marks in the dust, then they go back to the space craft and zip away.

It does look like it leaves one guy sort of unaccounted for, since there's only one set of footprints going back, but there's all sorts of ways to account for him, really. Like he takes off the space suit and goes downstairs and out the door. There's no spare space suit stashed around the house, but the guy who went back outside could of been carrying it. Hell, he could be carrying it with the other guy in it. Just leave one set of footprints so as to fuck with our brains.

Nobody can figure out how the two guys—the one who snatched Vaughn and the one she Kweezinarted—got inside in the first place. The apartment is isolated but it's got spy cameras and alarms and it's damn solid. They must have got a key somehow.

Maria

I was lying in bed watching the cube, a twentieth-century American flatscreen adaptation of *Cyrano de Bergerac*, which was funny and fascinating, and I must have become too absorbed in it. Dallas had gone to the kitchen to get us some wine. I didn't notice how long he'd been gone, and I almost let the first attacker sneak up on me. If he'd had better aim he'd be alive.

I can't feel much remorse for killing him. Disposing of him. Nothing but disgust. This other little man disgusts me too, but in a different way, many different ways. I know him in such excruciating detail.

I sat up and was reaching for the cube controls, to turn up the sound, when a little dart hit the sheet stretched between my knees. It was like the stinger darts, with a bit of bright orange string attached. There was a shattergun right next to the control box—we had shatterguns like some houses have ashtrays—and I picked it up without even thinking, and when the big stranger, *huge*, sailed into the room, aiming a gun at me, I thumbed the trigger.

Dallas said there was no way you could miss with a shattergun, but I very nearly did. It wasn't even pointed at him when I jammed down on the trigger.

There was a sharp bang, and the walls and the bed were drenched with blood. Half his body was spinning like a crazy top, bouncing off the walls and floor and ceiling. The other half was everywhere. The air of the bedroom was full of globs of blood, bright red spheres that pulsed as they fell slowly toward the floor. Intestines draped a crazy blue design across the far wall and the cube console. White

bloodstreaked bone fragments twirled and glittered. Globs
of yellow fat. His heart bounced off a wall and the ceiling
and drifted toward me, still beating.

I didn't notice all this in the time it took me to draw one
breath and scream. But then I felt a sting, and there was a
dart in my left breast, and the universe crawled almost to a
stop.

The nasty little man later explained, holding up a note
before my frozen face for a couple of weeks, that it was
zombi, a harmless drug. Harmless! I wish we could have
traded places and he had to look at me for twenty years. I
would do all sorts of things that are not in my nature. It
would be fun to hold him down and urinate on him. For
about a week.

No. He might enjoy it.

He sailed slowly into the room, putting the dart gun into
the waistband of his trousers. He made a gargoyle face and
covered his mouth with both hands, and for a few hours
succeeded in not vomiting.

I knew that it was some sort of drug, but wondered
whether it could be lethal. Was I dying with infinite
slowness? Fourteen weeks of medical torture for five days
with Dallas; only two when I was well enough for love.
Then this.

So the nightmare had materialized, though it wasn't *my*
insides everywhere. Had they killed Dallas in the kitchen?
They probably gave him the same thing I had. Maybe we
both were dead. I couldn't remember whether that million-
pound reward was "dead or alive." With slow panic
I realized there were a lot of things I couldn't remember. I
didn't know how old I was and couldn't figure it out. I
couldn't remember the name Dallas was using. I knew it
was a politician in Julius Caesar's court, a character in a
Shakespeare play, but I couldn't remember the name.

The ugly man slowly pulled the dart out of my breast and
rubbed the spot with his thumb. I couldn't feel it; that's
when I realized I couldn't feel anything. My body was slack
and paralyzed.

He peeled the blood-soaked sheet off my lower half and

spent a long time staring at my nakedness. Dallas had loved this new body with abandon, several times a day. His body was still new, too. That was helping me accept it as mine, this hypersensitive overgrown babyish figure.

He put his filthy hand under my leg and the other arm behind my shoulders and picked me up. We took a long voyage upstairs. On the way we passed Dallas, facedown but relatively unmarked. He was spattered with blood, but no more so than the walls and ceiling. Oh God, God. I wish You were still there, somewhere, and would send help. Though we weren't supposed to ask for this kind of help; Thy will be done.

One sharp memory: being a girl in the convent lying bleeding praying, ecstatic in the certainty of God's grace. I tried to hold on to the feeling and it drained away, like trying to hold on to a handful of dry sand.

There was a man in a space suit waiting outside the air lock, carrying a bundle. The ugly little man pushed the cycle button and let go of me. Falling three feet on Ceres is like falling an inch on Earth. But a lot slower, even in real time.

The other came in. They talked to each other, but the words were pitched too low for me to understand.

He unzipped the space suit and stepped out naked. He was sleek and handsome. The ugly one also took his clothes off; I memorized every square centimeter of both of them. If I ever got to the police I would be able to draw exact pictures of them. Then the police would hand me over to the Stileman Foundation.

They shook out the bundle: street clothes, two space suits, and a plastic thing I didn't recognize. The handsome one put on the street clothes, the ugly one put on one of the space suits, and together they stuffed me into the plastic thing, growling at each other, probably about this body.

I could tell that I normally knew what the plastic thing was, but I couldn't associate a name with it. It was to go into space with, if there was an accident. My skin stuck to it here and there. It was probably very cold. Oxygen hissed into it, and it inflated, I suppose to a perfect sphere. Most of it was silver, but there was a transparent window close to my face.

We passed through the air lock, the man pushing me along and carrying the extra space suit, waiting hours for each twenty-second cycle. I hadn't used the air lock but remembered Peter Quinn saying that's what it was, twenty seconds, and it seemed like two or three hours. How long did this drug last?

I wondered whether Quinn had betrayed us. How could those people have gotten in, otherwise?

We were a long time outside, and the window rolled away from me. I slept for some time. When I woke up I could see peripherally out of the window, but had a hard time figuring out what I was looking at. Finally I realized it was the hull of a small spaceship, but it was so shiny that the hull was a curved mirror. The little man looked tall and lean in the reflection. We went through another tedious air lock.

Inside, he unzipped the balloon and carried me to an acceleration couch. There were four of them. The ship was a fairly new standard-model Rocketdyne, apparently ordinary except for the mirror finish outside. It was a little faster than Fireball, but if we were headed for Earth, it would still take more than a month. What would that be if this zombi drug didn't wear off? A hundred years? Two hundred?

At least I could sleep. After he'd spent about an hour strapping me in, my eyes slowly closed.

Waking up was interesting. Mind fast and body slow: I was wide awake but my eyes were just slits, a tiny bit more information coming in every few minutes. I seemed clean; he had wiped the dried blood off my upper body. I could see him off to one side, blurred, ambiguous. With sudden indignation I realized he was stimulating himself sexually, rubbing up and down, staring at me. Each cycle of his hand took about ten minutes. The whole process could take *days!* Would I be the first woman in history to be bored senseless while being sexually abused?

Maybe, in a way, I wasn't being actually abused, since he didn't know I could see him. He could just as easily be raping me, I realized, and about thirty seconds later had an odd ghost of a feeling around the lower chest, loins, scalp, extremities: adrenaline. I tried to will my eyes to shut. If he knew I could see him he might indeed rape me; men can be funny about being observed. Women are funny about it, too. Dallas and I had talked about voyeurism; Italian attitudes are different from American, but I said there was a commonality. The ultimate violation of privacy. He said that, nevertheless, it was the only crime in the world that didn't exist until it was discovered; if the woman didn't know she was being looked at, the crime had no effect on her. I told him he was a pagan and didn't understand sin. It wasn't necessary for the victim to know, for the sin to exist. He tried to wax anthropological on the subject, more than half kidding, and I pretended to get angry and moralistic, also kidding, since fornication, rather more serious than peeping, was one sin I had to confess to regularly. We did a lot of that kind of game-playing, silly attitudinizing, and I missed that frivolous side of him with a terrible sudden ache. I laughed more with him, and harder, than I ever had with a man. With two of the sisters at the convent, Dominica and Laraine, before we were old enough for *ginnasio*, when we went to the orchards outside of the walls, we would talk about things in the world, about men, especially about the gardener and the driver, and sometimes we would laugh so hard, that terrible guilty laughing, that we would cry and our cheeks would hurt from the stretching, and we would be hoarse when we got back, and once the Mother Superior asked us about it and we started laughing again, *inside the walls!* That was so wicked we laughed until we peed ourselves.

Oh well. The one thing you can never find again, after you lose it, is innocence. I did manage to force my eyes completely shut. Spare the man the knowledge that his trivial sin had been observed, and therefore existed.

Dallas

I handed back the draft of Big Dick's Vigilante Committee report. "Fast work. You really think it could be a floater, though?"

"Aw hell. That was before I knew about Doc's ship gettin' stolen. That's gotta be it."

"So she could be anywhere in the Belt," Baird said, "if they are indeed the ones who stole the Rocketdyne. Or headed for Earth, most likely."

"Gives us a window," Big Dick said. "Hell, more than a window. They an't gonna be wastin' any time; we got the Rocketdyne's params—push 'em through the machine an' you prolly get ETA accurate within an hour or so. Day, for sure."

One of the cleanup crew came up from downstairs, hauling along the largest piece. It had an arm and a leg and a head, horribly caved in. It was flayed from the chest down and scooped out inside. It looked like something you might see hanging in a butcher shop, except for the face. "You guys know who this is?"

"Huh-uh," Dick said, "and I never forget a rib cage."

"I gave him his immunosuppressant series last week, him and his two buddies. A little guy and a big weight lifter type. They'd just come from Earth, took jobs up at SORF."

"Just mechanics, or what?"

"I dunno. Went up, gave 'em the pops, came back. Didn't seem like no Stephen Hawking."

"Do me a favor," Baird said. "Find out what names they were going under, what day they came in."

"That's easy enough. I got 'em right off the pickle boat." He carried the half-corpse back down.

"Pretty sight. What does it take to make you doctor guys wanna puke?" Dick asked Baird.

"Patients who don't pay. We get to them sooner or later, though, and the feeling passes." He turned to me. "You'll want to head for Earth as soon as possible. But don't do it. Not until you can find another stealthed vessel."

I heard the words but couldn't put them together. Like Dick, I don't see that many scooped-out corpses. "I'm sorry. What was that?"

He repeated it, slowly: don't go tearing out after them. "You might as well wave a flag at the foundation. They'll be keeping an eye on anyone who leaves from the Belt over the next few days. So hold it. Wait until we can find a stealthed spaceship."

"Right." I crossed the room in one slow step, picked up Eric's reader, and turned him on.

"Long time no see," he said. "What's new?"

"Plenty; no time now. Try to get me Bill Baron."

"Okay." The phone screen lit up with a ringing pattern, and Bill appeared.

"Bill. It's Dallas."

He inclined his head. "Looks more like Fernando Lamas. You remember him?"

"No, look, I got my face laundered. Let's see . . ." Try to think. "First night we had dinner together on *adastra*, you had the pheasant. It tasted like greasy chicken."

He laughed. "Okay, you're you. What's happening with all this murder business? A new hobby?"

"Yeah, sure." I hesitated. "Don't want to talk over the phone. Can you come over to my place?"

"Okay." I gave him the address. "Jesus—did you just have another murder over there?"

"Practice makes perfect," Dick said sotto voce.

"Afraid so. I think the place is safe for the time being, though."

"Is Maria all right?"

"That's part of the problem."

He reached for the screen. "We'll be right over."

"What was that all about?" Baird asked.

"Friend of mine. He has a stealthed Sasaki."

Dick whistled. "That's a real truck. He's into big-league smuggling, eh?"

"What do you mean, smuggling? How can you have smuggling here if there aren't any laws about it?" I hoped I hadn't compromised the Barons. I could have called later.

"The term's not accurate," Baird said. "What we mean by 'smuggling' is secretly tapping an income source, usually a precious-metal or rare-earth variegate—they're criminally easy to mine; you just place a few textbook charges, stake out a Kevlar tarp, blow a hole, scoop up the gravel, take it back to Earth and sit back and count your money."

"But if everybody knew where it was," Dick said, "the market price of the stuff would nosedive. One small variegate of gold would have more gold than Fort Knox. So that's why they use stealthed vessels." He shrugged. "It an't anything people disapprove of. I've spent months at a time lookin' for a variegate I could retire off of."

"That's where the Rocketdyne came from," Baird said. "Guy who loaned it to me comes up here about two months a decade. Makes his pile and goes back to Earth in a regular ship, rented. Nothing secret about it, though I don't suppose he tells the foundation where his money comes from."

"Gonna be hell to pay when he finds out it's stolen," Dick said.

"We've got eight years before he comes back," Baird said. "A lot can happen."

I went down to meet Bill and Doris so as to prepare them for the blood-spattered hallway before they came inside. The big pieces had been photographed, bagged, and hauled off to the dump, and a cleanup crew was working on the walls, but it still looked like a set left over from a grisly horror movie. Dick and Baird went on to work, saying they'd check back in the evening.

Bill and Doris were glad to be rushed upstairs. I started fixing coffee.

"I'm going to need a big favor. But I can't tell you everything about why I need it."

"Maybe we don't want to know that much about it," Doris said, "if it involves this double murder."

"Single murder. At first they thought I was dead too, but it was just a drug."

"We at least ought to know why the Stileman Foundation's after you," Bill said. "What did you do to deserve such a big price on your head?"

"Not what I *did*. What I know." I served the coffee and sat down with them, paused, and took a deep breath. "This is hard to believe. But I can prove that the foundation's been taken over by a secret inner circle that will do anything—murder, kidnapping, blackmail—in pursuit of its goal. Which is world domination."

Bill gave me a look. "Do you feel all right?"

"Why would anybody want to rule the world? They'd have to *run* it."

"I know. And in fact, they don't put it that baldly; they just think the 'phems are doing a bad job and 'we' ought to step in and clean things up. The 'we' is a group of about a hundred handpicked immortals.

"They wanted me, I supposed for my visibility, and when I refused they tried to kill me. That failed, so they set me up as a murderer. Maria and I fled out to here, and they sent a couple of thugs after us. They knocked me out and either kidnapped Maria or killed her." I gestured downstairs. "She killed one of them with a shattergun."

"But if they were after you," Doris said, "why didn't they kidnap *you* while they had the chance?"

"I don't know. It doesn't make sense. Maybe the survivor panicked after Maria killed his partner—it is a pretty brutal sight after all. Maybe he just grabbed her and ran."

"Wouldn't he look pretty obvious?" Bill said. "Running down Tsiolkovski with a protesting woman in tow?"

"Yeah, naked and bloody, too." I pointed toward the air lock. "He took her outside." Dick's Vigilante Committee report was over on the couch. I sailed over, picked it up, tripped, caromed off the window, and came back, slowly tumbling head over heels.

"Can you teach me how to do that?" Bill said.

I handed them the report. "There was another guy involved. They evidently stole a stealthed Rocketdyne, put her aboard, and used this rise in the ground to sneak away unnoticed. Probably headed back to Earth."

He studied both of the pages, nodding. "Look, Dallas. Anybody overhearing this would say you were crazy. *Dangerously* crazy, considering the string of bodies that leads to here."

"That's something they're counting on." I told them about the letter we'd sent to all the board members. "Have you been following the news?"

They both shook their heads. "Never," Doris said. "They change the names but the stories stay the same."

"They even published the letter as proof of my insanity."

"I did see that, actually," Bill said. "I mentioned to a friend that I'd met you in *adastra*—don't see that many celebrities—and he told me about the accusations. I looked it up and decided it couldn't be true. I flatter myself that I can read people pretty well. At least I ought to be able to tell a screwloose murderer after having a few meals with him. That's why we put an ad on the board. Did you see it?"

"Yes. But we didn't want to get you involved. Now I'm afraid I have to."

"What do you need?"

"A stealthed ship."

They looked at each other. "It's full of silver," Bill said. "I mean *full*. We were just about to head back to Earth."

"I don't see how we could handle a passenger," Doris said. "There are only two acceleration couches, and the life-support system couldn't handle three people, not back to Earth."

"Besides, we're taking three months. You'll want to go back as fast as possible."

"You're right," I said. "We calculated no more than five weeks for them."

"But you do need stealth," Doris said, "if you're even halfway right about the foundation. They'll have a welcoming committee waiting on Earth for anyone who leaves the Belt in the next few days." She bit her lip, concentrating. "But that's worth thinking about, too. They'll expect you to be hot on their trail, right? What if you did take three months? They wouldn't be as ready for you. Might even assume you weren't coming."

"That's right," Bill said. "We could split up; Doris could take a commercial flight home while you and I crawled back to Earth."

"Or vice versa," Doris said. "You might find it easier to get along with me than him, cooped up."

"You're both too generous. But I don't think I could do it. After three months I *would* be crazy. What if I was a week late? What if they decided I wasn't coming and . . . disposed of her?"

Bill sipped his coffee reflectively. "That's playing into their hands, though, thinking like that. They want you to come charging in. You ought to put them off-balance."

"They've got *me* off-balance. How would you feel if somebody snatched Doris?" He gave me a patient look. "Sorry. I know a couple of months doesn't compare to seventy years."

There was an awkward silence. "Men," Doris said. "A gallon of honey is no sweeter than a thimbleful."

"We could offload," Bill said slowly. "Without the silver, the ship would be light and fast."

Doris nodded. "You could go in alone. Bring the ship back later. We have six or eight years left before we have to go to the clinic. We could amuse ourselves here."

I was stunned. "You know you'll probably lose it." Say it. "They'll probably kill me."

"We know," Doris said. "We can buy another."

"One thing you can always get in Novy is a spaceship," Bill said.

Crimewatch Ceres

26 *apryél*

LIBEL ACCUSATION?
(WHO'S CALLING WHO A WHAT?)

0258 Michel Gulyaev, proprietor of Girls Girls Girls, says that Bonita Morris, who owns The Come & Get, has told her customers that he's nothing but a greasy overcharging pimp and his girls never wash. He says that's unfair restraint of trade and her girls are so ugly they have to do it in the dark. She says where do you think you are with this "restraint of trade," Leningrad? and she's willing to line up all her girls and boys one for one with his, high noon on Tsiolkovski, starkers, and let the public decide who needs a bag over whose head or, for that matter, body. This is the kind of duel we like to report on.

SUSPICIOUS DEATH

0940 Real estate agent Peter Quinn was found dead in his office this morning of an apparent "cerebrovascular accident," a stroke. Clinic says no way that's possible; he was in last month for a checkup and was fine. Visual inspection of the body by the medics revealed apparent electrical burns to the scrotum and penis, as they say in the medical world. Medic thinks he was tortured to death.

This reporter and the other people at the inquest couldn't think of anything Quinn would know that would be worth torturing him to find out, so the assumption is that the torturer did it for jollies.

Quinn has been around for a long time, and everybody knows he was a straight man in a crooked profession. If this reporter finds the jacknik who did it, he will personally toss his scrotum and penis, as they say, out the air lock—one inch at a time—and will send out invitations for the ceremony.

After about an hour—which is to say several months, subjective time—Maria had sorted things out and found a way to make the most of her situation. There was no way to tell how long she would be in this state, or whether she would survive it, but even without religious belief, she was still a person with a long habit of meditation: working out things in the solitude of her mind, yes, but also taking quiet pleasure in the thought that isn't thought, the silent hum of the body and brain just existing. That might be what saved her.

It's not possible to describe in words exactly what she was doing, what she *was,* over the nearly twenty years that passed while the stealthed ship crawled past the orbit of Mars. One contraindication cited by Vitaslow's manufacturer was that it could have an adverse effect on the patient's mental health, if there was any prior evidence of instability, which was probably an understatement. Maria's case was more complicated than the label-writer might have expected, though. It didn't hurt her. Perhaps it drove her more sane, as she evolved from resisting her state, to accepting it, and finally to savoring it.

The ugly little man moved through her universe as slowly as a planet through the Earth's night sky. She ignored him for months at a time. On occasion, with the speed of a glacier, he put a towel between her and the acceleration couch and removed it, evidence that some kind of metabolism was creeping along within her body. She knew intellectually that she had gone many days without food or water and wondered how long that would take to kill her.

After twelve days, or nineteen years, she slowly began to perceive new things. Smell came first, mostly the little man's food and body. Then came the subtle body senses her memory identified as proprioceptive: equilibrium and the positions of her bones and muscles. That was good for weeks of sensuous imagining, as she discovered her body anew, cell by cell.

The world began to speed up around her. One awakening, she could suddenly taste the staleness of her mouth and feel the damp rough fabric of the towel she was sitting on; the cold metal and plastic of the acceleration couch. Breathing in deeply, she could feel her chest expand, and hear the air rushing down her throat.

"Coming out of it?"

She looked at the ugly little man and remembered the thousand tortures she had devised for him. "Water."

Maria

I hadn't really thought about the man for a long time, ever since I forgave him and stopped using him as a focus for my anger. It was Briskin who was doing this to us. I assumed the little man just wanted a million pounds and immortality, for which a lot of people would kill, let alone kidnap. But that was not exactly it.

When I was able to croak one word, he brought me a bulb of water, which I sucked dry in seconds, once I managed to get it to my lips; and a Coke, sweeter than sin. Two weeks of torpid peristalsis woke up; I managed to undo the straps and just made it to the toilet.

The caffeine roared in my ears and brain, and I delighted in the swift rush of time, the real sounds and smells, even the annoying grind of the toilet's macerator, even the fiery pain in all my joints muscles holes—*must be lactic acid buildup from forced inaction*—and I laughed out loud at my brain working in a linear, let's-identify-and-solve-this-problem, way again. Though I did like the other way.

Behind the mirror (a ghastly apparition, but who wouldn't have been?) there was a medicine rack with chewable noraspirin; I shook out three and loved the crunching concussion in my jaws and ears, biting down; the astringent vinegariness going up *inside* smelling from inside my mouth and the chalky promise of swallowing it, glowing with pain I felt so good I could explode. I sucked on the water tube like a baby coming out of the womb and into the world's hunger and thirst. I touched myself and had a hammering chain of orgasms that made me choke and cough on the water.

"Are you all right in there?" All I could answer with was laughter and more coughing.

Feeling almost human, I zipped up into the shower and rubbed the waterbrush all over my skin, fast and slow and soft and rough, body screaming STOP DON'T STOP! dangerous perverse giddiness as the difference between pain and pleasure dissolved and the man pushed the door open—

"Are you all right? I heard you—"

"I'm fine. Go away." The words hurt my throat. Maybe I should have asked him to do my back first. The patch I couldn't reach with the brush itched and crawled. Then I figured out how to hook the brush against the side of the shower bag and back up against it.

I vacuumed myself dry—rubbery lips of the recycler, a weird ecstasy—and found a paper jumpsuit in the closet. It was a couple of sizes too large, and made me look like a little girl playing dress-up. I saw my stupid smile in the mirror and thought again of Dominica and Laraine, and stifled childish giggles in the paper sleeves that overhung my hands. Dominica and Laraine are dead of old age now; that thought helped calm me down. More or less composed, I went back into the cabin.

He was looking at me with an expression difficult to read. He wasn't an ephemeral. Interesting that I couldn't tell until I saw him in real time. "I'm surprised an immortal would take such chances for a million pounds."

"I'm not a bounty hunter," he said without inflection. "This is a favor for a friend."

"Charles Briskin." He hesitated, and nodded once. "I don't think much of your taste in friends."

"Obviously not. You blew one of them to bits."

I suppressed a wave of nausea at the memory. "Tell me what you would do if you had a price on your head and somebody came through the door, aiming a gun at you. You can't blame me for that."

My feelings were more complicated than that rationalization, of course, but I didn't want to give him my guilt for a weapon. I drifted toward the acceleration couch. "But I am sorry I killed him. Since it had no effect on the outcome."

"Oh, it had an effect. He was going to bring Mr. Barr along. I didn't feel I could take care of both of you without help."

"You'd need help guarding two sacks of potatoes?"

"Didn't want to leave you under all the way to Earth." He took the dart pistol out of his waistband and inspected it. "We weren't supposed to use this on you more than once. Staying in suspended animation for too long is supposed to be unhealthy." He put it back. "If you give me any trouble, I will use it, though."

"Don't worry." Maybe I could take it from him while he slept. "What would I do if I overpowered you? I don't know how to fly."

He smiled. "Not true. Sir Charles said you're a better pilot than I am."

"So you're going to tie me down while you sleep?"

"Nothing that complicated. Lock you up in the head." That gave me a strange image, having *been* locked up in my head for a long time, until I realized he was using the nautical term.

I felt an odd closeness to him, not from having spent almost twenty years naked in his presence. It was the well-documented irrational bond between prisoner and jailer, terrorist and hostage. Maybe that's a symmetry weakness in neural connections. When we love someone we allow ourselves to be imprisoned by him, solid bars of shared life, and this person who brings actual bars insinuates himself, by association, backwards into our heart. What a strange thought. Yet I did feel this closeness to someone about whom I knew absolutely nothing except that he abducted me for Charles Briskin, eats right-handed and masturbates left-handed.

"What is your name?"

"You don't have to know that."

"I don't know what to call you."

"Don't call me anything." He turned away, looking resentful or petulant, and switched on the cube. He did feel some guilt, I realized.

"Why me, rather than Dallas?" I asked, and braced

myself for the answer. Dallas wasn't worth anything dead.

"Like I say, I wasn't after the million pounds. Sir Charles said if we could only take one alive, it was to be you."

That was bad: he must know about Baird Ulric. They would want to examine me, compare his methods with the clinics'. After all this, was I going to die anyhow, and on a dissecting table?

"He wouldn't say why. He called us on the way out and changed the primary target from him to you. Murray —the man you killed—thought that he figured Mr. Barr would come charging after you anyhow. I think it's simpler than that. For some reason, you *are* more important than him."

He looked at me quizzically and I shrugged. "Who knows why a crazy man wants what he wants?"

"He is not crazy. He's a visionary."

"Whatever you say. You have the gun."

"I do indeed. You might give that some thought." He thumbed the cube input button. "News: abduction, Ceres."

"No references since 6 March 2078. Continue?"

"No." He turned to me. "They never have acknowledged that you disappeared. That's very interesting."

"We lived a completely hermetic existence," I said, "being afraid of people like you. If Dallas was knocked out the way I was, nobody yet knows we're gone."

"Possible."

Then a memory came like a blow. "No. There was that other man. The one who met you at the air lock. Did he—"

"He was just a lowlife we recruited up in SORF, a fairly competent pilot. Never knew who you were. All he knew was that there were two dead people downstairs, and he'd better not be found with them."

"But Dallas wasn't dead."

"No; he got the same dosage as you. I suppose it would wear off sooner, since he's bigger. So he's probably looking for you by now."

"If he has any sanity left. Lying helpless for twenty years watching a body decompose."

He raised his eyebrows. "It really did feel like twenty years?"

"At least." Dallas had practiced Zen, though, when he was younger. He spent a year in Antarctica just watching the wind blow the snow around. I hoped he could still find that, to help him through.

"What did *you* think about? A million ways to kill me?"

It took me a minute to come back to him. I was *with* Dallas, the way the granular snow rattled against the ice floes, the sudden smell of the penguins that day the hairs in his nose freezing when he stepped outside the tent and breathed the midnight sun the aching slow cra-a-a-ack of the iceberg calving food freezing solid while he ate.

"What? Excuse me." I shivered with the Antarctic cold. How did that happen?

"Did you think about a million ways to kill me?"

"No. That's not my nature." A little truth. "I thought of many ways to hurt you, to embarrass you. Usually involving the dart gun."

"You can disabuse yourself of that. I've been immunized against the zombi drug." That was a quick lie, an obvious bluff. He wasn't a good improviser. "At least I didn't take advantage of you. That would have been easy."

"You thought about it." Pretty obviously, at the time.

"Of course. Not violent rape, but, uh . . ." He waved a hand at his lack of romantic vocabulary.

"I would have killed you. If I survived the experience, I would have killed you."

"I understand."

"I don't think you do. Several days of helpless agony, for your minutes of satisfaction. I thought about the possibility quite often."

"No . . . what I mean is . . . I was raped once myself." His voice broke. "Eighty-two years ago. Sometimes it bothers me that he must be dead by now. So I'll never be able to . . . punish him. To kill him. That's all I meant by saying I understand."

"Oh." It must have been terrible, against your will. Dallas and I had used that channel, exploring, but gently, slowly. My body was overcome with the sweetness of the memory of it, and trying to imagine what it felt like to Dallas, and I had to concentrate on listening:

"It hasn't been easy, watching you for two weeks, thinking about you. Even for a Stileman, your body is remarkably flawless."

Brand-new, I almost said.

He blushed. "I don't suppose there's any possibility . . ."

The man really was a born romantic. "None. Nobody but Dallas."

"That's what I thought." Was there a note of relief in his voice? "But I'm afraid we will be forced into some intimacy. I don't have anything like handcuffs or rope. I can't leave you here alone while I use the head. You'll have to come with me."

"That's ridiculous."

"I assure you I don't care for the idea myself. But if you were to take control of the ship while I was indisposed, you could kill me with a six-gee burst of acceleration, or kill us both by opening the air lock."

"I wouldn't do either. You may have my word."

"Those are my orders. If Murray were still alive, he could watch you."

"You'll have to carry me."

"That's all right. You're weightless." He snatched my wrist and I tried to pry his fingers away; but it was impossible; I was still weak as a child. "Don't resist. I'll have to shoot you."

He let go, satisfied. But it occurred to me that I was a lot less weak than I should have been, after two weeks of total flaccidity. When I first woke up, I could hardly raise my hands to hold a drink, even without fighting gravity.

The Coke, of course. I was burning all that sugar. It's as simple as $C_6H_{12}O_6 + 6O_2 \rightarrow 6CO_2 + 6H_2O +$ energy; now where did that come from? Biology class in *ginnasio*, I guess, but I must have forgotten that long before the turn of the century.

But no, it's not that simple, I recalled from somewhere,

nowhere; it's not as if your stomach were a furnace that burned glucose and turned it into energy. The Coke goes down into the small intestine, is converted into monosaccharides, wanders to the liver, goes through glycogenesis. . . .

I could pin that down. It was 1997, eighty-four years ago, when I first found out I had cancer and read about the body compulsively for months.

It didn't really matter where it was coming from; how it was being processed. I could feel strength growing in me like a vessel filling. "Could I have something to eat?"

"In a minute. First we have to go to the head."

He grabbed my wrist lightly and we started floating aft. He wasn't looking at me. Now or never. I saw an opening and, with a speed that surprised me, grabbed the pistol from his waistband, then pushed it against his abdomen and pulled the trigger!

Nothing happened.

He casually twisted the gun out of my hand and pushed me away. Smiling, he took a dart out of his jacket pocket. "Safety first." He loaded it and I closed my eyes.

I heard the gun fire, a quiet snap, but didn't feel anything. When I heard the door to the head, I cautiously opened my eyes. The dart was caught in the loose folds of paper between my breasts.

I stifled the impulse to rush to the controls and injure or kill him with a burst of acceleration, as he'd said. Morality aside, I might not be able to figure out the unfamiliar panel before he came out. Instead, I tore the orange string off the dart and pressed it into the paper fabric; it held. I grasped the dart carefully hidden in my right hand, point out, and floated with my eyes closed except for a slit. Just come within arm's reach.

The toilet cycled and he returned, unfortunately with the gun out. Had he reloaded it?

He floated in front of me for most of a minute, not saying anything, just staring. Then with no warning he slapped my cheek hard.

In one instant I cried out, he fired, and I poked his hand

with the dart. The pain from the slap sparkled away as the zombi took effect. We drifted away from each other, slowly rotating.

Another twenty years. I wondered if *he* would stay sane. Which one of us would come out of it first?

I retreated into a familiar place, pulling the calendar in after me.

The Barons decided that the best place to stash their load of silver, while Dallas was borrowing the ship, would be with a friend who owned, or at least sat on, a small rock not far from Ceres. It would also give them a chance to show Dallas where the brake and accelerator were, and make sure he knew enough to change lanes before making a left-hand turn.

The ship, *Shadow*, was parked in the high-security area, a fenced-in gravel field with servomech perimeter guards. The fence didn't have much practical value in a conventional way, since in a thirtieth of a gee, anyone could hop over it. But anyone who tried would land in several places at once.

There was also an individual human guard living inside *Shadow*, a young man who was ecstatic at being able to take his accumulated wages on a misguided tour of Tsiolkovski. He traded places with Dallas and the Barons when they came out in the mating crawler, and took it back to Big Dick's central tower.

"It's not much, but it's home," Bill said.

"It'll do the trick," Dallas said. He knew too many wealthy people to be surprised at the shabbiness of the ship's interior. Some millionaires become indifferent to luxury; some actively reject comfort and style in a reverse, or perverse, display of status.

Doris was rational about it: "We only live in it for a couple of months a decade. I'd feel silly prettying it up, especially after we spent so much to stealth it. Like gilding gold."

Bill was checking the pantry. "*Damn* that walking appetite! We'll have to restock before Dallas takes it in."

"We should tighten up our contract with the boy," Doris said. "Three meals a day, thus and so."

"If you wouldn't mind mating with my ship up in the SORF, I can offload meals from it."

"Good idea," Bill said. "The markup on Tsiolkovski is murderous."

There were two acceleration couches forward. Bill and Doris climbed up and strapped themselves in and told Dallas to lie down on the aft bulkhead. "We'll do one gee max," Bill said. "Plenty to get us off this pebble." He typed in a few lines; evidently his ship's AI was not the garrulous kind. "Ready?"

"Fire away," Dallas said.

He called the control tower and got clearance—"Go anywhere as long as it's up"—and then typed one character. Gravity came on in a slow surge.

Odds and ends clattered around in the pantry and galley. "He never cleans up, either," Doris said. "I'll give him a good talking-to."

They accelerated for about a minute, long enough for Dallas to feel some relief when it stopped. "Come on up," Bill said. "Show you how to fly it."

Dallas floated forward and hovered next to Bill. He typed AUTHORIZE and told Dallas to put his thumb on the print pad. He did and the machine asked back BY WHOM?, and Bill put his thumb there. OKAY.

"It's pretty smart. Once authorized, an imbecile could take it anywhere within its range. Watch this." He typed in

GO IN A RANDOM DIRECTION FOR TWO MINUTES, THEN TURN ON STEALTH AND TAKE US TO LUANNE DUNCAN'S ASTEROID IN THE SHORTEST TIME POSSIBLE WITH ACCELERATIONS NOT TO EXCEED ONE GEE FOR TEN MINUTES EACH WAY.

It responded with SECRET WORD?

"Luanne's code. Turn around, please, Dallas." He typed in an eight-letter word. "Okay." The screen said HIT ANY KEY. "Better get settled again."

Dallas rolled left, then right, as the ship yawed, then it

accelerated briefly. After two minutes, it pitched and yawed again, and then blasted for exactly ten minutes. He went forward again and the screen was blank except for the top line: STEALTH . . . TIME TO DECELERATION 87 MIN 23 SEC, which was counting down.

"What happens if the computer breaks down?" Dallas asked.

"It won't," Doris said. "We've used it for twenty years with no problems."

"No moving parts," Bill said.

"Ours went loony on the way out. Gave us a hell of a time."

"Guess it could happen," Bill said. "You'd have to destealth and call Mayday." He laughed. "Just tell them you're Dallas Barr; you'll get plenty of help."

For the next hour and a half, the three of them prowled around the ship, making sure Dallas knew what to do in case this or that came up. They had to consult the manual for most of the emergency procedures, since the worst that had ever happened to them was an ullage problem in the drinking-water tanks that made the faucets hiss and spit in microgravity.

Luanne Duncan was a pleasantly batty Scotswoman who baked scones and made "proper tea" for them, no easy trick on an asteroid barely a kilometer wide. It would take an hour for a dropped sugar cube to hit the ground.

Dallas let the Barons visit while he unloaded the silver. It was a tedious process since he had to use an EVA chair in the virtual absence of gravity: fill your lap up with rocks, then give it a little burst to move out of the hold, wait two seconds, then a counterbalancing burst, then a slow rotation; when you reach 180 degrees, gently throw the rocks downward; come back around, stop the rotation, small burst to go back to the hold. That was the pattern when everything went perfectly, which happened about two trips out of a hundred.

The bright chunks of silver were rather conspicuous against the dark magnetic hoarfrost of iron-nickel particles that clung to the asteroid's surface like fur. Dallas draped the black Kevlar blanket over the pile, battened down the hatches, and collected his hosts.

Bill rode the floor on the way back while Dallas "piloted," though piloting was nothing more than being careful in explaining to the spaceship what you wanted it to do.

GO BACK TOWARD CERES, ACCELERATION NOT TO EXCEED ONE GEE, MATCH ORBIT WITH SORF, UNSTEALTH 500 KILOMETERS FROM SORF.

If the stealthing was still turned on too near the Synchronous Orbit Repair Facility or any other place with guidance and communication equipment, it could interfere in dozens of frequencies. Not especially stealthy at close range.

Dallas put the Barons on the shuttle along with all of the expensive leftover wine from Fireball. It would be a long month back to Earth, he said, but he wanted to arrive sober and mean.

He didn't know what a long month *was*.

Maria

WE kept rotating and bouncing off the walls. Once each six months or so I would come close enough to the console to read the numbers, which I assumed were estimated time to deceleration. That gave me an objective measure of the time stretch: it took about a minute for each tenth-of-a-second number to change, so we were slowed by a factor of about six hundred. It took me several rotations to figure that out; arithmetic was just plain not there for me; I had to go through a tortuous chain of logical inference to come up with that number. We'd gone halfway to Earth this second time I'd been zombied; two weeks divided by six hundred comes to what? Or was it times six hundred, or plus or minus, or to the six-hundredth power? I knew the words but couldn't make them produce any new numbers.

It was frustrating, but only frustrating. I got through the last long wait and I would get through this one.

It occurred to me that given as much time as I had, perhaps I could reinvent arithmetic. I could remember from college that a fellow Italian had done that, making up arithmetic from scratch, and I could even remember that his name sounded like a musical instrument in English—and even *how the room smelled* the day we learned about him—and that the girl in front of me was named Helena and she'd let her boyfriend touch her breasts in the dark, but not look at them—and that the boyfriend was the *matricola* Paco, who was small but handsome and wore bluejeans that were so tight he seemed to walk on his toes, and you could see enough to tell he wasn't circumcised—but for the life of me I couldn't remember what that man's name was or how he reinvented arithmetic, or why, actually. Was his arithmetic better than the kind we learned in school? Did it come up with the same numbers? It seemed to me that it would have to, though I wasn't sure why.

This time around I was more comfortable in my ignorance, my stupidity, knowing that it was temporary. Some circuits were disconnected, but the brain, or the mind, probably knew what it was doing. If all of your cognition worked the way it normally did, you might find a couple of decades of deaf-and-dumb-and-paralyzed confinement rather terrifying.

For about a couple of days, the little man and I converged on each other, coming together in the middle of the cabin, close to where we were when this started. I could see his head bump my knee, but couldn't feel it.

He looks very strange, as I must. But at least my mouth isn't open. His eyes are wide and his mouth is stretched open as if in a voiceless scream. Not smart. Losing water fast, mouth drying out.

For the brief time I was out of this state, I wasn't able to think about it enough. Integrate the experience into my life, as they say. Figure out what's good and bad about it. In a way it's like being handed an extra twenty years, free. Two twenties for me. Will that make me older than Dallas?

It does something to your relationship with time, other than just slowing it down. Afterwards. The intensity of memory, like erasing the time between then and now.

More than that. I "remembered" Dallas's Antarctica retreat as if I had been there myself.

It's a wonder to me that the people like Claudia Fine, constantly taking different drugs to alter their perception of reality, don't take this one for their peculiar pleasure. It's not new; someone must have taken it for fun by now.

Maybe some ephemerals do take it this way, as a kind of artificial immortality. Of course it would be different with an ephemeral; most drugs were. Maybe it would drive you mad.

It might not mix with other drugs, either. Twenty years of grief and you would be tearing your eyes out. Twenty years being drunk would be no pleasure. And it might be maddening to a person like Claudia, not being able to *do* anything, month after month.

As if we weren't all locked up in the head anyhow.

GET ME TO EARTH AS SOON AS POSSIBLE bought Dallas almost an hour of 3.8 gees. The machine pointed out that if it were to take him literally, it could accelerate at top thrust until it ran out of fuel, which would be forty-two minutes at about eight gees. That would probably kill Dallas, and his corpse would fly by Earth at about two hundred kilometers per second. The machine assumed he would rather slow down and actually *land* on Earth and be alive at the time. It also left a reserve of fuel for mid-course maneuvering. WOULD YOU RATHER ARRIVE DEAD IN 18.2 DAYS OR ALIVE IN 31?

Dallas was not sure whether the machine knew what a rhetorical question was, so he answered it straight.

He read a book a day, as much to calm himself as anything, and played a lot of chess with Eric, and they hashed over plans. Eric suggested that they land in Anchorage, the only spaceport in anarchistic Alaska, destealthing as soon as they were out of Pacifica airspace. Dallas agreed that that was better than his own nonplan, which was to land it in the middle of the most desolate place he could find. Some government would surely confiscate the ship, and they wouldn't be able to get away fast. In Anchorage they could just bond it for either Dallas or the Barons to pick up later. Then begin Step Two.

The problem was figuring out what Step Two was going to be.

Dallas

EVEN if I knew where Briskin was, it wouldn't be smart to charge in on him, confront him directly, give-me-back-my-woman-or-else. What woman? Or else *what,* loony? I had to assume he'd be ready for me.

The revised, refined plan was to arrange a local "media event," buying time on a number of Alaskan stations, presenting my story in a venue that Briskin presumably would not be able to control. Even assuming that the foundation dominated the mainstream stateside newsnet— and so could edit anything I said or did before it went out to the consumers—they couldn't control all the maverick little Klondike stations. That was one reason they were popular in California and the West; independent from network control, their programming was wildly uneven but not often dull.

So I could reach a couple of million people for a few minutes. That was enough to ensure that Briskin couldn't air his own version of my little homecoming speech, later.

Money was going to be a problem. I had a gold bar worth maybe a quarter of a million dollars, American. (Alaska prints its own bills and mints coins, but its currency is strictly tied to the American economy.) I'd need a platoon of bodyguards, all of them professional enough to disregard the million-dollar price on my head, once they found out who they were in fact protecting. Eric suggested that I hire people from the actual States, since they at least had to belong to a union.

Then I had to buy a few minutes of live airtime, and not in a cheap, unwatched period. That would cost ten times as much as the guards. And there had to be some left over, since after the broadcast I would want to either jump into a hole and pull the hole in after me, watching the fireworks from safety, or else make an immediate and public move toward Briskin. It would depend on his reaction.

I've been reading about paranoia, trying to understand, to second-guess, the man. Something inside me fights the approach, though. The psychologists write about delusional fixity and displacement of responsibility, psychotic decompensation, and so forth. But they don't mention evil. I have to believe that his actions are evil. It's absurd to call something a medical problem when its symptoms are a desire for world domination and the casual employment, enjoyment, of homicide.

With Eric's help I searched my recollections of the two contacts with Briskin over and over. One advantage of being a machine is that you don't get bored. *I* was going out of my skull saying the same things repeatedly, in slightly different ways. But it was potentially invaluable, especially if we could pin down something Briskin said that might give us a clue to the actual size of the Steering Committee. Or the thing's actual existence: it had belatedly occurred to me that his might be a committee of one. The killers and the kidnapper were probably just hirelings, no matter how big the outfit was. Had he actually done anything that couldn't have been done alone, given enough money and madness?

He'd said there were about a hundred members, with another fifty being considered for the privilege. But he didn't mention any names; didn't really provide any details. Maybe it was all fantasy, part of what a psychologist would call his delusional system, a made-up family. Eric pointed out, though, that actually paranoid people are observed to do exactly the opposite as the illness progresses: they organize all the people who are out to get them into a "paranoid pseudocommunity" united for the sole purpose of harming them.

Which, he noted, was exactly what I would sound like, telling the world about this sinister underground that had made attempts on my life all over the Earth and as far out as

Novysibirsk. I had no more objective evidence for my version of it than Briskin would have for his. All you could say for sure was that an unusual amount of homicide had crystallized around me.

For a moment the universe slipped on its axis and I was the actual insane one, killing people left and right and constructing a fantastic elaborate delusional system to blame my crimes on an innocent person. From this viewpoint, inside my own delusions, would I ever be able to tell the difference?

At least I did have news stories to verify my recollections. It was unlikely that a professional killer could have wandered into my bathroom by mistake. Coincidentally hired by the Stileman Foundation, according to its spokesman, Charles Briskin.

Shadow was the roomiest spaceship I'd ever traveled in. The hold that would normally be full of silver on the return trip was rigged out as an interesting gym. Besides the Stiktite exercising treadmill that almost all small ships had, so you wouldn't be too tired out when you returned to Earth's gravity, there were trampolines mounted on the forward and aft walls. Tumbling in three dimensions was more interesting than endless miles of rip, rip, rip on the treadmill, and it let me work off the anxiety about Maria and the hostility that I was brewing up toward Briskin.

One of us, at least, was going to be sane when I confronted him.

Maria

I spent about a year looking forward to a slow and agonizing, if technically painless, death. I assumed that when the clock ran down to all zeros, the ship would rotate 180 degrees and begin deceleration. The little man and I would descend gracefully to the aft bulkhead and be crushed and smothered by our own body weight, at four to six lazy gees. If there was no reason, such as delicate or loose cargo, to decelerate slowly, you strapped in and did it quickly, to save fuel. We were both delicate and loose, but I didn't expect the ship to divine that.

It would be like falling off a roof onto the sidewalk and then having a grand piano lowered onto you.

A red light came on when the clock read 00:10:00.00; ten-minute warning. For a hundred hours I watched it blink stroboscopically, off and on for twenty seconds at a time. A buzzer growled. Then the ship rotated, the little man and I both slid over to the port side. I struck facefirst, and for a long minute heard the cartilage in my nose crackle. When a few days went by with no sign of blood, I decided it hadn't broken.

I couldn't see the clock, but supposed it was just as well. Neither could I calculate how long it would take us to fall. Would we know when it started? Probably not.

I slept as much as possible. Perhaps I would have the luck to be asleep when acceleration began, and drop headfirst, unknowing, to the release of a crushed skull or broken neck.

Awake, I tried to find the quiet place where I had been so many decades ago, ready to let myself die and join God. It wasn't there anymore, no more than he was. Neither, for that matter, was the rage that I'd felt as a young girl, the heretical rage at the insult of death that overwhelmed me after the earthquake had taken everybody but Madre, the rage that the sisters cured with loving patience. What I felt was almost petty, like being annoyed: yes, I'm going to die someday, and it will be about as profound as turning off a light switch, or the Universe, but I would rather take a stab at a thousand years or so before I run out of brain cells or luck. If we were bargaining over this thing, I would grudgingly take death now, but just as soon not have it happen in slow motion, an hour-by-hour catalog of bones snapping, muscles tearing, and organs rupturing until the lights faded out. But after the lights went out there would be no memory, nothing, so as Dallas was occasionally moved to say, fuck it, the hell with it, fuck it the hell with it fuck it the hell with it fuck it hell fuck hell fuck . . . what's that smell?

I could smell the metal of the bulkhead. A whiff of sweat and urine. I could feel where my bones were. Throbbing pain in my bumped nose and fire in all the muscles and joints—much faster than last time, every few seconds a new person, new and slightly less comfortable than the last one.

There is a God, it came to me in a rush, and he is reviving me so that I can feel pain before I die. As soon as I'm able to move, the fusion torch will light and I'll be slammed back against the aft bulkhead. To consider for a few agonizing seconds the eternal consequences of my newly embraced atheism.

I closed my eyes and waited obediently to die, but instead I kept surviving and the roll call of pain got longer and longer. Sinus headache, diaper rash, stubbed toe, infected sore where the dart had gone in, stomach cramps, kidneys, and bladder. If I didn't die soon I would have to go to the toilet.

My calves flexed without my thinking about it, and I floated aft, toward the head. It was a wonderful experience, again, to relieve myself, variously, but overall not really worth the wait. I wadded up the clothes I had been wearing for the past twenty years and unfolded a fresh paper tunic from the cabinet. "Might as well die looking fresh," I said out loud, and my reverberating voice was weird in my ears.

I kicked up toward the acceleration couches. The clock on the control console said + 09:43:23 CORRECTION URGENTLY REQUIRED. I touched the couch, and the console spoke:

"Acceleration cannot proceed until one or both passengers are properly secured. Please strap yourselves in and press any key to resume guidance sequence."

I pushed aft and port and retrieved the little man, whose frozen face was still contorted in a rictus of horror. Sweet dreams, I hoped. I took the dart pistol from him and started to maneuver him into the couch; then remembered it saying "one or both." That would be a lovely irony, if the torch lit while I was in the process of saving his worthless skin.

I suppose it could hear me. "Will you wait to accelerate until after both of us are strapped in?"

"Yes. Guidance revision sequence will not be initiated spontaneously. The pilot must press a key."

Before strapping him in, I took off his shirt and tried to rip off the sleeves, to tie his arms down, but didn't have the strength. Then I saw I could use the sleeves as bonds without separating them from the shirt. Inelegant but adequate.

I contemplated further immobilizing him by pulling his pants down around his ankles, giving him a few years of embarrassment, but didn't do it, on the off chance that he would enjoy exposing himself or, rather, having somebody else expose him.

I strapped myself in and touched a key. The console counted down from five, we made two pairs of swings and dips in pitch and yaw, and then deceleration slammed in. I watched the accelerometer climb to minus six gees, and then my lids closed.

What was it like in the old days, with airplanes? Hearing the engines scream, the wind whip by. All I heard was little creaks and pops as the ship debated with itself whether or not to break up under the strain. Then a pair of crashes from the pantry: something not properly secured.

It was very hard to breathe. It went on for a long time. I tasted blood and realized I had caught the side of my tongue between my teeth, how stupid, and extricated it with difficulty.

Then it was over. The clock showed we'd been blasting for thirty-one minutes. I felt as if somebody had been massaging me with a cricket bat for that long. My tongue was raw and swollen; all the blood I'd swallowed wanted to come up. Some cool water helped, and I found an antacid that at least covered up the heavy taste of blood. The little man seemed about the same. Too much to ask, to have him bite *his* tongue.

I studied the control console. There was not much to it; a fairly standard American idiotproof layout. I never could understand people who would trust AI circuits so completely that they didn't even install readouts and controls for the thousands of things that would have to be done if you were actually put in charge of the ship. Every year several people disappear into space. Most of them probably spend their last days shouting at an unresponsive screen.

"Show me where we are," I asked the machine.

The screen split into two pictures, one a diagram of Earth with a circular orbit around it, the other an image of the actual planet. "We are currently in geosynchronous orbit over longitude thirty-nine degrees east, which is Kenya. My basic algorithm precludes coming closer to Earth while stealth mechanisms are in effect."

That explained the mirror finish outside. "Suppose I ask you to change that part of your algorithm?"

"It violates international law to operate a stealthed vehicle any closer to Earth."

"I didn't ask you about the law. Will you take me to Earth?"

"It violates international law to operate a stealthed vehicle inside geosynchronous orbit."

"I understand that. Will you break the law for me?"

"I cannot."

Not surprising. "All right. Turn off the stealth and take us to Maui."

"I cannot deactivate stealth measures without proper authorization." That gave me a cold ripple; we could go around that track until we ran out of air.

I unhooked the microphone and thumbed it. "Mayday. Mayday." I doubted that Briskin was sitting somewhere over Kenya, waiting for us. "I'm in a stealthed ship, name unknown, in geosynchronous orbit above thirty-nine degrees east. Please answer."

The console answered. "No communications are allowed while stealth conditions are in operation. I cannot deactivate stealth measures without proper authorization."

"What is proper authorization?"

"Place thumb in identification square."

Of course. "Just a moment." I untied the man and pulled him over. Pressed his thumb to the square. A small STEALTH OFF message blinked on and disappeared.

I tied him back up and strapped him in. Strapping myself in, I paused to think. Maybe I had better not go straight to Maui. Maybe I'd better not stay here, either. You had to assume that when a spaceship suddenly appeared out of nowhere, various authorities would notice.

How much power did Briskin actually have? Did everyone in authority accept his version of what had gone on in Yugoslavia? Dallas and I had chewed on those questions a few times, and I'd had forty more years to think them over. With no new data, unfortunately, other than the fact of my kidnapping, although that was not insignificant.

Wait. "Where were you programmed to land?"

"I was not programmed to land. I was only asked to wait in a parking orbit above thirty-nine degrees east."

"Are there any other spaceships in the vicinity?"

"Yes. A stretch Mercedes is closing on us at thirteen hundred meters per second. Range four hundred eighty kilometers."

"Take us to Maui. As fast as possible."

"Very well. Sixty-second countdown—"

"Take us *now!*" I had been leaning forward into my straps with the tension. The sudden acceleration was like a huge soft animal rolling over on me. I did manage not to bite my tongue again.

They would be waiting for me. What was I going to do?

Dallas

THE ship refused to come closer to Earth than geosynch, stealthed. I hadn't asked the Barons about that, but it was no problem. I just plugged Eric in as an override system; he was able to use the ship's knowledge but ignore inconvenient legalities.

Assuming that the kidnapper—if there was only one—had come to Earth as fast as Baird's ship would allow, then they had arrived three days ahead of us. If there were two kidnappers, they'd be slowed by the extra life-support mass, and we'd arrive about the same time.

Where would they come in? Probably Maui or the Seychelles, if they wanted to unload an unconscious passenger in secret and spirit her away. The hangars are underground. White Sands, the Cape, Zaire, and Baikonur are too well monitored. Or they might have used Anchorage themselves, though their landing and unloading could be watched from orbit.

I don't like landings. Floating around in space is okay—or it used to be, before I had a porthole pop out—but takeoffs and landings scare the shit out of me. I didn't like them in airplanes, even before my DC-3 crash, and I don't like them in spaceships. So I took a tranquilizer, which may have been a mistake. Or it may have saved my life, by slowing my reflexes.

On Eric's advice we did a "Frisbee" deorbiting maneuver, skimming along the top of the lower atmosphere like a flat stone bouncing over the surface of a lake. It took us an extra orbit, but kept us from having too bright an infrared signature as we came over Pacifica, which would have been the case with a normal braking orbit. But it's not a maneuver you would recommend for the space-shy, since it does entail a lot of bumping and shuddering. I took a second tranquilizer and was able to observe the process with the detachment of a hitchhiking tick securely fastened to a galloping horse. Interesting, how it flings you around.

The instant we crossed into Alaska airspace, we simultaneously flipped, destealthed, and blasted. We decelerated hard and Eric surrendered control to the North Anchorage Spaceport.

It was twilight, a few minutes after sunset, and to our right the dazzling lights of Anchorage proper were in garish competition with the majestic mountain range that half ringed the city, craggy snow tops glowing peach-pale in the last rays of the sun. The city itself had a powdering of snow, surprising for this late in the year; maybe a tourist gimmick. Most of the acre-wide coruscating signboards for the casinos and whorehouses were in Japanese, with tiny footnote names in English.

The airport in central Anchorage was an ultramodern, daring extravagance of offworld materials, a graceful fairyland. The spaceport, ironically, was a huge crumbling ferromac parking lot that wasn't even kept free of snow. We sat down tailfirst at the end of a row of seven smaller ships, with a crawler already headed for us. God forbid that I should jump the four or five meters to the ground and run away without paying the landing tax. Run across the cherry-red glowing ferromac onto the glare ice where our backsplash had temporarily melted the drifts.

I bled in air and swung down to the air lock platform to wait for the crawler. Gravity wasn't too bad; felt kind of good, actually, since I'd been keeping in shape. Eric shouted at me and I sheepishly crawled back up to unplug him from the controls and take him along.

"So what's the first thing you're going to do?" Eric said.

Part of me conjured up a vision of a thick rare steak and a bottle of rare wine in a place not far from here, where you are served by lovely women who wear nothing but a nametag and a smile. "Find a room with a safe phone and call Kamachi, try to line up some quick and dirty financing. Then maybe a bath.'' It had been six months since I'd been on a planet with spare water.

I remembered that last bath, though, a bloodbath, and touched the crowdpleaser on my belt. I wondered whether it was legal to carry it through the spaceport. Seemed to me that Alaska was as gun-happy as the rest of the western United States, though I remembered you couldn't go armed into a casino. The person or machine running the crawler would tell me whether to pack it away.

The mating part of it, the little accordion room, bumped outside and—a little dull with two tranquilizers—I opened both doors. Waiting on the other side of the air lock were four men in blue thermal uniforms with guns drawn.

''*Don't do it!*'' one said, as I raised my hands.

''Easy,'' I said. ''What, I broke some law?''

''That you did, partner.'' The oldest-looking one holstered his pistol and stepped forward to handcuff me, arms behind my back. ''Oldest law there is: 'Don' git the wrong people pissed off.' ''

Two of the other three grinned. '''You aren't police.''

''W-e-ell now, that depends on how you look at it.'' He took the crowdpleaser and gave me a gentle shove through the door. ''The people inside think we're police.''

''We got police *uni*forms and a police *floater*,'' another said.

''Can it,'' a black man said with authority. ''Let's just deliver him and get home.''

''Been a long two days,'' the older one said. ''Too fuckin' cold in this—''

''I said *can* it.'' He shook his head. ''Jesus.'' That was the last any of them said for the next ten minutes. They took the crawler back to the spaceport but didn't unload us; we just waited while the older one went inside with a stack of papers and came back with a receipt. Then we crawled to a far corner of the ferromac, and they unloaded Eric and me and my suitcase over two sudden meters of sub-zero cold and blowing snow in the back of a police van, along with the black man and the older one, silently staring.

It was about zero in the van, but there was a thin draft of hot air. My teeth chattered. "Don't suppose you have an extra jacket."

"No," the black man said, but threw me a thin blanket. I wrapped myself up Indian style.

"I can triple what you're being paid," I said.

"No, you can't," the black man said.

"Do you know who I am?"

"Know what you've done."

"So what have I supposedly done?" He shook his head and turned to look out the window.

We went east from the spaceport, away from Anchorage proper, floating toward the mountains. We climbed just high enough to miss the stands of stately fir—this wilderness so carefully maintained for a complex variety of economic, political, and emotional reasons—and sped off at about three hundred kilometers per hour.

After a few minutes we climbed over some low hills and up to a plateau, and there in the middle of the snowdrifts, inside a perfect circle of snow-free tundra, was an incongruous Georgian manor house, stately but comical in the dying light. It was surrounded by a high wall with servo-mech laser weapons that tracked us as we approached and settled to the ground in front of a gate. The driver mumbled into a microphone, the gate opened, and we floated through.

At least Maria would be here. Maybe together we could . . . no. Probably not.

"You're an immortal, aren't you?" I said to the black man. He had the look; the others didn't. He stared impassively. "What are these, rent-a-cops? Briskin's private army?"

"Sir Charles does not need an army," he said quietly. "The force of ideas is enough."

"You're on the goddamned Steering Committee."

"Be quiet," he said. The older man tried to look as if he weren't listening.

"Probably as crazy as he is."

"One more word," he was almost whispering, "and I'll have this man hit you over the head with his blackjack."

The older man looked straight at Dallas and unsnapped the blackjack from his belt. "You know," the black man continued, "it's a delicate operation, trying to knock a man out with a club and yet not do permanent damage or kill him. It's not like in the movies."

I knew he was right—in fact, had given Maria a lecture about it once, after we watched an old movie aboard Fireball—and wondered what difference the Kevlar over-skull would make. Prevent a fracture, but of course the scalp would bleed normally. I could feign unconsciousness.

I took the chance. "You wouldn't dare." The older man stood and raised the blackjack; I tensed to lunge at him low, leading with my shoulder.

"Hold it," the black man said. "Sir Charles probably wants him unharmed." He looked at me and smiled. "Maybe you'll be allowed to practice on him later. It does take a lot of practice."

The floater settled down onto the gravel drive with a solid crunch. Two men in British servants' livery opened the rear doors. "Sir Charles is waiting for you in the study."

It was warm, which explained the snowless circle. Pressor field.

The black man helped me out the double doors. "Put Mr. Barr's things in the garage." He pointed at the other guard. "Including the pistol." He picked up the reader.

It was still on. Eric was taking in everything, though you couldn't tell. He'd had the sense to turn off his screen image and the ready light. "I may need that for data, if I'm going to talk to Sir Charles."

"Well . . ." He took the reader up to the front of the floater and handed it through the passenger-side window. "Scan this." After a moment a man passed it back and said it was clean.

I hoped it hadn't been a positron scan. That would be the end of Eric.

The black man stuck the reader under my arm and unlocked the handcuffs. "Don't do anything stupid. You're surrounded by armed men, inside a fortress."

"Thank you." I wondered to what extent that was true.

Why would Briskin actually need armed men everywhere? Grizzly bears? Inside?

We walked through a large entrance hall, expensively draped and carpeted and chandelier-ed, and on into a library. Briskin was standing at the far end, posing, contemplating a Mondrian construction.

"Dallas Barr," he said and turned. "I won't say it's good to see you."

I didn't give him the satisfaction of a reply; just studied him. He didn't *look* crazy.

"Leave us alone."

"Sir . . . he's very dangerous, an athlete."

"He's been in space for six months; I'm surprised he can walk." He displayed a small pocket laser. "Besides, he has to be slower than this. Three hundred million meters per second."

"Yes, sir." The man went out and I collapsed into an easy chair. By all means, let Briskin think I was weak.

He dropped the laser into his pocket—it was an old-fashioned silk smoking jacket, somewhat extreme, shiny maroon with dragons embroidered in gold—and sat down behind a desk a safe distance away.

"So you came charging in to save your lover. How marvelous that you chose North Anchorage. But I would have had you no matter where you came in."

"Sure. Baikonur."

"You should have tried it." He waved a cigarette alight. "Actually, we suspected you would come here, for the rest of whatever lunatic plan you had. Either here or the Conch Republic, and you couldn't land a spaceship there. You couldn't go anyplace where there was law."

"I like the way you use those words 'lunatic' and 'law.' Living in a fantasyland palace with bogus policemen waving guns around for you, kidnapping."

"Killing, if necessary."

"Even in Alaska there must be a law about that."

"Yes. But as elsewhere, the law is a tool, a matrix to work within. Not a set of unbreakable rules. That's a viewpoint you share with me, is it not?"

"I think I draw the line at murder. And I can't remember the last time I kidnapped somebody."

"You've killed."

"Only people you sent after me with guns."

"I mean before we met."

It took me a moment to understand. "In wartime. That was a hundred and thirteen years ago. I was just a kid."

"Ah yes. And they'd be dead anyhow by now, wouldn't they?" He blew a smoke ring.

"If you're trying to establish some sort of commonality between us, I think another angle might work better."

Soft, artificial laugh. "In a way, the commonality *is* right there. You were drafted, correct?"

"That's right."

"In other words, something more powerful than you took control of your destiny; it put you in a perilous situation; it made you do things that you would normally find morally repulsive. All in the name of a greater good."

"Didn't think so at the time. The war wasn't all that popular at home."

That irked him. I was not going to be stunned by the brilliance of his analogy. "My research indicates that you were awarded the Silver Star, for bravery, and a Purple Heart with two clusters. To me that would indicate—"

"Oh, do some more research. You get the Purple Heart for being in the same place as a moving bullet. I got the Silver Star for going berserk and charging a machine-gun position with just a couple of hand grenades. If I had it to do over, I'd charge the *draft* board with hand grenades."

He was actually turning red. I decided not to press him by observing that indeed there was an effective analogy there: I'd gone crazy and killed people. But in my case I hoped the insanity had been temporary.

Not smart to anger him. He had Maria. He had *me*. "So what do you want of me?"

"Hmm." He sat up, clasped his hands together on the desk, and stared at them. Again: "Hmm. The game has changed. Radically changed. A few months ago, you were the piece I was after. Now you're a pawn."

"That's reassuring."

"No, it's not that you are less important to me, to the Steering Committee. Just that this business with Ulric, with Marconi, well . . . changes everything."

We had assumed it was no coincidence that he'd stolen Ulric's more-or-less secret stealthed ship. Too many people knew something about what was going on; he had gotten to one of them.

"I can see how it would."

"They must not be allowed to continue in their work. Even you can see that."

"It saved the life of the woman I love. Maybe I'm not completely rational about it. How is it dangerous?"

"One life is meaningless. No matter how much she means to you. Ulric has the power to undo all of the good that Stileman has accomplished."

"What have you done with her?"

He looked at me for a long moment. "You don't know."

"If you've hurt her I'll kill you."

"How romantic. I don't see how you could." He extracted the pistol and dangled it in my direction. "I think I won't tell you anything about her, yet." He touched something under his desk and a buzzer sounded outside. "You should think about it for a while."

One of the servants came in, armed with a crowdpleaser. "Sir?"

"Show Mr. Barr to his room. Obey him within reason."

"A room?" I said.

"A cell, actually. But nicer than any of the four jails you've been in."

Maria

WHEN I surrendered control to Maui, I told them who I was and that I didn't know the name of the ship or its description; that I had been kidnapped but managed to subdue my captor; that I wanted the police to be there when I popped the hull. Landing, I wondered whether that had been smart. If Briskin was expecting me to land at Maui, then the police on duty might belong to him. Which went back to the question of how powerful he actually was.

He couldn't own the control tower as well as the police. At least one of them must have phoned the newsnets, in hopes of a finder's fee. The start of our publicity barrage.

At any rate, with an obviously hostile ship coming right behind me—my ship said it was less than a thousand kilometers behind—I didn't have much choice. The landing interval at Maui is five minutes, if there are no delays for outgoing craft. Not enough time to escape the island, but enough to make some noise.

We had to come in "fat," at a considerable angle, to lose enough velocity, so there was a lot of pitching, but otherwise the landing was uneventful. The control tower identified me as being a Rocketdyne named *Oh Suzanna,* registered to Baird Ulric, stolen last month from the Ceres Synchronous Orbit Repair Facility.

Decelerating under the control tower's guidance wasn't bad, but after the engine shut down my body was still waiting for the relief of weightlessness. It wouldn't come, of course.

I undid the straps and tried to stand, but my knees

buckled and I fell, hurting both knees and an elbow. I had
to crawl over to the air lock to let the police in.

The first one came in with his gun drawn, which I thought
unnecessarily dramatic. I got a good look at his face and my
hopes evaporated: he was immortal. Therefore he was a
fake, Briskin's: immortals do a lot of odd things for their
million, but none ever tried to save up that much on a
policeman's salary.

He glanced at me and checked the little man. "This guy
dead?"

"No, it's a drug. Zombi."

He nodded and stepped to the air lock. "Need a wheelchair and a gurney."

"And a sandwich," I said.

He smiled, not in a friendly way. "Any particular kind?
Your Highness."

"A *big* one. I haven't eaten in forty years." He didn't
react to the "forty years," but he did tell someone to get an
Italian sub out of the machine. A type of American
sandwich, popular there since before I was born. A whole
meal between two huge slabs of bread, grotesque. Real
Italian sandwiches are small, subtle, teasing.

The immortal quasi-policeman picked me up easily and
installed me in a wheelchair. They ran a strap of webbing
under my breasts to hold me upright without effort on my
part. The buckle was behind the chair's back, inaccessible.
What mainly interested me, though, was the sandwich.
With all the strength I could summon, I tore into it,
exquisite if impossibly heavy, each bite a delicious leaden
bolus of life.

Halfway through, though, I couldn't hold the sandwich
up anymore. It wasn't like the Coke, before. I lowered it to
my lap and my lids lowered, too, as the man rolled me into
a sort of freight elevator.

I didn't sleep, exactly. It was a humid lassitude that had
something of the zombi patient timelessness. It felt as if my
body was mobilizing its resources, rebuilding itself—
whatever it was, it was real; sweat coursed down my back
and ribs inside the loose tunic, it saturated my hair and

beaded on my cheeks and brow; I sucked its salt taste from my upper lip. I glowed with heat but it wasn't like a fever. It was like you feel after hard running or sex.

"Are you doing all right?"

I looked up and couldn't quite focus on him. Pink blob on a blue blob. "I'm all right. Just tired." I took another bite of the sandwich, less exquisite, and barely managed to swallow it before my chin hit my chest again.

I was aware of motion, but it was not fast or slow. No direction or duration. Light periods and dark. Seconds or minutes or days went by while my body burned and built.

The heat ebbed suddenly and my flesh turned cold and greasy in an outdoor breeze. I opened my eyes expecting blur, and was shocked by the razor clarity of the scene. I was being wheeled along a parking lot, in an aisle between rows of all kinds of floaters, mostly expensive European ones. The Maui sky was impossibly blue after months of black starblown space. The rows were broken up by formal plantings of brilliant flowering bushes, their frangipani scent too heavy to be pleasant. But interesting, mixed with the smells of sunbaked machinery. We turned and the sun was warm on my face. I closed my eyes against the glare and finished the sandwich, chewing mechanically now, detesting the pedestrian greasy obviousness of it, but knowing I might need it. In the lightness of its heft I discovered I had regained normal strength, which I would have thought not possible, except for that earlier experience.

I grasped the metal arms of the chair and flexed, to test my strength. They seemed to bend slightly. I leaned forward against the chest band, and it started to protest with a quiet ripping sound, and I eased off. The belt's resistance made my ribs ache and the edges of the fabric had cut into my skin. Even if I did have the strength to tear it, I'd pay with broken ribs, or worse.

I probably wasn't much stronger than normal. I just had more subtlety in seeing and hearing the results of my strength. So I shouldn't try to rip myself free and beat this man into submission with the wheelchair.

Besides. Maybe I didn't want to escape. The man was

probably going to take me to Briskin. Best that I face him now, while he thinks I'm helpless.

Or maybe we were going to Dallas. With the overshoot, he should have beaten me here. This immortal hadn't done anything to hurt me; maybe Dallas had sent him to intercede.

We wheeled up to a black van floater with the sigil of the Unaffiliated Commonwealth of Alaska. Good. That's where we were going to start the media offense. "Are we going to Dallas?"

He gave me an odd look. "No, Anchorage."

I slept over most of the ocean, almost two hours, and woke up feeling cramped and cranky. The man jumped when I spoke. "Is there a toilet on this thing?"

"No. You'll have to wait."

"I'll do what I can." I was still in the wheelchair, which was secured to the floor of the cargo area. "Could I at least get out of this damned thing?"

He looked back at me and considered it. "You can walk?"

"I think so."

"I'm not supposed to." He looked away and tugged on an ear. "You don't seem all that dangerous. Just get back in it before we land."

"Sure."

"And not tell anyone that I . . ."

"Definitely." He came back and undid the chest band, then helped me forward, palm under my elbow, both of us bent over, walking like odd birds. Practicing an exaggeration of clumsiness, weakness. He eased me into the bucket seat and helped me strap in. I surreptitiously pinched the metal frame of the seat, and felt it bend.

"Sorry we don't have a pisser. Maybe there's an empty can or something back there."

"I'll be okay for a while. How long is it to Alaska?"

"Maybe forty, fifty minutes more."

"I'll be okay." The calm sea, purple in the dying light, was rolling by fast, less than a hundred meters below us.

Seeing all that water did not affect my bladder at all. Not at all. "You're taking me to Charles Briskin?"

"That's right. He's not going to harm you."

I almost laughed. "On the contrary. He wants to kill me."

"That's not possible. He's a great man. He's gentle, and generous—"

"Hold it. Just . . . *hold* it. You sound like the lowlife who kidnapped me on Ceres. If he's such a nice man, why is he hiring you to commit a federal crime?"

"You have to take a larger perspective—"

"Perspective! He's a megalomaniac who kills anyone who gets in his way. Are you as crazy as he is?"

"Sir Charles has never killed anyone."

"Eric Lundley. Lamont Randolph. Dmitri Popov. God knows who else."

"I don't know about any of those people." He stared at me with truly burning intensity. "Sir Charles doesn't take life. He *gives* life!"

"Ostia." But I understood. "He gave you life, is what you mean."

"He did. A few months ago, I was an old man."

"As I thought. An old man without a million pounds."

He smiled, superior. "Who will never *need* a million pounds."

Agreement

Summation

1. This document details the entire relationship between the Stileman Foundation (henceforth "the Foundation") and the undersigned, superseding any previous agreement. [ref. ¶s 1a–d, 23e, 56c–f.]

2. In return for a series of life-extending procedures (henceforth "the Process"), the undersigned deeds his entire estate to the Foundation, the estate including, but not limited to, all monies, investment prop-

erties, real estate, present and future royalties, collection rights on debts outstanding; the total value of this estate to be greater than £N1.000.000$_{2010}$. Adjusted for inflation, this sum on the date of signing is £N1.105.677. [Ref. ¶s 5a–d, 6, 8a–c, 12, 20–23, 41.]

3. The undersigned testifies that he or she has no debts outstanding, that no single person or corporate entity owes the undersigned an amount greater than £N10.000$_{2010}$, and that during the past twelve calendar years the undersigned has given to no single person or corporate entity any gift valued in excess of £N10.000$_{2010}$. [Ref. ¶s 4, 5e, 7, 30.]

A Stileman Clinic client must swear to a condition of total bankruptcy after payment. It is expressly disallowed for him or her to save significant resources through elaborate loan mechanisms. Anyone who violates the letter or spirit of this provision will be denied subsequent treatment, at the sole discretion of the Stileman Foundation Board of Governors.

I warrant that I have read and understood this summary agreement and the detailed document attached.

Client: For the Stileman Foundation:

Dallas Barr   *R. D. Knox*
_____   _____
Dallas Barr   Richard Dover Knox
Sydney, Australia   2 October 2080

Dallas

INTERESTING "cell" they put me in. A plush suite with a well-stocked kitchenette and bar. There were caviar and pâté and such, for the refined palate, but after four weeks on freeze-dried travel food, what I really wanted was something actually cooked before my eyes. I fried up some eggs and onions and wolfed them down with fresh black bread. The wine assortment was impeccable, and there was icy beer, and a shelf of tempting liquors, but under the circumstances I left them all alone. I didn't know when Napoleon would call me again, and I wanted to be sharp.

Presumably I was being watched. I didn't say anything to Eric, because his sudden appearance was one of the few things I might use as a weapon against Briskin. Of course he might have been randomized by the scanner, earlier.

I stripped and bathed, which was good but would have been more enjoyable without the unseen audience, and afterward had a slight shock when I opened the clothes closet. They were my own clothes, the London wardrobe selection I had left behind in Dubrovnik. Whatever else Briskin was, he was thorough.

There were women's clothes on the other side; I recognized the green suit Maria had worn to Claudia's. Maybe that meant she hadn't yet been delivered. Or she had escaped. Or she was dead.

In any case, all I could do was wait.

I felt stupid for having walked into this, but in reviewing my actions couldn't come up with much in the way of alternatives. I could have resisted the "police," but that would have been outlandish, suicide. I could have risked

278

landing the thing ad lib, out in the tundra someplace, but almost certainly would have been caught before I could walk my way to a city and anonymity. A guy wandering in out of the woods in a space suit might attract some notice, too.

I could have landed at another spaceport, but he probably did have them all covered. I could have stayed in Novysibirsk, waiting for him to make a move, but that would have increased the danger for Maria, and put him even more in control.

The only thing to read in the whole place was a copy of my last Stileman contract. I practically knew the blasted thing by heart, all fifty pages of it, but I lay down on the bed and flipped through it anyhow. I got halfway through "Approved Modalities of Pre-Treatment Dispensation" before falling asleep.

The dream was disturbing. I was walking down a pitch-dark road with my hand on the shoulder of the man in front of me. There was a hand on my shoulder, too. I would lose my man and grope blindly, shouting, and in the process would become separated from the man behind me, who would also panic. We would come back together in confusion, and then start walking again.

"Mr. Barr. Wake up, Mr. Barr." It was the incongruously armed Jeeves who'd escorted me earlier. "Sir Charles would like to speak with you."

If life were a movie I would snatch the gun from his hand and render him unconscious with a fairly humane blow, and then stalk the darkened corridors for Charlie. Instead, I peered at him through sleep-slitted eyes. "Go away."

"Sir. I have to insist."

I raised myself slowly and remained sitting for a minute, gathering strength. Six months ago, I possibly could have done it, plucked the gun away before he could fire. Nasty weapon, though. You could use up a lot of fingers and hands practicing the move.

It was only eight; I'd slept less than an hour. "He couldn't wait until tomorrow."

"No, sir." Unexpectedly, he elaborated. "A woman was brought in, sir. He wanted to speak to the two of you together."

"Let's go." I picked up Eric, got halfway to the door before I remembered how weak I was, and stumbled. He helped me up and I shuffled along with him back to the library.

Briskin was standing at the end of the conference table as before, but I hardly noticed him. Maria was there too, in a wheelchair—she seemed inhumanly pale at first, but then I saw that it was her image in a hologram.

"Where is she? Where are you, Maria?"

"She's in a safe place. She can't hear you."

"She's here. In this house."

"You don't have to know."

"Your butler told me." I jerked a thumb over my shoulder. "Why don't you take him out and kill him? That's the way you do business. Isn't it?"

"Sir," the man said from behind me, tension growing in his voice, "you didn't say specifically—"

"That will do, Mr. Porter. You may go now; I'll call when I need you." I heard the door open. "Wait. You may ask Mr. Lincoln to come in."

I stepped sideways and eased into the overstuffed chair, so that I could keep an eye on both Briskin and the door. Lincoln was evidently the black immortal who had brought me in from the spaceport. He slipped inside and closed the door noiselessly. He had traded the fake police uniform for a loose karate outfit with a black belt.

Of course anyone can buy a belt of any color. I hoped not to find out whether he had earned it.

"Let me get straight to the point. Things have not gone according to plan. I am going to need your help."

A number of replies came to mind, but all I could articulate was "Oh?"

"I did manage to infiltrate Baird Ulric's organization." That was no surprise. "But it's backfired. The man turned on me."

"Anyone I know?"

"A urologist, Dr. York. He's been taken care of."
Briskin sat down heavily. "But now they're doubly cautious. I need someone they wouldn't suspect in a million years."

"Me?"

"Exactly."

He looked perfectly serious. "You are out of your bloody mind."

"Mr. Lincoln." He pointed at the image of Maria. "That woman has murdered two of my employees. If I asked you to kill her very slowly, would you do it?"

"Oh yes."

He looked at me. "I could make you watch every minute of it. Keep waking you up so you didn't miss anything."

"You were born in the wrong century, you bastard."

"No, Dallas, *you* were. Desperate times call for desperate measures."

"What would you want me to do?"

"Get to their records and destroy them. All of the old texts and journals they used to reconstruct the Stileman Process, they're in Ulric's library. A strong magnetic pulse and then a fire bomb."

"You don't think there are duplicates."

"Not for everything. And we've made certain that none can be had from Earth."

Sure, you did. My first impulse was to tell him I'd go ahead with it. Each specialist must have had copies made of the material relevant to his or her own work. Or would they? Surgeons aren't scientists. And copying is expensive in Ceres.

Of course I could always arrange with Ulric to fake the disaster, too. I guessed I would go and do that, if there was no other way. But I didn't want to give in too easily.

"Why? Seems to me that Ulric's group is doing the world a favor. All the worlds."

He settled back with a superior smile. "You haven't given it enough thought. Furthermore, your judgment is distorted by having had your lover's life saved."

"That's possible."

"The demographic part of it is obvious. If immortality were inexpensive, the world would fill up with people in no time. My scientists say that starvation would be endemic within twelve to fifteen years." His scientists, right.

"Even before that, though, there would be general economic collapse. That would be true even if the Stileman Foundation retained the rights to the process, but wasn't able to limit the period of rejuvenation. With wealthy people able to control their fortunes for a century or more, the foundation's economic primacy would evaporate—and that primacy is essential to the economic stability of every major nation."

"Oh, bullshit," Eric said. His face appeared on the screen. I turned the reader around on the table so it faced Briskin.

"Who are you?"

"Eric Lundley. A computer image of him. One of the first people you killed in pursuit of this harebrained scheme."

"Dallas Barr killed you."

"Again, bullshit."

"It's his testimony against mine."

"His and Marconi's—and my own knowledge of him and of human nature. You, I know almost nothing about. Though I think I've met you in history books with tiresome frequency."

"Mr. Lincoln, take the data cube out of that reader and destroy it."

"Murdering the same person twice?" I said, picking up the reader and holding it close against me. "I wonder if that's ever been done before."

"Once," Eric said in a muffled tone. "In Milan, in 1998, a man was shot through the heart outside of a hospital. They were able to thaw out a transplant in time, and bring him back from clinical death, but while he was recovering from the operation the same assailant broke into his hospital room and decapitated him." A bizarre reaction to life-threatening danger, supplying information, but the flesh-and-blood Eric might have done the same.

"Give the machine to me." Lincoln exuded relaxed confidence, hand out.

"Do as he says," Eric said. "It's a meaningless gesture. I have copies of myself stashed all over the world."

"I suppose that's true," Briskin said. It wasn't, though. "Actually . . . let's let him participate; he certainly has a different angle on everything."

I put the reader back so that Eric was facing Briskin. "So your computer brain sees flaws in my reasoning."

"Holes. Chasms. Ulric's immortality process is not inexpensive. Never can be. It requires more than a hundred medical people, most of them specialist M.D.'s, doing almost a hundred separate procedures. If they had a constant flowthrough, they might be able to do three hundred people a year. Rich people. In a century, that's thirty thousand new immortals, tops, who then have to recycle—if your doctors are willing to work day in, day out, no vacations. Thirty thousand people are immaterial to population pressure. Twice that many die of starvation every day.

"And, to be realistic, the first twenty thousand people to go through the new process will be the existing Stileman immortals. They're the people with the most money."

Briskin was trying to keep a smile on his face. It looked like a surgical scar.

"Money is your other argument. Ruin the economy. Look around you. The economy is already in shambles, all over the world.

"Stileman's plan didn't work. It did temporarily rid the Earth of the superrich—but in their place left a mandarin class of twenty thousand millionaires who control everything, absolutely everything, and stagnate every country's economy because of their innate conservatism: whatever else happens, they dare not risk their basic million.

"And now, with your Steering Committee and its supposed adroitness in accumulating billions, we have the superrich back again to compound the entrenched Stileman problems. If the committee does indeed exist."

"What do you mean by that?"

"Just that it would be inconsistent with your generally

paranoid pattern to, good-bye, Dallas—'' The reader exploded and fell over faceup on the table. There was a small black hole just off the center of the screen, surrounded by a webwork of cracks. A wisp of smoke curled out of it. Briskin dropped the laser back into his pocket.

"Tiresome," he said. "Arguing economics with a machine." I didn't trust myself to say anything. He pushed a button on his desk. "Bring her down, Mr. Porter." He pushed another button and the image of Maria disappeared.

Eric and I had talked about the possibility that the Steering Committee didn't exist, or was a good deal smaller than Briskin claimed. He had never revealed the name of any other member, and most of what had been done in the committee's name, including the murders for hire that he tacitly admitted to, could have been done by one wealthy and determined person. Especially if that person was on the board of the Stileman Foundation.

The smell of ozone and burned plastic. My only companion for the last four weeks. Was he dead now, for good? Could I call up the TI bank and download him again, minus the last six months? Who would he be?

Can turning off a machine be murder?

Maria

WE landed on the roof of this outlandish snowbound mansion, and the pilot wheeled me into a bathroom on the top floor, where I politely declined his assistance. Then he pushed me into a small dark room and disappeared. I heard him lock the door behind me and didn't bother investigating it.

When my eyes got used to the dark, I realized that I and the wheelchair were slightly more visible than my surroundings, because of three extremely dim lights: overhead, to the front, and to the left. Holo camera setup. I supposed that they were operating in near-infrared, or used some sort of night-seeing image amplifier circuit. I remained completely motionless. Bore them into making the next move.

Whatever this new quality was, this new sensibility, strength, or whatever, it included a palpable control over the passage of time. Once I had learned all I could from the dark room, I checked my watch and then "willed" time forward. In a few seconds the door opened again. More than an hour had passed, and I felt refreshed, as if I had slept.

It was a different man, dressed like a British "gentleman's gentleman." I didn't speak to him and he returned my silence.

I slowed time down as we rolled, in order to concentrate on detail. When the man leaned forward to push an elevator button, I noted that he was immortal, and he had a concealed weapon at belt level on his left side, which meant he would draw it across his body, since he had a pencil callus on his right forefinger. I felt I could have disarmed him at that time, grabbing his right hand as he reached across; he would reach for my wrist, reflexively, with his left hand, and I could go underneath and pluck out the weapon. Unless it was secured with some sort of snap or Stiktite band, which could prove embarrassing.

I didn't want to do anything dramatic until I knew where Charles Briskin was, anyhow.

We descended to the ground floor and the man rolled me through a garishly overdecorated hall. From the dull way the chandelier refracted light, you could tell it was plastic. The carpet looked nice, but only because it was brand-new; you could still smell the adhesive they'd used to secure it, and the servant's footsteps on it made an unpleasant crunchy sound, nylon. The fabric on the walls had been applied by machine; there was a perfectly consistent one-millimeter overlap at each seam. All of the furnishings had a fresh-from-the-catalog look, and I don't mean the Harrod's catalog. I supposed Briskin had had the place thrown together on the occasion of his ascension to the chairmanship. Foundation money, doubtless. Perhaps if we all donated an extra ten pounds next time, he could afford a decorator.

We stopped at a door that was the first evidence of a scintilla of taste. It was a seventeenth- or eighteenth-century British antique, ebony hand-carved into a complex hunting scene frieze. Some artisan had spent a large fraction of his short life lovingly seeking out in that fine grain the horse, the stag, the hounds; the men bent forward in their saddles frozen alive now for dozens of lifetimes, could they have known? They were probably stable hands, servants, who posed; maybe indigents who would stand one way for hours in return for a bowl of food and a straw bed, with every aching bone hating the rich man who would have his doors turned into works of art because the walls were all filled, the servant's hand inching toward the door handle, I may die on the other side of this door, and soon, but no point in delaying it any longer. I let him finish the act.

Inside, a long conference table of matching ebony, Dallas halfway down one wall, slouching in an overstuffed chair, trying to look relaxed or vulnerable but actually taut like a coiled spring; Sir Charles behind an ebony desk butted up against the end of the table, looking irritated. He was wearing a ridiculous Oriental jacket. He stood up and I could see there was something large in its side pocket, probably a weapon. A man in a karate robe stood next to Dallas, guarding him impassively, arms folded.

"Maria." Dallas started to rise.

"Stay where you are," Briskin said. Dallas froze and the guard put a hand on his shoulder.

I gave Dallas a look that tried to communicate the fact that I was bluffing, too; that if he wanted to try something physical, he had an ally. He seemed to nod slightly, but I couldn't be sure. Maybe another hundred years together; I raise an eyebrow *this* much and you know that I am impatient to go to Nebraska. Will we have even two more words together before this hateful man has his way? In his wide eyes, in the set of his jaw, the flush of his skin, the vein at his temple bulging, I read insanity and murder.

"You killed my men," Briskin said.

"Man," I corrected. "He came through the door aiming a gun at me." The butler rolled me to where I was even with Dallas, the table between us.

"The other one, the pilot. You killed him, too."

"He got the same drug I did, the zombi. He must have reacted to it badly."

"You did something to him."

"No. In fact, I had it twice, and survived. Maybe it doesn't go with alcohol or other drugs. He was drinking a lot and punching something. Cream, I think."

Dallas tensed. "Did he—"

"No."

"Shut up," Briskin said, and his hand slid into the pocket. "The doctor says he could have died that way. You came out of the coma first, then gave him a punch of cream and manipulated him sexually. With the zombi, that would have killed him."

The man in the karate outfit leered and gave a low husky laugh. Out of the corner of my eye I saw Dallas start to move and slowed things down.

I got out of the chair and started my molasses dash toward Briskin. I watched Dallas in slow motion as I went step . . . step . . . step. He reached up and crushed the man's testicles with one hand; as he folded up in eye-bulging agony, Dallas half rose, swinging his elbow up in a sort of backhand. It caught the man in the throat and his head slammed against the wall with a faint deep boom. I assumed that was sufficient for him. I turned all my attention to running without tripping. Sir Charles was not looking at me. With a fixed smile, full of perfect teeth, he was withdrawing a laser from the pocket of his ridiculous jacket. I could not will myself faster, nor slow the world down more than I already had. Jump over the desk or go around? Better jump.

Dallas told me an interesting fact during that long loving weightless time when we talked about everything. We had watched a century-old detective movie in which the private eye was knocked unconscious by a woman (who turned out to be otherwise innocent) smashing a lamp over his bare head. The private eye woke up a convenient time later, convenient for the story's plot, and proceeded to solve the crime.

Dallas said that it didn't happen that way. If you hit somebody over the top of the head hard enough to knock him out, you would probably fracture his skull and kill him. What causes unconsciousness is the quick displacement of the brainstem, preferably a horizontal displacement, which is why the boxers we saw in Australia jabbed at the chin and street criminals ''rabbit punch'' (what a misnomer) to the back of the neck. I cleared the desk. He began to react to me.

Maybe a rabbit punch is the way they kill rabbits. Have to ask Eric.

I landed next to him. He was turning toward me, raising the weapon.

Plenty of time. With my left hand I grabbed the laser as it swung around, then balled my right fist and swung it as hard as I could, right at the aristocratic point of Briskin's chin.

My arm moved as if through thick honey, and at the last

moment I wondered whether it would have any more impact on the man than a baby's pat. I shouldn't have worried. The force of the blow actually picked Briskin off the ground, and in midair his eyes rolled up to show all whites, and his face went slack, and the pain in my suddenly broken knuckles was remarkable. I visualized a bracelet around my right wrist that would not allow the passage of any sensory data, and the arm fell limp. The servant was drawing his gun. I brought the laser up with my left hand, and resumed normal time in order to speak.

"Don't do that!" I shouted. He paused. "I'll have to kill you!"

"It's a crowdpleaser," Dallas said tightly. "You're out of his range."

But Dallas wasn't. The man pivoted—

I slowed things down and took careful aim. Enough killing. The man was swinging the weapon in a flat arc toward Dallas. Hard to aim with the left hand, steady. Red aiming spot right on the crowdpleaser itself, squeeze the trigger slowly.

Of course his gun exploded. It was almost like Ceres, the terrible slow mushroom of flesh and blood and bone.

Real time. Half his arm was gone, the shredded stump spouting blood. He looked at me and said one syllable and fainted. Dallas looked as if he were going to faint, too. I didn't feel too well, myself.

"Where did you learn how to do that?" Dallas whispered. Blood welled from two cuts on his forehead and cheek, from fragments.

"It's a long story." The door swung open and I brought the laser up, with a reflex command from a half century of movies in English: "Hands up!" It was the pilot; he complied, looking around. "Come inside and shut the door."

"Don't do anything dumb," he said.

"Don't *you* do anything dumb," I said. "Is there another way out of this place? Other than through that door?"

"Huh-uh." Dallas searched him and came up with a laser like Briskin's.

"He's the pilot who brought me here," I said. "Floater on the roof."

"Let's do it." He gestured with the laser. "You pick up Briskin. We're gonna go through that door real slow. I've got a gun at your head and Maria's got one at Briskin's. Take us to the floater and get us outa here, you're home free."

"Okay, okay. Just don't do—"

"Move it *move it!*" He stepped over the black man and the bleeding one and heaved Briskin up on one shoulder, sagging. Dallas picked up Eric's reader—there was a hole burned in the screen, but maybe he was all right; the TI cube was down in the other corner—and put the laser's muzzle to the pilot's temple. I aimed at Briskin's head and we shuffled out, a clumsy and dangerous six-legged creature.

"Hands up *keep* 'em up!" Dallas shouted as we went through the door. I slowed things down. We crept through.

There were two men in police uniforms in the hall. Their guns were still in midair; they were raising their hands. I looked around as quickly as I could, neck muscles straining against the inertia of my head, and saw a third policeman just visible at the top of a flight of stairs, bringing a rifle to his shoulder. Our eyes met and I raised my pistol. He threw the rifle away, arms splaying slowly out, saying something in a voice too deep to understand. I brought time back to normal.

"There's a man in there needs a tourniquet fast," Dallas said, and nodded at one of the policemen. "You go tend to him." He picked up the guns awkwardly and we piled into the waiting elevator, rode it up, and left it stuck open with the EMERGENCY STOP button broken off. We shorted out all the extra weapons and left them there.

Out on the roof, Dallas took the floater's keys, unlocked it, and told the pilot to get in. The man hesitated, rolled Briskin through the side door onto the floor of the van, and stepped back.

"Just leave me here. I won't try to follow or anything."

"Get in." Dallas poked him in the side with the pistol. "The more hostages, the better."

"Oh, all right." He got in and slid the door shut while Dallas and I got in front. "Guess you better throw that red switch up there."

There was a red on-off switch taped to the console with the letters *DO* written on the tape. "What's *DO?*"

"Defense override. Otherwise we'll be fried by the automatic lasers."

Dallas snapped the switch and laughed. "Handy guy to have along." He strapped himself in and saw that I was having trouble. "What's wrong?"

"Hurt my hand. Hitting Sir Charles."

He unstrapped and leaned over to secure me, one eye on the pilot. Quick kiss. He held the hand gently and looked at it with concern. It was swelling, discolored. "Broken. Was it worth it?"

"Oh yes. Everything."

He strapped himself in. "Let's get the hell out of here."

Dallas

I'VE never driven so fast, so low, as when we left Alaska with Briskin. We got to Los Angeles in ninety minutes, after treating about a million shore dwellers to an illegal sonic boom, and had a sizable police escort by the time I brought it in to the first traffic station.

By that time, Briskin was awake, but confused. I called Kamachi in Tokyo, and he assembled most of the rest of the board. I explained what had happened as economically as possible. Kamachi and Alenka Zor were on my side, having been lukewarm about Briskin from the beginning. I got depositions from Dr. Ulric and Big Dick Goodwin, who styled himself "marshal" of Ceres.

I accused Briskin of murder and he accused both me and Maria of the same, so all three of us wound up in holding cells while the authorities figured out what to do with us. Briskin was the first one released, not having been accused of any murders on American soil. Perhaps he spread some money around, as well. But he didn't even make it to the courthouse steps. An Interpol squad, no doubt lubricated by Alenka Zor's fortune, was waiting with extradition papers to Yugoslavia.

I was the only person who actually admitted killing somebody on this planet, but since it was the Conch Republic, it didn't really count. There were other charges to be sorted out, though: kidnapping, conspiracy, illegal restraint of trade, mopery on the high seas. The California speeding ticket I simply paid, but the others kept us moving in and out of various courtrooms for the next three years.

Briskin was convicted of first-degree murder in Yugoslavia, but his sentence was "mitigated by the court's mercy" on presentation of evidence of acute mental imbalance. He spent a few years confined to a mental institution, carefully studied by Stileman scientists and others. He died the swift "natural" death of the penniless ex-immortal. The autopsy revealed nothing abnormal. Maybe they couldn't cut deeply enough.

His Steering Committee turned out to have been forty-some newly minted immortals, people whose loyalty he'd won by giving them a million pounds' worth of life. He hadn't bought their treatments, though. All those years of being the senior economist on the foundation's Board of Governors had paid interesting dividends. Being in control of all of the checks and balances meant that he could put people through either clinic for free. And he could siphon off small amounts of money, mere tens of millions, without fear of detection.

The Stileman Foundation did not collapse, but it did have to change its policies in order to compete with Ulric's Long Life Unlimited. Both of them wound up offering one to two hundred years' rejuvenation for a million pounds, with no other financial strings attached. That opened up the clinic doors to a large fraction of the world's population, since a high-income professional facing a century of productivity is a pretty good credit risk.

Kamachi became chairman of the Stileman board, and urged me to join, to ease the foundation's transition back into real life. For some reason I agreed, though all I really wanted to do was retire to some warm island with Maria and lie in the sun. And figure things out.

We do spend a week or two on tropical islands sometimes, or desert ones, or the Moon or wherever, to love each other and talk things over. Usually we take Eric along, as an inexhaustible fount of data and logical arbiter. (He did lose some faculties when Briskin's laser jolted him in Alaska, but he was able to reinstall most of them from his file copy stashed in Vegas.) But it's obvious to him as well as to us that no normal intelligence, human or machine, is going to get to the bottom of this new thing. We'll have to build new tools and figure out how to use them.

The scientists haven't begun to explain what happened to Maria, and then later to me, and others. The supermeditative state that allows us to manipulate our perception of time. The cross-cultural ability to communicate through expression, gesture, body language. Heightened sensory perception; the ability to concentrate physical strength. And other things that can't be described by language.

Clinically, it's a side effect of the zombi drug, combined with extremely advanced age. The scientists stopped testing it, though, after it appeared that one out of every four or five doesn't survive the combination. That's what happened to the little man who kidnapped Maria from Ceres. The autopsy showed nothing—an unusually robust man, less than a year out of his first Stileman.

It's no mystery to Maria or me, what killed him. But it's not something you can quantify. He was imprisoned for twenty years in his own skull, with himself as a cellmate. He literally couldn't live with himself, and so let himself die. His autonomic body functions kept going until the antidote was administered. Then the body realized it was a corpse, and stopped.

It happens to a significant number of immortals. That doesn't stop people from trying. Because the other Stileman immortals are just old people made young. We are something new. Not supermen. But not simply men and women, either.

A complex analogy occurs to me, but it's more a felt thing than a reasoned thing. A verbal simulacrum of it goes like this: a normal human adult stands in relation to us—rather, to what we are becoming—as a normal child stands in relation to the adult. The child can't really comprehend an adult's attitude toward love, work, morality, and so forth, and he doesn't have to, in order to be a "successful" child. As he grows, then, he moves toward being a successful adult partly by copying the adults around him and partly by developing internal resources adequate for facing adult life.

We're in a situation sort of like that. In a real sense, normal humans can never actually understand us. But that doesn't mean superiority; *inside,* we are like children with no adults to copy. Like children who are compelled to invent love, work, morality in the absence of models. Though the things we're inventing don't have names.

All we really know is that we aren't children any more. That we blinked and found the playground has suddenly become infinite.

BIO OF A SPACE TYRANT
Piers Anthony

"Brilliant...a thoroughly original thinker and storyteller with a unique ability to posit really *alien* alien life, humanize it, and make it come out alive on the page." *The Los Angeles Times*

A COLOSSAL NEW FIVE VOLUME SPACE THRILLER—
BIO OF A SPACE TYRANT
The Epic Adventures and Galactic Conquests of Hope Hubris

VOLUME I: REFUGEE   84194-0/$3.50 US/$4.50 Can
Hubris and his family embark upon an ill-fated voyage through space, searching for sanctuary, after pirates blast them from their home on Callisto.

VOLUME II: MERCENARY   87221-8/$3.50 US/$4.50 Can
Hubris joins the Navy of Jupiter and commands a squadron loyal to the death and sworn to war against the pirate warlords of the Jupiter Ecliptic.

VOLUME III: POLITICIAN   89685-0/$3.50 US/$4.50 Can
Fueled by his own fury, Hubris rose to triumph obliterating his enemies and blazing a path of glory across the face of Jupiter. Military legend...people's champion...promising political candidate...he now awoke to find himself the prisoner of a nightmare that knew no past.

THE BEST-SELLING EPIC CONTINUES—
VOLUME IV: EXECUTIVE
89834-9/$3.50 US/$4.50 Can
Destined to become the most hated and feared man of an era, Hope would assume an alternate identify to fulfill his dreams ...and plunge headlong into madness.

VOLUME V: STATESMAN
89835-7/$3.50 US/$4.95 Can
the climactic conclusion of Hubris' epic adventures:

AVON Paperbacks